B.U.G.F.O.R.C.E.™

B.U.G.F.O.R.C.E.

THE SIEGE OF STONEWALL

Dedric Knox

B.U.G.F.O.R.C.E.

TABLE OF CONTENTS

DEDRIC KNOX

Prologue

Return to the Small

The hum of the chamber rose again.

The same vibration that had once heralded their escape from the microscopic world now called them back. The air thrummed with excitement, the smell of sterilized metal mixing with faint ozone and the copper taste of anticipation. Around the platform, engineers proceeded in silence, their eyes reflecting the pulsing light of the Miniaturization rays.

Captain William Jones stood at the threshold of the pod, the weight of memory pressing on his shoulders.

They had fought their war.

They had saved humanity.

And yet, somehow, this moment—the return—felt so much heavier. He looked to his side.

1st Sergeant Miller pulled on his gloves, jaws tight, the old humor buried beneath purpose. "Hard to believe we're going back in on purpose," he muttered. They had been in the regular world for three years now.

"Yeah," Jones replied. "But this time, we build instead of burn."

On the far side of the platform, Dixie ran her hand along the sleek curve of her harness, the micro-lattice fibers glinting under the light. Her gaze was steady but far away. "Ground feels too big up here," she said softly. "I want to hear the wind hum again." Jones smiled slightly. "You'll get your wish, Corporal."

Dr. Sharma gave a nod from the control booth. "Vitals steady. Neural sync confirmed. Time dilation lock engaged."

Her voice softened as she added, "See you on the other side, Captain." Jones nodded, then stepped into the pod. The Hum intensified light swallowed his form. The world unfolded around them. It was vast, towering, alive!

Grass blades rose like emerald towers. Pebbles became boulders. A single drop of dew shimmered like molten glass, suspended in a web of silver filaments. The air itself pulsed with life—thick with micro-sounds, layered with motion invisible to the human eye. They were small again. Shrunk to Micro-Operatives scale once again. They were home.

Jones exhaled, his breath fogging faintly against the inside of his helmet. "Welcome back to the frontier."

The new BUGFORCE Base awaited them just beyond the conversion perimeter—a sprawling field installation built into the roots of an ancient oak, where root walls curved like natural fortifications. Engineers had carved tunnels through the root-fiber, reinforcing them with resin plating and sap-resin lights that glowed like amber veins. The air inside buzzed faintly with power, and every corridor hummed with renewal.

The insignia of BUGFORCE had been carved into the heartwood above the main gate—half leaf, half shield—newly gilded, still wet with lacquer.

As they entered, a voice echoed from the base loudspeakers:

"Welcome to Outpost Genesis—Home of BUGFORCE."

Dozens of technicians and Micro-Operatives were already at work. Ground Division engineers maneuvered micro-lift haulers loaded with cut root-segments, while

Water Division specialists calibrated the filtration wells that would feed the base's water reserves. The smell of soil and machine oil mingled, a perfume of rebirth.

Sergeant Miller surveyed the activity with his still blue eyes with a grunt of approval. "Feels strange seeing the place brand new. Like walking into your own ghost before it's died."

Dixie's eyes lifted to the high canopy—glimpses of sunlight filtering through miles of leaf. "Strange," she said, "but alive," Dixie remembered their first encounters as Micro-Operatives and thought to herself *this feels like home.*

At the far end of the base, an assembly platform waited—tall enough to fit a beetle transport and three scout skimmers. Around it, a unit of recruits was receiving final briefings, their new armor still unscuffed, their helmets shining like polished amber. They looked up as the veterans passed, straightening at the sight of the trio whose names had become legend.

"Captain Jones!" one called, saluting. "Sir—welcome back!"

Jones returned the salute with a modest nod. "At ease, Micro-Operatives. You're standing on the future—don't let it sink under your feet."

The command bay of the new BUGFORCE Base was smaller than the old war rooms, but cleaner, brighter—a place for strategy, not survival.

A holo-map shimmered in the center, displaying the surrounding landscape in glowing detail: Reed Flats, Lotus Lake, the Broadwater Basin, and—at the farthest edge—an unmarked site still under construction. This site's name flashed in pale green letters:

Stonewall Outpost — Phase I Rebuild.

Dr. Sharma appeared on the screen, her expression earnest.

"Captain Jones. Your orders are confirmed. At Rootrise Turn 5 tomorrow, Ground Division and Engineering Corps will escort your convoy to the Stonewall site. Establish perimeter, provide overwatch, and assist in securing the ridge."

"Understood," Jones said. "How many teams?"

"Five engineering units, two logistics crawlers, and full Ground Division security. You'll travel under standard convoy protocol. Expect the terrain to be unstable. The soil there still carries deep hive scars." Jones gave a grim smile. "We've walked worse ground."

Dixie leaned over the map, tracing a fingertip along the projected route. "Reed Flats, through the Hollow Verge, then north along the Broadwater shelf. That's at least one Traverse."

"About five miles," Miller said, adjusting his sidearm. "Three days at convoy pace."

Jones nodded. "Then we start at Rootrise."

Later, as night settled over the base, the hum of machinery faded to the rhythm of quiet breathing, of Micro-Operatives preparing for what came next. From her perch on a root ledge above the courtyard, Dixie looked out into the vast world—each blade of grass shimmering with dew, each drop reflecting stars like distant fires.

"It's strange," she murmured. "We fought a war to get out of this world. Now we're building a home inside it."

Miller leaned against the wall beside her, arms crossed. "Maybe that's the point. We learned how to survive. Now we learn how to live."

Jones joined them, his gaze sweeping over the construction crews below. The root walls pulsed faintly with the life of the great oak above—a reminder that even amidst ruin, life endured. He spoke quietly, but his words carried:

"Tomorrow, we move to Stonewall. The base there will be more than a fort—it'll be the start of something new. Humanity's first real hold in this world. Our proof that we're not running anymore."

Dixie smiled, wings twitching in the dim light. "Then let's build it right."

Jones nodded, his eyes reflecting the glow of the sap-lamps.

"Stonewall will stand," he said. "Not because of the walls we raise—but because of the people inside them."

The night wind stirred, whispering through the roots and leaves above. A sound that could almost have been a word. Hope, perhaps. Or simply breathe.

And beneath that vast, living canopy, three veterans of an impossible war stood ready to begin again, returning not as conquerors, but as builders, defenders, and guardians of a fragile new dawn.

Chapter 1

New Recruits, New Rules

The transport chamber hissed as its inner seals released, filling the hangar with a faint metallic haze. From within stepped a line of wide-eyed recruits, each no taller than a small tac, their Micro-Armor humming faintly with the telltale static of fresh shrink induction.

Recruit Keller stumbled as his boots hit the steel floor. To him, it stretched like a canyon, every groove in the metal a trench. He clutched his helmet awkwardly under one arm, trying not to gape at the sight of the older operatives waiting in formation. Their armor bore scratches, dents, and stains that told stories the recruits hadn't lived yet.

"Eyes forward!" barked Sergeant Brin, his voice amplified through the comms so that it rattled in their helmets. "You're Micro-Operatives now, not star-struck ants at a picnic. Fall in!"

The recruits shuffled into line, boots banging like drumbeats in the yawning chamber. Keller found himself next to a tall, slender woman whose armor was still flashing calibration lights. She gave him a nervous grin before snapping her attention forward again.

At the far end of the hangar, a massive banner displayed: BUGFORCE — Micro-Operatives of Earth. Beneath it, the emblem of the four divisions radiated in holographic blue: Ground, Tree, Water, and Air.

Commander Havelock stepped into view. His armor served as a patchwork of scars and medals; the surface was pitted from acid burns and stinger strikes. He scanned the recruits, his one good eye narrowing.

"You think the first missions were the hard part?" he growled. "That was survival training. Out there in the wilds, we held the line long enough to prove the Micro-Operatives program wasn't a fool's dream. But now…" He gestured to a diagram flickering to life in the air above him — an Outpost, jagged and crude, yet formidable. "Now we build."

The schematic rotated, showing walls pieced together from stone and wood at the base of a single tree and sitting as though it was a part of the tree's root system, glass shards, and metal. Towers bristled from the corners, with firing slits sized for crossbow bolts and micro-charges. A single word glowed across the base of the hologram: STONEWALL.

"This outpost," Havelock continued, "will be the first permanent human holdfast at Micro-Operatives scale. It will be tested. It will be attacked. And you—" his eye swept across them like a blade, "—you will bleed for it."

A silence settled, broken only by the hum of generators. Keller swallowed hard. Beside him, the slender woman muttered under her breath, "Great pep talk, pop." Havelock's gaze immediately fell on her. "Name, recruit?" The tall, Slender woman answered, "Recruit Juno, sir."

"Juno, if you survive the month, you'll thank me for honesty. Bugs don't give speeches. They give stingers, mandibles, and acid. And they'll be here soon."

He stepped back, nodding to Sergeant Brin. "Take them through orientation. They fight tonight." The recruit's face was drained of color.

Orientation was little more than a blur of shouted orders, weapon racks, and hurried drills. Keller fumbled with his Micro-Lance — a collapsible spear humming with a faint electric charge. The weapon felt both too heavy and too fragile, like a toy pretending to be lethal.

"You'll get used to it," muttered Corporal Dixie, a veteran assigned to oversee their squad. Her scarred armor smelled faintly of scorched chitin. "Or you won't. Either way, keep it pointed at something ugly." Keller tried to laugh, but it came out as a cough.

By the time night fell, the recruits were gathered onto the assembly platform at the edge of camp. Beyond the lights, the wilderness loomed: towering grass blades swaying like trees in the slight breeze, the ground alive with the rustle of unseen things.

Stonewall was half-finished in the distance, its walls jagged silhouettes against the gloom. Teams of operatives scurried like ants across the scaffolding, welding, bracing, hauling.

"This," said Corporal Dixie, pointing with her lance, "is where you'll earn the name Micro-Operatives. Not in drills, not in simulations. Out there, against what's coming."

A sound rose from the darkness. A clicking, distant at first, then multiplying — the sound of legs. Many legs. The recruits were alarmed and frozen. Dixie's faceplate lit with a grim smile. "Welcome to Stonewall."

Dixie squawked at the new recruits, ordering them to load onto the Bastion Hauler. The Bastion Hauler is a land-based crawler engineered to transport and deploy prefabricated fortifications directly into contested zones. The Bastion Hauler is a siege engine and mobile base-builder with a complement of 25 Micro-Operatives. Dixie continues to herd the recruits into the hauler. While the recruits were loading, a familiar figure stepped onto the assembly platform. "WHAT DO WE LOOK LIKE, DIX?" yelled Captain William Jones. Dixie, with a playful grunt, said, "Same bunch of robots the academy spits out, Captain!" Captain Jones turns and calls for First Sergeant Miller, "TOP, let's go, brotha." Both Sergeant Miller and Captain Jones get into the hauler with Dixie and the recruits. The navigator grabs the radio, and his voice crackles across the radio, "BH-6, we are clear to move out." After a short pause, a voice from the other side of the radio advises you that you are clear to move out, BH-6. As the Hauler moves forward, two Crawler Haulers line up behind the Bastion Hauler to form a small convoy. As the Convoy continues, overwatch is provided by three Scarab Tankettes formed around the convoy, one in the front taking the lead, and two on either side of the convoy. A Dragonfly Skimmer provided overwatch from above. The Convoy and the overwatch team pushed forward with the recruits towards Stonewall.

The convoy rolled, tracks whispering over steel grit and seed husks, the Hauler`s belly lights strobing a steady march tempo down the centerline. Inside, the recruits swayed on mag-straps, helmets clacking, every bump a quake.

"Span marker in three," called the navigator from the forward blister. "Two. One. Span elapsed."

A chime rippled through the hauler. Captain Jones glanced at Dixie. She answered with a tilt of her chin that said, " Keep *them occupied.*

"Alright, robots," Dixie sang over the squad net, "roll call by eyes, not mouths. Check your lances, check your vibro-brakes, check your neighbor."

Keller checked his Micro-Lance, thumbed the charge to a low hum, then glanced at recruit Juno. She had a strip of black tape around her wrist with tiny hash marks inked to it—counting what he didn't know. She met his look and waggled the lance tip. "Keep it pointed at something ugly," she murmured, borrowing Dixie's line. Keller managed half a grin.

The world outside was a forest of towering grass and ruin. A fallen screw the size of a silo lay on its side, polished by rain; a thicket of moss climbed a river-stone that would've been a warehouse back at human scale. The lead Scarab Tankette—low, armored, its carapace plates welded in a beetle's pattern—crested a pebble and flashed a green light: route clear. The Dragonfly Skimmer circled above, wing membranes oscillating with a high, almost musical whine that Keller felt through his ribs more than he heard.

"Contact," the Skimmer pilot Dea Anne whispered, and the squad net went thin and sharp. "At grid Gnat-Nine. Heat blooms. Pheromone density is rising. Say again: rising."

A coldness stitched up Keller's spine. Corporal Dixie's voice lost its playfulness. "Wedge up. Scarabs form a chevron. Crawler Haulers, close hulls. BH-6, keep pace and don't stop to sight-see."

"Copy," rumbled First Sergeant Miller with a slow and weighted reply, singing through his heavy white mustache. "Recruits, eyes left and right. Remember your drills: segment seams, antenna base, joint pits. If it spits, it's acid. If it clicks, it's talking to friends."

They felt the ants before they saw them—vibrations like muffled thunder through the hauler's frame. Then the grass parted and something black and purposeful lanced into the beam of the forward light: a worker ant the length of a canoe, matte armor slicked with dew, mandibles flexing against nothing with a sound like snipping steel.

The lead Scarab fired a thump charge that blossomed into a crackling net. It sprang wide and clung to chitin; the ant convulsed, legs windmilling, wedge-body skidding.

"Left flank, two more!" yelled Juno, voice pitched high but steady.

They came like knives, fast and angled to cut past the tankette and climb the hauler's rear. The side Scarabs barked micro-charges, peppering the joints with sparks, slowing but not stopping. The ants flowed around their fallen nest-mate with an alien intelligence that wasn't exactly thinking. "BH-6, deploy Toothpick, pattern Theta," Jones snapped.

The hauler's side bay irised open and belched a rack of prefabricated barricades—meter-high spike bundles that unrolled and self-anchored into the soil like porcupine spines. The first ant hit the hedge at speed; its legs tangled and it pitched forward, mandibles chewing reflexively through wood slivers while the Scarab on the right slid sideways, took the joint seam, and fired a bolt. The bolt sparked, the ant spasmed and then went still. "Smell wall's going up," said Top. "Pheromone Foggers, pulse."

Under the hauler, nozzles hissed, and the world filled with a bitter, almost citrus haze Keller tasted through his filters. The fog was brewed to scramble insect scent trails—overlaying false panics, dead-ends, and enemy markers. The remaining ants stopped, feeling signals the humans could not, antennae sketching agitated figure eights.

The pause ended. Three more bodies boiled out of the grass, using the stalled workers as steppingstones, mandibles already slick with atomized acid. The fog made their aim sloppy. One jet splashed across a barricade; the wood hissed into mush. "Open the rear!" Dixie barked. "Second squad, out and brace!"

The back ramp peeled down. Cold air slapped Keller's faceplate. He followed Juno into the open, boots sticking to a leaf-damp earth, shoulders squared against the instinct to curl small and hide. The world was too big. The ants were too close.

"Here!" Juno stabbed her lance at an ant's foreleg as it cleared the spike hedge. The prongs kissed the softer pit at the joint, and a blue thread of current snapped. The leg buckled. The ant spilled forward, close enough for Keller to see the scratch scars on a mandible from an old fight, and the beaded texture of its eyes.

"Keller!" Dixie's voice with the snap of a whip. He didn't think. He lunged, driving his lance up beneath the jaw hinge the way the diagrams had taught him. The ant's body went rigid, then slack, mandibles still chattering on reflex. He had to work his lance free with both hands. "Nice pin," Juno said, breath ragged. "You and me? We'll make it a habit."

Overhead, the Dragonfly Skimmer dropped low and flared its wings. The oscillation shifted, deeper, a tremor more than a sound. The ants faltered, legs splaying. The Skimmer's aft turret walked a line of flechettes across the ground in front of them, carving a no-go strip that glittered with sharp, humming wire. Confusion turned to retreat: the ants pivoted in the fog, bumping into one another, their perfect traffic broken.

"Don't chase," Top warned. "We're not here to teach them lessons. We're here to make it to Stonewall in one piece. Load up."

They loaded and the ramp sealed. Keller's hands shook as he seated his lance on the rack. Juno leaned back against the bulkhead, helmet resting on it with a hollow thunk. Through the red wash of the cabin lights, Dixie walked the aisle, checking faces, clapping a shoulder here, adjusting a strap there. When she reached Keller, she didn't say anything, just tapped the notch on his lance where the prongs had blackened. The look said: good.

"One span to go," the navigator called. Calm returned in brittle layers. The world outside became motion again, green and gray, and the occasional metallic flash of something human-made and lost.

They crossed a gravel field—a planet of boulders to them—then a spill of ancient birdseed where hulls had to belly-crawl through a tunnel of husks that smelled like stale grain and dust. A desiccated leaf arched overhead like a collapsed cathedral. All the while, the Skimmer scribbled lazy circles above them, and the Scarabs shifted formation with the grace of veteran brawlers: fists that knew when not to clench.

The second Span passed in a rush of small alarms—mites scattering from light, a spider's filament strung like an invisible trip line over the route (cut, marked, avoided), a sudden gust that made the hauler lean into its tracks until Keller imagined the whole convoy sliding away like a toy down a drain.

And then the world ahead stepped down. The grass thinned. The ground rose, firm and tamped, until the flank tankette flashed its lights twice and the Skimmer buzzed its happy chord, and the recruits pressed to the viewports to gawk.

Stonewall rose from the earth like the ribs of some buried giant. Splinter-timbers locked into glass-shard braces; bottle-green panels from a broken vial caught the last light and glowed; scrap-metal plates overlapped like scales. The gate was an old hinge salvaged from a hinge, thick and pitted and new again. Watch posts jutted from the corners, crossbow ports already manned, their crews snapping salutes as the convoy rolled under.

Inside the wall, the air smelled like oil, cooked fungus, and something Keller couldn't name that felt like hope. Teams swarmed the Bastion Hauler before it settled: loaders peeling off the remaining barricade bundles; engineers swearing affectionately at the scuffed Scarab skirts; medics pushing stretchers they wouldn't need, not this time. The new recruits exited the Bastion.

Captain Jones stepped down hard and fast, helmet off, face flushed. Top followed, impassive. Dixie unclipped, turned to face the recruits, and held one fist up. The Hall quieted.

"You did what Micro-Operatives do," she said, voice plain. "You moved. You adapted. You didn't get clever when clever would get you dead. That's the job."

The Fort Commandant, Major Edgar "Buster" Gregg, stood at the end of the platform, his still Austere blue eyes focused on them. For a moment, no speech came. He just nodded once, slowly, like a promise that wasn't words.

Juno bumped Keller's shoulder. "See? Pep talk by silence. That's what I'm talking about"

Keller didn't answer. He was looking past them, past the bustle and the walls, at the horizon where the grass was bluer, and the ground rolled, thinking of the path they'd cut and the ants that now knew a new smell and would come testing again. His hands had stopped shaking. He wasn't sure when.

The Bastion Hauler side bays yawed open and began disgorging their cargo: brace-frames, hinge-ribs, thorn hedges, rolls of vibration mesh. The hauler was a furnace of industry, feeding the bones of a fortress that would hold or break depending on how well they fed it.

"Recruits," Top said, "welcome to Stonewall. Stow the jitters, grab a crate, and follow your sergeants. The outpost won't build itself, and the bugs won't wait for an invitation."

As night settled, Keller shouldered a beam with Juno at the other end. He could feel the weight—real, honest, shared. Somewhere beyond the wall, a click traveled through the grass and was answered farther off. He tightened his grip, breathing steadily in his mask.

The hurried construction of Stonewall Outpost was a testament to humanity's desperate foothold. As the final bracing timbers were slotted into place and the watch towers bristled with crossbows, a palpable sense of fragile victory hung in the air. Captain Jones, his face still bearing the grime of their recent engagement, surveyed the ramparts. Beside him, First Sergeant Miller stood with his usual stoic silence, a sentinel of unwavering resolve. Corporal Dixie, her squad of eight recruits, including Keller and Juno, awaited orders, their initial baptism by fire having clearly etched itself onto their young faces. Their purpose now was clear: to secure the perimeter, a necessary ritual of deterrence and vigilance as the last vestiges of Stonewall's defenses were erected against the encroaching darkness.

The Dragonfly Skimmer, piloted by Dea Anne, a figure as sharp and focused as the craft she commanded, ascended silently, its oscillating wings a blur against the bruised twilight sky. Below, the Scarab Tankettes, squat and purposeful, dispersed like metallic beetles, their rounded hulls a stark contrast to the sharp angles of the half-finished fortress. They moved with a practiced precision, forming a protective cordon around the active construction zones. Captain Jones, his voice crisp over the squad net, briefed his team. "Perimeter sweep. From the hinge gate to the eastern scrapwall. Miller, you take point with the tankettes. Dixie, keep your recruits tight. No heroics, just eyes forward. Dea Anne, keep us covered from above. We're not looking for a fight, but if one finds us, we'll be ready." The recruits, a mixture of apprehension and newfound grit, adjusted their helmet mounts, their Micro-Lances held at the ready.

As they advanced, the terrain revealed its hidden dangers. Blades of grass, still towering like ancient trees in the dim light, rustled with unseen movement, each tremor a potential threat. A spider's silk, shimmering like a death trap, had been strung across a well-worn path, a silent realization to the colossal life teeming just beyond human scale. Miller's lead Scarab calmly dislodged the filament with a controlled burst from its forward-mounted emitter, the tiny, humming strands dissolving into dust. Keller, his senses heightened by the recent encounter, found himself scanning the dense undergrowth, the memory of clicking mandibles and scuttling legs a persistent phantom. Juno, walking beside him, offered a brief, reassuring nod, her own gaze sharp, ever vigilant, a silent acknowledgment of their shared trial. The air, thick with the scent of processed fungus and damp earth, carried the distant, rhythmic pulse of Stonewall's ongoing construction, a symphony of survival that now, for them, included the quiet hum of their own vigilance.

The wind that hissed through Stonewall Outpost's crenelated parapets wasn't wind at all, just a night draft that started two miles away on the human scale. But to Micro-Operatives, it carried grit, scent, and the soft static that meant the weather was turning. Captain Jones felt it prickle across the plates of his AEGIS-CHITIN Mk II Armor as he surveyed the perimeter catwalk, helmet visor set to low tint, eyes flicking from the rubble-stitched kill zone to the dark seam of the Drain Gully where things liked to come from.

First Sergeant Miller paced ten steps behind, big for a half-inch, shoulders square beneath his segmented pauldrons. He carried the squad link on his forearm screen like it was a prayer book, thumb skimming over the ready lights of eight tiny icons arrayed in a diamond formation.

"Perimeter One is sound," Miller reported, voice calm. "Sonic spikes all green. Clay webs unbroken. Trip-filaments holding."

"Out in the gully," Jones said, nodding toward the shadowed trench that served as the outpost's moat. "We've had too many 'quiet' shifts lately."

Miller made a noise that could have been an agreement or just a cough in the mic. "I'll never say quiet on patrol, That's a curse."

They reached the outer bastion where the wall bent into a blunt angle facing the Drain Gully. The ground beyond—

pebbles the size of boulders, splinters like felled trees, brittle curls of old leaf—rolled away in a broken field. A strip of pale dust marked a common insect trackway. The squad moved there like a shadow stitched to Jones's heels: Dixie, the scout; the rookie recruit Jaro and Sal with the Shock-Net launchers; Quill the engineer; Oates the medic; and the two riflemen, Juno and Keller—the latter still wearing his armor too stiff, still learning the way of weight and fear.

Dixie, kneeling at the parapet, craned her neck. A cascade of numbers scrolled across her visor, reflected faintly in her irises. "Picking up kinetic spikes," she said. "Lots. They're… pulse rhythmic. Coming fast."

Miller went still. Jones felt his heartbeat meet the timing of those words like a hand closing around a knife. "Type?"

"Standby, Captain." Dixie thumbed her sensor wand forward on its rail. "Ground impacts eight to twelve meters out, inbound arcs… oh, that's not good." She sucked a breath through her teeth. "Oriental rat fleas. Twenty signatures minimum. They're in a rush pattern."

Even for hardened Micro-Armor, that word sent nerves slicing up spines. Fleas were more jump than flesh: compressed, spring steel bodies with legs like biomechanical trebuchets, a hunger that traveled on a vector, and mouthparts designed by nightmares. Their jump windows were microseconds and miles at once.

Jones glanced over the kill zone. Their perimeter was built to break a crawler wave, not a string of ballistic predators. "How long?"

"First contact in thirty seconds." Dixie's voice remained steady, but she lowered the lance and reached for her rifle in the same breath. She turned, her visor bright. "Eight-man squad, prepare to fight!" Her call lashed into the air. It moved them.

Miller's voice boomed on the squad net, deep as bedrock. "You heard the scout. Battle rattle! Jaro, Sal—load Shock-Nets. Quill, drop arc beacons on my mark, set them two meters staggered, low. Juno, Keller—left sector rifles. Dixie, you're with me midline for jump-timing. Oates, back of the stack—no hero runs."

"Roger," came the chorus, eight voices snapped down to their clean bones.

Jones felt the rhythm take hold: the discipline he'd drilled into them, the thousands of rehearsals run on phantom threats. He checked his own loadout—Neuro-Stunner clipped to his thigh mount, carbine mag readouts humming steady, pulse-charge at eighty-nine percent. He dialed his visor to Jump-Solve mode; the world tinted, became a lattice of arcs and probable landing points.

"Captain?" Miller said on a quieter channel. "You'll keep that Stunner for the breach team if we lose the wall?"

"We won't lose the wall," Jones said, gentle and iron together. "But yes."

"Copy," Miller acknowledged.

Dixie snapped a finger toward the Drain Gully. "Eyes up. They're cresting."

They came like punctuation marks fired from a slingshot—small, dark commas tracing high parabolas on the dusty air. For a split second, each flea was motionless at apex, legs tucked, a clock spring twisted to murder. Then they dropped, accelerating, angular bodies gleaming the color of old cloves.

"First wave three," Dixie counted. "Impact in five—four—three—"

"Anchor nets," Miller barked.

Jaro and Sal shouldered their Shock-Net launchers—twin-barreled devices whose spooled wire hummed with trapped thunder. Jaro fired; the net spat out, a silver lattice blossoming with brutal elegance. It caught the first flea just above the kill zone and wrapped it in a crackling shroud. The flea screamed—a sound half-felt, a buzz drawn through bone.

"Two caught!" Sal shouted; her own net fanning open to snag another in mid-arc. The second screamed, legs splayed like ruined bows, body jerking as electricity sailed through it.

The third hit dirt, skittered, and surged like a thrown dagger.

"Left sector!" Juno called, laying into it with Micro-Bolt rounds. The flea jerked, twisted, leaped again—an ugly, arching bound that cleared the first line of caltrop glass.

"Keller!" Jones snapped.

Keller's shots came wide—too high, chasing the arc instead of the landing. The flea hit the wall and clung, hooked feet finding purchase on rough stone. It flexed once, legs compressing like loaded springs.

Jones moved without thinking. He slammed the muzzle of his carbine into the joint space between the flea's head and thorax and double-tapped. The rounds thudded like hammers into dense chitin. The flea kept coiling. He thumbed his underbarrel, and the pulse-charge went off point-blank, a white-blue blink. The flea convulsed and released, falling, spasming in the dirt. "Reset," Jones said, voice even. "They'll come again."

And they did. The fleas surged in a cadence—triplets and pairs, then the nasty trick of a single long quiet followed by a cluster. They fell into the kill zone and tangled in shock, thrashed across clay webs and left smoking prints, leaped up the wall and were slapped flat by rifle fire and pulser grenades. Quill's arc beacons crackled to life, erecting thin ghostly curtains that stitched the open ground with ion haze;

two fleas hit those in mid-jump and lit up like wicked stars, tumbling in crooked spirals.

Dixie's voice never stopped. "Apex—now. Next window… mark… mark. Angle three low incoming, watch the ricochet. Sal, swing right two degrees—good hit. One loose, centerline, impact in two—one—now!"

Miller flowed along the rampart, the quiet storm of a First Sergeant in his element. He swapped rifles, slapped magazines into trembling hands, turned fear into motion, motion into aim. "Keller, breathe. Breathe, or I'll come take your lungs personally. Juno, don't lead the shadow—lead the fall. Quill, I need a resin burst on sector yellow, they're learning the web pattern."

"Learning? They're fleas, Sarge," Quill muttered, but he palmed a cartridge anyway and slammed it into the dispenser port. A wave of quick-cure resin spat from hidden nozzles, glistening like poured amber across a strip of broken ground. The next jumper hit it and stopped as if God had pressed a finger onto the world. Sal's bolt ended it.

Jones tracked the count in the back of his mind even as he shot, even as he moved to where the pressure built. Eight down in the first minutes. Three more in the nets, thrashing themselves toward stillness. Two scorched, two split by arcs, one smashed against stone so hard his hands rang. "We're at sixteen," Dixie called. "Four unaccounted. Watch for the curveball."

As if obeying, the battlefield went thin and strange. The fleas stopped coming from the open gully mouth. The dust trail that had flurried with their approach went still.

"They're cycling," Jones realized. "Re-vectoring."

"Which means—" Miller began.

"—they're going to flank," Jones finished. He spun and scanned the right-hand spillway. It was narrower, a runnel that led along the footings of the wall toward an angle where the stone met old, crumpled foil. Perfect springboard, perfect cover.

"Squad, Right Two!" Miller roared. Captain Jones shouted, "Shift! Dixie, eyes!"

"Got it—there!" She pointed. Four dark commas, low arc, coming from the foil seam, like knives thrown underhand. "Jaro!" Jones barked.

"On it, Captain."

Jaro's last net sang and blossomed. Two fleas hit it. The third sailed under, shadow rippling over Jones's boots. The fourth clipped the wall and vanished into the shadow of the parapet, legs whispering, gone. "Lost one inside!" Juno yelled, feet already moving.

"Negative!" Miller snapped. "Hold the line. Captain—"

"I've got it." Jones didn't wait for permission.

He vaulted down a ladder rung, slid into the narrow run of rock between the parapet and the inner wall. It was dim and close, the air tasting like metal and old sun. He could hear it—tiny claws on stone, the churn of a spring winding.

The flea came at him from the shadow, a blur of hardness. He threw himself sideways, and it grazed his thigh, hooks skittering over armor, turning his skin cold where bruises would bloom later. It hit the stone, clung, and turned, legs compressing.

Jones didn't raise his carbine. He hit the activator on his thigh mount and drew the Neuro-Stunner.

It was not a pretty weapon. It didn't make holes; it made endings. Thin as a baton, flanged with emitters, it lived for close quarters. He thumbed it to wide fan, and when the flea launched, he stepped into it and cut the air with an invisible blade.

The Stunner's field hummed. The flea hit it mid-spring and froze, arrested in a physics that didn't care about muscle.

It dropped at his feet, legs twitching in a fractional tremor. A second pulse stilled it completely.

"Clear," Jones gasped. He realized he'd been holding his breath after all.

He climbed back up into the sunlight and the sound of his squad finishing a fight: The last flea died on a resin strip, a single line of smoke curling up and away like someone writing a name he couldn't read.

Silence landed. It wasn't complete—the outpost hummed with its generators, and somewhere a wind vibrated through an old wire—but it was silent enough to carry the truth that everyone was still here.

Miller rolled his shoulders, jaw working as if chewing through an old memory. "Twenty," he said at last. "Dixie?"

"Twenty," she confirmed. "My counts match. No second wave signatures."

"Scavenge cycle," Jones ordered, voice gentle to bleed the adrenaline out. "Sal, Jaro—retrieve nets, watch your gloves. Quill, check arcs, and reset beacons. Juno, Keller—police the brass, check the resin before it sets hard. Oates—sweep for bites and breaks."

They moved. They always moved. It was how you stayed human after the fight.

Keller came to Jones, helmet under his arm, face pale under the grit. "Captain… I—thanks for the save."

Jones studied him for a heartbeat. The kid's hands were steady now. That mattered. "You saved yourself," Jones said. "You took a breath when the Sergeant told you. You listened to Dixie's windows. Next time you'll put those rounds on the landing."

Keller nodded like a penitent, then surprised Jones by smiling—a small thing, but real. "Yes, sir."

Dixie joined them, sensor wand slung. She tapped the flea carcass Jones had dropped below the parapet with the toe of her boot. "You walked it with the Stunner? Show-off."

"I was out of time," Jones said.

"You're not wrong," she conceded. Her visor flicked as she scrolled through her recording. "On the playback, wave three tried to calibrate to our web spacing. Quill, your resin shift threw them dumb again."

Quill grunted from where he pried a beacon out of a rock crack. "Good to know dumb is still an option."

Miller approached, the shape of him cutting what was left of the moon-lit sky. He rested his fists on his hips and looked out over the kill zone—the shattered nets, the stilled bodies, the small curls of smoke. His voice went quiet in a way that always made the squad lean in to hear. "This is how they'll come at Stonewall," he said. "Not today, not tomorrow. But they will. They'll come learning. They'll come fast. We do not gift them a wall to practice on."

Jones nodded. "We tighten. We stop thinking like we're waiting and start thinking like we're shaping. Quill, adjust clay web lines to irregular spacing. Mix your resin with grit so it looks like nothing until it's everything. Dixie, write me a new jump-window drill. Pair Keller with Juno until they breathe the same." Dixie saluted with two fingers, "already putting it together, Cap."

Jones let his gaze travel the horizon, where the Drain Gully cut a jagged smile across the broken field. Stonewall Outpost crouched against that seam, like a knuckle planted in dirt. They'd hold it. Not because it was pretty, nothing was pretty at this scale—but because it was the hinge on which the route to the farms swung, and behind that hinge were people who would never even know a fight had happened on their behalf. Jones found Miller's eye. "Supper's going to taste like ozone."

Miller sniffed, a shadow of humor crossing his blunt features. "Better than dust. Barely."

Oates finished his sweep and held up a scanner. "No bites. Jaro's got a mesh burn, but it's on the surface. Keller's going to have a beautiful bruise."

"I'll wear it with honor," Keller said, half-grinning now.

"Wear it with padding," Miller said dryly. He took one last look at the field, the bodies already cooling toward the color of the earth. "All right.

Reset and rotate. Patrol Two takes over in twenty. We're not done with the night yet."

They packed the fight away piece by piece, rolled the thunder back onto spools, and brushed the resin with sand until it disguised itself as ground. The wind—no wind—moved again, and with it the thin, clean smell that lived after storm and fire: the smell of a wall that had held.

When the relief squad clanked up the stairs, Jones passed them on the rampart and clapped each shoulder. He felt the buzz of their armor through his gloves, like the last ripples of a bell that had been struck.

"Captain," Dixie said, falling into step beside him as they headed inward. "When I said, 'prepare to fight'… they really did."

"They will again," Jones said. He looked at the outpost's inner court, where banners painted with the BUGFORCE insignia moved in the warm draft. "And again, after that."

"And again," Miller echoed from behind, steady as a heartbeat.

Stonewall stood. The morning leaned toward a gold that never quite reached the ground at their scale, but it was enough to paint the edges of their armor and turn the resin's dull surface to a ribbon of light before it hid itself. The squad walked those battlements like owners, and guardians, and something harder to name.

On the far edge of the field, a tiny speck jumped and vanished, nothing more than punctuation in a sentence already written.

"Let them come," Jones murmured.

Dixie adjusted her visor, recording the horizon. "We'll be ready."

Chapter 2

Building Stonewall

When the first squads of BUGFORCE arrived at the lip of the drainage culvert, they found nothing but broken ground and hostile soil. The place was little more than a scar on the earth, surrounded by creeping weeds and the constant hum of insect wings. Yet to Captain William Jones and First Sergeant Miller, this spot was destiny. It would be here, on contested ground, that the Micro-Operatives would raise their first lasting bastion: Stonewall Outpost.

The materials were meager, but the ingenuity was boundless. Scavenger teams hauled pencil shafts from the Overworld above, each sharpened to a crude point. Driven into the dirt at Micro-Operatives scale, they took hold deeper than expected, settling firm and true, becoming palisades thick as timbers, unyielding like stone. Behind them, bottle caps—once useless scrap—were overturned and pressed into the mud, where the ground seemed to accept them, sealing their edges as armored plates that deflected both mandible and stinger. The rough beginnings looked more like a junk heap than a fortress, but to the weary soldiers, it was a promise. The work was relentless.

Micro-Operatives squads rotated between combat patrols and construction duty, knowing the enemy could strike at any moment. Ant scouts probed the lines while fleas tested the wire traps. Yet every attack only stilled the Micro-Operatives' resolve. With every hour of toil, a new section of wall rose, a trench deepened, or a rampart lined with razor blades set edge-out, gleaming like the fangs of a predator.

Within three spans of constant labor, Stonewall Outpost began to take form. The Command Bunker, carved beneath a rusted tin shard, became the nerve center of the garrison.

Wax paper sheets served as roof insulation, held down with pushpin anchors driven deep into the soil. From here, comms relays crackled with static but held, allowing messages to reach distant units patrolling Reed Flats and Lotus Lake.

The outer wall was christened "The Pencil Line." Each shaft had sunk at a tight angle, forming a bristling barrier that no swarm could easily penetrate. Behind it, pits lined with broken glass fragments and sharpened nails created deadly kill zones. Bottle caps, polished to shine, doubled as both shield plates and reflective signals—sunlight glinting from their surfaces became an early-warning code for approaching patrols.

The heart of the outpost was the Stonewall Parade Ground, a flat span of compacted soil where squads drilled daily. Though small by human measure, it was vast to the Micro-Operatives, capable of mustering three full platoons. Around it, the quarters were simple dugouts lined with matchstick beams. At night, fireflies harnessed in glass beads cast their glow, illuminating the fortress in a spectral haze.

The final act of completion came with the raising of the BUGFORCE Emblem above the gate. Painted onto the inside of a soda-can shard, the six-legged beetle symbol stood stark against the blue of the sky. For the first time, Micro-Operatives looked upon a fortress that felt truly theirs—built not from borrowed human tools alone, but from sweat, sacrifice, and stubbornness.

The true genius of Stonewall lay not in its size, but in its symbolism. It told the insects that BUGFORCE was no longer a bunch of nomads. They had claimed ground, held it, and fortified it—and the ground had answered back. Stonewall was no longer merely built upon the earth; it was *threaded into it*, its walls braced by unseen strength, its foundations gripped by something older than stone. The Micro-Operatives felt only stability beneath their boots, but the insects saw more. They saw roots where there should have been soil. Bark pressing through scrap and stone, a living boundary forming around human will. Stonewall was a defiance etched into the earth—and answered by it.

Stonewall Outpost would go on to serve as the anchor of the entire frontier campaign. From its walls, scouts would launch missions into Reed Flats, supply convoys would ferry across Lotus Lake, and the first assaults on the Beamhive Gate would be staged. Its ramparts became the line Micro-Operatives swore to hold at all costs. Every plank, every shard, every bottle cap carried the memory of hands that bled to set it in place.

Once the construction slowed, the fortress settled into a rhythm. Dawn at Stonewall was marked by the buzz of the firefly lanterns dimming and the whistle of morning drill. Recruits marched across the Parade Ground, their micro-armor clattering in time as they practiced shield walls and fire team formations. Veterans supervised, their armor scarred from past battles in Reed Flats, reminding the younger ones of what awaited them beyond the walls.

Mess was a communal affair. Meals of condensed nutrient paste, ground seeds, and droplets of dew collected in a thimble cap. Recruits took droplets and shared shoulder to shoulder. In downtime, soldiers etched their names—or sometimes just initials—into the wooden ribs of the Pencil Line. Each mark was both a claim of presence and a vow of protection.

Training never ceased. Archery ranges used needle-tips as targets, and sparring pits allowed warriors to test their exo-rigs against one another. Engineers experimented with traps and barriers, constantly repurposing scavenged debris into defense tools. Every day was a blend of vigilance, innovation, and solidarity.

The true test of Stonewall came sooner than expected. On a moonlit night, a column of ants emerged from the culvert, testing the outpost's resolve. They came silently at first, slipping between shadows, mandibles clacking softly like the clicking of knives. The sentries spotted them only because a glint of moonlight caught on a polished exoskeleton.

The alarm sounded. The walls shook as warriors scrambled to positions, shields raised, weapons braced. The Pencil Line held as the ants threw themselves at the barrier, only to be met with spears and falling shards hurled from above. Razor blades embedded in the earth shredded their legs, forcing them into the kill pits where glass and nails awaited.

For hours, the fighting raged until the last ant retreated into the night, dragging the bodies of its fallen kin. When dawn broke, Stonewall's defenders were bloodied but unbowed. The fortress had not only survived—it had proven itself. From that moment forward, the phrase "Stonewall Holds" was not just an oath. It was truth forged in battle.

The Engineers of BUGFORCE were unlike any others. Where a human engineer would survey land and steel, they worked with scavenged fragments of the Overworld and the shifting soil of the Micro-Operatives scale. Their eyes measured not in meters but in grains, every mound of dirt, a ridge, every pebble a boulder. With them marched the Ground Division, soldiers who turned design into reality, their spades and mauls working as tirelessly as their rifles. Together they faced the question that haunted the outpost's birth: Could Stonewall truly withstand the swarms?

Ants were the most immediate and familiar enemy. Patient, organized, relentless. Their assaults came like tides, not as individual skirmishers but as entire companies of living machines. To counter them, Engineers sank bottle-cap plates into the soil at the base of the Pencil Line. These curved domes forced ants upward, breaking their phalanx cohesion and exposing their soft undersides to spear thrusts.

Moats lined with ground glass were carved into arcs, each shard angled to cut through chitinous legs. Above, razor blades were embedded as vertical barriers—so sharp and so alien that even the ants hesitated at their glimmer. Yet no defense was perfect. Engineers knew ants would eventually bridge pits with their own bodies. Plans for rolling barricades made of thimble rims were drafted, but resources remained too scarce. For every ingenious trap laid, there was the gnawing awareness that the ants' sheer numbers might one day overwhelm them.

Roaches presented a different terror. They were not tacticians but juggernauts. Their armored shells could shrug off a spear strike, and their scuttling movements ignored terrain where smaller insects balked. Against them, the Ground Division devised crushing corridors—narrow alleys lined with stacked matchsticks. When a roach forced its way in, squads could collapse the corridor by pulling weighted string lines, burying the beast beneath a cascade of rubble.

Engineers also experimented with fire traps, igniting oil-soaked fibers when roaches entered choke points. But the outpost lacked steady fuel, and the risk of burning the entire structure made commanders wary. The solution, as with all things in BUGFORCE, was improvisation: spring-latch harpoons fashioned from small bent safety pins, capable of piercing even a roach's hide when released at close range.

Still, whispers grew among the rank and file. Roaches could burrow, and every time a patrol reported strange tremors beneath the soil, a new rumor spread. What if the enemy simply came from below, bypassing the Pencil Line entirely?

The wasps were the greatest nightmare of all. Ants could be outmaneuvered, roaches crushed, but wasps brought death from above. Their wings thrummed like storms, and their stingers struck with the power of spears. For the Micro-Operatives, even a single wasp could devastate an entire squad.

To answer this threat, the Engineers constructed canopy screens of woven thread, strung between the tips of pencil shafts. These nets sagged under dew but could tangle wings long enough for soldiers to strike. In the open, squads carried mirror-shields made from foil fragments, angled to flashlight into wasp eyes and disorient their dives. On the outpost's ramparts, crossbows built from bent staples waited, each one capable of firing a needle-bolt skyward with surprising force.

Yet for all their ingenuity, nothing silenced the dread that swelled whenever a shadow passed overhead. Veterans told stories of entire platoons scattered by a wasp's sudden strike. The fortress might stand against ground assaults, but would its walls matter if the enemy simply swooped in over them?

As defenses grew more elaborate, so too did the doubts. Every new trap, every sharpened shard, reminded the soldiers of the enemies it was meant to stop—and the inevitability that one day those enemies would test them. Around the firefly lamps at night, murmurs spread: Was Stonewall really solid and defendable?

The Engineers debated endlessly in the Command Bunker. Some insisted that the layers of traps and barricades made Stonewall unassailable. Others, grimmer, argued that the outpost's very visibility was its weakness. The insects were too many, too adaptable. Sooner or later, they would find a weakness.

Captain Jones never showed doubt publicly, but even he wondered. He walked the Pencil Line at dusk, running a gloved hand along the jagged barriers. They were strong, yes—but they were finite. Ants and roaches were not. And the sky, with its endless wings, remained beyond their full control.

The Ground Division drilled harder, turning tension into discipline. Micro-Operatives learned to swap between ant-fighting formations, roach-trap deployments, and wasp-defense drills in minutes. Engineers revised their blueprints constantly, scavenging for more shards, more caps, more blades. Every defense was a compromise: strong in one direction, vulnerable in another.

Stonewall Outpost was not a fortress of comfort. It was a fortress of necessity, stitched together from human refuse and Micro-Operatives' resolve. Its walls could repel, its traps could kill, but its true strength was the men and women who believed in it.

And yet belief was fragile. Each new raid tested it. Each shadow overhead strained it. Even as the emblem shone bright above the gate, the unspoken question weighed heavily on every heart: Would it be enough?

In the weeks that followed, Stonewall earned its reputation through blood and persistence. Ant waves broke upon the Pencil Line. Roach incursions were repelled with harpoons and collapsing corridors. Wasps were blinded, tangled, and occasionally slain. The outpost held—but only barely. Every defense that succeeded was matched by a near-disaster.

The Micro-Operatives began to understand the truth. Stonewall was not invincible. It was not impregnable. But it was a stand. A rallying point. A declaration that BUGFORCE would not yield, the earth without contest.

When new recruits arrived, the veterans told them the same line: Stonewall may not stand forever—but while it stands, we hold the line. And for that, the Engineers kept building, the Ground Division kept training, and the outpost's battered walls became something greater than stone. They became hope itself.

Chapter 3

A Fortress in the Wilds

Stonewall Outpost stood tall against the miniature Horizon. Micro-Operatives are at their assigned post in the watch towers, and Micro-Operatives are on perimeter patrol, keeping an eye out for any involvement that may compromise the outpost.

Stonewall was a success! Global Command was proud of this accomplishment. To ensure that Bugforce continues to gain ground and hold it. The High Command brought a long-awaited idea into fruition. The idea was to separate BUGFORCE into four divisions: Ground, Water, Tree, and Air. These divisions will be stationed across the earth in the field that they are named after.

Major General Rueben Edwards created the Specialist IV rank designation for unit scouts. After training, they held the designation MSO (Master Scout-Operatives). They received some of the best training in the world, and each one was assigned to a different Division to study and examine the approach of the enemy. General Edwards was big on acronyms. He is the one who coined the term BUGFORCE, which stands for Biological Unit Guard: Field Operations Reconnaissance Control & Engagement.

Corporal Dixie Lake, a legend in her own right, was given the first appointment because of her bravery in past battles. Dixie was assigned to the Tree Division with her comrades, and friends Captain William Jones and 1st Sergeant Richard Miller. After 7 Moonspans of quiet at the Outpost, Dixie reported that the ants are preparing to attack. Corporal Dixie Lake's report cut through the quiet hum of Stonewall Outpost like a sharpened splinter. "I have movement on the perimeter preparing to attack," she announced, her voice tight with the grim certainty of experience. Her red hair seemed to crackle with the same energy as the unease that had settled over the perimeter. For the past seven Moonspans, an unusual stillness had masked a growing threat, and now, Dixie's keen eyes had detected the subtle, yet undeniable, shifts in the surrounding foliage. She noted strange insect activity gathering around Stonewall's perimeter, a disturbing pattern of movement that spoke of an organized, coordinated advance, far beyond the usual skirmishes.

Captain William Jones, his bald head gleaming under the outpost lights, immediately moved to Dixie's side. His chitin exoskeleton, a witness to countless engagements, shifted with his purposeful stride. "Strange activity, Dixie? Elaborate," he commanded, his voice a low rumble that carried authority. 1st Sergeant Miller, his white handlebar mustache against his weathered face, joined them, his piercing light blue eyes scanning the maps laid out on the tactical table. The prospect of a full-scale assault, especially after the initial success of the Bugforce reorganization, was a sobering one. The new BUGFORCE divisions were untested in large-scale conflict, and the enemy's precise timing suggested they were aware of this vulnerability.

The true gravity of Dixie's report began to dawn as the forward observation units relayed their findings. Not only were the ants massing, but they were employing tactics never seen. Swarms of beetles, heavily armored and seemingly impervious to standard projectile fire, advanced in tight formations, with armored chitinous plates. The ground troopers began loading into the Scarab Tankettes, the Ground Division's primary assault vehicles, but now they were being countered by an equally formidable, yet alien, force. Above, the air began to thrum with the beating of a thousand wings. The enemy was deploying their own aerial units, a menacing cloud that promised to overwhelm the Sky Division's emerging defenses. Dea Anne, the Chief Warrant Officer, already prepped in her flight suit, was receiving urgent updates, her bright red hair a streak of defiance against the encroaching darkness, as the threat to Stonewall Outpost escalated from a potential engagement to an immediate and critical threat.

Specialist Diaz, the Ground Divisions Entomologist, was stroking and pulling on his long mustache while listening to insect chatter over the Insect-Comm Decoder or the IDC-1. Diaz quickly raised his hand and shouted stop while he continued to listen to the insect chatter. He looked at the Ground Divisions Major Gregg, whom he calls *buster*, Jones, and Dixie, and spoke out saying, "They are just taunting us." Let's hold our ground; this is an act of psychological warfare. Specialist Diaz's declaration hung in the air, a stark counterpoint to the rising panic. "Taunting us?" Captain Jones echoed, his voice a low growl. He turned from the tactical map, his gaze locking with Diaz's. "Psychological warfare? Diaz, we're facing an organized invasion force, not a debate club." 1st Sergeant Miller, his expression unreadable beneath the stern lines of his face, adjusted his grip on a data-slate. "If it is psychological, it's effective. The sheer scale of their deployment, the uncanny timing… It's designed to sow doubt, to make us question our own strength, our new strategy." Corporal Dixie Lake, her own brow furrowed, tapped her lance against the stone floor. "They're not just attacking our defenses; they're attacking our minds. Since the 14th turn of Deepfall, it's been this way. A feint here, a display of overwhelming force there, always just outside our effective range, but visible enough to remind us of what we're up against. They're trying to wear us down before the real assault even begins."

The realization settled over the command center with a chilling finality. The ant and beetle forces weren't merely engaged in a frontal assault; they were orchestrating a meticulously planned campaign of attrition, a war of nerves waged on the very foundations of Micro-Operatives morale. The heavily armored beetle formations, the menacing aerial swarms – these were not just military assets, but tools of terror, designed to inspire fear and uncertainty. Each observed movement, each intercepted transmission of insect chatter, was being twisted and amplified into a narrative of Micro-Operatives' vulnerability. Specialist Diaz, the entomologist, had identified the pattern, the subtle cues that spoke not of brute force alone, but of calculated manipulation. He had heard the whispers in the insect chatter, the boasts and threats that served no tactical purpose beyond undermining the defenders' resolve.

Captain Jones, a man who had faced down countless biological horrors, felt a prickle of unease he hadn't experienced since his early days. He understood the strategic value of intimidation, but this felt... personal. "So, they're not just trying to break our lines," he mused, his voice resonating with a newfound gravity. "They're trying to break our will. Diaz, your analysis is critical. We need to counter this, not just with force, but with our own unwavering conviction. We hold the ground, and we hold our minds." 1st Sergeant Miller nodded, his eyes narrowed in grim determination. "14 Phases of this psychological siege. Suddenly, the Insects disappeared from the Micro-Operatives' view. It's time we showed them that Micro-Operatives resolve is as unyielding as our chitin armor." Under Captain William Jones's watchful gaze, a new strategy began to take shape, one born not of brute force but of resilience and adaptation. While Specialist Diaz worked to decipher the subtle nuances of the enemy's psychological onslaught, Jones turned his attention to the Tree Division's unique strengths. He recognized that to effectively counter the enemy's aerial and ground maneuvers, they needed elevated vantage points, positions from which to observe and intercept, and to do so without revealing their full strength. "Dixie," Jones declared, his voice cutting through the hushed tension, "we need eyes in the sky, but the ants control the air. We will take the fight to the trees themselves." With that, he directed a contingent of his division toward a grove of young Willow saplings, a half-span west of Stonewall Outpost, now referred to as the Willow Stand. Here, under his direct supervision, they began the painstaking work of constructing new watchtowers, not from milled lumber or prefabricated materials, but from the very essence of their environment: carefully selected twigs and stripped bark, woven and layered with an instinctive precision that spoke of generations of arboreal warfare.

Corporal Dixie Lake, her red hair a vibrant contrast against the muted greens and browns of the Willow Stand, worked alongside her comrades, her lance serving as a versatile tool for both construction and defense. The saplings, young and pliable, were coaxed into forming sturdy scaffolds, their branches intertwined with bark to create platforms that would offer a commanding view of the surrounding terrain. Each twig, each piece of bark, was placed with deliberate care, a validation to the Micro-Operatives' ability to leverage their environment. The enemy's relentless psychological warfare, designed to erode their will, instead served to sharpen their focus. Jones understood that by engaging in this meticulous, creative endeavor, they were not only building physical defenses but also reinforcing their own mental fortitude, demonstrating to the ants that their attempts at intimidation were fostering only a deeper sense of purpose and unity within the Tree Division.

As the watchtowers slowly rose amongst the willows, they became more than just structures; they were symbols of defiance. The enemy's perceived invincibility was being chipped away, not by overwhelming firepower, but by the quiet determination of Micro-Operatives building their own strategic advantage from the ground up. Captain Jones observed the methodical progress, the focused intensity of his three Micro-Operatives, and felt a surge of pride. This was the true strength of the Bugforce reorganization – the ability to adapt, to innovate, and to draw upon the specialized skills of each division. The ants might believe they were engaging in a war of attrition, but they failed to account for the Micro-Operatives' unwavering determination and their profound connection to the very earth they fought to protect. The Willow Stand, once a quiet grove, was transforming into a silent, potent threat, poised to observe and respond to the insidious machinations of the enemy.

As the Tree Division completes the new builds of the watchtowers, Captain William Jones expands, and they're into a full-fledged Tree Division post that includes a Command room, Barracks, Supply Vaults, Medical Hollow, Workshops, observation perches, and Escape root tunnels. Willow Stand was equipped by its Tree Rangers with Camouflage Canopy Nets, Pheromone Disruption Towers, and a host of other defenses. As this area was completed, Captain Jones extended efforts to the Elms near the swampy Reed Flats and Lotus Grove, where Broadwater widens into Lotus Lake, with low-hanging trees mixed with floating lotus blooms. As Willow Stand solidified into a formidable Tree Division post, Captain William Jones oversaw the deployment of advanced defenses. Camouflage Canopy Nets draped the sprawling branches, rendering the post nearly invisible from above, while Pheromone Disruption Towers pulsed with unseen waves, confusing any airborne threats. It was this type of ingenuity and dedication of the Tree Rangers that would later build a compact force capable of immense strategic impact. Juno, a Tree Ranger whose Russian heritage was etched in her stark features, her purple-dyed hair a vibrant defiance against the muted greens and browns of the forest, felt the weight of it all. Strapped into her green and bark brown exoskeleton armor suit, she moved with a precision that belied her diminutive stature. From her perch on an observation spire, she surveyed the meticulously constructed Command room, the spartan Barracks, the secure Supply Vaults, and the life-saving Medical Hollow. Even the humming Workshops and the shadowed escape root tunnels spoke of a larger purpose. She reflected on their existence, on how their small frames housed such vast responsibilities. They were but specks against the grand canvas of the world, yet their vigilance, their very survival, hinged on their ability to protect what was precious. The captain's attention now turned to the Elms bordering the swampy Reed Flats and the serene Lotus Grove, where Broadwater widened into the tranquil expanse of Lotus Lake. Here, low-hanging branches mingled with the ethereal dance of floating lotus blooms, a deceptively peaceful landscape that masked potential vulnerabilities. The Tree Division's expansion was not merely about building structures; it was about extending their watchful gaze, about weaving a more comprehensive defensive network. It was in these quieter moments, between the calculated movements and the hum of technology, that Juno's thoughts often drifted. She recalled her induction, the stern pronouncements about the gravity of their mission. The contrast between their physical size and the immense scope of their duty was a constant, gnawing awareness. Recruit Bryan Keller, his husky frame already hinting at the strength that would one day elevate him to Class II Operator, often found himself alongside Juno, discussing their roles. He, too, was eager to serve as a scout, his ambition burning as brightly as Juno's purple hair. He admired her efficiency, her quiet competence. He understood, in his own way, the burden they all carried. The serene beauty of the Lotus Grove, so inviting and tranquil, could easily become a deceptive trap. As they prepared for the next phase of reconnaissance, the air thick with the scent of damp earth and blooming flora, Bryan felt a surge of determination. They were small, yes, but their commitment was boundless, their perseverance forged in the fires of necessity, ready to face whatever threats lay hidden beneath the tranquil surface of the lake. These three Tree Sector Division areas assisted Captain Jones and his squads with better overwatch and increased scout operations for the Stonewall battlefield. After the completion of the Ground and Tree Division's Outpost, the High Command sent Commander Arlen Veyra to look at establishing a PT-Boat Marina to establish supply routes and security on the water in the area.

After 3 Moonspans in Climbmoon, the Roc-Cargo arrived at Stonewall with Commander Arlen Veyra. After the Cargo plane landed, Commander Veyra was met by Troopers of the Ground Division. These Micro-Operatives led the Commander to the Stonewall command; they led her to a large door that led to the operations center. This room had a picture of a large, winged insect embedded in the door with the word Hivewatch inscribed on it. Commander Veyra walked into a darkened, round-shaped room with a large round table in the center. The table is a glowing, hex-mapped projection table displaying Stonewall's perimeter, swarm movements, and resource levels. As she looked around, she observed Operator stations in recessed alcoves with control slates, linked to surveillance beetle-cams, perimeter sensors, and Bastion Hauler logistics. as she looked up to the dome ceiling in amazement she was greeted by Major Edgar Greg of the Ground Division at Stonewall. "Commander, I hope your trip was pleasant, Welcome to Stonewall you can call me Buster". Commander Veyra, a seasoned officer from a PT Boat Squad, offered a crisp nod in return. "Major, the journey was uneventful, though the necessity of such a lengthy transport underscores the urgency of our situation." She reached into the breastplate of her own, more streamlined exoskeleton, a darker, iridescent chitin that spoke of aquatic deployments. From a concealed compartment, she withdrew a data-slate, its surface flickering to life with the holographic insignia of BUGFORCE High Command. "My orders are clear, Major. I have been assigned direct oversight of Harborpoint Command. My mandate is to ensure its operational readiness and to assess its strategic vulnerability in the face of ongoing swarm movements." The projection table's ambient glow illuminated the stern lines of her face as she awaited Greg's response, her gaze sharp and assessing.

Major Edgar Greg, a man whose imposing six-foot frame was encased in a formidable chitinous exoskeleton of deep brown and rust colored armor, gestured towards one of the operator stations. "Harborpoint, yes. A critical nexus. We've had our concerns, Commander, particularly regarding the integrity of their defenses. Lieutenant Edwina Hernandez has been instrumental in bolstering our river patrols around Harborpoint, a woman of unparalleled dedication and foresight." He paused, allowing the weight of their shared responsibilities to settle. "Your presence here, Commander Veyra, is a welcome reinforcement. High Command clearly recognizes the escalating threat, and I believe your expertise will be invaluable in coordinating our different assets."

Veyra's eyes scanned the hex-mapped projection, tracing the faint red vectors that indicated swarm incursions and the pulsing blue nodes representing resource caches. The constant ebb and flow of data on the table was a witness to the relentless pressure Stonewall endured. " Lieutenant Hernandez`s efforts are noted and appreciated, Major," Veyra stated, her voice even. "But oversight at Harborpoint requires a broader perspective. I will need access to their full sensor logs, their defensive matrices, and a direct line to their command structure. The Roc-Cargo brought me here, but my focus now shifts from transit to protection. The time for passive observation is rapidly receding." At that moment, Lieutenant Edwina Hernandez walked into Hivewatch and saluted Major Greg, saying, "Reporting as ordered, sir." "Yes, would you please escort your new Commander to Harbor Point?" Ordered Major Greg.

Lieutenant Hernandez escorted Lieutenant Commander Arlen Veyra to PT Boat SR-01 UWS Dart. The Dart left Stonewall Outpost, headed south to Harbor Point Command. As the boat approached Lotus Lake, the Commander's eyes rose in pride as they approached the first Water Division Base. Lieutenant Commander Arlen Veyra, a veteran of countless patrols and swift amphibious assaults, found herself gazing out at the shimmering expanse of Lotus Lake. The sight of the Water Division's first base, a meticulously constructed network of docks and fortified structures, stirred a flicker of pride within her. Beside her, Lieutenant (Junior Grade) Edwina Hernandez, her demeanor a blend of youthful resolve and seasoned professionalism, offered a subtle smile. As PT Boat SR-01 UWS Dart glided towards one of the main slips, Veyra's gaze was drawn to the figures assembled on the dock. Micro-

Operatives Sailors, their uniforms immaculate, stood at rigid attention, awaiting the arrival of their commander. The anticipation in the air was perceptible, a silent acknowledgment of rank and the gravity of their shared mission. This was not merely a docking procedure; it was a presentation of readiness, a affirmation to the discipline ingrained in every member of the Water Division.

The Dart eased into its berth with practiced precision, the mooring lines expertly secured by the awaiting crew. Commander Veyra, disembarking with a fluid grace honed by years of naval service, was met with a crisp, unified salute. The sailors' eyes, sharp and focused, conveyed a silent respect that transcended mere protocol. Lieutenant Hernandez, by her side, provided a brief, hushed introduction to the officers presenting their compliments. Veyra returned the honors with a nod, her gaze sweeping across the impressive array of PT boats docked within the harbor, each bearing the insignia of the Stingray Class. She saw not just vessels, but instruments of war, meticulously maintained and ready for deployment. The pride she felt moments before solidified into a quiet determination. This base, this force, was an integral part of the larger defense, a crucial focal point against the encroaching swarm.

"Commander Veyra," Lieutenant Hernandez began, her voice resonating with quiet authority, "Welcome to Lotus Lake. Your presence here is an honor. We are prepared for your assessment, and all divisional assets are at your disposal." Veyra's gaze lingered on the water, the vast, blue canvas that was both their primary conduit and their greatest vulnerability. The strategic significance of Harborpoint, of Lotus Lake itself, was underscored by the sheer scale of the Water Division's presence. She recognized in the disciplined formations and the pristine condition of the vessels a formidable capacity. The journey from Stonewall had been a necessary prelude, but now, standing on the solid ground of this vital outpost, her true work, the work of safeguarding their fragile domain, was about to begin.

*****

The last hammer fall rang a tiny bell against the vastness of the world. From the ridge line of bark that crowned Stonewall Outpost, the Micro-Operatives watched the final brace slide into its socket, a wedge no larger than a fingernail to them, a timber girder to those who carried it. The brace locked with a soft, satisfying click. For a breath—one collective breath—the outpost went quiet. Wind bled across the moss fields and through the willow crowns; the river beyond spoke in its endless tongue. Somewhere far off, a fly skimmed the air, its wings a cathedral's worth of stained glass and thunder.

"Mark it," 1st Sgt Miller said, and his voice on the net was more exhale than order.

Below, the carpenters chalked the brace with a charcoal sigil. A final line on a long map.

They had worked in Steps and Spans—half-inch footfalls and hours stitched into six-hour Reaches—until the days no longer felt like days but braided lengths of effort. Now the

fortification lay completed in a ring of pale wood and braided wire, sunk posts, tuned membranes, and sap-cured shields: a necklace tight to the throat of Stonewall. It was not one wall, but systems within systems, layers, the way the bark itself formed its slow concentric story.

Captain William Jones stood in the western bastion with his hands behind his back, staring out at the moss flats that sloped to the Broadwater River. He had a catalog of each piece in his head, and yet, seeing it whole, he felt small in a way he hadn't since his first patrol in Reed Flats. The ridge looked like nothing from the broad scale of things, no more than a scab on a branch. But under his boots, it was a city's works: palisade teeth, culvert gates, hinge-bridges, sap-bladder baffles, bolt towers, listening webs spidered from dew-thread. People. So many of them. Each is as small as a seed. Each carrying a lift the size of a duty.

Miller joined him. He leaned his elbows onto the top rail, a motion as familiar as prayer. "All tied off," he said. "Tree Division logged the last guyline. We're sealed."

Jones nodded, as if that wasn't exactly what he'd been waiting to hear. "And the river?"

"Boom anchored. Stingrays on station. Lily-pad pontoons slotted to the shallows, decoy rafts out in a lazy 'S' to catch a vanguard. If anything, bigger than a water flea brushes that boom, we'll hear it in Hivewatch before the ripples finish their sentence."

Jones's gaze followed the line of water to where the Broadwater bent its back like a bow. The Stingray-class PT boats were there, silhouettes tucked under a root-arch's shadow, their manta profiles barely breaking the film. In training briefs, the river was a corridor. In truth, it was a moving world: a pane of glass that could turn to teeth when the wind rose or when the larger lives of the wetland shrugged. Their boats were knives along a leviathan's flank.

"Do you ever..." Jones began and then stopped. Finishing the sentence in his head, "Feel small and obsolete in this world we're in," Miller's mouth twitched. "Yes."

They stood in that shared admission. In the wind, the palisade cracked and settled. The newness of it felt like a young scar.

Corporal Dixie Lake saw the whole fort differently than either of them. She perched on a signal mast, harness clipped, a skimmer hooded behind her like a waiting bird. From this height, the palisade's geometry lay itself bare: a spool of defensive thought, spiral and spoke. Canopy lines stitched to the crowns of the willow stand. Vinecrawler clamps sunk in bark. The Branch Bastion—new and haughty—perched on a cradle of living wood like a siege tower that had decided to become a treehouse. Between them, lanes of fire marked by chalk, whisper-lines drawn on rails where nobody would see them but those who needed to.

A dragonfly crossed the sun, and for a moment, it was a frigate blotting a star. She watched its shadow glide across the inner yard where recruits shouldered coil and ration pods. If she looked to the far marsh, the reed heads were a city of spires; if she looked closer, the lichen at her boot was a forest. Scale did not change the feeling. It only magnified its weight.

She keyed the net. "Skimmer teams check in."

One by one, the Tree Division voices answered: Thorn 1 green, Thorn 2 green, Liftpod Beta docked, Vinecrawler Roma anchored, and spines cold. She liked the choir of it— workmen's music, each bar proof that hands had made something that would hold.

"Tethers on the west line hum a little," said Thorn 3. "We tuned them for wind from Lotus Lake, and she's giving us Broadwater echoes."

"Noted," Dixie said. "Tune a half-fret down. Give the wind its throat."

She looked to the far side, where the Ground Division had sunk trap-lattices into the soil. What a magnificent pettiness, she thought suddenly; what a human thing, to take a world that did not notice you and insist it be shaped to your size. Not to dominate, but to fit. To survive. She closed her eyes against the thought's sharpness, then let it cut her anyway. They were half an inch high on a good day. This wall wouldn't stop the broad world; it would only stop the world that had learned to see them.

"Thorn 1," she said softly, "eyes on the culvert."

"Already on it," came the reply, warm with a scout's gladness.

Down in the culvert—where an ant column might once have found a cool and shadowed road—Master Operatives Coto and Kess slid the final grate into the slot they had carved in old bark. The culvert looked like a canyon's mouth. Their grate was a portcullis. Sap-sealed hinges. A false gate behind with a tunnel that dog-legged into a killbox.

"We're done," Kess said, more to herself than to Coto, as if the gate might argue.

Coto wiped resin from his gloves and straightened, back popping like a string of twigs underfoot. His lantern haloed the carved walls. He could still see the marks of chisels where they had hewn the first angles. He could still feel the shudder in his legs from when the ant vanguard had tested the old weave last Reach—calm, relentless, blind to anything but mandate. Smallness had a different meaning when the tunnel filled with mandibles the size of your helmet.

"Done," he echoed, and it sounded, for a heartbeat, like a prayer.

They stood shoulder to shoulder with the grate between them and whatever might come. In the dark, with the lamplight steady, the two of them felt it roll through them— the idea that their work was a stitch in a longer cloth. The wall would not save them by itself. The grate would not. The tuned membranes and sap bladders would not. But together, they might turn a rush into a hesitation, a hesitation into a decision, a decision into a retreat. And sometimes that was all the distance between a name on a memorial plank and a laugh by the morning fire. "You hear that?" Kess murmured.

Coto cocked his head. Beyond the grate, the river's whisper, the familiar hush of the reed-winds, and a faint, just-felt thrum—the palisade wires singing to the air. The outpost had a voice now. It had always had voices, but this was a voice made by their hands. He smiled, and the resin cracked on his lips.

*****

Hivewatch, the command room at the outpost's core, was never truly quiet, even when no alarms sounded. It carried the soft sounds of a hundred far places braided into a single hum: ticker-lines from the listening webs; pulse murmurs from the lily-pad pontoons; the ghost of footfalls from patrols transmitted through taut threads to tiny bell-points; the tremor of the river boom like a sleeping thing's breath.

Lieutenant Song stood at the central board. She set her palms against the map—bark with inlaid thread, pins for squads, shell flakes for towers—and felt the warmth of the work beneath her hands. Around her, scribes marked logs with a discipline that was everything and nothing like the river's. Jones came in without announcing himself. He never did in Hivewatch; it was not a place for pomp.

"Looks different now," he said. "When the pins have all got homes."

Song nodded. "When the lines close," she said, and then added, "No gaps. Not on the board."

They both knew the gaps remained in the world. Gaps of weather, of luck, of a wasp's sudden hunger, of a mudslide when the Broadwater River changed its mind. But on the board, tonight, the story was closed.

"Stingray calls outbound?" he asked.

"Two boats out to shuffle the decoys," Song said. "One patrolling the boom. Reports all quiet—if quiet is what we call the Broadwater River when it goes around us like a god ignoring a whisper."

Jones stared at the river's icon, a ribbon of blue pigment. "Quiet is good," he said. "Quiet is a gift."

He looked down at his own hands. They were nicked despite not lifting a hammer today. "Command cuts you with paper and time," Jones said.

"Sir?" Song asked, and he realized he'd left the net open.

He clicked off, then on again, evenly. "Nothing," he said. "Just listening."

On the inner parapet, a handful of recruits sat with their backs to the fresh palisade, canteens shared, helmet clasps against their throats unhooked in the soft way of those who will clip in again without prompting. Recruit Keller, still marveling at everything, traced a finger along the grain of a rail. The wood's ridges rose like mountains. In a splinter, he saw a cliff face. In the resin bead, a lake. The world would not meet him in the middle. He had to go to it.

"Think it'll hold?" asked a recruit who sat beside him, his armor still wearing the old calibration flicker.

"From ants?" Keller said. "From fleas? Spiders? Wasps?" "From all of it," he said.

Keller considered. "All of it? No." He saw the disappointment on his face and felt he'd failed some test. "But it'll hold long enough," he added quickly. "Long enough for Thorn to drop a sap charge. Long enough for a Stingray to rake a bank. Long enough for 1st Sergeant Miller to put a squad on a rope and do something the wall can't."

He regarded him for a beat, then smiled. "Good answer."

"My sergeant said walls are for time," Keller added. "Not safety. Safety's a story we tell our kids; time's a favor we buy our friends."

He snorted a laugh. "Your sergeant says a lot."

"He's got a lot to say."

They watched as a Liftpod came down, ghostly on its vine and pulley. It carried crates—bandages, bolt spools, bread pods—and two cooks who waved as if in a parade. From the other side of the fort, the Vinecrawler edged into its berth, clamps finding the grooves they'd been carved to find. It looked like a beetle that had decided to become a house and then changed its mind again.

Keller felt the little sting under his ribs that meant pride and fear in the same breath. "We're small," he said, trying the words out, as if speaking them might shrink the truth to size. "We're very small."

"We are," the recruit said. Then: "And look how big we build when we mean it." They sat in that duality, and the wall behind them warmed as it drank the day's heat.

Dusk came in a slow bleed of color, the sky a wet leaf held to flame somewhere beyond the treeline. River light softened. Branch shadows lengthened and joined. The palisade glowlines—a thin run of biolumens painted in scallops—woke by degrees, a necklace finding its purpose.

On the outpost's eastern rim, a chaplain in grease-stained sleeves hung a small bell from a wire post: not for prayer, not exactly, but for marking. He rang it once. It didn't carry far. It didn't need to. The tone folded into the hum of Hivewatch, into the thrum of tuned guylines, into the hush of reeds, into the tired laughter of a cook.

Miller walked the interior circle. He tapped a post here, tightened a lash there, put his big palm on the bark in places where men and women had worked until their hands forgot other shapes. He stopped by a gap that wasn't a gap—the planned sally where a rope ladder could be dropped in a handful of heartbeats. He pictured it in use: a squad gone and back through it like water through an embankment. He pictured it never in use. He pictured both and let neither be a promise.

He found Jones at last on the south wall. The captain had a folded paper in his hand. It looked like an order but was only a list of names: those who had carried, and cut, and held and held and held. "Going to read it?" Miller asked.

"Not tonight," Jones said. "Tomorrow. When they're tired enough to hear it as more than praise."

"Never thought of praise as a burden," Miller exclaimed.

"It can be," Jones said, mouth corner turned. "It can be the heaviest thing we put on a person." They leaned into the rail as if it could lean back.

"You ever wonder," Miller said, "how big it is?"

"You mean the marsh?" asked William.

"No," Miller said, and his hand made a little circle that could have been the outpost or a galaxy. "All of it. Everything that doesn't care what we name it."

Jones thought of Lotus Lake—bigger than any single day and still a puddle to the sky. He thought of the dragonfly's wings like a cathedral, then like a shard of sunlight. "Every time I look at a map," he said.

"And still we draw lines on it," Miller said. "Still, we build."

"Still," Jones said.

They let the word settle like dust.

*****

Dixie coasted the Skimmer along the inner wind, feet brushing sparks from the glowline where she passed. She could have flown out into the open to feel the broader drafts, but tonight she wanted the cord of the walls near. She wanted to trace the shape they'd made against a world that did not notice their shapes unless they taught it.

She dipped a wing over the Branch Bastion, where sentries had chalked tally marks of construction days into a plank. She dipped again over the lily pad pontoons, now little mirrors of the first stars. She felt how the outpost breathed—

how the tuned wires took the wind and made of it a quiet instrument.

"Thorn flight," she said into the net, "this one's for you."

She rolled the Skimmer, let the masthead flags graze her wake, and came out of it not with any acrobat's flourish but with the ordinary grace of a thing designed to move between branches. The cheer from the inner yard was a handful of voices and the rustle of many more smiles.

She leveled out. "You're small," she whispered to the Skimmer, to herself, to the wall, to the river, to the sky. "We are all so very small."

*****

At Hivewatch, Song pinged an acknowledgment she did not need to make and did anyway. On the culvert, Coto and Kess shouldered their tools and started the long climb up. On the west redoubt, Jones folded the list of names and tucked it into his pocket like a charm.

Night thickened. The world beyond the wall brought its own announcements: frog-song like drums; a wind-change that made the guylines go from low to lower; the Broadwater putting its shoulder at the boom with a sudden lift and then sighing off it. The little bell was taken down. The glowlines found their final brightness. Sentries rotated. The kitchen banked its fires.

At second watch, a water flea struck a decoy raft with enthusiasm that would have been comic in daylight. The raft flipped smartly, sending a ripple that traveled the tied line into a tiny arm at Hivewatch. The arm thumped a pad no bigger than a seed. A mark was made in the log. No alarm sounded; the world had merely said I am here, and the outpost answered, We know.

Keller lay on his back and looked at the sky, and the sky was too large to look at. He picked a small piece of it—the space between two needles far above—and let his eyes rest there, and in that framed window he saw a star drift, though it might have been a beetle's lamp or a far skimmer. He thought of his mother's kitchen, of the way a kettle's steam had looked like clouds in the morning light. He felt the wall under his shoulder blades like a promise.

They were small. He was a fact inside that fact. He could vanish into the scale of it. But someone would still need to tune the guylines at dawn, to check the sap seals, to walk the boom, to carve another notch in the tally plank when the sun came up. He could do that. It did not make him bigger, and it did not make the world smaller. It made a bridge between them. He slept. The wall did not.

Before dawn—a gray hour without edges—the river threw a fog up that touched every surface with a wet finger. The glowlines dimmed. The watch changed. In Hivewatch, Song stretched her knuckles one by one and felt each joint crack like tiny faults slipping in the crust of an enormous world. The first skimmer patrol went out under Dixie's hand with hardly a sound. On the water, the Stingrays added their wakes to the fog, stripes on a sleeping cat.

Miller found a brush and worked sap polish into a spot where the rail had been rough. It was too small a task for a first sergeant and yet just right for him. Jones climbed to the parapet with the folded list.

He called the names without rank, without unit. Carpenters first, then riggers, then sap-slingers and sappers, then Thorn flight, then Stingray crews, then cooks, medics, and scribes. He spoke them into the cool, and the fog caught his breath and made it visible and then took it. When he finished, he did not make a speech. He only touched the rail and said, "It will not be enough. But it will be enough today."

That was not the sort of thing a captain said. It was how a man felt.

Dixie, circling, heard it over the net without wanting to. She smiled and kept the skimmer level.

At the culvert, Kess ran her palm over the grate, invented a superstition, and told no one. Coto, already halfway up the ladder, sang two bars of a song without words. Keller's new friend put on his helmet and tapped the brim, and he mirrored him, and when their visors touched, it clicked like a small bell.

The sun came up slow, stained by fog, and touched the palisade with a child's careful finger. The outpost glowed like something living. The world around it stretched and yawned and did not notice.

Inside the wall, the Micro-Operatives rose. They were half an inch tall, and they were impossibly large. They took their places along the ring they had made together. They listened to the wind, to the river, to the quiet within the quiet, and they heard—not safety—but time. And they began to spend it, carefully, for one another.

Chapter 4

The First Probe

Fog lay low over the Broadwater River. A thin skin of mist stretched between the moss lands and the river like a quiet veil, softening edges, turning every branch and post into a silhouette. Stonewall Outpost woke slowly in that hour before dawn when light had not yet committed, and the night still whispered through the willows. The wall's glowline had dimmed to its lowest hum, and the river boom thrummed lazily under the water's shifting weight.

In Hivewatch, Lieutenant Song sat alone with a cup of barkbrew cooling beside her. The boards murmured softly, a blend of water and wind—a song she knew by heart. She let her fingers rest on the vibration threads like a harpist listening for discord. Usually, the dawn hours were the stillest. Not this morning.

Something beneath the western palisade shivered. A thread jumped, not sharply but with a deep, pulsing rhythm, as if the bark itself were exhaling. Song leaned forward. "That's new," she whispered to herself. She pressed her ear against the board. The pulse came again. Not wind. Not water.

Out on the western parapet, Recruit Keller squinted through the mist. The night watch had passed quietly, with only frogs and the occasional water flea bumping against the boom. His armor was still damp from the fog, and the rail beneath his gloved hands felt slick, like the back of some living thing. Below, the moss stretched toward the tree line, pale and damp, beaded with dew.

Then the bark tremor reached him. It started as a tickle through his boots—a subtle, beneath the wood. He thought at first it was his imagination, a phantom of long watches and too much silence. Then the tremor came again. Not constant, not chaotic. Rhythmic. "Uh, sarge?" he said softly into the comm bead. "You feel that?"

A pause, then Sergeant Miller's voice crackled in his ear. "Feel what, Keller?"

"The floor's… breathing," Keller said.

*****

Far overhead, in the early gray canopy, Dixie Lake's skimmer floated between branches like a leaf on a breeze. She loved these hours—the air cool, the forest half-asleep, the world larger and quieter than anything made by Micro-Operatives. From her vantage point, Stonewall was just a patterned ridge, a ring of geometry set into the living wood.

She banked gently along the western perimeter, letting the updraft from the Broadwater River lift her wings. That was when she saw it: scouts. Tiny, quick-moving shapes at the far tree line, barely visible through fog. At first, she thought they were bark beetles foraging. But then one paused. Raised its antennae. Another joined it. Then another. A line formed—not a march, not yet, but the hint of one.

Dixie narrowed her eyes. "Hivewatch, this is Thorn lead," she said softly into the net. "We've got movement west, tree line. Not birds. Not beetles."

"Copy, Thorn," came Song's voice. "Describe."

"They're small. Fast. And they're tasting the air."

The mist thickened between her and the tree line, swallowing their forms again. But she knew the pattern. She'd seen it before, in Reed Flats, the day before the first nest fell: scouts first, quiet as whispers, charting paths before the swarm.

She tapped the underside of her skimmer. The machine responded like a living thing, wings shifting pitch.

"Recommend quiet watch, no alarms yet," she added. "They're feeling us out."

"Understood," Song replied. "Keep eyes on them. We'll listen."

By mid-watch, the tremors had spread along three sectors of the western wall. Riggers in Tree Division paused their dawn checks to place palms against the bark. Sappers in the culvert line crouched, listening to the ground the way soldiers once listened to train rails.

The vibrations came in rolling pulses, as distant footsteps magnified through wood. Not marching, not coordinated—but moving. Always west to east.

Inside Hivewatch, the map board came alive with faint tremor sigils. Song traced them with a stylus, connecting dots. The pattern resembled a fan spreading toward the wall. A testing line. She glanced at the chronometer. Still pre-dawn. Still quiet.

On the southern river boom, a Stingray Sailor named Ibarra leaned over the prow, watching for ripples. The fog clung low to the water, muting sound. Then he saw them—

small dark bodies floating downstream. At first, he thought it was driftwood, but its orientation was wrong. They were ants, dead or sacrificed, moving like offerings. A dozen at least, carried by the current, bumping the boom's nets. "Command," he whispered into the bead. "You seeing this?"

Jones answered himself, his voice low. "We see it." He stood above Hivewatch now, watching the river in person. His hands were behind his back, but his jaw was tight. Scouts on land. Scouts in water. Bark tremors. Something was unfolding out there in the fog. But the forest didn't shout. It whispered first.

By the time the sun's first light revealed itself through the canopy, the quiet had become electric. Sentries leaned forward on their rails. Skimmers hovered in slow loops overhead. The Stingrays held station at the boom like cats watching a mousehole. Hivewatch's vibration threads thrummed softly under Song's hands. No columns yet. No assault. Just tremors. Just shadows.

*****

Dixie pulled her skimmer into a hover above the tree line and stared into the fog. For a heartbeat, she thought she saw a black wave ripple through the moss. But when she blinked, there was only mist again. "They're coming," she whispered to herself. "They're just not ready yet."

The sun rose like a pale coin through the fog—distant, dim, indifferent. Its first rays spilled over the Broadwater River and caught on the dew-beaded moss land to the west. For a brief moment, the world seemed suspended: the wall lines gleamed faintly, the guylines hummed, and the mist curled like smoke around the willow trunks.

Then the fog began to move. It wasn't wind. It was pressure—soft at first, then growing. The mist rippled in long, shallow waves as if something immense were pushing through it from beneath. From the parapets, sentries leaned forward. From Hivewatch, Song's stylus paused midair. Dixie banked her skimmer higher, wings whispering.

Through the whitening fog, a dark seam appeared on the moss. Thin. Straight. At first glance, it could have been a fallen branch. But the seam widened, split, and began to spread laterally, like ink bleeding into cloth. The moss dimmed under the sheer number of tiny bodies pressing across it. It was ants!

Hundreds at first. Then thousands. Flowing out of the tree line in three uneven columns, moving fast—faster than a Micro-Operative could sprint, faster than the eye could count. They came on six legs apiece, heads down, antennae twitching, their chitin shining faintly where sunlight cut through the mist. They did not march in perfect rhythm. They swarmed, like rivers finding their own paths downhill.

"Contact, western moss land," Keller's voice cracked over the net. "They're—holy— they're everywhere—"

"Hold your line," Sergeant Miller snapped back. But even Miller's voice had a thinness to it; a strain stretched across disbelief. None of them had seen a swarm like this this close to Stonewall.

In Hivewatch, the vibration threads lit up all at once. A forest of pulses climbed the board like wildfire. Song's fingers danced from thread to thread, her calm voice on the net a steady drum against the rising storm.

"Three main bodies," she announced. "Left column cutting low through the reed edge. Center column on the direct line to the west palisade. Right column peeling north along the ridge." "Are they coordinated?" Captain Jones asked.

"Negative," Song replied. "No standard rhythm. Columns are… overlapping. Some groups are slowing, some are accelerating. This isn't organized command—it's instinct."

Jones's gaze swept the board. "Instinct's still enough to break a wall if we treat it like a drill."

He turned to Miller, who stood ready at the door with his field jacket half on. "Sound the wall-bell. Quiet signal, then full. I want everyone awake."

Miller nodded once and hurriedly left Hivewatch. Moments later, the low chime of the wall-bell carried through the outpost—a muted, deep note meant to stir sleepers without startling them. Then the second bell rang sharper. Troops scrambled from bunks. Thorn flights unfurled wings. Ground Division squads rushed to assigned parapets, pulling on gear as they ran.

On the western parapet, Keller watched the black line split like water meeting rocks. The ants flowed toward every dip in the terrain, every root hollow, every ramp. They climbed over one another in living bridges, their bodies forming arches and mounds as if they were one writhing organism. There was no banner, no trumpet—just the relentless hiss of thousands of feet over moss. "They're fast," Keller breathed. "Too fast."

Below him, sappers sprinted to light the moss-fire lanes—thin lines of pre-treated lichen meant to burn fast and bright, not to kill but to disorient. Sparks flared, racing along the lines like veins of light. Flames licked upward, and the first rows of ants hit them headlong. Some faltered. Others ran straight through, bodies smoldering, antennae waving furiously. It barely slowed them down.

From her perch above, Dixie had the clearest view. The black rivers of ants wound toward the wall in irregular braids. Some surged straight, others peeled off suddenly and followed invisible scent paths toward lower terrain. She counted at least five sub-streams that seemed to be acting independently, their patterns colliding in chaotic bursts.

She tapped her net bead. "Hivewatch, Thorn lead. Swarm confirmed. Not a unified push. Multiple instinct columns. Fast but messy."

"Copy," Song said with excitement. "Mark their vectors."

Dixie tilted her skimmer, slicing through the fog like a silent blade. Her chalk sprayer hissed, laying bright white tracer lines in the air above each visible column. From the parapet below, the defenders watched as her glowing arcs outlined the paths of approach—a painter sketching the outline of their doom.

The first antennae touched the palisade. They came up the slope in waves, hitting the lower lattice of the wall like a sudden tide. Some climbed over one another immediately, creating living ladders. Others fanned out along the base, probing for seams, tapping the wood with their jaws. The sound of mandibles on timber echoed up through the parapets: click click click click click—fast, staccato, like rain on a drum.

"Hold fire," Miller's voice came through the net, hard as iron. "Let them commit. Don't waste sap or bolts on sniffers."

The defenders watched. The ants pressed closer. The black line at the base thickened. They weren't testing with one or two scouts anymore—they were massing.

Keller swallowed. "Sir…how many is that? Brin answered without looking at him. "Enough to ruin your breakfast, Keller."

Near the culvert mouth, the right-hand column broke formation altogether. Some groups turned north, drawn by reed trails. Others began to cluster at the old maintenance shaft, their antennae quivering wildly. Sappers watching from above felt their stomachs tighten. That shaft had been sealed—but only recently and not yet reinforced with permanent grating.

"They're smelling it," one of them whispered. "On the wall", Song's voice cut in. "All units, mark the shaft. The right flank is veering. Not coordinated, but they've found something."

"Copy," Jones said. "Contain it." Back at the center line, the largest column finally hit the palisade in force.

The first wave collided with the wall base like water against stone. The second wave climbed over the first. In seconds, a vertical mound of ants had formed bodies stacked three, four, five layers thick, climbing their living brothers to reach the wooden face. Their movements weren't elegant, but they were fast. A few slipped into gaps between logs. Others fell, only to be trampled by those behind.

It looked less like an army and more like a black flood, one that didn't understand walls, only forward.

The Micro-Operatives leaned over the parapets and stared. Some whispered prayers. Others checked their bolt rifles with trembling fingers. They had expected the ants to come eventually. But not like this—not in chaotic, overwhelming torrents before dawn.

Dixie hovered above them, gazed hard. "They're not coordinated," she muttered. "But they don't need to be."

The black line pressed closer. The wall began to hum under the weight. And deep beneath the palisade, the bark tremors that had begun at dawn now pulsed like a drumbeat.

The first probe had begun. It began as a clicking whisper—mandibles tapping bark like hail on a roof. Then came the climbing. Ant bodies pressed tight against one another, forming living bridges that spanned cracks, ladders that reached the lower parapets. They were fast, relentless, and heedless of casualties. Those crushed beneath became rungs for those above.

The Micro-Operatives finally opened fire. Bolt rifles along the western parapet cracked in near-unison. Blue-white flashes tore into the climbing masses, sending bursts of ant bodies tumbling down the slope. Sap launchers belched sticky green arcs, splattering across writhing clusters and hardening in seconds, gluing dozens in place mid-climb. Some ants thrashed violently, snapping limbs and antennae; others simply kept climbing over their stuck comrades, indifferent to their fate.

"Fire in waves!" Miller barked over the net. "Don't burn your barrels. Front line, two volleys. Second, pick targets climbing high!

The trained rhythm kicked in. Micro-Operatives fired, stepped back, reloaded, and rotated positions like cogs in a machine. Despite the chaos, their discipline made the parapet hold—for now. Below, along the slope, sapper teams were already putting improvised plans into action. "Roll it!" someone shouted.

Three moss-sealed barrels, normally used to store surplus sap, were tipped from a ledge. They tumbled down the slope, cracked open on jagged roots, and burst into slick pools at the wall's base. Ants rushing up the incline suddenly found their feet sliding; dozens toppled backward, carrying others with them in a chain reaction. The slope became a writhing, slippery mat of bodies. "Light it!" Brin ordered. A scout struck flint and tossed a resin torch.

The sap ignited with a whoosh, flaring bright green and orange in the fog. It wasn't a wall of fire, but a series of unpredictable burning patches that broke the ants' flow, forcing them to split and surge around flames. The burning sap smoked thickly, creating choking clouds that clung low to the ground, confusing their pheromone trails. "Not bad," Brin muttered, impressed despite himself.

Overhead, Dixie dove. "Thorn flight with me," she called over the net. Her skimmer folded its wings slightly, catching an updraft, and she plunged toward the center column where ants were massing hardest. From her harness, she pulled the chalk-resin bombs—small, gourd-shaped charges filled with quick-hardening foam. Thorn flights didn't have the raw firepower of Stingray boats or wall sap cannons, but they could strike with precision.

"Marking drop lines!" Thorn Two shouted. White tracer smoke curled from their wingtips, painting arcs over the swarm. Dixie's team released the bombs in tight formation. The gourds burst on impact, releasing expanding foam that filled every crack it touched. Whole clusters of ants were suddenly cemented together, their climbing halted mid-stride. Others stumbled into the sticky mess and became part of the snarl.

"Direct hit, center line," Song's calm voice confirmed from Hivewatch. "They're slowing."

"Only slowing," Dixie replied. "They're not thinking. They're reacting. Which means we can trip them if we keep changing the terrain."

At the culvert mouth, the right-flank column reached the maintenance shaft. Ants swarmed its edges, sensing the weaker seal. Sapper crews there had only minutes to reinforce.

"Get that grate locked!" Coto shouted. His hands flew across vine lashings, tightening knots as fast as his fingers could move. Kess hammered resin wedges into the cracks, teeth bared in concentration. "Here they come!" one of the lookouts yelled.

Ants poured toward the shaft like water finding a drain. Some threw themselves bodily at the seam, wedging their heads into cracks and biting. Resin flakes flew. One ant got halfway through a gap before Kess drove a spike hammer into its thorax with a sharp thunk. The creature spasmed and fell. Coto shouted to two engineers behind him. "Get the sap bladder!"

They rolled forward a swollen membrane sack used for sealing leaks. Together they shoved it into the shaft entrance, punctured its plug, and watched as thick, expanding sap foam filled the space. Ants rushed it, biting, climbing over, but the foam hardened fast. Within moments, the entire entrance was sealed with a pale, living wall. "Great's holding," Kess gasped. "For now." Coto nodded, sweat slick on his brow. "Then we just bought the wall ten more minutes."

*****

Downriver, the Stingray boats moved. The Broadwater River's surface was slick with fog, but the moment the ant swarm began spilling toward the western bank, the Stingray crews pivoted in near-perfect unison. Their slim, manta-shaped hulls cut through the mist like blades. "Fire grid B," Hernandez shouted to command from the lead Stingray.

Micro-bolt cannons along the hulls raked the shoreline, chewing into ant clusters approaching the water's edge. The bolts burst like miniature grenades on impact, scattering chitin fragments across the mud. A few of the ants tried to raft themselves—locking legs, floating on bodies, but the Stingrays swung broadside and unleashed a rolling volley that shredded the makeshift bridge before it formed. The boom lines thrummed with the current, holding firm. For now, the river flank is secure.

*****

On the western parapet, Keller found himself reloading faster than he'd ever practiced. His hands shook at first, but Brin's barked orders kept him focused.

"Don't look at their numbers," Brin growled. "Look at the spot you're killing. That's your world. One spot at a time."

Keller lined up his sights and fired into a climbing knot where ants had nearly reached the parapet lip. His bolt punched through three at once. Another fell backward, taking ten with it.

His world shrank to that one patch of wall, that one swarm of legs and mandibles. The enormity of the tide faded under the rhythm: aim, fire, reload, step back. Next target. Next breath.

"Western wall holding," Song's voice echoed through Hivewatch. "Culvert sealed. Stingrays clear."

Jones exhaled, hands gripping the railing above the command floor. "Good. Keep them reacting. Don't let them find a rhythm."

The ants didn't break. They didn't strategize. But they didn't stop, either. They kept pressing, climbing, colliding, as if their numbers alone could substitute for thought. It was overwhelming—a black sea smashing itself against Stonewall's edges.

But the Micro-Operatives weren't static defenders. They were builders, riggers, pilots, and fighters, using every tool at hand. Fire, sap, chalk, foam, boats, rifles—woven together through drilled teamwork and battlefield improvisation.

Where the ants surged strongly, defenders shifted positions fluidly. Where sappers saw weak points, Thorn flights marked them for bombardment. When rifles overheated, crew swapped weapons and manned the sap hoses. Where sap barrels burst early, someone would roll debris into place to redirect the swarm. For every chaotic push, there was an answer. Not perfect. Not elegant. But enough.

Slowly, across the western approach, the black line began to fragment. Not because the ants faltered, they didn't—but because the defenders had turned their instinct into confusion. Fire patches burned pheromone trails. Foam blocks forced them into collisions. Sap slicks made the ladders collapse. Stingrays punished anything approaching the river. Thorn flights broke clusters before they could mass.

The first clash was not a clean line of battle. It was a storm meeting a wall of ingenuity—a hundred improvisations overlapping like scales on armor.

Keller ducked as a clump of ants tumbled from the wall, smashing against the parapet below him. He met Brin's eyes. The sergeant nodded once. They were still holding. But the tremors hadn't stopped. If anything, they were getting stronger.

The wall roared like a living thing. From the parapets, the sound of rifles, sap launchers, and mandibles blurred into a single, relentless pulse. Every tremor along the bark, every thunk of bolt into chitin reverberated inward, through ladders and braces, into the very spine of Stonewall. Inside the outpost, the world fractured into zones of urgency.

Hivewatch sat at the center like a beating heart. The vibration threads were alive beneath Lieutenant Song's hands—an entire map in motion. Dozens of pulse markers crawled across the board as the ant columns shifted, split, and surged. Runners moved through the chamber like blood cells, grabbing chalk-marked slips and sprinting for stairways. Above them, the walls of Hivewatch creaked with each impact.

"Left flank, lower slope…ladder collapse." "Center western palisade reporting heavy pressure," another added. "Sap reserves dropping to yellow."

"Right flank—" a third voice rose, "—we've got movement near the storage tunnels!"

Song's stylus darted like a blade. "Relay to Kess: storage tunnel pressure, eastern lip. I want two squads diverted now. Thorn flight Bravo, break off from high cover and give me eyes north of the sally gap. Stingrays remain on grid B—don't chase stragglers."

Her voice never rose. It didn't need to. It moved like a current beneath the storm, holding the center steady.

Near the inner courtyard, Sergeant Miller pushed through a crush of scrambling squads. Sappers dragged barrels. Ground Troopers carried bolt bundles to parapet lifts. A pair of Tree Division riggers hoisted a broken parapet railing onto their shoulders, rushing it toward the western wall like stretcher bearers. Miller caught them by the arm.

"Which sector?" he barked. "C-three parapet, sir—ants almost over the lip."

Miller didn't hesitate. "Go! Keller's up there. Don't make me come haul you myself." They vanished into the smoke, boots thudding on the bark-plank causeway.

Miller looked up; Thorn skimmers were streaking overhead in tight arcs, their wings cutting through morning fog as they painted chalk lines over new ant flows. The skimmers' tracers drew living maps in the air, marking trouble before it arrived.

"Smart kids," Miller muttered, then caught a glimpse of Dixie banking hard over the northern tree line. "Showoffs."

At the western gate platform, a squad of engineers and civilians converged without waiting for orders. Sap barrels, spare planks, and coil bundles were dragged together to form a makeshift barricade behind the gate doors.

"These barrels are for storage," one of the supply clerks protested weakly.

"They're for living now," a rigger snapped back. "Get me more vine lashings!"

Within minutes, the empty gap behind the gate had transformed into a bristling wall of improvised obstacles. If the outer gate went down, the ants would face a gauntlet of sticky traps, angled boards, and quick-release braces. No manual called for it. But every Micro-Operatives working there had seen floods, fires, or collapses before. They knew how to improvise when systems fail.

On the northern flank, Thorn Flight Bravo peeled off from high cover as ordered. Their lead, a wiry pilot named Sel, spotted a cluster of ants diverting toward the sally gap, following some errant pheromone line. It wasn't a major column—yet—but if they reached the gap, they could spill straight into the supply lanes. Sel clicked the net twice. "Bravo on the sally run."

Four skimmers dove low and quick between the willows. They weren't carrying heavy ordnance, but their chalk-foam gourds could block narrow approaches. In perfect formation, they released their charges in a zigzag line across the moss path. The foam expanded instantly, forming an uneven barrier that forced the ants to break stride and scatter.

It bought time. Not much—but enough for Miller to reroute a squad down the interior ladders to seal the gap from the inside.

Down near the culvert tunnel, the maintenance shaft groaned under renewed pressure. Ants had begun piling against the sap-foam seal in numbers, clawing and chewing. Resin flakes rained into the tunnel like snow. Inside, Kess and Coto worked shoulder to shoulder with three volunteers from the mess crew, shoring up braces and wedging crates against the foam bulge.

"This is insane," one of the cooks muttered, shoving his shoulder against a crate.

"Welcome to the war," Coto grunted, tightening a lash. The tremors through the foam wall vibrated up his arms like the heartbeat of something huge. He didn't like how steady it was becoming.

From above, Song's voice crackled through the tunnel comm tube. "Culvert team, status?"

"Holding," Kess answered. "But if they keep this up, we're going to need more foam."

"Copy. Reinforcements enroute," Song replied without hesitation.

At the base of the parapet lifts, a group of civilians— scribes, cooks, and two water haulers—had organized themselves into a resupply chain without waiting for orders. Bolt boxes and sap canisters were loaded onto pulley lifts and cranked skyward by sheer muscle power. One of the scribes, her ink-stained hands slipping on the rope, she bared her teeth and pulled anyway.

"They're not soldiers," Miller thought as he passed them. "But today, they're part of the wall."

He stopped beside them long enough to help heave a particularly heavy crate onto the lift. One of the cooks, sweat plastering his hair to his forehead, grinned at him. "Don't worry, Sergeant," he said breathlessly. "We'll keep your shooters fed." Miller slapped the man's shoulder. "And we'll keep you breathing."

Hivewatch' s pulse board began to spike on multiple vectors. Song's eyes moved rapidly between them. She saw it clearly: The swarm wasn't coordinated, but Stonewall had become a maze of shifting signals. Every improvised block, every fire lane, every Thorn chalk line was warping the ants' pheromone trails. Some columns doubled back. Others collided with each other. Instinct fought instinct.

But that didn't make it safe. It made it chaotic. "Multiple pheromones overlap," an operator reported. "We've got ant groups colliding near western C-five!"

"Let them crash," Song said evenly. "Bravo flight, mark C-five with foam. Ground squads, reposition to cover the aftermath." She was orchestrating a battle of improvisation—using the ants' lack of coordination against them.

*****

Inside the storage tunnels, a dozen defenders formed a barricade out of stacked ration crates. The narrow corridors funneled everything into tight choke points. When a half-dozen ants finally managed to chew through a soft seam and spill inside, the defenders met them with sap sprayers and pikes.

The ants didn't coordinate their attack; they simply charged, each trying to climb or bite the closest thing. The defenders exploited that, tripping one ant into another, toppling their formation like tumbling stones. It wasn't elegant. It was gritty, hand-to-hand survival in narrow tunnels.

Throughout the outpost, communication threads tied everything together. Hivewatch called vectors. Thorn flight drew chalk lines. Stingrays hammered the river edge. Squads shifted like water, plugging gaps as they appeared. Civilians carried supplies. Engineers improvised braces. No one stood still.

And slowly, despite the swarm's overwhelming speed and numbers, Stonewall didn't break. It bent, flexed, and answered.

In a brief lull between orders, Song looked down at the pulse board. Her fingers hovered above the vibrating lines. It looked like chaos. But underneath the chaos, she felt something steady. Teamwork. Residents of Stonewall Improvised, instinctive, but real.

The ants were many. The Micro-Operatives were few. But the Micro-Operatives talked to each other. They adapted. They shared intent.

And for the first time since the black line appeared, Song allowed herself a single, slow breath. The wall still held.

The first sound was not a roar, nor a crash. It was a deep, wet pop—like sap splitting under pressure.

Down in the maintenance tunnels near the culvert line, Coto froze mid-swing as the foam wall bulged inward, pulsing like a lung about to exhale. Kess dropped her hammer and pressed both hands against the crate barricade they'd wedged into the seam.

"Did you hear that?" one of the cooks whispered. Before anyone could answer, the foam split down the center, a jagged crack zigzagging like lightning through the hardened sap. A dozen glinting mandibles punched through the fissure, snapping and scraping. Resin shards sprayed like snow. The air filled with the high, dry clicking of ants tasting daylight.

"Back," Coto bellowed. "Everyone back!" He shouted. They stumbled over tools and crates as the wall burst open. The foam cracked apart in great, brittle slabs, and the ants poured through—not in disciplined ranks but in a frenzied surge, tripping over one another, climbing the broken edges, scrambling across the floor. A black wave spilled into the tunnel like water breaching a levee.

Kess swung her hammer in both hands, smashing the lead ant square in the head. It crumpled, but two more replaced it instantly. The mess crew grabbed pikes from the rack and braced shoulder-to-shoulder. "Hold the line!" Kess shouted, voice echoing down the tunnel.

*****

Up in Hivewatch, Song saw the right flank tremor lines spike so suddenly that her stylus snapped in half against the board. Her eyes widened. "Culvert breach!" she barked. "Sector E-two! Interior tunnels compromised!" "Culvert breach!" she barked. "Sector E-two! Interior tunnels compromised!" The CommNet flared alive with overlapping voices:

— "We've got black inside!"

— "Foam wall down!"

— "They're in the tunnels—repeat, inside the wall!"

*****

Miller didn't wait for orders. "First platoon, with me!" he roared, already sprinting down the inner causeway toward the culvert access ladders. The floor shook beneath his boots as distant impacts rippled through the wall.

*****

Jones appeared in the Hivewatch doorway, cloak thrown over one shoulder. "How bad?" "Secondary column found the maintenance shaft," Song replied crisply. "No coordination—just brute force. They cracked the foam. If they reach the inner yard—" They won't," Jones said, and he was already moving.

*****

In the storage tunnels, chaos erupted like dry tinder. The ants didn't form ranks or flanking maneuvers—they flooded, filling every crevice they found, mandibles clacking, antennae thrashing. Some skittered along walls. Others crawled across ceilings, upside down, snapping at anything that moved.

The Micro-Operatives weren't ready for ants inside the wall. "Rally at the third junction!" Coto yelled, shoving a young engineer toward a side passage. "We need to bottleneck them!"

They fell back through a narrow corridor, dragging debris as they went. Kess and the mess crew shoved overturned carts and broken barrel halves into the passage, forming a hasty barricade just wide enough for two defenders abreast. The ants came colliding into it seconds later.

Pike's jabbed through gaps. Sap sprayers hissed, coating the leading insects in sticky resin that hardened mid-lunge. The front ranks piled up into a struggling, black mass—but the ants behind didn't stop. They climbed over the immobilized, jaws gnashing, eyes reflecting torchlight like a field of glass beads. "Where's Miller's squad!?" Kess shouted over the commotion. Miller and his squad arrived like a hammer.

Miller's boots hit the tunnel floor just as a group of ants leaped over the barricade. He didn't hesitate—he shouldered his bolt rifle and fired point-blank, the blast punching through three bodies in a burst of blue-white. His squad poured in behind him, forming a firing line across the corridor.

"Line up! Line up!" Miller barked. "Short volleys—don't cook the barrels!"

Bolts flashed, sap splashed, pikes stabbed. The air filled with smoke, resin fumes, and the metallic tang of crushed chitin. The tunnel became a meat grinder, the defenders carving through wave after wave of ants that had no plan beyond "forward."

Even disorganized, their weight was terrifying. Every time one cluster fell, another pushed in from the breach. Some scuttled over their dead with horrifying speed, using bodies as bridges. One particularly massive soldier ant slammed against the barricade hard enough to crack a cart plank, its head shoving through like a battering ram.

Miller lunged forward, planted his boot against its face, and fired down its throat. The explosion splattered the ceiling. "Keep firing!" he roared.

✵✵✵✵✵

Above, Dixie banked her skimmer low over the western yard as Hivewatch relayed the breach. She could see it now—

ants slipping through vents and crawl gaps, not as a disciplined assault but like an infestation spreading into cracks. Her stomach knotted.

"Thorn lead to Hivewatch," she snapped. "Give me an opening above the culvert tunnel."

Song didn't need to ask why. "Roof access hatch three, clear. Watch the boom cable."

Dixie swooped low and pulled a sap-charge gourd from her harness. These weren't meant for precision; they were meant to flood a space, to drown a gap in sticky resin.

She dropped through the hatch, wings flaring in the cramped tunnel air, and hurled the gourd down the breach corridor behind the ant surge. It shattered in a glorious green bloom, resin foaming outward to seal the rear. The ants in that section became entombed in hardening sap, thrashing uselessly as the foam closed around them.

Kess blinked through smoke and sap mist. "Nice timing, Thorn." Dixie tipped her head, grinning resolutely. "Next time, maybe fix your foam wall properly."

*****

Back in Hivewatch, the tremor lines on the right flank began to even out. The breach surge had spent itself in a furious, disorganized rush. Once the tunnel bottlenecks held and the Thorn sap charge cut off reinforcements, the remaining ants inside were mopped up by coordinated squads.

"Sector E-two stabilized," Song reported calmly. "Interior breach contained."

Jones stood beside her, arms crossed, eyes fixed on the board. "They found the crack," he murmured. "And they exploited it. Without even thinking."

"Instinct doesn't need a battle plan," Song replied. "It just needs a gap."

As Miller's squad cleared the last stragglers, Kess slumped against the wall, sap speckles across her face, hair sticking out like straw. Coto dropped beside her, hammer across his knees. Around them, bodies—both ant and Micro-Operatives—littered the tunnel. It smelled like resin, sweat, and crushed bark. "We patched it," Coto said hoarsely. "For now," Kess answered.

Above them, the wall still shook. The swarm outside hadn't relented; this had only been one probing tendril. But Stonewall had met it fast, hard, and together. The breach that might have turned into a rout had instead become a rallying point.

*****

Dixie climbed back out through the hatch, wings slick with sap, and looked west toward the still-boiling swarm. "They're learning," she muttered.

And below, in the tunnel, Miller cracked his neck and reloaded. "So are we." For a heartbeat, everything in Stonewall hung on the edge between holding and breaking.

*****

The swarm pressed the wall in black waves; mandibles clattered against wood and resin. Smoke from burning sap lanes coiled into the air like dark ribbons. The Broadwater River mist hadn't fully burned off, so the entire western perimeter looked like a battlefield painted in shadows and flame, flashes of blue bolt-fire cutting through the haze.

But then something shifted. Not in the ants—they kept swarming, chaotic and tireless—but in the defenders. After the culvert breach was sealed, after squads had fallen into rhythm, after Hivewatch stitched their movements together like thread in cloth, Stonewall stopped merely surviving. It began to push back.

"Ground Division, form staggered lines along C-three through C-five!" Miller's voice cracked over the net like a whip. "Tree Division—mark climbing clusters for suppression fire. Thorn flight, on my signal, strafe the center column's flank. Stingrays, grid B plus five."

Orders rolled out like a drumbeat. Within minutes, squads repositioned, engineers shifted sap hoses, Thorn pilots banked for low runs, and Stingrays drifted closer to shore to deliver crossfire. The wall transformed from scattered defensive outposts into a single, interlocking machine.

*****

77

On the western parapet, Sergeant Brin pointed his sap sprayer down at a dense climbing knot. "Cut it here," he told Keller, who adjusted his rifle to cover the same cluster. "One, two, three—"

They fired in tandem. The sap jet splattered across the knot's base while Keller's bolt burst near the top. Ants at both ends froze or fell, and the middle section collapsed like a bridge with no supports.

"That's how you do it," Brin said. "Two-man kill zones. Keep it up."

Further down the parapet, other pairs mimicked the maneuver. It wasn't a planned tactic—it had emerged in the chaos—but Hivewatch picked up the pattern and began relaying it intentionally.

"Section C-four adopting Brin's ladder-collapse," Song called calmly. "All western parapets adjust fire patterns."

Within moments, the entire line was systematically knocking down ant ladders faster than they could form.

*****

Out on the Broadwater River, the Stingray boats swung into a new pattern. Instead of static firing positions, Hernandez ordered alternating lateral sweeps, their manta hulls gliding parallel to the shoreline like silent predators. Each sweep unleashed volleys of micro-bolts that raked the flanks of ant clusters approaching the river edge.

"Stingray One to Hivewatch—shoreline is ours," Hernandez reported. "They can crawl all they want; they won't cross water today."

"Copy," Song replied. "Maintain grid. You're our knife on the edge."

Ant groups that tried to raft themselves again were cut to ribbons midstream, their bodies drifting downstream like broken twigs. The river boom thrummed approvingly.

*****

Above, Dixie led Thorn flight in low strafing runs just behind the western palisade. It was dangerous flying—tree trunks, rope lines, and lift cables everywhere—but Dixie's wing mates trusted her implicitly. They dove between posts and platforms, dropping chalk-foam gourds at key convergence points.

"Marking C-three flank," Thorn Two called, streaking past Keller's position like a flash of silver-green wings.

A moment later, foam blossomed across the slope in a jagged zigzag, cutting off one of the instinctual pheromone trails. The ant column behind it crashed into its own flank, momentarily jammed up in a mass of confused bodies. Miller saw it from below and seized the opportunity. "First platoon, forward push! Hit the jam while they're tangled!"

Squads descended from the wall through vine ladders, meeting the swarm just outside the palisade for the first time that morning. Sap-sprayers opened wide, coating the floundering mass. Bolt rifles picked off climbers trying to peel away. Pikes held lines against stragglers. It wasn't a reckless sortie—it was a targeted strike into a vulnerable choke.

They didn't need to destroy the swarm. They needed to fracture its rhythm.

*****

At the culvert tunnel, Kess wiped sweat from her face and caught Coto's eye. "Think we can flood the slope?"

Coto looked at the sap line valves built into the lower supports. They were meant for controlled maintenance, not combat. But sap under pressure was heavy and fast.

"Yeah," he said slowly. "We can."

With two mess crew volunteers, they cracked the maintenance valve and redirected a thick sap flow down a carved runoff groove. The viscous green torrent rolled downhill like liquid glass, coating the lower approach under

79

the right flank. Ants tried to climb over it, but it stole their footing, sending them skittering back down into their own lines. Those that got stuck became snarls, tripping the ones behind.

Hivewatch picked up the shift instantly. "Sector E-three slope is flooding," Song announced. "Redirect squads to exploit the collapse."

Brin's team moved like clockwork, pouring focused fire into the now-slick slope, turning what had been a pressure point into a killing ground.

*****

In the inner yard, civilians and support staff were no longer just hauling supplies—they were directing flows. A young scribe stood on a crate with a whistle, signaling pulley lifts to send bolt crates to parapets that were running low. Two cooks commandeered a ration cart and turned it into a mobile sap carrier, hauling extra bladders to where they were needed most.

Jones watched them for a brief moment from the parapet stairs. These weren't soldiers. But in that moment, they moved like part of the defense, weaving into the machine.

He keyed his net. "All units, listen up. We're not just holding anymore. We're shaping. Keep your heads. Keep your lanes. We're going to bleed them dry."

*****

Hivewatch itself had transformed. Where before the board had been a web of panic, it now showed structured chaos. Song and her operators relayed Thorn chalk lines to ground squads, Stingray sweeps to parapet teams, valve floods to Thorn flights. It was like watching a knot tighten— every instinctual swarm movement met by a coordinated, improvised response.

"They're turning on themselves," one operator whispered, pointing at two overlapping tremor lines near C-four. Song nodded. "That's the idea."

*****

By mid-cycle, the difference was visible from the air. Dixie banked high and looked down upon the western slope. Earlier, it had been a uniform black tide. Now it was splintered into dozens of struggling streams:

some trapped in foam zigzags,

some slicked down by sap flows,

some being hammered from the river flank,

some simply colliding with each other, their pheromone lines knotted like tangled string.

"They're not thinking," Dixie said over the net. "And we're making them pay for it."

She dove again, skimming just above the parapets, wings leaving vapor trails in the mist. Her team followed like silent hawks.

*****

On the wall, Keller reloaded and glanced at Brin. "Are we... winning?"

Brin poured sap residue over the rail and gave a crooked grin. "We're making them regret knocking."

*****

Below, Miller's platoon held the outer slope briefly before climbing back inside, their boots sticky with sap, armor scratched but spirits high. They had struck, not merely endured.

*****

In the tunnels, Kess and Coto watched the sap-flood groove harden into a glossy slope that ants couldn't grip. They laughed breathlessly, realizing it had actually worked.

*****

And in Hivewatch, Song stood at the center of a storm of voices and signals. Her hands hovered above the board—not overwhelmed now, but orchestrating.

The swarm didn't stop. Instinct couldn't decide to retreat, not yet. But the momentum shifted. The ants had surged before as a chaotic flood; now they were reacting to the defenders—splitting where the defenders directed, stumbling into obstacles that hadn't been there a moment before, being carved into pieces by a coordinated, improvisational force that knew how to talk to itself. Stonewall was no longer a static ring of wood and sap.

It had become a living weapon, and the ants, for all their numbers, were starting to falter. Class III Specialist Diaz, a five-foot Hispanic male whose jet-black hair was neatly trimmed above a bristling mustache, adjusted the sensors on his IDC-1 Chiterscope. His brown and black chitin exoskeleton armor, designed for both protection and subtle camouflage against the very creatures he studied, hummed faintly. He'd been tasked with monitoring the swarm's communication, an endeavor that had grown increasingly crucial as the battle for Stonewall raged. For hours, his readings had been a confusing noise, but now, a pattern, or rather, the lack of one, was emerging. The Chiterscope indicated that the ants' language, usually a complex symphony of chemical signals and subtle vibrations, was muffled, lacking any discernible direction. Their pheromone trails, the invisible highways of their collective will, appeared broken and fragmented, a stark contrast to the overwhelming, unified pressure they had initially exerted.

Diaz's brow furrowed as he zoomed in on a particularly dense cluster of activity near the breached culvert. The Chiterscope's visualization, normally a vibrant, flowing network, showed only intermittent blips and dead ends. It was as if the very concept of coordination had been surgically removed from the swarm's collective consciousness. He relayed his findings to Hivewatch, his voice calm but tinged with a developing understanding.

"Hivewatch, Specialist Diaz reporting. Readings confirm a significant communication breakdown within the swarm. Pheromone trails are fractured, and directional intent is… absent. It's not a directed assault; it's sheer, unthinking momentum against a wall of organized resistance." The implications were profound. Their enemy, an organism renowned for its flawless, instinctual coordination, was unraveling from within, its inherent logic shattered by Stonewall's relentless, adaptive defense.

The realization settled over Diaz like a heavy cloak. They weren't just fighting an enemy; they were observing the disintegration of an entire ecosystem's governing principle. The battle was no longer just about repelling waves of insects; it was about witnessing the consequences of disrupting a fundamental biological imperative. As he continued to monitor, he saw individual ant clusters falter, not from direct fire, but from the sheer inability to receive or transmit directives. They bumped into each other, veered off into non-existent paths, and ceased their relentless advance not because they were killed, but because their purpose had been rendered incomprehensible. Stonewall, a machine forged in desperation, had inadvertently introduced chaos into the very heart of the swarm's existence.

For Spans, the battle had been noise and pressure—a black tide hammering the wall without pause. But sometime in the late morning light, as the fog finally burned off the Broadwater River and the glowlines dimmed beneath the sun, a strange thing happened.

The swarm began to lose itself. Not all at once, not like a routed army. The ants didn't scream or blow horns. They simply started… turning the wrong way.

At sector C-five, a dense knot of climbers suddenly stopped scaling the wall and began milling in place, antennae thrashing. Two subgroups collided head-on near the sap-flood slope, each following a conflicting scent path. One cluster tried to push left, another right; neither yielded. A writhing ball of bodies formed, climbing over each other but going nowhere.

"They're jamming themselves," Keller said in disbelief from the parapet, watching the pile grow until it rolled back down the hill under its own weight. "Yeah," Brin grunted. "Keep shooting."

*****

On the western flank, Thorn Flight Bravo streaked overhead, chalk bombs spent, wings glinting. From above, Sel could see the pheromone lines like faint trails in the dust—some clear, others broken, some doubled back on themselves. What had begun as three columns now looked like a spiderweb kicked by a boot.

"Command, Bravo," Sel called in. "The swarm's fractured. Trails are overlapping. They're following ghosts out there."

Song's voice came back steady: "Maintain pressure, Bravo. Keep them off balance."

Sel tilted her wings, banking over the foam zigzags that Dixie had laid earlier. Ants still tangled in the hardened resin were now being crawled over by other ants who couldn't find the original path. The result was a tangled mound, like a knot in a rope that only tightens the more it's pulled.

*****

Down by the river, Hernandez watched through Stingray One's periscope as a fresh group of ants tried to raft themselves again. But this time, their formation was sloppy. Some ants followed a fading trail into the water; others veered north toward a nonexistent bridge. A third group, confused, began circling the bank aimlessly. "They're lost," one of the gunners muttered.

"Then make 'em stay lost," Hernandez replied. She gave the firing signal, and a clean sweep of micro-bolts tore through the half-formed raft, scattering limbs and bodies downstream. The river took the rest.

The Stingrays resumed their slow lateral sweeps, not hunting, just maintaining a knife-edge. No ant made it across.

*****

Inside the culvert tunnels, Kess leaned against the wall, chest heaving, as Miller's squad cleared the last stragglers that had trickled in since the breach. The ants were no longer pressing in mass—they came sporadically, like drips from a leaking pipe, each following outdated scent markers that no longer led anywhere.

"Breached corridor is secure," Miller reported into his bead, voice rough. "Nothing left but confused wanderers."

Song's reply came crisp. "Seal it and stay alert. They're unraveling but not gone."

Coto and two mess crew hauled the last of the resin slabs into place, plugging the breach gap fully this time. "Let's see 'em chew through that," Coto muttered, jamming the wedge tight.

*****

Out in the yard, the improvised resupply chain had become so efficient that for the first time since dawn, they had surplus crates waiting at the base of the lifts. A cook leaned on the pulley rope, exhausted but grinning. "We might actually live through this."

A nearby medic gave a short, shaky laugh. "Don't say that out loud."

The laughter didn't travel far—it didn't need to. The defenders on the wall had started to hear the difference. The clicking, climbing, scratching chaos at the base wasn't as thick anymore. Instead of a rolling drumbeat, there were pockets of sound—a tangle here, a collapsing ladder there, isolated groups getting stuck or turning circles. And beneath it all, the deep bark tremors that had begun at dawn… eased. I was as if a giant creature under the moss had started to roll over and fall asleep.

*****

On the parapet stairs, Jones stood with his arms folded, scanning the battlefield. The slope beneath Stonewall looked like a black patchwork quilt: some sections slick with hardened sap, some burned to ash, some foamed into static knots, some littered with bodies. The ants were still there, but the shape of their attack had dissolved.

"They're pulling away," Miller said, climbing up from the culvert tunnel, armor streaked with resin and ant ichor.

"Not because they decided to," Jones replied. "Because their instincts are chasing a dozen dead ends at once." Miller nodded. "Still counts as pulling away."

*****

Dixie banked high above the wall, letting her skimmer catch a broad updraft. From here, the ant retreat looked almost like a tide going out. There was no clean line of withdrawal—just streams thinning, peeling back toward the tree line, some veering off entirely, others disappearing into moss depressions as though the ground itself had swallowed them.

"They're not retreating in formation," she said softly into her net. "They're just… unraveling."

Song's voice came up from Hivewatch. "Copy, Thorn lead. Western sectors report ant activity down to thirty percent. No new surges detected."

Dixie circled once more before letting her skimmer rise into the thinning sky. Her wings caught the sun. Below her, the wall held firm—scarred, smoking, but intact.

*****

Keller leaned over the parapet rail, panting, rifle empty, arms shaking with fatigue. He stared at the slope as the ants peeled away in broken streams. A few lingered near sap patches, nibbling at hardened foam as if confused about why their path no longer worked. One lone ant climbed halfway up a foam column and just stopped, antennae waving helplessly.

Keller spat over the side. "Yeah," he said hoarsely. "Run back to whatever pit you crawled out of." Brin clapped him on the shoulder. "They're not running, kid. They're just lost. But lost is good."

*****

Hivewatch grew quieter. Runners no longer sprinted in frantic bursts; they jogged, exchanged short nods. Song's stylus moved more slowly across the board now, circling.

dissipating tremor signals instead of drawing new ones.

"Sector C-three clear. Sector E-two is stable. Northern Sally Gap nominal," an operator reported.

Song allowed herself a long, controlled breath. She glanced up at Jones, who was still at the parapet window. He met her eyes and gave the smallest of nods.

She didn't smile. But her hand, resting on the vibrating threads, eased.

*****

By late third Span, the black lines had thinned to nothing. A few scattered groups still wandered at the tree line, but the main mass had pulled back, their pheromone network collapsed under its own contradictions. The western slope was a graveyard of tangled bodies, hardened sap, foam knots, and burned moss lanes.

The first probe was over. The ants hadn't been beaten in a traditional sense—they had simply spent themselves against a wall that refused to break, a defense that bent, redirected, and talked to itself while their instincts clashed and tangled.

Stonewall stood. Smoke curled lazily into the blue sky. The sound of clicking mandibles faded back into the forest like a nightmare receding at dawn.

The air after battle always felt too big. The Broadwater mist was gone, burned away by the midday sun. In its place hung thin smoke, rising from scorched moss lanes and sap fires guttering out along the western slope. The palisade was streaked with green sap, black scorch marks, and crushed ant bodies. Foam ridges jut like strange sculptures, hardened mid-chaos. The hum of the wall was quieter now, but not silent; it thrummed as a heartbeat slowed after a sprint.

Keller stood at his post on the western parapet, his rifle hanging limp at his side. His hands were sticky with resin; his hair matted to his forehead. He looked down at the battlefield and saw a map of their improvisation:

Zigzag foam barriers cutting broken trails,

Hardened slicks shining like glass,

Burned moss lanes marked where fire had redirected columns,

Dead ants heaped in tangled piles where instinct had collided with defense.

For the first time since dawn, Keller let himself sit, back against the parapet rail. The wood was warm under his armor. His heartbeat slowed. He could finally hear himself breathe.

Brin walked past, doing the habitual post-battle check of every position. "Eyes open," he told Keller, though his tone was softer than usual. "Just because they're gone doesn't mean they're gone." Keller nodded. "They'll come back."

Brin stopped, met his eyes, and gave a small, grim smile. "Yeah. But now we know how to make them bleed for every inch."

*****

In Hivewatch, the vibration threads had gone still. Operators leaned back in their seats, rubbing their eyes. The chalk-marked battle board looked like an artist's mad sketch: overlapping arcs, crossed-out trails, notes in every margin. Song stood alone in the center, stylus tucked behind her ear, surveying the mess.

"Clean the board," she said at last. Her voice was steady, but the edges of fatigue showed.

One by one, the chalk lines were wiped away, leaving only faint ghosts of where the swarm had pressed hardest. She kept her eyes on the western vector where the first tremors had been felt at dawn. Nothing moved now. The bark threads were quiet. But she didn't mistake quiet for safety.

Jones entered from the parapet walkway; his coat marked with smoke and sap. He stood beside her silently for a long moment.

"Casualties?" he asked.

"Casualties?" he asked. Lieutenant Song advised, "Three wounded. No deaths." Song's fingers tapped the board lightly. "Two structural breaks in C-five and the culvert maintenance shaft, both contained. SAP reserves are down to forty percent. The Thorn flight burned through all foam gourds. Stingrays held with minimal expenditure."

Jones nodded slowly. "Better than I expected for a swarm that size."

She turned to him. "They weren't organized. If they had been—"

He finished for her. "We'd be counting bodies, not barrels."

They shared a look—victory tempered by clarity.

"This was a probe," Jones said quietly. "And probes don't stop. They learn."

Song returned her gaze to the blank board. "Then so will we."

*****

In the culvert tunnel, Kess sat cross-legged on the floor, hammer resting across her lap. Sap specks coated her arms like freckles. Around her, the freshly sealed breach gleamed pale green. Coto slumped nearby against a crate, head tilted back, eyes closed.

"You realize," Kess said, "we held that line with four cooks, a hammer, and one Thorn sap bomb."

Coto snorted without opening his eyes. "Yeah. Maybe they'll promote the kitchen."

Laughter rippled through the exhausted tunnel crew— not loud, but real. The kind of laughter that survived fear and came out clean on the other side. Above them, the drip of hardening sap was the only sound. A beautiful sound.

*****

On the river, the Stingray crew sat on their decks cleaning micro-bolt barrels. The Broadwater River flowed on, indifferent, carrying away ant bodies and foam fragments. Hernandez leaned against the prow, helmet off, eyes narrowed at the tree line. "They came close to the water," one gunner said. "Yeah," Hernandez replied. "And next time they might not get lost." He tapped the hull with his boot. "Good thing we didn't either."

*****

In the inner yard, civilians moved among the Micro-Operatives like a second wave—not of fighters, but of healers and rebuilders. Medics tended to burn and bite wounds. Engineers reset broken lifts. Scribes cataloged spent ammunition and sap reserves. Two Thorn pilots sat against a wall with their wing's half folded, chalk dust streaking their faces like war paint, passing a water gourd back and forth wordlessly.

Dixie landed her skimmer on a scaffold overlooking the western slope. The wind caught her red pig-tailed hair as she looked out over the battlefield mosaic they'd created. She'd seen swarms before. She'd seen panic and collapse. But this… this had been different.

They hadn't held because of fortification alone. They'd held because dozens of minds adapted faster than instinct.

She keyed her net softly. "Hivewatch, Thorn lead. Perimeter is clear."

Song's reply came back like a long exhale. "Copy, Thorn lead. Well flown."

Dixie smiled faintly and turned her gaze back to the forest. "They'll come again," she whispered. "Next time, smarter."

As evening approached, smoke drifted upward in thin streams. The sun slanted low through the trees, casting long shadows across the palisade. The battlefield's quiet had a weight to it—not peaceful, but watchful, like the forest itself was holding its breath.

Jones walked the wall slowly, Miller at his side. They passed teams repairing cracked rails, scraping sap residue off platforms, cutting away foam to clear firing lines. The damage was visible, but so was the resilience. "They came hard and fast," Miller said. Jones nodded. "And disorganized. Like water finding cracks." "We sealed the cracks… for now," The captain said as he looked out into the distance.

They stopped at Keller's parapet post, looking down at the western slope. It looked like another world—a place where instinct and intellect had met and ground against each other until one gave way. Miller folded his arms. "This wasn't their full force." "No," Jones said. "This was their question."

"And our answer?" asked Miller.

Jones looked over the field and spoke evenly. "Not enough to end it. But enough to make them think."

Miller smirked. "If they could think."

"They don't need to," Jones replied. "They just need to learn."

*****

That night, the outpost lights burned late. Thorn pilots swept the skies in lazy patrol arcs. Hivewatch kept a skeleton crew on the vibration board. Civilians brewed bark tea for exhausted squads in the yard. The sap fires had all been doused, but the smell lingered—a mixture of scorched moss, resin, and ant ichor.

Keller lay on his bunk, still in his armor, staring at the ceiling. Every time he closed his eyes, he heard clicking. Not loud. Just soft. Like the memory of rain.

But beneath that sound lay something else: pride. They'd held. Against thousands. Against the instinct that didn't understand fear. They stood their ground.

Outside, the forest was quiet again. But every Micro-Operative at Stonewall knew that quiet no longer meant safety.

It meant time.

Time to repair.

Time to learn.

Time before the next wave. Because this had only been the first probe.

Chapter 5

Cracks in Command

As the Emberglow phase pressed down on Stonewall Outpost like the lid of a great chest. The last streaks of twilight had bled away beyond the western tree line, leaving the world bathed in lanternlight and the faint silver wash of the stars. The fortress stood in uneasy stillness.

The western slope was a scarred landscape—foam zigzags hardened like chalky rivers, sap floods glistening in strange, glassy sheets, ant carcasses curled and blackened where they had fallen. The forest beyond loomed quiet, but not empty. Every Micro-Operative on the wall could feel it: the sense of something watching from the dark.Parapet patrols moved in pairs, boots tapping softly on bark-reinforced planks. Thorn pilots, grounded and exhausted, lounged near their launch towers, eyes on the sky. The hum of the tremor threads under the fortress was faint, but constant—a low heartbeat beneath their feet. No large movement yet. Just scattered scout signatures, rippling through the network like distant footsteps in a cave.

*****

Inside Hivewatch, scribes and tremor analysts worked in muted coordination. Thin lines of ink crisscrossed parchment maps; sap lanterns hung low, casting pools of amber light over the central projection table. A handful of division aides clustered around a secondary thread display, whispering to each other about the readings.

"Still no major formations," one muttered.

"Doesn't mean they're gone," another replied, glancing toward the west. "They're out there. Learning."

*****

On the parapet, Captain William Jones walked the length of Sector C-3 with his hands clasped behind his back, cloak trailing faintly in the night breeze. He paused by a broken sap barrel left from the previous day's firefight. Hardened resin crusted the lip like amber blood.

Below, the slope stretched down toward the tree line. In the lanternlight, the zigzag lines of hardened foam looked almost like runes carved into the earth. Symbols of resistance—or of a story mid-telling. He leaned on the rail, staring out at the tree line. No movement. No glints. Just silence. *Miller's right,* he thought. Quiet's a liar.

Farther down the wall, Keller leaned over the parapet, staring west. His rifle was slung across his back, but his hands gripped the rail so tightly his knuckles paled beneath the dirt and sap. This was his first real night after a battle. The adrenaline was gone. What replaced it was something stranger—not fear, not calm, but a kind of sharpened alertness. He glanced at the hardened sap field and whispered, almost to himself, "We actually did it."

A veteran nearby chuckled softly. "Yeah, kid. We did. First probes are always messy."

"Think they'll come back tonight?"

The older Micro-Operatives spat over the wall. "They're ants. Of course, they'll come back. Question is how many and how smart."

*****

In the culvert tunnels, Kess ran her hand along a recently sealed breach plug. Sap still oozed faintly in the seams, warm and tacky. She and Coto had spent most of the day shoring up supports, hammering reinforcements into the inner shaft walls, and rerouting drainage lines. Now, in the quiet, the tunnels smelled of drying sap and burnt wood. Coto crouched near the main flow valve, tightening a bolt. "If they find this tunnel again…"

"They will," Kess interrupted. "The question is how fast."

She tapped the seal with the butt of her tool, listening to the sound. Solid. For now.

*****

Overhead, Thorn pilots flew lazy patrol arcs under the stars, wings gliding silently through the cool air. From that height, Dixie Lake could see the entire slope bathed in a faint lantern glow. It reminded her of looking down at a wound that had scabbed over but not healed. She adjusted her goggles against the wind and muttered into her comm bead, "They're holding their breath down there."

Hivewatch crackled back faintly: "So is the forest."

*****

Back in the command room, Hivewatch, Major Edgar "Buster" Greg stood over the projection table, pale eyes flicking between thread readings. He didn't speak. He didn't have to. Everyone in that room could feel the weight—not of an impending attack, but of something else settling in: questions.

How long could Stonewall hold? How much sap remained in the reservoirs? How many more waves before the cracks widened—not in the walls, but in the people?

Colonel Havelock had not yet convened the council, but the air already carried the static of disagreement. The Colonel's arrival earlier that evening had been noticed by everyone. Micro-Operatives on the parapet whispered about the mobile commander who'd ridden in from the Western Front. Officers spoke in quiet, clipped tones. Thorn pilots speculated in the mess.

The fortress had survived its first test. But beneath the calm lantern light, fault lines were forming. Jones turned from the parapet at last. The night was clear. No movement.

But his stomach tightened anyway. Stonewall felt different tonight. Heavier.

Not because of what waited in the forest… but because of what waited in the war room.

*****

The Hivewatch war chamber was unlike any other space in Stonewall Outpost. Built into the base of the great central trunk, its bark walls were reinforced with sap-steel ribs, their surfaces smoothed and etched with faint operational glyphs. Tremor threads crisscrossed the floor like glowing veins, converging at the center beneath a broad circular table carved from heartwood. Sap-lanterns hung from the ribs in concentric rings, their light warm but subdued, as if even the walls knew to lower their voices tonight.

The chamber filled slowly—rank by rank, voice by voice—until the air itself seemed to thicken with authority.

At the head of the table stood Colonel Dorian Havelock, commander of the entire Broadwater theater. His presence was as bold as his uniform. Silver insignia caught the lanternlight in sharp glints, and every motion he made carried the weight of someone who had given orders that shaped campaigns, not just battles. He surveyed the room with the calm precision of a surveyor marking terrain: deliberate, exacting, unblinking.

Arrayed to his right and left were the division leads:

Major Aria Vance, Air Division—tall, hawk-eyed, her posture precise, Thorn flight insignia stitched into the breast of her coat. She carried herself like the sky was her personal domain.

Major Edgar Greg, Ground Division—broad-shouldered, his forearms still faintly stained with sap from spending the day overseeing parapet repairs firsthand. A veteran of countless sieges, he carried his weight like part of the wall itself.

Commander Arlen Veyra, Water Division—soft-spoken, with the stillness of a deep river. Her uniform smelled faintly of Broadwater River mist.

Major Rowan Duskveil, Tree Division and Strategic Operations—pale-eyed, analytical, with the quiet gravity of someone who watched more than he spoke. The other officers sometimes joked that he could see tremor lines in his sleep.

Opposite them stood Colonel Havlock.

Fresh from the Western Mobile Command, his travel cloak hung loose over battle-worn armor, still dusty from the forest trails. His presence was lean, and spearpoint sharp command forged not in chambers but in endless marches and ambushes. His reputation had preceded him: a commander who distrusted fortresses, who believed mobility—not walls—won wars against instinct.

At the far side of the table, slightly apart from the brass, stood Captain William Jones and 1st Sergeant Richard Miller, their armor still streaked with soot and resin from the first probe. They didn't have seats. They weren't here as decision-makers. They'd been invited by Major Duskveil to provide something the room sorely lacked: the ground truth of those who'd fought on the parapets themselves.

Duskveil stepped forward into the circle of lanternlight, clasping his hands behind his back. His voice was soft, but it carried. "Colonel Havelock has convened this council at the BUGFORCE headquarters request. The matter before us is strategic." He let the word hang, the tremor threads humming faintly beneath their boots. "Following the first probe, we must determine whether to fortify Stonewall as a permanent bastion or prepare to abandon it and return to mobile warfare doctrine."

The words dropped into the chamber like a pebble into a still pond. The ripples were immediate. Greg exhaled heavily through his nose. Vance straightened. Veyra's expression didn't change, but her fingers tightened slightly on the table's edge. Jones and Miller exchanged a silent glance—they had guessed something like this might be coming, but hearing it laid out aloud still landed like a hammer blow.

Colonel Havlock stepped into the lanternlight, the room shifting subtly toward him. His boots made no sound on the thread floor. "Let's not waste time pretending this is anything but what it is," he began. "You fought well. I respect that. But courage doesn't change doctrine. Fixed positions don't survive instinct swarms. They never have. I'm not here to congratulate you—I'm here to make sure Stonewall doesn't become a monument to stubbornness." The statement sliced through the air like a clean blade.

Major Greg leaned forward, brow furrowing, but he held his tongue. Vance's eyes narrowed slightly. Veyra's calm remained like still water before a coming ripple.

Havelock's voice was steady, clipped. "Major Duskveil, this chamber recognizes your experience. Present your observations."

Duskveil gestured to the map table. The projection above it flickered to life: a rendering of the western slope, still scarred from the first probe. Foam zigzags etched white paths through dark moss; sap flood lines shimmered faintly like frozen rivers; the culvert breach blinked red at E-2.

"You held," Havlock said. "But this was a disorganized swarm. Pheromone lines were tangled. They tripped over each other. Next time, they won't. And when they coordinate, this fortress becomes a fixed target. And fixed targets," he paused, scanning the officers, "die." Silence, heavy, and deliberate. The sound of the tremor threads seemed louder in the stillness.

Jones shifted his weight but said nothing. Miller's jaw clenched faintly. They were soldiers, not strategists—but they understood enough to know that if the brass started debating whether the walls should stand at all, the next battle might not be decided on the parapets.

Major Duskveil broke the silence like a whisper slipping through cracks. "That is the question before us," he said. "Hold the line… or move before it's too late."

Colonel Havelock's gaze swept the room once more. "Then let us begin."

The lanterns flickered as if the chamber itself inhaled. The debate was about to start—not between soldiers and ants, but between visions of war itself.

For a moment, no one moved. The tremor threads hummed faintly beneath their boots, the only sound in the chamber. The lanternlight carved long shadows across the faces of the officers gathered around the map table.

Colonel Havelock let the silence stretch just long enough to make everyone uncomfortable. Then, with the weight of a gavel, he spoke:

Havlock didn't hesitate. He took two steps forward, boots whispering against the thread floor, and planted a hand on the western edge of the map projection. "Stonewall is a tactical marvel," he said flatly. "But tactically impressive is not strategically sound. You survived a disorganized probe. Good. But instinct learns. Next time, you'll face a coordinated swarm. And when that happens, this outpost becomes a fixed kill zone. For you."

His words didn't echo. They didn't need to. The stillness in the room gave them weight.

Major Edgar Greg leaned forward, knuckles pressing against the edge of the table. His voice came out low, gravelly. "We held this wall," he said. "And we'll hold it again. These walls multiply our strength. Without them, we're chasing ants in circles."

Havlock met his gaze evenly. "And when the next wave comes coordinated? When they hit the culvert, the parapets, and the air lanes simultaneously? What then, Major? You think sap floods and foam lines will hold forever? You'll run dry before they run out of bodies."

Greg's brow furrowed. "Then we stockpile more. Reinforce harder. Adapt faster."

Colonel Havlock's reply was cold. "They don't build stockpiles. They are the stockpile."

Major Aria Vance tapped two fingers lightly on the air sector of the map. "Our Thorn flights still have maneuvering room," she said. "If we strengthen the launch towers and expand the outer perimeter clearing, we can maintain aerial superiority. Air arcs are our advantage."

Havlock turned to her with the calm precision of a blade changing direction. "For how long? Canopy growth is already reclaiming the northern lane. You'll lose air corridors in weeks. You can't hold the sky forever with thorn wings alone."

Vance didn't flinch. "If we can hold long enough for reinforcements from the eastern river front, we won't have to."

"And if those reinforcements never come?" The Colonel shot back. "If Headquarters decides to shift priority elsewhere? You'll be flying in a box while the swarm builds its ladder." Her jaw tightened, but she didn't look away.

Commander Arlen Veyra cleared her throat softly, her voice like still water. "The flotillas rely on this outpost. Stonewall is our anchor. Without it, Broadwater River patrols become wandering targets with nowhere to refit."

Havlock didn't miss a beat. "And if Stonewall falls, your flotillas are trapped. Anchors cut both ways." Veyra fell silent, her expression unreadable.

Major Rowan Duskveil lifted his pale eyes from the map. His voice was measured, quiet, but every officer leaned closer to hear him. "Colonel Havlock, your position is to withdraw now? Abandon Stonewall and revert to mobile doctrine?"

Colonel Havlock straightened. "Yes. We shift to strike columns. Ambush along pheromone trails. We fight in motion. BUGFORCE was designed to move, not to entrench."

Major Buster Greg watched him carefully, hands clasped behind his back. "And you believe this is strategically sound."

"I've lived it," Havlock answered. "Fixed positions invite annihilation. Mobile doctrine bleeds the swarm dry over distance. It's how we've survived every major instinct surge west of here." All eyes turned to the two figures standing slightly apart—Captain William Jones and 1st Sergeant Miller. They weren't seated, but their testimony carried the weight of mud, sap, and blood.

Jones stepped forward, the lanternlight catching the soot stains on his armor. "The wall held," he said simply. "Because we made it hold. Not because it's perfect. Because we were here. If we abandon this place, the ants pour through the Broadwater valley. There's no second line. No fallback. We give this up, and we give them everything behind it."

Colonel Havlock folded his arms. "And how many times do you think you can do that before you break? Before the sap runs out? Before they adapt?"

Jones met his eyes without blinking. "As many times as it takes."

Miller took a half step forward beside him. His voice was rough, the kind that carried from parapets to trenches. "This isn't just timber and sap. It's the line. Pull it, and the whole forest feels it snap."

A murmur rippled through the officers. The entire Stonewall crew—Greg, Vance, several aides—nodded faintly. The Colonel stayed stone-faced.

Havlock turned to the room, his voice rising—not in fury, but in conviction born of doctrine. "You're mistaking.

symbolism for strategy. I've fought these swarms in the open. I've seen what happens to fortresses that think they're untouchable. "This outpost has even fallen once, that's why we rebuilt," indicated Colonel Havlock. "The swarm doesn't tire. It doesn't negotiate. It just keeps coming until the wall is gone—or you are."

Greg slammed his palm on the table, the sound cracking through the chamber. "And you're talking like someone who's never had to stand shoulder-to-shoulder while the wall shakes under your feet. You think mobility saves everyone? It scatters them."

Havelock raised his fist. The room froze. His tone was cold steel. "This is not a brawl," he said. "This is strategy."

Duskveil leaned forward, folding his hands on the table. "We have two paths," he said quietly. "Fortify and hold… or abandon and return to mobile doctrine. Both carry catastrophic risks. There is no third option."

Havlock's voice cut through. "Then choose the one that keeps us alive."

The tremor threads beneath the table shivered faintly. A thin line pulsed westward, like a distant heartbeat.

No one spoke.

For the first time since the probe, it wasn't the ants pressing the walls. It was ideas pressing the command. The council broke just before midnight.

No decisions had been made. No hands had been raised. No doctrines rewritten. But as officers filed out of the Hivewatch war chamber, the air had changed—like the ground after a lightning strike, the smell of something split and smoldering lingered.

Colonel Havelock exited first, silent, flanked by aides who scribbled notes as they walked. His expression gave nothing away. He moved like a man carrying the weight of both roads in his head—neither chosen, both heavy.

Major Vance fell in behind him, eyes distant, already calculating air route clearances. CCommander Veyra walked with slow, measured steps, as if she were following a current she hadn't decided to resist yet.Major Duskveil stayed behind in the chamber, standing by the projection table with his arms folded. He stared at the western slope rendering, the pulsing tremor threads, the bright foam zigzags and sap lines etched like veins across the moss. To anyone watching, he looked like a teenager who just had an argument with his parents.

Jones and Miller lingered at the doorway. Neither spoke. They didn't need to. They'd seen that look before—in officers before a storm, not of weather, but of orders.

By the time the officers reached the outer corridors, the whispers had begun.

Pairs and trios gathered in alcoves and along the trunk's inner spiral ramp, their voices low but sharp.

"...he's not wrong. If the next swarm coordinates, this wall won't hold."

"—and where do we run? There's nothing between here and the Eastern Bridge."

"Greg's losing his temper. Vance doesn't look convinced either way."

"Havelock's not showing his hand. That's what worries me."

Major Greg marched down the corridor like a storm cloud, two Ground Division officers at his side. "We've held lines worse than this," he growled. "Havlock is trying to fight the last war, not this one. Stonewall's the shield. Without it, Broadwater's naked."

A lieutenant jogging to keep pace nodded fervently. "Sir, morale's with you. No one wants to abandon the outpost."

Greg stopped and jabbed a thick finger at the younger officer's chest. "Morale's only worth something if command doesn't fracture. Keep your squads steady. No rumor-mongering. Understood?"

"Yes, sir."

He turned and disappeared deeper into the trunk, heading for the parapet stations.

*****

In the upper flight tower levels of the Skyspan Aerodrome, Vance stood on a narrow balcony with two Thorn squadron leaders. The forest spread out before them in silver moonlight, the canopy undisturbed. One pilot muttered, "If they pull out, we're blind."

The other countered, "Mobile warfare means more flight ops, not less. Maybe we'd actually get to strike instead of hover."

Vance listened, saying nothing for a long time. Then she exhaled through her nose and said, "Stonewall's not just a wall. It's runways. Without it, our charges become half-blind raids. But…" She paused, looking west. "…Havlock isn't a fool."

The pilots glanced at each other, uncertain which way she leaned. That was exactly how she wanted it.

*****

In the tunnel sector, Kess leaned against a newly sealed wall, arms crossed. She and Coto had overheard snippets as officers passed through.

"They're arguing upstairs," she muttered. "We're the ones who'll patch it either way."

Coto smirked tiredly. "If they abandon this place, the Culverts'll be the first highways the ants reclaim." She didn't laugh. Neither did he.

*****

In the mess hall, Micro-Operatives clustered in uneven groups. The energy was different—tense, questioning. Someone had gotten wind of the debate. They always did.

A sergeant slammed his cup down. "They're not actually talking about pulling out, are they?"

"Havlock is," someone replied. "He's some big-shot from the west. Says mobile doctrine wins wars."

"And Jones?"

"He's standing his ground. So's Miller. Greg too. Air's… who knows." The room buzzed like a hive before a swarm.

Near the top of the trunk, Major Duskveil stood alone on the observation deck, the forest stretching out black and endless before him. He wasn't whispering, or arguing, or rallying. He was listening.

He traced invisible lines in the air with his finger, following tremor patterns in his mind. He could already see factions forming like cracks in ice:

Hold the Wall — Greg, Miller, Jones, the Ground ranks, parts of Air.

Return to Mobile — Havlock, some Thorn officers, a few logistical strategists.

Undecided currents — Vance, Veyra, the quiet middle, waiting for someone to tilt the scale.

No sides had been declared. No lines drawn. But they would be.

The ants hadn't yet adapted. The forest was still listening.

But inside Stonewall, the first fractures were already spreading, silent and slow, like roots working their way into stone.

By the following morning, the debate had escaped the war room.

It moved through the outpost the way moisture seeps into wood: slowly, invisibly at first, then everywhere at once. It wasn't shouted in streets or scrawled on walls; it was carried in conversations during patrol shifts, whispered in bunkrooms, traded across mess tables. Everyone had heard something. No one had the full story. But they had enough to start choosing sides, even if quietly.

*****

In the Air Division flight decks, Thorn pilots gathered around a cracked barrel they'd turned into a makeshift coffee table. Wing rigs and glider harnesses hung from overhead beams, swaying slightly as warm updrafts rose through the trunk.

One pilot leaned back in his chair, boots propped up. "You hear Havlock wants to pull us out?" he said, voice half-amusement, half-disbelief.

A veteran wing leader snorted. "Havlock is old doctrine. They love their mobile columns. Hit-and-run, burn the forest from the shadows. Sounds glamorous until your wings tear and you've got nowhere to land."

A younger pilot chimed in, "Maybe he's not wrong. If the ants start coordinating, these launch towers won't mean squat. We'll be boxed in before we even clear the canopy."

The wing leader shot him a look. "You box yourself in when you stop fighting for the sky. Stonewall is the reason we have clear lanes at all. Without it, you're flying blind."

Laughter rippled uneasily. No one outright disagreed, but neither did anyone shut the conversation down.

Even here, high above the parapets, the fault line was visible.

*****

In the Ground Division barracks, the atmosphere was heavier. Squads sat cleaning their weapons, tightening armor fittings, or playing quiet rounds of dice on overturned crates. The walls still smelled faintly of charred foam and resin—a scent that didn't wash out easily. A corporal spat into a bucket. "Pulling out? That's a joke. These walls held. This is our ground."

Another squad member shook his head. "Yeah? And when they come back smarter? You saw what they did to the culvert. Next time, they'll hit three points at once. Havlock ain't wrong to think ahead."

The corporal pointed a cleaning rod at him like a spear. "And where exactly do you plan to run? You think the forest cares? Stonewall's the only thing between them and Broadwater. You give this up, you might as well light the valley on fire yourself."

The others muttered. Some nodded. A few stayed silent.

It wasn't open mutiny. Not yet. But you could hear the lines being drawn in the rhythm of their arguments, in the tone of their disbelief.

Deep below, in the culvert tunnels, Kess and Coto were working on reinforcing the secondary flood gate. The air down here was damp, thick with the smell of wet bark and sap. Hammers rang softly against wood and steel.

Coto wiped his brow with a sap-stained sleeve. "You think they'd really walk away from all this?"

Kess drove a spike into the tunnel wall, the sound echoing. "Command's been doing stranger things lately. If they think the wall's gonna fall, they'll want to fall back before it happens."

He grunted. "Yeah, and we'll be the ones the ants use as their first hallway once we're gone."

They shared a look. It wasn't defiant or fearful—just tired. They'd spent the last three nights sealing breaches, rerouting water flows, and patching stress fractures in the lower structure. To them, debates about doctrine sounded like theories, while the tunnels were consequences made real.

*****

In the mess hall, where rumors coagulated like steam, groups of Micro-Operatives gathered over trays of barkbread and nut broth. A sergeant slammed his cup down on the table. "Jones says hold the wall," he declared. "And if Jones says it, I'm in."

Someone down the line countered, "Yeah, well, Havlock has fought more swarm pushes than anyone here. If he says mobility saves lives, maybe we should listen."

Another voice cut in: "And what about Greg? You think he's gonna pack up and run? He built half these defenses with his bare hands."

The mess buzzed with layered voices. There was no single chant, no dominant faction, just dozens of personal interpretations, colliding like currents beneath the surface.

*****

Even the recruits felt it. Keller sat on a parapet crate, helmet on his knees, listening to two older NCOs argue quietly nearby.

"…can't keep doing this forever. We're one coordinated push away from being buried alive."

"…and if we run, then what? You think they'll stop? You think they'll give us time to dig in somewhere else?"

Keller didn't speak. He just stared out over the wall, at the hardened foam lines zigzagging down the slope. A day ago, this fortress had felt invincible to him. Tonight, it felt like it was balanced on a knife's edge—not because of what was out there, but because of what was happening inside.

*****

Across Stonewall, the debate was no longer confined to officers. It was alive—in wings, in boots, in wrenches, in whispers.

No one had raised flags or declared factions. But everyone was quietly, instinctively aligning, like iron filings under an invisible magnetic field.

And as the tremor threads pulsed faintly beneath their feet—steady, distant—one fact lingered in every mind:

The ants weren't the only ones adapting.

Night wrapped around Stonewall like wet bark. Outside, the forest lay silent, moonlight pooling in the foam zigzags below the walls. Inside, however,

Hivewatch didn't sleep.

Sap-lanterns burned low. Tremor threads hummed with faint signatures. Scribes dipped their pens in ink and copied data onto fresh parchment. In the center of the war chamber, the projection table glowed with a pale amber light, its shifting map layers throwing distorted shadows up the bark walls.

The commanders had reconvened, this time in a reduced council—no lower officers, no ground sergeants. Just the core brass.

Colonel Havelock stood at the head, coat unbuttoned now, the wear of command etched sharper around his eyes. To his right: Duskveil, pale-eyed and steady, surrounded by a cluster of silent analysts. Across from him, Greg leaned against the edge of the table like a man waiting for someone to finally admit the inevitable. Vance and Veyra took their usual positions, shoulders squared but expressions taut.

On the table, Duskveil's analysts had prepared two simulation overlays, both built from real-time tremor data, supply tallies, and swarm behavioral models pulled from the first probe.

Duskveil stepped forward, voice quiet but cutting through the chamber.

"Two scenarios. Two paths," he said. "No third option."

The map projection shifted. The first scenario unfurled like a scroll — labeled simply:

SCENARIO A — HOLD THE WALL

Amber lines traced Stonewall's defenses. Foam zigzags pulsed faintly. Sap flood channels were highlighted in gold, launch towers in blue, and culvert seals in red. A timer appeared in the corner: T+ 1 Cycle and 3 Spans.

Duskveil's analysts began the sequence.

Spans 0–8:

The simulation showed scattered swarm activity at the forest edge — early probes, tremor signatures like faint ripples. Foam reserves held steady. Air sorties maintained wide arcs. Ground forces rotated through parapet stations without strain.

Greg nodded faintly. "That's how it should look."

Spans 9–15:

Multiple tremor vectors began to align on the western slope. Swarm density doubled. Foam barriers held, but the sap reservoirs began ticking down in the sidebar tally. Thorn patrols intercepted two climbing columns in the north sector, burning through 8% of their aerial payloads in a single night.

Vance leaned forward. "That's sustainable. Barely."

Havlock didn't comment. He didn't need to.

Spans 16–24:

A new line appeared—bright red—cutting under the wall. The culvert branch. A simulated ant vanguard split off and attacked the secondary seal point. Casualties spiked among the lower tunnel defenders. The foam zigzags held, but tremor feedback indicated a coordinated three-point assault.

SAP reserves plunged to 38%. Thorn flights were forced to narrow their patrol arcs to stay supplied. The launch tower icon blinked yellow — "overextension warning."

Greg grunted. "We'd adapt. Rotate squads, plug breaches faster."

Havlock arched a brow. "With what sap?"

Turns 25–36:

The western wall was hammered. Three simultaneous surges hit the parapets, culvert, and northern ridge. Foam lines were overrun in two sections. Flood channels held back the main mass, but the culvert branch breached, overrunning lower tunnel defenses. Casualty markers flared red across the projection.

A single black line — the swarm's simulated advance vector — punched through a breach point in Sector E-2. The model estimated 60% casualties before stabilization... assuming reinforcements arrived on time.

If they didn't, Stonewall fell.

The projection froze on a grim image: red swarm vectors flooding through a broken culvert breach while thin blue defender lines collapsed inward.

Silence. Heavy. Only the tremor threads buzzed beneath their boots.

Duskveil turned to the brass. "Projected outcome: Stonewall holds with severe casualties and total depletion of sap stores. Viability beyond 36 hours depends entirely on timely reinforcements from the east."

He paused. "Probability of timely reinforcement under current supply and route conditions: 42%."

Greg folded his arms, jaw tight. "Still standing."

Havlock finally spoke, voice cool. "Barely. You're calling a bloodbath a victory."

Duskveil gestured, and the map shifted again. New label:

SCENARIO B — MOBILE WITHDRAWAL

The walls faded into ghostly outlines. Amber lines pulled back from the outpost into the forest interior. Thorn patrol routes fanned out wider. Stingray patrols shifted east to cover Broadwater crossings. Mobile ambush points appeared along pheromone routes like scattered embers.

Havlock straightened. "This is how we survive."

The analysts began the second sequence.

Span 0–8:

Stonewall's defenses were dismantled in controlled sequence. Sap barrels drained into portable tanks. Ground squads loaded onto haulers. Air units began running escort sweeps. The wall became a skeleton.

Greg muttered under his breath, "That's abandonment."

Spans 9–15:

The swarm arrived at Stonewall to find it empty. Red vectors surged over the walls, unopposed. The fortress was consumed like dry bark. But outside, along pheromone routes, mobile strike teams hit supply columns and vanguards, peeling swarm layers away piece by piece.

Havlock tapped the table. "This is what we do best."

Vance watched silently as Thorn arcs stretched farther east, their icons blinking yellow under increased strain.

Spans 16–24:

Broadwater valley lit up with hit-and-run engagements. Mobile teams inflicted steady casualties on swarm trail formations. But the swarm didn't stop. It simply flowed around.

A new set of red vectors appeared sweeping into the eastern river basin. Without Stonewall, the Broadwater choke point opened. Civilian caravan markers blinked along retreat paths. Panic markers spiked.

Duskveil's analysts annotated: "Swarms bypass fortified position; strategic delay successful but fails to contain."

Span 25–36:

The mobile groups were forced into constant retreat. Thorn patrols overextended; launch tower resupply was non-existent. Stingray flotillas were caught between supporting ambush teams and defending the eastern crossings.

Swarm density in the Broadwater Basin hit 180% of previous projection. The valley was lost in the model, even if mobile forces survived.

The simulation froze again: Stonewall was a black crater. Red swarm vectors flooded through Broadwater like ink in water. Blue mobile forces hovered at the edges, alive but strategically displaced.

Duskveil folded his hands. "Projected outcome: Mobile forces survive, swarm slowed but not contained. Broadwater valley and Stonewall lost. Civilian displacement unavoidable."

Havelock's face was stone. He stepped forward. "Survival. Adaptation. Live to fight another day."

Greg barked a laugh with no humor. "At the cost of everything behind us."

Vance rubbed her temples. "Air won't last long without towers. If we run, my flights become raiders, not guardians."

Veyra finally spoke, voice quiet. "And the flotillas? Without Stonewall, they become islands waiting to drown."

The two maps hovered side by side in the dim light:

One, a fortress standing against the tide, bloodied but defiant, gambling everything on reinforcements.

The other, a fluid shadow war, surviving but ceding the heart of the valley.

Havelock stared at both without blinking. The silence stretched.

Duskveil broke it, softly: "Two roads. One breaks the wall to save the army. The other breaks the army to save the wall."

The tremor threads pulsed beneath their feet—steady, distant, alive.

Outside, the forest remained silent.

Inside, leadership was running out of comfortable lies to tell themselves.

Dawn bled slowly through the canopy, staining the upper towers in a thin orange haze. Dew clung to the parapet railings, dripping in steady rhythms like the ticking of a slow clock. Patrols changed over; Thorn pilots ran pre-flight checks in strained silence. The fortress looked calm. Inside, it was anything but.

*****

The Hivewatch chamber filled once more—tired eyes, fresh uniforms, brittle voices. No one had truly slept. Some hadn't even changed their coats from the night before. The air was sharper, the usual courtesies thinner. What had begun as a strategic question was about to become a fault line.

Colonel Havelock stood at the head of the table, hands clasped behind his back, jaw set like carved stone. Behind him, the dual scenario maps still hovered—Hold the Wall on one side, Mobile Withdrawal on the other—casting a pale glow across the officers' faces.

Major Vance stood with her arms folded tightly, expression unreadable. Commander Veyra traced idle circles on the table's edge with one finger. Major Greg planted both fists on the wood, his weight leaning forward like a battering ram ready to charge. Duskveil stood opposite him, cloak thrown over one shoulder, every line of his posture screaming: decide.

Jones and Miller had been summoned again—not to lead, but to witness. They stood near the chamber doors, silent, the only ones still bearing soot and battle-wear. Duskveil occupied his usual position beside the analysts, pale eyes scanning the room like a man charting weather patterns before a storm.

Havelock's voice cut through the silence. "We have seen the models. We have heard the arguments. This council will now deliberate and advise on operational direction."

The Colonel didn't wait for permission to step forward. "The wall will fall," he said flatly. "Maybe not tomorrow, maybe not with the next probe. But it will. Every swarm in history adapts. It's only a matter of time before they find the weak seam. And when they do, this fortress becomes a grave. Our doctrine was never meant to be static. We bleed them in the field, not on the ramparts."

Greg let out a low laugh—one that didn't reach his eyes. "Doctrine," he said, the word dripping like sap. "Tell that to the squads who held the parapets while your doctrine was off running drills in the western woods. You're talking about abandoning a fortress that's already won its first fight."

"Won?" Havlock shot back. "You call that a win? You burned through a third of your sap in one night. Half your Thorn payload. If that's victory, I'd hate to see defeat."

Greg slammed a fist on the table hard enough that inkpots rattled. "This fortress is the line. You give this up, and everything east of here is tinder waiting for a match. You think your ambush columns will stop what's coming? You'll be picking at the edges while the valley burns."

Havlock leaned forward, his voice like a blade drawn slow. "Better to bend than break. Better to survive to fight again than to chain yourself to a wall you know can't hold forever. This place isn't sacred. It's a position. And positions are only worth what they can buy you in time."

Vance finally broke her silence. "And what about the sky?" she said sharply. "If we run, Thorn flights lose their towers. We become raiders, not guardians. Our wings are sharp, but they can't cover an entire basin alone."

Havlock turned to her, voice steady. "You adapt. New towers. Forward strips. Air was never meant to nest."

Her lips thinned. She didn't answer, but her hands tightened around her folded arms.

Veyra spoke next, quietly. "And the flotillas? Without Stonewall, our moorings are exposed. We rely on these walls to keep the Broadwater corridor stable."

Havlock's response was immediate. "Then move your flotillas east. Out of the choke. You can't anchor to something that's sinking."

Veyra lowered her gaze. She didn't agree—but neither did she argue further.

Greg leaned across the table, his voice rising. "You're not talking strategy anymore, Colonel. You're talking retreat. Call it what it is."

"And you," Havlock replied, "are talking about a siege you can't win. Call that what it is."

The two men locked eyes—one forged in siege craft, the other in mobile campaigns. The temperature in the room changed.

Major Duskveil raised a hand sharply. "Enough."

Silence snapped back into place like a trap closing.

Duskveil stepped forward, voice quiet but cutting. "The models don't favor either path cleanly. Hold the Wall buys time—but bleeds resources fast. Mobile Doctrine preserves the army—but loses the valley. Either way, something breaks. The question is what we are willing to lose first."

His words hung in the air like smoke. No one challenged them.

Then Havelock turned to Jones. "Captain," he said. "You fought on the wall. Speak plainly."

Jones glanced around the room—at Greg, at Havlock, at Vance and Veyra, at Duskveil's still gaze. He straightened. "The wall held because we were here," he said. "If we run, they'll flood through. If we stay, they'll hit harder next time. I don't pretend to know which path saves more lives. But I know this: whatever choice you make, we'll be the ones bleeding for it."

Miller added, quietly but firmly, "And if you pull us out, tell the squads yourself. Because they won't hear it from me." For a moment, that landed heavier than any model projection.

Colonel Havelock stepped into the center of the room. His voice was cold, precise. "Enough of doctrines and recriminations. This is not a debate club. This is command."

He looked to his officers one by one. "Major Vance. Commander Veyra. Major Greg. Major Duskveil. Captain Jones. Sergeant Miller. Understand this—whatever we decide, it will not be unanimous. The forest will not give us time to soothe egos."

His gaze locked on Greg and Duskveil in turn. "We will not turn this into a civil war of doctrine, I will break both your commands before the swarm has the chance."

The room went still. Even Greg didn't reply.

Duskveil's analysts shifted uneasily. The tremor threads beneath their boots pulsed faintly, echoing the tension above.

No decision was made that morning. Havelock adjourned the leadership with clipped orders for readiness drills and aerial reconnaissance expansions. But as the officers filed out into the pale dawn, the fracture line was no longer hidden.

Greg left with his jaw set, flanked by Ground officers. Havlock stayed behind for a moment, staring at the map projection like a man already imagining different roads. Vance walked alone. Veyra lingered by the door, torn between currents. Duskveil remained by the table, silent, tracing fault lines only he seemed to see.

Jones and Miller watched them all go. Neither spoke. But both understood something clearly now:

the next battle wouldn't just be against the ants.

Chapter 6

The Swarm Rises

At night, the forest was a cathedral of breath and filament. Dew beaded on willow whiskers and clung to the undersides of leaves like constellations, each droplet catching the faintest glimmer of starlight. Far from the lantern crown of Stonewall, sound moved in narrow threads—one twig tick, one moth-whisper, one distant drip counting seconds no one owned.

The scouts moved inside those threads. Sergeant Brin led the first pair, a slim silhouette where bark met shadow. He wore moss-darkened armor with every buckle wrapped in cloth, every stitch soot-rubbed to kill the shine. At his shoulder, Scout Talla slid her palm along a root rib's curve and felt the wood's cool pulse as if asking permission. They had slipped a span into the tree line, then three, then more, because the forest kept giving them distance.

"West-by-north," Brin murmured, voice the thickness of a breath. "Keep the wind."

Talla's answer was a brush of fingers against his sleeve: aye.

Behind them, a second pair—Jaro and Fenn—ghosted through fern shadow, trading the lead every dozen steps so neither rhythm grew predictable. Their packs were lean, their kits fewer than fear might prefer: coil line, chalk, sap whisperer, a purse of dust to mark a trail if running turned to fleeing. No rifles—too loud. Each carried a thorn-bow and three short sap charges that would glue a corridor closed or buy three heartbeats of distance. In the last hour, they hadn't spoken. They'd only listened. At first, the forest had been the forest. Then, it wasn't.

Brin felt it before he heard it—an almost-murmur, the way a wall hums before a kettle boils. He raised two fingers. Four bodies melted flat to bark and moss as if they had never been separate from it. Talla's lips shaped the question without sound: Wind?

Brin tilted his head. Not wind. A texture. A far, spreading shudder that didn't belong to trunks or river, more like the way a thousand tiny feet might press the world's skin at once and then again and then again—too even to be random, too vast to be close.

He took the sap whisperer from his belt—a leaf-thin disc pressed against the bark of a knee-high root. It tremored. He closed his eyes. Let the threads inside his fingers absorb it.

"Large movement," he breathed, no louder than the leaf's own veins. "West curtain. Broad front."

Jaro's eyes flicked toward the black beneath the boughs. "Ants?"

"Ants," Brin said. And then, because the forest kept speaking, "—and something heavier."

They moved again, slower now, trading distance for certainty. The moss felt damp enough to drink but too springy to trust; every other step they sank and rose with a plant's lazy breath. The murmur grew. The shudder turned to pressure. The pressure resolved into layers.

Talla stopped so suddenly that Fenn nearly stepped into her. She lifted a hand and drew a tiny half-circle in the air. Edge.

Beyond the next low ridge of roots, the ground dropped into a shallow basin where the willow canopy opened like a throat. Starlight ran down the bowl's curve, and in that pale wash the scouts saw movement enough to make the air look granular.

Ants—thousands—filling the bowl's lower lip and filling up toward the ridge in silent ropes. Not in a single mindless rush. In lanes. In waves that didn't collide.

A line on the basin's far side lifted and rippled. The ripple shimmered and separated from the ground and became a wasp column, wing-cases closed, bodies angled forward, legs working in tight, synchronized twitches that carried them at a march rather than a flight. Between the ant lanes and the wasp marchers, beetles moved like armored stones—broad backs, grinding mandibles, a rumble in the bark that made the scouts' teeth buzz.

Jaro's fingers found Brin's forearm. "Not ants alone."

Brin nodded once, slow, as if any sudden thought might make noise. He slid a lens from his throat pouch and raised it to the basin's rim. The glass was darkened, tuned to catch faint pheromone haze. The air above the lanes shone with veins of pale smoke—scent trails laid and re-laid until they thickened. He tracked them backward, following the way they braided and unbraided.

They converged on three points: a fallen limb black with ant traffic, a cracked stump where beetles tested their jaws on sap-hardened bark, and a wasp roost where winged bodies clustered like seed pods, vibrating in call-and-answer tremors.

No chaos. No chance. Just design.

He passed the lens to Talla. She looked, swallowed, and didn't hand it back. Her other hand crept to the sap charges at her hip the way a player's hand finds a lucky coin.

"The siege wasn't an accident," Fenn mouthed, eyes on the wasps' still wings. "It's a hand."

Brin's jaw moved once, a thought his teeth could not grind into something softer. He watched the lanes. Ants never looked like obedience until you saw this—rows that never tangled, pauses where empties yawned and then filled exactly, beetles adjusting pace to match the ant flow without forcing it.

And the wasps—an army taught not to lift until a signal passed through their bodies like lightning choosing a path.

"Back," Brin breathed. "Two points, two routes. We mark and run."

They ghosted away from the basin rim in the reverse of their approach—half-steps, weight spread, whole bodies attentive to not making bark complain. Once they had put a dozen root ribs between themselves and the basin, Fenn risked a glance eastward. Through gaps in the leaves, far beyond the scouts, a dull amber pulsed on the horizon where Stonewall's lantern crown would be, if you pretended you could see that far. He imagined the wall, the foam zigzags, the culvert seals. He imagined the bowl they had just seen emptying into those shapes. They moved faster.

Halfway home, the forest offered them a message of its own: a line of abraded bark on a knee-high run, fresh, the size of a scout's hand, smoothed by dozens of chitinous bellies. It curved—not toward Stonewall directly, but to the left of it, toward a low saddle in the land where the wall's western and northern sap sheds touched.

Talla crouched, tracing the groove with one knuckle. Flank route.

Brin took a breath and tasted the air's memory. The scent was thin but present—wasp musk under ant acid, with a fainter, tarry thread that might have been beetle spit. He looked up through the lattice of willow hangings into the dark without stars.

"Two fronts," he said. "And a hammer."

They moved again—no longer a drift but a line. Jaro ranged ahead to clear a path that was more absence than trail. Fenn looped wide and returned twice, signaling with the smallest hand signs: clear, clear, caution. Talla stopped once to scratch a mark into bark with chalk and then blew a puff of dust over it to hide the shine: if they had to run this way with half the outpost at their backs, they'd want breadcrumbs.

The murmur thickened behind them. It wasn't pursuit; it was attendance—as if the forest itself had come to watch, its voiceless congregation turning to face a single altar.

They broke the tree line and hit the first run of Stonewall's outer roots at a controlled crouch that looked like falling. The sight of the wall—lantern crown dim, silhouettes pacing—shouldn't have made their lungs loosen, but it did. The parapets looked smaller than ever and more necessary for the same reason.

The gate sentry on the low door didn't ask their names. He saw Brin's hand in the signal slit—two fingers, then three, then a flat palm—and unbarred the door like a man relieving a held breath. The scouts slid through. The bar fell back into its brackets with a sound that hadn't meant safety since the first probe. It meant for now.

"Hivewatch?" the sentry asked, voice careful.

Brin nodded. "Run it."

They climbed the inner stair at a speed that never looked fast, how scouts always moved when the message was a blade too big for one tongue. Voices chased them: the scrape of a cook's ladle in a cauldron, a medic's easy lie to a wounded man, a sergeant's sardonic prayer about double watches. Above it all, the threads—the vibration grid—hummed a line so faint you might call it your own blood in your ears if you needed a reason to sleep.

The stairwell to Hivewatch smelled of resin and sweat— the smell of urgency wrapped in bark.

Sergeant Thomas Brin took the steps two at a time, though his footfalls were no louder than falling dust. Behind him, Talla, Jaro, and Fenn moved in practiced silence. They had run for most of the return, but now, inside the outpost's heart, their pace was deliberate. Information carried too fast was as dangerous as information carried too slow.

The outer corridor gave way to the war chamber's double doors, their sap-steel hinges humming faintly with the tremor feed from the floor below. Two sentries stood watch, weapons lowered but hands ready. One caught sight of Brins mud-darkened armor and the leaf disk clipped to his belt, and he didn't hesitate.

"Hivewatch," the sentry called inward. The doors opened like a lung exhaling.

Inside, the chamber was already stirring. Sap-lanterns burned higher than usual. Tremor threads glowed with a restless pulse. Scribes moved between tables with parchment rolls hugged tight against their chests. Analysts clustered around the projection well, its surface alive with thin gold lines that sketched out the western forest in shifting, trembling strokes.

Major Edgar Greg stood beside the projection, pale eyes half-lidded as he traced phantom patterns in the air above the map. He didn't look up when Brin entered. He simply said, "Report."

Brin crossed the floor and set the sap whisperer onto the rim of the projection table. A soft click sealed it into the receiver. The chamber stilled.

A heartbeat later, the tremor feed bloomed.

It began as a low, granular hiss—like sand pouring through hollow wood. Then the patterns emerged: steady, layered pulses moving east from the tree line in broad, deliberate sheets. The analysts exchanged quick, sharp glances. This wasn't the scattered noise of random scouts. This was organized movement.

Duskveil who was also at Hivewatch, leaned closer, fingers hovering just above the glowing map. "Scale it," he murmured.

An operator twisted a dial. The tremor map zoomed outward, the delicate gold threads revealing the basin Brin`s team had observed. The image filled with living dark—ants in lanes, beetles in grinding formations, wasps clustered in tremoring roosts. The vibration signature was unlike anything recorded since Stonewall's founding.

Colonel Havelock arrived without sound, his cloak trailing like a dark banner. His eyes took in the map in a single sweep. "How far?" he asked.

"Less than a couple Reaches," Brin said. "And growing. It's not random. They're assembling."

"Numbers?" Vance's voice came from the doorway— she was still in her flight leathers, goggles hanging around her neck.

Brin looked at Talla. She stepped forward and answered clearly, "Thousands. At least. Ant lanes in six separate bands. Beetle groups flanking each. Wasps grounded, wings folded. They're waiting for a signal."

At that, even Greg stopped mid-stride. The last time wasps had been part of a ground column was in the Fall of Embergate, and that fortress had been overrun in three Spans.

"Let's see it," Duskveil said softly.

Brin passed over the pheromone lens. An analyst placed it in the reader. The map overlaid faint scent lines, glowing like spider silk across the basin. Three thick braids converged at distinct points: a fallen limb, a cracked stump, a wasp roost pulsing at rhythmic intervals.

"They're being… directed," Talla added, voice quiet.

Duskveil, nor Greg answered. They didn't have to. Everyone in the room saw it: the way the trails moved like veins, the way the wasps vibrated in chorus, the way ants shifted lanes without collisions. This wasn't the forest's usual swarm behavior. It was a military geometry drawn in pheromone and instinct.

Havelock folded his hands behind his back, jaw tightening. "We assumed the probe was opportunistic," he said. "We were wrong."

Veyra slipped in quietly, having heard enough from the hall to forget ceremony. "This is a siege," she murmured.

Duskveil tapped the wasp roost symbol. The projection magnified it until the roost's inner structure became visible as a pulsing node of light. "And someone," he said, "is conducting it."

For a long moment, no one spoke. The only sound was the tremor plate, thrumming softly beneath their boots, echoing the unseen army's march.

Finally, Havelock broke the silence. "Sound the quiet muster," he ordered. "All divisions. I want every lead in this chamber within the hour. And double the scouts on the north saddle. If they're planning a flank, I want eyes on it before dawn." A runner bolted from the chamber.

Greg stepped up beside the map, fingers tracing the flank groove Brin had marked in chalk. "They're coming with weight and brains this time," he muttered.

A newly assigned commander named Walter Raines entered last, drawn by the sound or perhaps by instinct. He took one look at the map, the wasp roost, the perfect rhythm of the pulses, and exhaled through his nose. "Well," he said quietly. "Looks like the debate just got louder." Raines was assigned by Headquarters to be a witness to the debate of whether to hold the outpost or become mobile again, and report back to the high command.

Havelock's gaze didn't shift. "No," he said. "It's over. Now we prepare."

B.U.G.F.O.R.C.E.

The tremor feed kept singing—low, patient, inevitable.

*****

The Hivewatch chamber did not dim that night. The lanterns burned steady and low, their amber light throwing long shadows across trembling maps. The tremor threads beneath the floor thrummed like distant drum lines, steady enough that a scribe's inkpot had started to leave concentric rings on the table without anyone touching it.

Around the projection well, Duskveil and his analysts leaned close, their movements quiet, their voices hushed but fast. Scrolls, pheromone overlays, and tremor frequency charts layered the table like sedimentary rock, each a fragment of something bigger.

Brin's scouts had been dismissed to rest, but their discovery sat alive in the data, refusing to sleep.

The Patterns

Duskveil stood at the table's center with his sleeves rolled to the elbow, his stilled eyes reflecting the golden tremor light. He had been tracing pheromone trails and vibration intervals for hours, his thin hands moving like a conductor trying to catch a tune only he could hear.

"They're not random," he murmured, almost to himself. "They're measured."

An analyst beside him adjusted a dial on the roost overlay. The tremor intervals from the wasp nest amplified— soft thud-thud... thud-thud... thud-thud—steady as a heartbeat.

Vance, leaning against the doorframe with her flight goggles dangling loosely from one hand, tilted her head. "That's not swarm noise," she said. "That's... a signal."

"Exactly," Duskveil replied. "Wasp roosts usually hum in layered frequencies. Different clusters, different tempos.

It's messy." He pointed to the projection. "But this—this is a unified rhythm. Something is keeping them all in time."

"Could it be environmental?" asked one of the younger analysts.

Duskveil shook his head slowly. "No. This isn't wind, or heat, or moonlight. It's intentional synchronization."

On another section of the map, tremor analysts had isolated the ant lane formations. Under Greg's direction, they overlaid the pheromone network and played it forward as a time-lapse. What emerged wasn't the chaotic, self-organizing churn of a typical instinct surge. Instead, it was structured flow: lanes forming, splitting, and rejoining at predictable intervals, like a trained army rotating ranks.

Greg leaned over their shoulders, arms crossed. "I've fought ants before. They don't do this. Not unless something's telling them to."

"They're responding to something," Duskveil corrected quietly. "And it's consistent across three species. Ants, beetles, wasps. Their signals are being braided."

The Braided Code

A second analyst tapped a fresh sheet onto the board. It showed pheromone plumes in faint white lines, overlaying vibrational pulses represented as concentric rings. Where the two overlapped, they formed nodes—bright intersections pulsing rhythmically.

"Look here," the analyst said, pointing at a node near the wasp roost. "The ants lay trails first. The beetles adjust their route to the pheromone. Then—" she flipped the transparency—"the wasps echo with vibration bursts exactly 3.7 seconds later. Every single time."

Vance straightened, frowning. "They're waiting for instructions."

"Yes," Duskveil said. "And they're relaying them. Whoever or whatever is coordinating, it's not just issuing commands—it's orchestrating."

He traced a finger along the pheromone braids, following them backward through the basin. Most led to obvious staging sites—fallen limbs, rotted stumps. But one thread diverged north, thin and erratic at first, then sharpening, like a wandering thought finding clarity.

Duskveil tapped it twice. "This one."

An operator zoomed the map outward. The thin thread led away from the basin and into a dense grove where the tremor data was still faint. "We don't have a good reading there," the operator warned. "Our western thread sensors don't reach that deep."

Greg leaned forward. "If something's giving orders, that's where it's hiding."

Havelock, who had been silent at the edge of the room, stepped into the lantern light. "What's the scale?"

"Unknown," Duskveil said. "But it's above the usual nest-signal range. And the rhythm—" He tapped the wasp roost node. "—is too uniform. This isn't one queen's pheromones. This is... centralized control."

The words landed like a dropped hammer. Even the scribes paused their writing.

Something Intelligent

Raines quickly spoke up, boots quiet on the bark floor. He scanned the boards, the maps, the analysts. "So," he said slowly, "the swarms not just bigger. It's smarter."

"Not smarter," Duskveil corrected. "Directed."

"By what?" Raines asked. "Some new hive strain? Cross-species pheromone matrix?"

Duskveil didn't answer right away. He stared at the node where all the threads braided together—three species, one rhythm, one hidden source. "Something," he said finally. "Something new."

Veyra crossed her arms. "We've never faced this before." "No," Havelock said. "We haven't."

The tremor feed kept pulsing. Duskveil adjusted the sensitivity, and suddenly the room was filled with layered intervals, like three different heartbeats lining up one after another until they snapped into perfect sync.

Thud-thud… thud-thud… thud-thud…

Vance swallowed. "That's not random."

Greg's voice dropped low. "That's a drumbeat."

The Realization

It was Duskveil who put it into words. Not loudly. Not dramatically. Just as a man who sees a truth, turns it over in his hand, and sets it on the table.

"They're not coming like a swarm," he said. "They're coming like an army."

The chamber went silent except for the steady rhythm under their feet.

Havelock finally broke it, voice cold and precise. "Then we will meet them like one."

The Hivewatch war table had seen battles fought upon its surface before — lines drawn in sap-ink; markers pushed like pieces in a game only half the players understood. But that night, as the officers and division leads gathered, it felt different. The tremor map was no longer theory. It was alive beneath their boots, a living pulse carrying the rhythm of something vast and deliberate just beyond the tree line.

Colonel Dorian Havelock stood at the head of the table, hands clasped behind his back, his gaze fixed not on the glowing projection, but on the faces gathered around it. Major Aria Vance of the Air Division, Major Edgar Greg of the Ground, Commander Arlen Veyra of the Water flotillas, Major Rowan Duskveil, Colonel Raines, Captain William Jones, and 1st Sergeant Miller. Every voice that mattered in Stonewall's defense was present. The scouts' discovery, Duskveil's analysis, and the growing tremor signatures had ripped away the last veil of uncertainty.

The projection well displayed the forest basin like a heartbeat under glass. Three species moved in braided formation, their lanes and pulses glowing faintly gold against the deep brown of the terrain. And farther north, a faint, unexplored tremor source pulsed like an unseen drum major keeping perfect time. No one spoke at first. The map spoke for them.

The Report

Duskveil was the first to break the silence. His voice was soft, but in that quiet, it carried.

"You've all seen the tremor logs. This is not a fluke. The pheromone signals are braided — three species operating in concert. The rhythm at the wasp roost is… singular. We believe there's a coordinating intelligence in the northern grove."

Raines leaned over the map, hands braced against the table. "You're saying they have a general."

"Something like that," Duskveil said.

Havelock's eyes flicked to Greg. "Numbers?"

Greg's jaw was set. "More than double the probe. Maybe triple. And they're not coming in a single wave this time. We're looking at simultaneous strikes — main push from the basin, flank from the northern saddle, wasps in reserve for air and breaches."

Vance nodded grimly. "Our Thorn pilots picked up faint wing vibrations on patrol. If those wasps take to the air in formation, they can harry the wall and hit supply routes simultaneously."

Commander Veyra traced the Broadwater's line with her finger. "And if beetles hit our moorings, we could lose the flotilla before they fire a shot. The sap lines run close to the bank. It's a soft underbelly."

Havelock took it all in without speaking. The drumbeat beneath their boots didn't care about their silence.

The Fracture Reopens

It was Raines who finally forced the conversation onto its fault line.

"You all know what this means," he said, straightening. "We're not facing a scattered horde anymore. This is an army. And you don't fight an army by sitting still and waiting for it to hit you on its terms."

Greg's response was instant, low, and dangerous. "And you don't abandon a fortress just because the enemy finally learned to knock."

Raines turned sharply toward him. "Stonewall isn't sacred, Major, nor is it a fortress it's an outpost made of wood and sap. And when it falls — and it will fall — those walls will bury every squad still inside."

Greg leaned across the table, shoulders squared. "We held once already. With less warning, less preparation. You'd have us scatter into the woods, run ambush lines like ghosts, and leave the civilians and supply stores here to burn?"

"They're a liability if they stay!" Raines snapped. "If we break into mobile formations, we can bleed this swarm across the forest. Stretch their lanes. Force them to fight where we choose."

"And surrender the wall?" Greg shot back. "Give them a fixed point they can occupy and reinforce? You'd hand them a foothold into the basin!"

The room's temperature shifted. This was no longer just strategy. It was identity. Greg was the wall. Raines was the forest. And the swarm outside had just raised the stakes.

Duskveil's Interjection

Duskveil's voice cut through the rising tension like a scalpel.

"Gentlemen," he said quietly. "The enemy is not giving us a choice between siege and field. They're preparing for both. Two prongs, one rhythm. If we hold, we must hold knowing we'll be flanked. If we move, we must move knowing we're abandoning a symbol that will be used against us."

Vance folded her arms. "If we retreat, we lose our towers. Our wings are sharp, but blind. We can't defend the basin from the sky without these perches."

Veyra added, "And the river routes go with them. You abandon the wall, you abandon the Broadwater's lock. We become a flotilla without a harbor."

Raines turned toward them. "Better a moving flotilla than a sunk one. Better wings that strike than wings broken against walls."

Greg slammed his palm onto the table. "This wall has never fallen. Not once."

"And that's exactly what makes it a prize," Raines said coldly.

The Division Deepens

Jones and Miller exchanged a look from their place near the door. Jones finally spoke, his voice cutting through the officers' rhetoric like a soldier's knife through rope.

"You're both right," he said. "And you're both wrong. The wall doesn't hold itself. We do. The forest doesn't bleed them alone. We do. Whatever decision comes, we'll be the ones fighting in the mud and on the ramparts."

Miller nodded once. "So figure it out fast. Because they're not waiting for us to agree."

The officers fell into a taut silence. Outside, a low tremor rolled through the floor like distant thunder. The swarm was still moving.

Havelock finally stepped forward, voice firm. "Enough. This isn't the time to draw swords against each other. The swarm is days — maybe hours — away. We will not splinter before the battle begins."

He swept his gaze across them all. "I'll hear operational proposals at dawn. But make no mistake: indecision will kill us faster than the enemy."

The war table pulsed beneath their hands. Three species. One rhythm. And a fortress balanced on a razor edge between holding and moving.

*****

The war table debate ended before dawn, but the argument didn't leave with it. It moved outward — into corridors, onto parapets, down into culverts and hangars and docks — carried in quiet conversations, in clenched jaws, in the rhythm of boots on bark.

The outpost awoke to the sound of preparation.

No horns. No speeches. Just the weight of thousands of hands working with the precision born of knowing what was coming.

*****

Air Division – The Thorn Wings

At the Skyspan Aerodrome, Major Aria Vance stood on the upper gantry, wind tugging at her flight jacket as the first light burned the fog into golden mist. Below her, Thorn skimmers and wing-rigs were dragged into formation, their glider membranes stretched tight and checked for micro-tears.

"Recheck every wing seam," Vance called down. Her voice carried like a blade through silk. "Any fray, any stretch, you bring it to me. No mid-air failures this round."

"Yes, ma'am," came the chorus from a dozen pilots and riggers.

Captain Sel, flight lead, moved among the crews with the quiet efficiency of someone who knew every rig by heart. She knelt beside a wing stretched across a frame and ran her fingers along the edge where resin met vein. "Tighter," she told the rigger, who nodded and hauled the line another inch.

Near the launch spurs, racks of sap bombs, flare bursts, and net canisters were being assembled into neat pyramids. Two junior flyers chalked symbols onto the bomb casings — not superstition, exactly, but not not superstition either.

Vance watched them for a long moment. Her division was the eye above the wall, the swift hand that struck first and last. But even she felt the gravity of what Duskveil had shown them. Wasp wings in formation were no laughing matter. If those creatures took the sky in organized swarms, the Thorn pilots would have to fight for dominance, not simply harass and retreat.

She descended the stairs to the deck where Sel was tightening a wing harness.

"Wing formations stay flexible," Vance said. "No rigid flight patterns. If the wasps fly in rhythm, we disrupt it. Scatter and stab. Think knife fight, not parade."

Sel glanced up, face serious. "And if they match us in the air?"

Vance met her gaze. "Then we stop thinking like pilots. And start thinking like hunters."

*****

Ground Division – Fortify the Bones

Beneath the wall, Major Edgar Greg stalked through the trenches like a storm given legs. The Ground Division had already thrown itself into work the moment the tremor map went live.

Teams moved in coordinated flows — sealing culverts with reinforced sap wedges, drilling brace holes into the outer roots, stringing trip-snares and pitch traps across the saddle approaches. Hammers rang against bark. Sawdust floated through the air like pollen.

"Recheck every culvert seal," Greg barked. "If I can find light between the wedge and the frame, you're doing it again!"

A squad was assembling portable sap sprayers, strapping them to bark runners like backpacks. The thick hoses coiled at their feet looked like sleeping serpents. These would be used to flood breach points when the beetles hit.

Kess and Coto were deep in the culvert tunnels, inspecting the foam lines and inner bulkheads.

"They'll go for the saddle," Coto muttered, tapping a wedge with his hammer.

"They'll go for everywhere," Kess replied. She braced her boots against the tunnel floor and drove the wedge one inch deeper. "But if they find the saddle weak, we're finished before the horns blow."

*****

On the upper ramparts, Miller paced the parapet, eyes on squads stringing new thorn-spike racks. His presence alone kept the pace brisk. "Ladders ready on every sector," he called. "You'll want them where you're not standing when the first breach hits."

Farther down the wall, Jones was walking the inner trench, speaking with squad leaders one by one. His voice never rose above conversational. He didn't need it to. When he stopped to talk, men and women leaned in. He checked their sap charges, reminded them where fallback points were, and ended each talk with the same quiet sentence:

"Eyes up. Breathe slow. You've done this before."

It wasn't a lie. But it wasn't quite the same either. This time, the enemy had a mind.

*****

Water Division – The River's Edge

On the Broadwater docks, Commander Arlen Veyra oversaw the flotilla's preparations. Stingray patrol boats bobbed against their moorings, crews moving over them like ants over their own hulls — tightening ropes, refilling charge pods, polishing the brass tips of harpoon launchers.

The river was still, a sheet of dull silver under the dawn light. But everyone working the docks felt it: this stillness was a held breath, not peace.

"Shift the inner boom two spans upstream," Veyra ordered. "If beetles test the moorings, I want them hitting the kill zone before they touch the planks."

"Aye, Commander!"

She stepped aboard the lead Stingray, its sleek, manta-like hull catching faint light. "Harpoon racks double-loaded. Depth charges primed. No wasted shots."

"Ma`am," said Bradley, the grizzled Executive Petty Officer, "if the beetles come heavy downriver, we won't have much room to maneuver" he said in a Scottish accent.

"Then we'll make room," Veyra said, her voice low. "This river's ours. If they want it, they'll pay in chitin and shell."

She looked out across the Broadwater River. Somewhere beyond those tree-lined bends, the swarm's flank element was gathering. If they found a way to push along the water, the Stingrays would be the only thing standing between Stonewall and a breach from below.

*****

Intelligence & Communications – Weaving the Net

Back inside Hivewatch, Major Rowan Duskveil had transformed the intelligence chamber into something resembling a spider's web.

New tremor plates were installed at the northern saddle, along the basin rim, and in the roots near the culverts. Runners scurried in and out carrying fresh signal leaflets, each one pressed with fine scent markings that could be passed hand-to-hand through the fortress without shouting.

"Interval calibration," Duskveil instructed his analysts. "I want signal lag down to two ticks or less between stations. If the flank moves, we feel it before we see it."

"Yes, Major."

He watched as three analysts synchronized tremor feeds from distant plates, their hands resting lightly on the surfaces, heads cocked like musicians listening for dissonance.

*****

On a far board, the northern grove — that unmapped source — was now ringed with thin, glowing arcs. A fresh scout team had been dispatched, their mission simple: place a listening node closer to the hidden signal and get back alive.

"Once the first beetle strikes, their rhythm will change," Duskveil murmured. "And when it does… we'll find the conductor. "Corporal Dixie Lake, a compact figure, and her red hair a stark contrast to the dark green, chitin exoskeleton armor suit she wore, adjusted the grip on her lance. Her clear, membranous fly wings, usually a symbol of her division's prowess, felt heavy against her back as she surveyed the dense northern grove. Beside her, Apprentice Rebecca Juno, her dyed purple hair peeking from beneath her green and black exoskeleton armor, checked the comms unit strapped to her wrist. Recruit Bryan Keller, a husky black male whose ambition to become a scout was evident in his every movement, scanned the tree line with an intensity that belied his recruit status. Their mission was clear: penetrate the unmapped source, the "northern grove," and discover the locus of the swarming intelligence that now threatened Stonewall. Class III Specialist Diaz, the division's entomologist, his jet-black hair and mustache framing a focused expression, finalized the calibration of their long-range listening node.

*****

"The tremor plates registered a significant energy spike from this sector," Specialist Diaz stated, his voice a low, even tone as he pointed to a flickering readout on his handheld device. "The pattern is unlike anything cataloged. It suggests a centralized nexus, not a distributed network." Corporal Lake nodded, her gaze fixed on the shadowed depths of the grove. The silence here was different from the expectant quiet of the outpost; it was a watchful, ancient hush, pregnant with unseen activity. Juno confirmed comms integrity. "Signal clear, Corporal. Diaz is receiving faint subsurface vibrations. Could be the root systems reacting to something significant." Keller, positioned slightly ahead, signaled a halt. A subtle shift in the undergrowth, a ripple in the dew-kissed moss, indicated movement.

The small team advanced, their exoskeletons providing a degree of camouflage against the bark and shadows. Corporal Lake's fly wings, though not designed for sustained flight in this dense canopy, allowed for short, controlled glides between branches, offering an aerial advantage for observation. They moved with the practiced silence of rangers, their senses attuned to the subtle cues of the forest. Specialist Diaz, his eyes now glued to his readings, detected a faint, rhythmic pulse emanating from deeper within the grove, a beat that seemed to resonate with the very sap flowing through the ancient trees. This was the anomaly they sought, the source of the coordinated threat, the conductor of the swarming intellect.

*****

The Sound of Readiness

By the time the sun fully cleared the eastern canopy, Stonewall had become something else.

Above: Thorn wings gleamed and bristled on launch rails.

Below: Culverts were braced, trenches armed, squads sharpened.

Along the river: Stingrays drifted in kill-zones, silent predators waiting for ripples.

In the walls: Tremor plates hummed in perfect calibration.

The fortress felt alive, its veins thrumming with both fear and resolve.

Arguments still simmered in corners — about hold or withdraw, about survival or sacrifice — but no one argued with their hands. They worked. They prepared.

And far beyond the tree line, the tremor rhythm grew louder.

*****

The mobilization of the divisions gave the fortress its steel and wings — but beneath the ramparts, down among the courtyards, warehouses, and root tunnels, there were hundreds who would never stand a post or man a wing. Civilians. Workers. Cook crews. Bark-menders. Sap-distillers. Children born beneath lantern light who had never once walked beyond the wall.

As tremor signatures thickened and scouts whispered of massing swarms, the civilian corridors became the quiet arteries of Stonewall's survival plan.

*****

Evacuation Corridors

Logistics crews worked by lanternlight to mark evacuation routes with chalk and resin tags. A series of root tunnels extended eastward beneath the secondary ridge, narrow and winding enough that ants would have trouble massing inside them. At the far end lay the Red Hollow staging point — a temporary fallback camp hidden beneath a grove of fallen logs three spans away.

Runners moved through the tunnels laying scent markers that could be followed even in darkness. Each bend was numbered. Each junction had a set of hanging chimes coded to divisions — three short rings for Ground, two long for civilians, a single low tone for wounded.

"Keep your lines tight," Logistics Chief Harrow told his team as they carried crates of ration packs and medical supplies toward the east shafts. "No open scents. If we leave a trail the ants can follow, we've just built them a highway."

A young quartermaster hesitated at a junction. "Sir, what about the second group? Families near the western tiers—"

"They move first," Harrow cut in. "The river flank goes soft, that's the first place to burn. No delays."

*****

Medical and Supply Stations

Inside the main warehouse cavern, sap stills bubbled and hissed as distillers worked through the night. Sap was more than a weapon; it was the lifeblood of the wall — adhesive, fire suppressant, sealant, and in emergencies, rations. Workers packed barrels into wheeled cradles that could be dragged down tunnels if a retreat was ordered.

*****

Nearby, the medical quarter was reorganizing itself into triage lanes. Medic teams rolled up cots, cleared clutter, and set aside splints and coag sap for mass casualty. The air was thick with antiseptic bark smoke.

"Separate the combatants from the civilians," Chief Medic Liora instructed. "When this starts, we won't have time to sort them on the floor."

Nurses with bandaged forearms lifted their heads as tremor vibrations tickled through the ground. It wasn't panic yet — but panic was close, watching from the rafters.

*****

Command Tension

At mid-morning, Colonel Raines and Major Greg crossed paths near the lower tunnel junction. They didn't stop to argue, but the glance they exchanged carried volumes. Raines inspected the evacuation markers, testing their scent durability with a practiced nose.

"Still pushing for this," Greg muttered.

Raines didn't look at him. "It's called being ready to move. You should try it sometime."

Greg's jaw tightened. "Or it's called scaring civilians before they have to be."

"They deserve the truth," Raines said, voice flat. "This wall isn't immortal."

"And neither are they if you shove them into the woods too early."

The silence that followed wasn't agreement — just stalemate. They parted without another word. The argument was becoming part of the outpost's heartbeat now, beating counterpoint to the swarm beyond.

*****

Civilians React

Word of the evacuation corridors spread like sap through roots. Parents gathered belongings quietly. Children asked questions their parents didn't answer. Some families volunteered to help in supply tunnels, lashing barrels and marking crates. Others stood in tight clusters in the courtyard, watching soldiers march past with expressions that were equal parts awe and dread.

A gray-haired distiller named Marna stopped Jones as he passed through with a ground squad. "Captain," she said, voice steady, "is it true they're coming in numbers like the old stories?"

Jones paused. "Yes," he said simply.

She nodded once. "Then we'll keep the sap flowing."

He met her gaze. There was no fear in it — just the quiet understanding of someone who had lived too many seasons to pretend walls never fall.

*****

Fortifying the Last Lines

Even as evacuation routes were prepared, fortifications inside the wall were being reinforced. Wooden doorways became choke points. Storage tunnels gained sap seal plugs ready to be slammed shut behind retreating groups. Lantern lines were rerouted to illuminate inner fallback rings, turning what had once been corridors for traders and workers into kill zones if the outer defenses failed.

Miller oversaw the civilian muster drills with his usual bluntness. "If the horn sounds three long, two short — you move east. You do not wait for orders. You do not pack extra. You do not turn back. Understood?"

A ragged chorus of "Yes, Sergeant" echoed back. Some strong, some trembling.

*****

An Uneasy Balance

By afternoon, the evacuation corridors were ready. Crates were stacked. Triage lanes cleared. Evacuation markers set. Civilians briefed. The wall had not moved, but the possibility of movement had been built into its bones.

Havelock stood on the eastern ridge for a moment, looking down at the tunnel mouths where faint lantern light spilled like veins into the forest. Behind him, the wall loomed. Before him, the path of retreat stretched toward the unseen.

It wasn't defeat. Not yet. It was insurance — and the act of making it was tearing at the edges of morale.

*****

The dawn that found Stonewell was thin and silver, a light that didn't commit to warmth. The air itself had gone still, stretched too tight between night and day. From the wall's crown, the forest looked asleep. From the forest's edge, it looked like a throat clearing itself before a scream.

And then, above that silence, a single set of wings unfurled.

Corporal Dixie Lake rose through the willow haze like something that belonged to both air and earth but trusted neither. Her fly-forged wings caught the first colorless light, iridescence flashing along green-black panels veined with copper filaments. Each downstroke hummed with the faint; musical buzz of living power harnessed to discipline.

"Recon air support, wings up," she whispered into her throat bead. "Arc One—west-by-north. Eyes wide."

"Hivewatch copies," came Duskveil's low reply, filtered through the signal threads. "Maintain altitude and silence."

*****

Below her, moving through the roots with predator patience, advanced Sergeant Josia Vek and his squad:

Specialist III 'Dizzy', Specialist III Cass Nova, and scouts Juno and Keller. Five shadows beneath the leaves.

Vek's gait was deliberate, almost casual, but the ground where he stepped didn't complain. His Augment threads—thin metal cords grown along his spine and into the muscles of his legs—absorbed vibration and fed it to his inner ear in patterns only he could read. Every step, every shift of air, every insect tremor in the soil arrived as data.

He raised two fingers. The squad stopped.

"Movement," Vek murmured. His voice was always soft now; the Augments made shouting painful. "Not near. Not small."

Cass Nova tilted her head. "You hear them?"

"I feel them," Vek said. "They're… marching."

*****

Overhead, Dixie banked, her wings shedding mist in long silver veils. The rising wind pulled at her hair, teased her goggles. She drew in a deep breath, tasting the air the way ground soldiers read tracks. The pheromone haze hit her throat like old copper—bitter and thick.

"They're close," she said into the bead. "One Spans west. The air's alive with scent."

"Copy," Duskveil answered. "Proceed and confirm."

*****

The Basin of Movement

The scouts reached the rim of a shallow basin where the willow canopy parted. Morning light spilled down in thin pillars, just enough to paint motion in the dark.

It wasn't a single swarm. It was lanes, dozens of them—ants moving in perfect braid formation, bodies gleaming like black water. The lanes didn't collide. They adjusted to each other, turning what should have been chaos into rhythm.

Vek crouched behind a ridge of bark, an Augmented left eye adjusting until every glinting body below was sharp

145

enough to count. "Ants by the thousands," he murmured. "Column discipline. Six bands. And—" He blinked once, internal lenses refocusing. "—beetles in the flank lines."

"Beetles confirmed," Cass added, sketching fast marks on his notepad. "Grinders. Armored class."

Dizzy closed her eyes, palm flat to the root beside her. "Pressure building. Intervals are wrong. Too even."

Above them, Dixie climbed higher, wings thrumming low and steady, until she had the basin from edge to edge in her field of view. She pressed her fingers to her comm bead.

"Hivewatch, I've got visual on wasps," she said. "Dozens. Grounded. Wings folded. They're vibrating— synchronized pulse. It's not feeding or defense. It's cadence."

A silence followed that wasn't hesitation—it was calculation.

Duskveil's voice came thin through the static. "Mark it. We're recording."

*****

When the Forest Breathed

The basin wasn't noisy; it was breathing. Vek's Augments made him feel every vibration as if it were a heartbeat beneath his boots. He frowned, adjusting his internal tuner. "The pattern's not random," he muttered. "Intervals—three short, one long. It's directional."

Dizzy swallowed hard. "They're taking orders."

Cass adjusted his resonator dish, catching faint scent lines rising from the ant lanes—thin silver streams visible only through polarized glass. They braided toward three points: a fallen limb, a split stump, and a roost dark with clustered wings.

Dixie angled left, wings whispering through the canopy. From above, the geometry made sense. Pheromone trails glowed like threads in sunlight, converging like veins toward

146

the roost. Even the beetles had positioned themselves with surgical precision.

"This isn't a swarm," she said softly. "It's choreography."

Her wings fluttered once—an involuntary shiver.

"Josia," she called down, "marking three convergence points. Ants and beetles following the same rhythm. Wasps acting as signal relay."

"Confirmed," Vek said, his mechanical iris narrowing. "And something heavier underneath them. The ground's… talking. I can feel the beat through the wood."

Then the forest changed key.

The wasp roost's tremor paused in unison. For a breath, even the ants froze mid-stride. Then, as if some unseen conductor had lifted a baton, every wing in the roost tilted halfway open. The sound that followed wasn't buzzing—it was music, low and controlled, a living drumline rolling outward through the trees.

"Contact event," Vek hissed. "They're aligning!"

Dixie banked hard, wings slicing mist. "I see it. They're preparing to launch."

Her chest tightened—not from fear, but from recognition. She had felt this once before, when the flies had rallied to her side against the spiders. This wasn't chaos. It was command.

*****

The Call and the Run

"Confirming species convergence," Cass whispered into the comm. "Ants six lanes. Beetles two flanks. Wasps reading cadence. They're forming for… something. We don't wait to see what."

Vek gave a single abrupt nod. "Fall back."

Keller and Juno dropped first, vanishing into fern shadow. Cass followed, leaving charcoal notes wedged into bark for retrieval. Dizzy moved backward with her hand still on the root, counting beats in her head.

Vek lingered half a second longer, Augment sensors widening their field until the entire basin's vibration grid mapped itself behind his eye. He blinked twice, committing the pattern to internal memory, then moved—quiet as fog.

Above, Dixie banked one last time, rising to clear view. The basin spread beneath her—a living pattern too deliberate to belong to instinct. The wasps lifted in perfect unison, wings cutting dawn like knives.

"Two roosts active," she said into her comm. "Flight formation confirmed. Wasp wings opening in phase sequence. They're—" she hesitated, realizing what she was watching— "they're forming units."

"Thorn Wing, disengage," Duskveil said sharply. "We need you alive."

"I'm already gone," Dixie whispered, folding her wings tight and diving into the shadow.

The wasp columns never saw her. They were looking forward, toward Stonewall.

*****

Return and Revelation

The scouts broke from the tree line just as the first tremors reached the wall. Lanterns flickered. Dust drifted from beams. The fortress had felt smaller every hour, but now it felt too small to contain what was coming.

The gate sentry saw Vek's signal—two fingers, then a closed fist—and unbarred the low door. The squad slipped inside, bark-dust in their hair, breath in shallow sync.

"Hivewatch," Vek said the moment the door closed. "Confirming multi-species alignment. Wasps in disciplined flight prep. Beetle breachers holding position. Ant lanes expanding. Whatever's leading them—it's intelligent."

"Source?" Havelock's voice, steel-flat.

Vek looked down at his shaking hands. The Augments translated the tremors through his bones even now. "North grove," he said. "It's breathing like a heart."

Dixie landed on the upper parapet, wings folding against her back, sweat glittering where her veins met graft lines. "They've started moving," she said. "Not in rushes—in lines. If that thing gives the order, we won't get a warning. We'll get a rhythm."

Havelock met her eyes. "Then we answer with our own."

The tremor underfoot changed again, heavier, closer. Somewhere beyond the wall, the swarm's cadence grew loud enough for every Micro-Operatives to feel it in their teeth.

The enemy wasn't swarming anymore. It was marching. The storm didn't come with wind this time. It came with rhythm.

By dusk, Stonewall's tremor plates pulsed like heartbeats under the floorboards, carrying the song of a forest preparing to march.

The swarm had begun to move in perfect unison—ants in braided rivers, wasps like black constellations crawling down from the stars.

Even the air seemed to vibrate with command.

But beneath that rhythm, in the low frequency only the augmented and the attuned could feel, something else moved — a second pulse, quieter, older.

*****

Sergeant Josia Vek caught it first. He was leaning on the western parapet, Augment sensors tuned low, his eye flickering with faint orange light. He frowned, feeling the layers separate: one pattern pulsing sharp and cruel, the other deeper, slower, deliberate.

"That's not swarm cadence," he murmured.

Miller looked up from the sap-line teams below. "Say again, Sergeant?"

Vek blinked, tuning the interference until the signal isolated.

"It's under the ants' march. A counterbeat. Someone's… talking through the earth."

Hivewatch confirmed it seconds later.

Duskveil's voice carried over the comms. "We're reading it here too. Intermittent pulses under primary rhythm. Pattern repeats every six seconds. It's not random."

"Could it be interference?" Havelock asked.

Duskveil hesitated. "Not interference, sir. Communication."

*****

The First Charge

The tremor of the approaching swarm arrived as pressure, not sound — the kind that flexed armor plates and teeth roots alike.

Then the first ant lanes burst from the treeline, black ribbons of precision fury.

"Fire the sap sprayers!" Greg's voice thundered across the parapets.

Green jets hissed through the air, igniting in viscous flame that rolled over the lead ranks.

Ants burned, shrieked, fell—but the lanes behind them adjusted, turning the fallen into cover.

The rhythm did not break.

From above, Dixie dove hard, wings flashing copper.

Wasps rose to meet her, dozens of them, moving in spirals that glittered like knives.

"Air to Hivewatch," she called, breath ragged. "Contact confirmed—wasp flight formation in full. Adjusting for dive intercept."

"Copy," Duskveil said. "Watch your altitude."

She didn't answer.

She was already diving through them, wings cutting smoke.

Below, Vek felt the beetle lines arrive.

Heavy impacts rolled through the soil, the kind that usually spelled doom for a wall.

But these were different. The beats were off—out of phase, deliberate, carrying that same low-frequency hum.

He dropped to one knee, pressed his gloved hand against the bark.

"Wait," he whispered. "They're... they're not ramming."

Greg's voice snapped through comms: "Report!"

Vek looked out over the western slope. The beetle columns had stopped short of the ant lanes, their shells shining slick black in the torchlight. Their mandibles clacked, but not in attack formation. It was signal patterning—staccato, metered, like coded light.

Duskveil's voice came again, sharper this time. "Sergeant Vek, describe that motion."

Vek's Augments decoded what his human eyes couldn't.

"It's not a charge. It's a broadcast."

A pause. Then, quietly: "They're calling us."

*****

The Hidden Accord

Hivewatch went silent except for the hum of the tremor plates.

151

Havelock stared at the projection. "That's impossible. Beetles don't communicate with us."

"Not openly," Duskveil said. "But they did… once."

The room turned toward him.

He continued, voice slow, deliberate. "Before Cycle 0 The Iron Root Truce. A peace pact forged between the first Micro-Operatives expedition and the Dusk Beetle clans under Queen Varaxes. The treaty was sealed in secrecy — even Hivewatch Command forgot its exact terms. But the archives mention one clause: If ever the swarm forgets its own nature, the Burrowed will remember theirs."

Havelock's eyes narrowed. "And you're suggesting—"

"I'm saying," Duskveil cut in, "those beetles out there are not part of the swarm. They're pretending to be. And now they're telling us to listen."

*****

Messages in the Earth

Vek stood again, eye glowing brighter as he returned the frequency. His Augments caught the pulses, translated vibration to sound.

Through the wall's heartwood came a faint voice, distorted by soil and distance.

<We are under their hive mind. But not bound to it. We crawl in their shadow, unseen.>

<When the signal peaks, we will turn.>

Dixie's comm crackled. "Hivewatch, say that again? I thought I heard—"

"You did," Duskveil said softly. "The beetles are ours."

For a moment, the enormity of it froze the room.

Greg looked out toward the battlefield where black shells glimmered under lantern fire. "You're saying we have spies in the swarm?"

"Not spies," Duskveil corrected. "Saboteurs."

*****

The Turning

The first true collision came minutes later. The ant lines surged, following the pheromone orders of whatever monstrous intelligence directed them.

Beetles joined the movement, stamping in unison. To the untrained eye, it looked like unity — a sea of black converging on Stonewall's western flank.

Vek's sensors blazed with feedback. "They're right under us. Now, now, now—"

The wall shuddered.

And then the earth cracked.

The beetle ranks turned sideways, opening gaps in the lanes that funneled the ants into kill corridors.

Hidden glands along their flanks ejected jets of slick resin that sealed ant paths shut.

Ants collided, tangled, broke formation.

The swarm's rhythm faltered.

From the wall, Miller saw it first. "They're fighting each other!"

Greg blinked, then roared. "By the roots, they're with us! Hit them now!"

Sap mortars fired, raining flame into the exposed lanes. The coordinated tide became chaos.

In the air, Dixie saw the confusion ripple through the wasp formations. They faltered, erratic, wings breaking their perfect cadence.

"Duskveil, confirm ground action—what's happening down there?" she asked.

"An old promise," Duskveil said simply.

*****

The Beetle Compact

In the battlefield glow, Vek caught glimpses of beetle sigils carved into shells — old markings, almost worn away, but now illuminated by faint green light. They weren't swarm runes; they were Micro-Operatives glyphs, archaic and solemn.

One beetle — a massive bruiser with mandibles polished like obsidian — paused at the base of the wall and slammed a foreleg into the ground three times.

Vek recognized the pattern immediately.

<We remember Stonewall. We remember the oath.>

He touched the bark beside him, replying through his Augments. "And we honor it."

The beetle turned, its armored head dipping in acknowledgment before charging back into the fray—not at the wall, but at the ants trying to breach it.

Dixie's voice came through comms again. "Vek, your friends down there are saving our hides."

"Yeah," Vek said softly. "Guess even the ground's got a conscience."

*****

Aftermath: A New Front

By full dark, the battlefield had changed. The ants had withdrawn in confusion. The wasps circled, leaderless and angry, until the swarm's unseen master pulled them back into the tree line.

The beetles—those who still stood—formed a rough half-ring around the wall's base, their shells flickering with faint green phosphorescence.

Greg stared down at them from the rampart. "We were never alone," he said quietly.

Duskveil's reply came over the link: "No. But the question is—how long have they been listening to us?"

Vek looked westward, sensors still tuned to the faint ground chatter. He heard words now not meant for him, beetle voices deep and resonant, speaking in codes older than any human tongue.

They were mourning their dead — and promising vengeance.

Dixie landed beside him, her wings folding tight against the wind.

"Never thought I'd say this," she said, staring down at the black hulks that gleamed like living tanks, "but it's nice having the bugs on our side for once."

Vek smiled—half human, half Augment glow. "Let's just hope they stay there."

In the quiet that followed, the wall pulsed once, faint but steady.

The tremor plates picked up a new rhythm—not the swarm's, not the beetles', but something merging both.

For the first time in days, it didn't sound like war.

It sounded like hope.

Chapter 7

The Accord Beneath

The dawn after battle arrived late. The light crawled across Stonewall like a guilty thing — pale, slow, unwilling. Smoke drifted up through the canopy in thin gray ribbons. Beneath it, the fortress felt smaller, as though the night had stolen a piece of its heart.

The air reeked of sap and charred resin, a scent that would not wash off for days.

Teams moved quietly through the wreckage, collecting fragments — not just the bodies of fallen Micro-Operatives, but broken armor plates, collapsed vents, even melted sap nozzles that had fused into the bark like amber fossils.

Miller's boots scraped against blackened wood. "Never seen ants move like that," he muttered.

Beside him, Captain William Jones surveyed the slope through a cracked scope. "They weren't moving," he said. "They were obeying."

Below the wall, dark shapes glimmered where the smoke thinned. Beetle corpses — and beetles still alive, their shells cooling in faint emerald light. None attacked. Some even helped move rubble, their forelegs working in slow, deliberate rhythm.

Kess watched one of them — a giant ground scarab easily five times her height — push aside a fallen ant husk, then drag another carcass into a trench. "You think they know what they did?" she asked softly.

Jones lowered his scope. "They knew before we did."

*****

Hivewatch: The Listening Table

Inside the command chamber, the tremor plates still quivered with residual signal. The patterns were faint, irregular, but recognizable to anyone who'd heard them in the night.

Major Rowan Duskveil stood over the central console; eyes hollowed from lack of sleep. "The signal persists," he murmured. "Shorter intervals now. They're waiting for a reply."

Colonel Havelock entered quietly, his uniform still marked with ash. "You're sure it's them?"

"I'm sure," Duskveil said. "Same resonance. Same pattern as the Ironroot glyphs on their shells."

He adjusted the dials, isolating the subsonic frequency until it filled the room — a low, rolling hum, too deep to be a voice, too steady to be chance.

"Translation?" Havelock asked.

Duskveil hesitated. "That depends on how much you want to believe in ghosts, sir."

The Colonel arched an eyebrow. "Try me."

Duskveil turned a knob, filtering the sound through harmonic analysis. The hum resolved into cadence. Cadence became rhythm. Rhythm became language — not words, but structured pulses that spoke of intent.

Through the static came three distinct phrases: <We held the line.> <The Accord endures.> <We await the Speaker.>

✻✻✻✻✻

Below the Wall

Outside, Vek knelt near the western slope where the ground was still warm from the battle. His Augments hummed faintly, picking up the same tremor Duskveil had detected. The vibrations ran through his bones, low and patient.

Cass Nova stood nearby, sketching the pattern into her field book. "It's beautiful," she said softly.

"Beautiful's one word for it," Vek replied. "Creepy's another."

A deep, resonant crack answered him.

The soil shifted.

Roots groaned.

From beneath the charred trench line, a massive shape began to rise — black carapace dull with soot, mandibles etched in intricate spirals that glowed faintly green. The creature moved slowly, deliberately, as if afraid to startle the air.

Dixie landed beside Vek, her wings folding tight. "Tell me that's not what I think it is."

Vek smiled, the Augment glow bright in his eye. "Depends. If you think it's a beetle who wants to talk instead of eat—then yeah."

The beetle's mandibles clicked once, then twice, then opened.

From deep within its throat came a voice like gravel dragged over metal.

<Parley> indicated the beetle. At that moment the beetle bowed and returned to continue clearing rubble. Dixie and Vek looked at one another is amazement.

*****

The signal continued all through the night. It pulsed beneath the fortress at intervals too regular to be nature, too subtle to be mechanical. It was the sound of something waiting, not impatiently but with the calm certainty of an ancient creature that had seen wars come and rot away.

Inside Hivewatch, the tremor table had become an altar. Every other operation had gone silent — no artillery reports, no weather feeds, no surface chatter. Just that single rhythm thrumming through the wood and soil.

Duskveil stood motionless, his eyes half-closed as if listening with more than his ears. The table's resonance thrummed through his hands like heartbeat and memory at once. "It's cleaner now," he murmured. "The distortion's gone. They're aligning their tone to match our plates."

Colonel Havelock watched from behind, his face lit by the faint green tremor lines. "You're saying they're tuning to us."

"I'm saying," Duskveil replied, "they already know our calibration."

He adjusted a dial, slowing the playback. The pulses broke apart into clean units—long, long, short, pause, repeat. Then again, slightly shifted, like a code being translated by someone fluent in a lost dialect.

"What does it say?" Havelock asked.

The reply came from the back of the chamber. Specialist Cass Nova had brought her notebook from the field and laid it open beside the table, sketches of tremor sequences drawn in dark graphite. "Same phrasing repeated every half span," she said. "We think it's an introduction. Or... an invocation."

Duskveil nodded slowly. "A name."

He tapped the table with one gloved finger. "Listen."

He re-ran the segment. This time, filtered and slowed, the tremor pattern carried a rhythm unmistakably alive — each vibration a syllable pressed into the body rather than the ear.

<VAR-A-XES.>

The sound seemed to move the air itself.

Dixie, standing near the threshold, felt her wings tremble in sympathy. "That's their queen," she said quietly. "The one from the stories. The Ironroot Monarch."

Vek, at her side, frowned. "I thought she was a myth."

"She was," Duskveil said. "Until she started knocking."

*****

The Chamber Below

The second pulse sequence began an hour later — deeper, slower, resonating directly through the ground beneath Hivewatch.

Vek's Augments caught it first. He pressed a hand to the floor and grimaced. "They're not just sending sound. They're mapping us."

"Mapping?" Havelock asked.

"They're scanning the fortress foundation," Vek said. "Finding a way up. Or inviting us down."

That idea sank into the air like a weight. For a long moment, no one moved. Then Duskveil stepped forward and adjusted the central dial, amplifying the signal. The table vibrated with new patterns, not words this time, but shapes — a spatial sequence, loops and spirals rendered in harmonic intervals.

"It's a location," Duskveil murmured. "Below the western slope. Old tunnel, possibly predating the first construction layers of Stonewall. They're asking us to meet them there."

Greg crossed his arms. "We can't just walk into a hole because a bug hums at us."

"It's not a hole," Duskveil said. "It's an old passage. The one they helped dig before the First Fortification was even raised. If the Accord is real, it began there."

Havelock exhaled slowly. "Then that's where it continues."

*****

Preparation

They sealed the decision quietly. By dawn, a small delegation had assembled at the base of the inner shaft — Duskveil, Vek, Dixie, and two Ground Division guards armed but discreet.

Each carried a resonance beacon tuned to the Ironroot frequency, a precaution in case the beetles' vibrations became hostile.

The tunnel entrance was rough, half-collapsed, the bark ribs dark with centuries of forgotten moisture. The air was heavy with scented decay — not rot, exactly, but the deep earthy musk of old roots remembering rain.

"Ever been down here?" Dixie asked softly. "Once," Duskveil said. "In training. It was sealed after the Black Sap floods. Supposedly unstable." Vek grinned. "Guess we're about to find out how unstable."

He adjusted his gauntlet settings, Augment lenses shifting from amber to dull green. The faint pulse of beetle vibration became visible — shimmering lines along the tunnel walls, faint phosphorescent veins that guided the way like stars buried underground.

"Follow the hum," he said. "They're showing us the road."

✳✳✳✳✳

The Descent

The passage sloped downward in slow, spiraling arcs. Each step took them deeper into a world that smelled of soil and echo. The hum of the beetle signal grew louder, resolving into multiple frequencies — high and low, layered like the harmonics of a living choir.

Dixie reached out, brushing a wall with her gloved fingertips. The bark was warm. "They've been down here recently," she whispered. "You can feel the movement in the grain."

"Don't touch," Duskveil said, though his own hand lingered a moment longer than it should have.

When they reached the third bend, the tunnel opened into a wide cavern lit by bio-luminescent fungus the color of deep emerald. The walls pulsed faintly, the same rhythm as the Ironroot signal.

And in the center, half-buried in soil and root, stood an enormous black carapace, motionless but alive — mandibles carved with the ancient sigil of the Beetle Queen.

Duskveil's voice was a whisper. "The Speaker."

The chamber hummed. Not with sound, but with the memory of vibration—a pulse carried through the roots, through armor, through marrow. The Beetle Speaker stood in the center of the cavern like a monument that remembered breathing. Its black carapace was patterned with faint green sigils that glowed in rhythm with its heartbeat.

When it moved, the ground seemed to shift slightly, the way deep earth adjusts when something very old turns its head.

Major Rowan Duskveil took one slow step forward. His voice was calm, but every syllable carried the discipline of a man speaking to a storm.

"This is Hivewatch Command. We acknowledge your signal. Identify yourself."

The beetle's mandibles opened. The sound that followed was not language as the Micro-Operatives knew it. It was pressure: long pulses, short breaks, tremor layers overlapping in harmonics too complex for unaugmented hearing.

Vek's Augments flared with blue light as he dropped to one knee, palm pressed to the soil. "She's using subharmonic structure. It's encoded speech."

Dixie looked at Duskveil. "Can you translate?"

"I can try," he said softly, adjusting the resonance module on his wrist. The small device began to hum in sympathy, its sensor threads glowing faint blue. He matched the pattern — frequency, amplitude, pause — converting vibration to modulated tone.

The words that emerged were rough, metallic, but clear.

<We are the Burrowed. Servants of the Deep Queen. We remember the Accord. We remember Stonewall.>

Duskveil exhaled. "They're confirming alliance." The beetle's next pulse shook dust from the ceiling.

<The Accord is threatened. The Swarm has changed.> <Something beneath the forest roots commands them.> <We cannot resist it long.> The Language of Tremors Duskveil glanced toward Vek. "Can you confirm?"

Vek's left eye flickered with readout data. "Same sequence. No deception tones. She's telling the truth."

Duskveil knelt and pressed his gloved hand into the dirt, closing his eyes. The resonance climbed through his arm and into his chest. He began to speak back — not with words, but with vibration. Each breath shaped the hum through the translator.

<We hear. We seek the source.> <Do you know the hand that commands them?>

The Speaker's carapace rippled faintly, the light along her mandibles shifting color from green to pale blue. A long pause followed — not hesitation, but grief.

<It was born of us, but not ours.>

<It burrows through song.>

<It calls itself the Hive Mind.>

The room went silent. "Hive Mind," Dixie repeated under her breath. "They've given it a name."

Duskveil nodded, expression unreadable. "Or it gave itself one."

The Speaker continued, slower now, as if choosing what truths to risk.

<The Mind consumes command.

Ants, wasps, locusts—bound by its rhythm.

Even our kind hears its voice. We resist, but the cost grows.>

She leaned forward slightly, her mandibles lowering toward the Micro-Operatives as if bowing.

<You broke the rhythm last night. The noise saved us.>

Vek blinked. "The counter-rhythm… when I disrupted their cadence."

"Yes," Duskveil said. "It weakened the Mind's signal."

<The Mind fears chaos,> the Speaker vibrated. <It thrives in unity. Your discord defends you.>

*****

Translation as Warfare

Duskveil called to Havelock, his voice crackling through the comm. "You hearing this, Colonel?"

"Every word," came the reply. "Keep her talking."

The beetle's lights dimmed, then flared again in a new pattern—rapid pulse bursts like Morse code but deeper, layered with harmonic undertones. Duskveil's translator struggled to keep up, modulating faster and faster.

<The Mind will come again. It learns. It adapts.> <We can slow it, but not alone.> <Renew the Accord. Share the ground between. Teach us your noise, and we will teach you, our silence.>

Duskveil frowned at that. "Noise and silence?"

Vek smiled faintly. "They mean tactics. We're chaos; they're endurance."

164

Dixie folded her wings, the faint hum still vibrating through the membrane. "Together, that's balance."

The Speaker inclined her head slightly — the gesture unmistakably human in meaning, alien in form.

<Balance. Yes. The deep must meet the light. Or all fall silent.>

*****

The Queen's Offer

The Beetle Speaker's mandibles clicked twice. A faint glow spread from her carapace into the surrounding soil. The ground itself began to pulse in a matching rhythm — not a warning, but an invitation.

A map appeared in light and vibration, etched across the chamber floor — root tunnels, fault veins, and swarm pathways stretching miles beyond Stonewall. At the map's edge, a single dark region pulsed faster than the rest.

Duskveil pointed. "What is that?"

<The Burrow Below.> <The Mind's Nest.> <Where the swarm's song begins.>

*****

The room felt colder. Dixie looked down at the glowing lines. "That's deep under Reed Flats."

Vek nodded grimly. "Too deep for flight. Too deep for light."

The Speaker's final message vibrated through their armor until it felt as if their own bones were answering.

<The Accord demands courage. The Mind demands silence. Choose.>

The glow faded. The chamber went still except for the faint hum of the translator cooling down.

Duskveil stood slowly. "Message received."

He glanced at his team—Dixie, wings twitching faintly; Vek`s, eye dimming from Augment overload; the guards, pale and wordless.

Then he looked at the massive shadow that was the Beetle Speaker. "We'll choose," he said softly. "But we won't choose alone." The cavern trembled once—then stilled.

The Beetle Speaker's shell dimmed, its green runes fading until only faint heat lingered in the air. Silence flooded back, heavy and expectant. For a heartbeat the Micro-Operatives thought the parley was finished.

Then the earth breathed. Fine soil sifted upward in concentric circles around the Speaker's forelegs. A fissure opened between the roots and from it rose a column of amber light, refracted through polished resin veins. Inside that glow a shape was forming—first silhouette, then substance.

It stepped forward with the grace of something that remembered how to crawl but had learned how to stand.

Two eyes gleamed, faceted like crystal but set in a humanoid face. Carapace armor flowed seamlessly into woven barkcloth. Its fingers ended in delicate black claws shaped for both grasp and gesture. When it spoke, the voice was layered — human tone over subsonic resonance

"I am Torr Var-Kin, voice of Queen Varaxes, bearer of the Ironroot Seal."

The words vibrated through the ground before reaching the ear, each syllable echoing in their bone.

Duskveil took a careful step forward, keeping his weapon holstered but his translator active.

"I am Major Rowan Duskveil of Hivewatch Command, Stonewall Outpost. We recognize the Seal."

Torr inclined his head, a motion precise enough to look learned rather than natural. "Then our memory was true. The children of the Sky and the children of the Burrow once built these walls together. The Accord still breathes."

Dixie's wings shivered involuntarily. "You look like us."

"Not quite," Torr replied, and for a moment his jaw split slightly along chitin seams that flexed when he smiled. "Your engineers left fragments of design in our lineage — machines that healed, metals that grew. We studied. We adapted."

*****

Formal Parley

Havelock's voice came faint through the comm-link above. "Hivewatch to Duskveil. Visual confirmation on the Envoy?"

"Confirmed," Duskveil answered quietly. "Bipedal hybrid. Intelligent, articulate, non-hostile." Havelock indicated "Proceed. Gather intent."

Torr turned toward the tremor plates embedded in the cavern floor, lowering one clawed hand until it touched the soil. The vibrations steadied, forming words that the translator rendered aloud:

"The Deep Queen sends greeting and warning.

The Hive Mind grows through the old tunnels.

Its roots drink our memories. We cannot contain it."

Vek's eyes flared amber. "You mean it's using your hives as relay stations?"

Torr nodded once. "The Mind wears our dead like armor. Every nest it consumes becomes a mouth. We came to tell you before we are silenced."

The weight of that sentence pressed the room flat.

Duskveil folded his hands behind his back. "Then Stonewall stands with you. The Accord is renewed."

Torr's head tilted, the motion insectile but oddly solemn. "Renewal requires proof."

He reached into a resin pouch at his side and drew out a fragment of ancient chitin, carved with both Micro-

167

Operatives runes and beetle glyphs. It pulsed faintly when exposed to air.

"The first Accord," Torr said, "signed by flesh and shell. Your Founders sealed it with blood and sap. The Queen asks for the same."

*****

The Blood and Sap Rite

A hush settled. Dixie exchanged glances with Vek and Duskveil. "You mean literally?" she asked.

Torr extended the shard toward them. "A drop only. One to mark that the living remember the dead."

Duskveil took a blade from his belt, cut the edge of his thumb, and let a single bead fall onto the fragment. The surface absorbed it instantly, glowing blue.

Vek followed, his Augment circuitry sparking faintly as metal met ichor. Dixie pricked her fingertip after theirs; her wing veins shimmered gold.

The shard responded, releasing a soft tone — low, resonant, and clean.

Torr bowed, mandibles clicking once in satisfaction.

"The Accord lives. The Burrowed will guard your foundations.

The Skyborne will guard our silence.

When the Mind rises, we fight as one."

*****

Departure

Without another word, Torr stepped backward into the amber light. The resin column folded around him like liquid glass, sinking slowly into the soil until only the glow of the Ironroot Seal remained. Then it, too, dimmed.

The chamber was still again, but changed. The very air felt heavier, older—charged with a pact that had waited centuries to be remembered.

Dixie let out a long breath. "Well," she said softly, "that was the strangest alliance meeting I've ever attended."

Vek chuckled, a dry, electric sound. "Let's hope it's the most peaceful one."

Duskveil looked down at the shard now glowing faintly in his palm. "Peace," he said. "No. This is preparation."

The echo of Torr Var-Kin's departure had barely faded before the cavern filled with the sound of breathing and boots on dirt.

Duskveil, Vek, and Dixie made their way back through the tunnels in silence. None of them spoke until the first glimmer of lantern-light from Hivewatch touched the damp walls.

Havelock was waiting. Behind him stood Major Greg, Major Vance, Commander Veyra, and two of the wall clerks who doubled as scribes. The air smelled of resin and soot.

"Report," Havelock said.

Duskveil placed the glowing shard of the renewed Accord on the table between them. "Queen Varaxes remembers us. The beetles stand with Stonewall. And the Hive Mind—whatever intelligence commands the swarm— is burrowing toward Reed Flats."

A low murmur rippled through the officers.

Vance crossed her arms. "You're telling us the beetles have been playing both sides?"

"No," Dixie said, wings rustling faintly. "They've been surviving in the middle. Pretending to obey the Mind until they could talk to us."

Greg leaned forward, heavy fists braced on the table. "And you trust them?"

Vek's Augment eye flickered. "They had every chance to kill us last night. Instead, they bled for us. That's trust enough for now."

*****

Debate

Havelock let the voices rise and fall before speaking. "We have two choices. We reveal this alliance to the garrison—rally the troops, show them the war isn't hopeless. Or we keep it sealed and let Hivewatch coordinate in secret."

"Reveal it," Veyra said immediately. "Morale's bleeding out. The men need to believe we're not alone."

Greg shook his head. "And when they see beetles walking our trenches? You think they'll salute? Half of them will torch the tunnels before they listen."

Duskveil touched the shard; its faint blue light pulsed with each word. "The Accord depends on silence. Varaxes's people live beneath the swarm's eye. If the Mind senses their betrayal, it will consume them first."

Vance frowned. "Then we're fighting beside allies no one can know about."

"Exactly," Duskveil said. "They are the shadow half of this fortress. We hold the walls; they hold the roots."

*****

Strategic Realignment

Havelock began pacing. "Fine. Then we need a framework. Dual command—one visible, one buried. Duskveil, you'll oversee the liaison channel. Vek, you maintain Augment contact. No transmissions above field level. Dixie, you coordinate air silence—if the beetle's surface near patrol zones, I want your flyers the first to see them, not the last."

Dixie nodded. "Understood."

Greg looked from one to the other. "We're rewriting the book here, Colonel. Code names, hidden ops, secret allies— we start living like ghosts, we stop being soldiers."

Havelock met his eyes. "Then call us what you like. Ghosts still fight."

He turned to the scribes. "Strike all record of this meeting from the day logs. Officially, the battle of the First Probe ended at nightfall. No mention of contact, no mention of envoys."

The scribes hesitated, then nodded. Ink scratched across parchment, erasing the moment as it was born.

*****

A Quiet Consensus

The council broke at last. Each officer left with new orders that no one could repeat. Only Duskveil lingered, studying the shard.

"Do you think they'll keep their word?" Veyra asked from the doorway.

Duskveil didn't look up. "They kept it for two hundred cycles without us remembering. The question is—will we keep ours?"

He slipped the shard into a sealed pouch and extinguished the lantern. The chamber fell into near-darkness, lit only by the faint green tremor running through the floor—the heartbeat of allies no one above would ever know existed.

*****

The next night, the tunnels breathed again. This time, the rhythm was measured—controlled, like the heartbeat of someone trying not to startle a friend.

Lanterns were dimmed. No guards beyond the first turn. No records kept.

Major Duskveil, Sergeant Josia Vek, Captain William Jones, and First Sergeant Miller descended together into the Ironroot Cavern where Torr Var-Kin had first emerged.

Each carried the same unspoken question: how far can we trust what we don't understand?

The air smelled of moss and resin dust, faintly sweet.

The hum beneath the floor had changed since last night; it no longer sounded like a foreign voice. It sounded like a pulse shared between both species.

Jones brushed a hand along the tunnel wall. "Never thought I'd walk into a meeting where the walls were listening."

Miller grunted. "Walls listen. Beetles answer. Big difference."

Duskveil smiled faintly but said nothing.

*****

The Speaker Returns

The amber glow flared again near the center of the cavern, forming a familiar silhouette.

Torr Var-Kin stepped out of the light as if it were a doorway he carried inside him. His faceted eyes glimmered under his brow ridges, reading each Micro-Operatives in turn.

"Commanders. The Queen honors your courage in silence. She has agreed to share what lies beneath."

He gestured toward the dirt floor, and the same living map rose from the soil—root veins pulsing faint green, tunnel arteries branching like capillaries. This time, new colors bled into the pattern: blue for Micro-Operatives patrols, gold for beetle burrows, red for swarm corridors.

Jones whistled low. "That's half the forest's nervous system right there."

Vek knelt, tracing a glowing strand. "They're showing us their flank routes. That's trust—or suicide."

Torr's mandibles flexed slightly. "Trust. Not suicide. The Accord requires mutual exposure. Our roots are open. Now show yours."

Duskveil nodded to Miller. "You brought the field charts?"

Miller unfolded a battered parchment packet and laid it over the glowing ground. The two maps—organic and mechanical—merged, aligning themselves as if guided by invisible hands. The beetle roots pulsed brighter where Micro-Operatives trenches crossed them.

"Now we see," Torr said softly. "Sky meets Soil."

*****

Negotiating the Alliance

The meeting stretched into careful rhythm. Vek translated the vibrations into tactical shorthand while Duskveil spoke for Hivewatch. Miller and Jones, still uncomfortable but curious, provided the field practicality others lacked.

Duskveil: "We need advance warning when the swarm moves underground. Your sensors go deeper than ours."

Torr: "We will listen to the soil and sing when it stirs. But when we sing, you must be ready to move faster than roots grow."

Miller: "We can rig seismic receivers to your rhythm channels—translate the vibration into signal beats for our comm lines."

Vek: "I'll sync my Augments to theirs. I can act as a live interpreter during movement."

Torr lowered his head slightly, mandibles folding in thought. "Agreed. But the Mind listens too. Your signals must sound like chaos, not command. Teach us your noise."

Jones gave a humorless smile. "Noise we can do. Half my squad's made a career out of it."

That earned a faint ripple of resonance from Torr—perhaps laughter, perhaps acknowledgment.

*****

The Pact of Roles

Once the maps dimmed, Duskveil spoke the final clause of the agreement.

"Stonewall will not reveal your alliance. You will not expose ours. When we strike at the Hive Mind's Nest, we strike together—above and below."

Torr stepped closer, towering over the humans but emanating no threat. "Then these are the roles of the Accord reborn:"

"The Burrowed will guard the unseen, watching the ground beneath your feet.

The Skyborne will guard the air, breaking the rhythm of the swarm.

The Rootbound—those who walk between—will carry message and balance. That is you, Josia Vek, Augment of the Bridge."

Vek froze. "The Bridge?"

"The Queen names you that," Torr said. "Your metal and marrow understand both signal and soul. Through you, our kin speak."

Duskveil looked at him, half proud, half worried. "Looks like congratulations and condolences come as one, Sergeant."

Vek gave a wry grin. "Story of my life, sir."

*****

The Quiet Understanding

When the meeting ended, the cavern lights dimmed again to soft emerald.

Torr placed one clawed hand against the soil. "When the Mind rises, we will answer the call. Until then, listen to the ground. It remembers you."

He faded once more into the resin light, leaving the chamber's pulse steady and calm.

Jones broke the silence first. "So we've got friends underground and enemies in the air. Sounds about right."

Miller nodded. "I'll take a friend I can't see over a command that don't listen any day."

Duskveil looked toward Vek. "You ready to carry a world on your circuits, Sergeant?"

Vek smiled faintly, his Augment veins pulsing green. "Already do, sir. Just never had anyone to share the signal with."

They started the climb back toward the surface. As they walked, the vibrations followed them, faint but steady — the beat of an ancient rhythm reborn.

*****

The tunnels were quiet again that night, but not empty. Torches burned low; their flames drawn thin by the steady breath of the earth. Each flicker cast shifting shadows along the ribbed bark walls — moving shapes that might have been roots, or memories pretending to be alive.

At the center of the Ironroot Cavern stood a ring of carved stones that had been unearthed only that morning. Faint symbols glowed on their surfaces — spirals, runes, and the crude outline of a Micro-Operatives hand pressed beside a beetle foreleg. The marks were old. Older than the fortress above.

Major Duskveil stood beside the relic, his voice hushed. "The Speaker said the Accord was not just a treaty," he murmured. "It was an oath. Taken by both sides — not written, not signed, but spoken into the soil so the ground itself would remember."

He turned toward Captain William Jones, First Sergeant Miller, Dixie Lake, and Josia Vek, who had gathered with a small escort. "You're not here as command," Duskveil said. "You're here as witnesses."

Jones nodded slowly. "We know the story, sir. We all learned it before our first Span in the ranks."

Miller's deep voice carried softly through the cavern. "Back before Stonewall was built, the first Micro-Operatives landed in the heartwood plains. They found the beetles waiting. Fought them for thirty Cycles before someone realized the insects weren't fighting for conquest. They were guarding the roots."

Dixie smiled faintly, her wings catching the green glow. "And when the war ended, both sides buried their dead together. That's where the Accord began — over a shared grave."

Vek crouched beside the stones, running a finger over the carved marks. "And now we renew it in the same place."

*****

The Return of the Speaker

A low hum answered their silence. The ground rippled once, and Torr Var-Kin stepped from the shadows at the cavern's far side, bioluminescent sigils faint along his arms. Behind him came three smaller beetles, each carrying resin urns that glowed like captured dawn.

Torr's voice carried easily through the chamber. "The Queen remembers the first Accord as we do. In that time, the Burrowed swore to guard the Deep. The Skyborne swore to guard the Light. Tonight, both shall swear again — not to peace, but to balance."

The urns were placed on the stones. One contained sap that glowed amber, one held Micro-Operatives blood still warm from ritual pricks of the finger, and the last shimmered with soil from the battlefield where beetle and Micro-Operatives had fought side by side. Duskveil gestured for Jones to step forward.

*****

Remembrance

Jones hesitated, looking down at the relic. "You know, I thought that story was a fairy tale," he said quietly. "My instructor at Skyspan called it the 'Day the Dirt Listened.' Said it was just a parable about understanding your enemy."

Miller snorted. "My grandfather used to tell it straight. He said the earth itself could keep promises. Guess the old man wasn't wrong."

Dixie folded her wings, eyes fixed on the glowing urns. "When I was a recruit, I thought the Accord meant we could stop killing. Now I know it just means we're not alone when we do."

Torr's mandibles flexed softly. "Even truth must have a cost. The Accord was never about ending war. It was about making sure war remembered who fought it."

*****

The Renewal

Duskveil raised his hand. "Then we renew it." He dipped his fingers into the sap and let a single drop fall onto the soil. Jones and Miller followed, each touching the resin until its glow deepened from amber to gold. Dixie leaned forward next, her wing veins shimmering faintly blue; where her sap met the soil, a faint chime rang through the chamber.

Torr extended one claw, pressing it gently into the mix. The sound that followed was neither speech nor vibration — it was something between the two. The ground answered with its own pulse, resonant and deep.

"We are the Ironroot Accord reborn," Torr intoned.

"By sap, by blood, by soil.

The Burrowed guard the depths.

The Skyborne guard the light.

The Bridge keeps them bound."

At his words, a faint ripple of green light spread across the cavern walls, traveling outward through root veins like veins carrying new life.

Vek closed his eyes as the vibration passed through him. His Augments flickered with the same rhythm. "It's syncing," he whispered. "The wall... the ground... the beetles. We're one signal now."

Oathkeepers

The hum faded into silence. For a long moment, none of them spoke.

Jones finally broke the stillness. "I wonder if the ones who first made this pact felt as small as we do right now."

Miller answered quietly. "Maybe smaller. They had no walls. Just faith that something bigger than them was worth trusting."

Dixie looked toward Torr. "And what happens now?"

Torr's compound eyes gleamed like twin lanterns. "Now the Deep Queen knows your names. When you fall, the ground will remember where to send your echoes."

He inclined his head once more, a gesture of both blessing and farewell. "May your noise guide our silence, and our silence strengthen your noise."

With that, the beetles withdrew, leaving the Micro-Operatives standing amid the faintly glowing stones. The last light of the sap dimmed until the only sound left was the slow, steady pulse of the earth — like a heartbeat shared between two ancient species. The day after the renewal, Stonewall felt different.

*****

The wind carried a low tremor that matched the heartbeat of the tunnels below, and the walls themselves seemed to hum faintly when touched. The alliance had not just been made; it had been woven into the fortress.

Major Duskveil noticed it first while studying the tremor plates. The resonance that had always jittered with random static now moved in deliberate cycles—two pulses low, one high, pause, repeat. It wasn't random background noise anymore. It was conversation.

178

He turned to Vek, who stood beside him with Augment sensors tuned.

"You feel that?"

Vek nodded, eye glowing faint green. "That's not the beetles. Their signal runs cleaner. This… this is something new. Something answering them."

*****

The Transmission

Without warning, every resonance line on the Hivewatch board spiked at once. The chamber lights dimmed, and a deep vibration filled the air, rattling the lantern glass.

Dixie burst in from the stairwell, wings half-spread, eyes wide. "I can hear it in the air—like thunder that doesn't stop."

Torr Var-Kin's voice crackled through the ground-link crystal they had kept from the ceremony.

"Do not be afraid. The Queen speaks through me."

The air grew thick; the tremor plates flared to life in a pattern too complex for human translation. Duskveil's translator struggled, then stabilized. The voice that emerged was layered—ancient, regal, and resonant with tones that seemed to echo inside the skull rather than the ear.

"I am Varaxes, Queen of the Burrowed.

I have heard your oath. The Accord breathes once more.

But the shadow beneath us stirs."

The sound pressed into every wall, filling the room with the sense of being watched by the earth itself.

"The Mind grows restless. It listens to our language, learns our rhythm.

Soon, it will speak."

*****

The Warning

Duskveil steadied himself against the console. "Your Majesty—how can we stop it if it understands us?"

Varaxes's voice was calm, almost kind. "You cannot silence knowledge once it is born.

But you can confuse it. The Mind craves unity—it dies in contradiction.

Where it seeks order, sow discord. Where it gathers, scatter. "Noise is your shield."

Vek frowned, the Augment glow flickering across his jaw. "Then we weaponize chaos."

"Yes, Bridge."

The way the Queen said the word filled the room with light. For a heartbeat, everyone could see their own shadows stretch and merge with the walls—as if the entire fortress had bowed.

*****

The Vision

Suddenly the tremor plates projected an image in raw vibration—pulses forming shapes in dust and light: a vast underground expanse shot through with glowing veins of amber sap. At its center lay a structure not grown but built— a spiral mound of chitin and stone, pulsing like a heart.

"Behold the Burrow Below," Varaxes said.

"The Mind's nest. It feeds on the sap rivers that once nourished us.

If it drinks them dry, the forest will fall silent forever."

Jones stepped closer, eyes narrowing. "That's Reed Flats. The southern marsh."

Miller crossed his arms. "You're telling us we have to go underground into that thing?"

"You must," the Queen answered.

"Only those who can walk between worlds—Sky and Soil—may end the song before it spreads."

Dixie's voice was barely above a whisper. "Then Stonewall won't be the front anymore. It'll be the launch point."

The Departure of the Voice

The light from the tremor plates began to fade. Varaxes's final words rolled through the chamber like a tide receding into deep stone.

"When the roots darken, call to us.

The Burrowed will answer.

Until then, remember—

the Mind listens."

The resonance stopped. Silence returned, thick and uneven.

For a long moment no one moved. Then Duskveil drew a slow breath. "She's given us our next war—and our deadline."

Vek looked down at his trembling hands. "If it's already learning our language, it's learning us."

Jones turned toward the tunnel mouth, jaw set. "Then we'd better teach it what we do when someone starts listening too close."

Dixie's wings unfurled, the chitin membrane shimmering faint blue in the lamplight. "Let's make some noise."

*****

Epilogue — Stonewall After Dark

That night, the fortress thrummed with a rhythm no one could sleep through—part human, part beetle, part something older still. The alliance held. The oath was alive. And far beneath Reed Flats, deep where light had never lived, a new rhythm answered back: slow, curious, hungry. The Mind had begun to speak.

Chapter 8

The Roots of War

The morning after the Accord renewal, Stonewall Outpost no longer sounded like war. It breathed.

A faint hum ran through its ramparts and chambers — not mechanical, not human. It was the deep, slow pulse of the wood and resin that made up its bones. The Micro-Operatives had long believed Stonewall to be a fortress built on roots; now they understood it had become one.

Captain William Jones walked the western wall with the early mist still hugging the bark. Every step sent a soft tremor through the planks, as though the ground were listening. The fog had not yet lifted from the canopy, and in the gray light the outpost's spires looked more like growing things than built ones.

Below him, squads cleared wreckage, scraping ant carapaces and hardened resin from the slope. The air was heavy with a new scent — not rot or decay, but sap and ozone, like life freshly broken open.

"Doesn't sound like victory," came a voice beside him.

Jones turned to see First Sergeant Miller climbing the ramp ladder, his uniform streaked with mud and scar burns. The big man's eyes were red from sleepless nights, but steady.

"It's not victory," Jones said. "It's breathing."

Miller gave a low grunt, setting his boot on the parapet. "You hear it too?"

"Can't not hear it."

They stood in silence for a moment, listening. The hum was low, constant, like a heartbeat underfoot. Every few seconds it would shift pitch, the tone rippling through the walls, as though the outpost were communicating with something deep below.

"You think it's them?" Miller asked quietly. "The beetles?"

Jones shrugged. "Maybe. Or maybe the Accord's just… alive."

*****

Hivewatch Reawakens

In the command hall below, Major Rowan Duskveil stood at the central console, its tremor plates alive with faint oscillations. Since the Accord, the readings had changed — no longer erratic spikes of battle but measured, harmonious beats. The fortress had become a conductor for subterranean sound.

"The resonance has stabilized," reported a technician, voice hushed. "We're receiving clear frequency pairs from the Burrowed network every four minutes. Pattern consistency ninety-three percent."

Duskveil leaned over the plate, his dark eyes reflecting the soft green glow. "She's keeping her promise," he murmured. "Varaxes is still listening."

Colonel Havelock entered quietly, his cloak dusted with sap flecks. "And what's she hearing from us, Major?"

Duskveil hesitated. "Everything, sir. Every tremor we make. Every word that shakes the floor."

Havelock's gaze hardened. "Then let's make sure what she hears sounds like order."

He moved to the table's edge, hands resting on the living wood. "Stonewall's heart beats again. I won't waste it. We use this—whatever it is—to reinforce every division. Air, Ground, Water, Tree. Every sector trains to the rhythm."

"You mean literally?" Duskveil asked.

"Yes. If the Mind listens for pattern, we'll drown it in chaos. If the beetles feel through soil, we'll speak to them in

183

sound. This fortress will become both a weapon and a warning."

*****

Signs in the Bark

Far below, in the trenches that wrapped the outer slope, Specialist Hale brushed sap dust off a piece of bark plating. The surface beneath glistened faintly — words carved not by hand but by natural growth. Spirals and glyphs, forming what looked like script.

"Sergeant!" she called. "You'd better see this!"

Miller dropped from the wall and crouched beside her. The markings pulsed once as if reacting to their presence. The letters weren't Micro-Operatives, and yet they formed a recognizable cadence.

Duskveil arrived minutes later, breath short from the climb. "Don't touch it," he warned, kneeling. The glyphs shimmered green again, faintly bioluminescent.

"What's it say?" Miller asked.

Duskveil tilted his head. "I don't know. But I think it's listening back."

The glyphs rippled once more, and from the soil beneath came a single resonant tone — low, deliberate, identical to the pattern of the Accord's seal.

The sound vibrated through the trench like a drumbeat.

"Message received," Duskveil murmured. "They're checking if we're still here."

*****

A Fortress Reborn

By afternoon, the hum of Stonewall had spread through every corridor. Beetle engineers moved beside Micro-Operatives repair crews, their clawed limbs working resin and bark together. The outpost looked less like a rebuilt fortress and more like a living hybrid — veins of green sap running through its foundations, glistening like circuitry.

184

Dixie landed in the courtyard, wings folding tight against her back. The air around her shimmered with humidity from the canopy above. She looked up at the parapets, where human and beetle banners hung side by side — one cloth, one chitin.

"You ever think we'd see this?" she said softly.

Vek's voice came from behind her. "See it? I'm not sure we're awake during it."

He approached, his Augments faintly glowing. "The walls hum at 12.7 hertz — low enough to be felt in bone, not heard in air. The beetles call it the 'breathing tone.'"

"Feels more like a heartbeat," she said.

"Same thing," he replied.

Dixie smiled faintly, then looked toward the western slope where the mist still lingered. "You think it's over?"

"No," Vek said simply. "It's changing shape."

*****

Tremors from Reed Flats

Evening descended with amber light bleeding through the canopy.

Duskveil sat alone at Hivewatch, the console vibrating softly beneath his hands. He had grown used to its pulse — steady, predictable. Tonight, it changed.

The rhythm faltered. Skipped. Then resumed in an irregular pattern, like a voice trying to speak through static.

He adjusted the sensors. The waveform stabilized just long enough for him to read it.

The signature wasn't beetle.

It came from farther east — beyond the Accord network.

Location: Reed Flats Basin.

The translation module printed four words onto the plate in pulsing light:

THE ROOTS ARE MOVING.

Duskveil stared at it, unblinking.

The fortress hummed around him, unaware.

Outside, the last light of day sank into the forest, and Stonewall — breathing, pulsing, alive — exhaled once like a creature ready to wake.

*****

The dawn came thin and bruised, crawling slow across the canopy.

It was the kind of morning that didn't belong to any side—neither peace nor war, just the space between breaths.

From the launch deck atop Skyspan Aerodrome, Major Aria Vance ran her glove along the leading edge of a Thorn Skimmer's wing, listening to the faint tick of resin plates expanding in the chill. The sound reminded her of heartbeats—too slow, too deliberate. Around her, the hangar crews worked in silence. Even the wind had learned to move quieter these days.

"Wings primed," she called.

Beside her, Dixie Lake stood at the threshold, helmet off, eyes on the horizon. Her flight grafts shimmered faintly, translucent wings catching the first fingers of light as if eager to move.

She didn't answer. She didn't have to. She was listening—to the same sound that now lived inside every wall of Stonewall Outpost: that deep, slow, rhythmic pulse. The Accord's heartbeat. The fortress and the forest breathing as one.

"Keep altitude below fogline," Vance instructed, voice measured. "Recon sweep west to east. No plume entry, no sonic trails."

Dixie smirked faintly, while checking Vance's Glider harness to insure it is tight. "Copy that. Silent as the sap."

B.U.G.F.O.R.C.E.

They stepped out together, dropping into the morning haze.

*****

The Flight

The canopy fell away beneath them, and the world opened like a scar. The forest was still wet from the night's dew, each leaf reflecting dull silver in the dim light. Below, the river snaked toward the Flats, its surface trembling with faint, unnatural ripples—like something alive was breathing just beneath it.

"Air One to Hivewatch," Vance whispered. "Thorn flight departing Skyspan. Bearing one-one-eight, crossing Broadwater at canopy level."

The reply came soft and filtered through static.

"Copy, Air One. Maintain low signature. Report all biological formations."

As they crossed the final stretch of treetops, Reed Flats unfolded before them—a drowned plain of mud, sap-pools, and tangled reeds stretching to the horizon.

It was not water. It was something pretending to be water. Still. Patient. Waiting.

Dixie slowed, wings catching a current that wasn't air. "You feel that?" she asked over comm.

Vance scanned her readouts. "Thermal inversion. Air's thick with moisture and... something metallic. Adjust filters."

The haze parted—and there, rising out of the Flats like the bones of a buried giant, stood the towers.

*****

The Breathing Towers

They were not towers in the human sense, but fungal spires—tall, ribbed columns of pale resin-flesh, each one capped by petal-like gills that opened and closed in rhythm.

The sound was low, organic, and disturbingly regular. Breathing.

The air between them shimmered with drifting particles—tiny, metallic motes that flashed like dust caught in sunlight, then vanished just as quickly. They rose and fell with the exhale of each tower, scattering light in shifting arcs.

"Fungal… but engineered," Vance murmured. "Structure's too symmetrical."

"They're alive," Dixie said quietly, eyes wide. "They're breathing with each other."

And indeed they were. Each spire expanded and contracted in perfect unison—an entire field inhaling as one body, exhaling as one mind.

Dixie counted under her breath. "Four seconds in. Four out. Ten at rest. Then again."

The pattern was exact. Measured. Purposeful. It wasn't just life—it was organization.

*****

The Metallic Plumes

A wind gusted through the Flats, and one tower released a jet of silver vapor that spread outward in a fine mist. It glittered briefly, then turned the air to glass. Sensors crackled. Readouts went blind.

"EMP trace," Vance snapped. "Metallic particulate."

Dixie banked left to avoid the plume, wings shimmering as she cut through clean air.

"Those spores—they're reacting to us!"

"They're listening," Vance corrected, pulling higher. "Hold vector."

The mist below rippled. The next tower opened, slower this time, releasing a thin stream of glittering dust that caught the early light like liquid mercury.

The plumes weren't random. They were signaling.

"Look," Dixie whispered. "They're answering each other."

Every tower across the Flats now breathed in the same rhythm, but with a half-second offset between them—a wave pattern, spiraling outward from a central point.

Vance frowned. "They're syncing. Like neurons."

Her hand hovered above the control panel, tracing invisible paths between the spires. "Each exhale triggers the next. Each plume marks a boundary. This isn't a field—it's a network."

*****

The First Visual of the Hive Mind

Dixie adjusted her scope toward the Flats' center. At first, she saw nothing but haze. Then—movement. Not above, but beneath the surface.

The mud itself trembled, a low ripple expanding outward from a dark core buried beneath the reeds. The towers bent slightly toward it, their gills tightening as though inhaling for something greater than themselves.

Then she saw it: a faint glow spreading outward in slow concentric circles—light traveling through mud and water, pulsing with the same rhythm as the towers.

"Mother of soil…" Dixie breathed. "It's under there." Vance turned sharply. "What is?" "The rhythm. The source. It's coordinating them." Dixie exclaimed The pulse quickened. The towers responded—each one tilting toward the light as if listening for instruction. The metallic mist thickened, swirling above the ground like a second atmosphere.

The Flats came alive. Dixie felt the tremor through her wings before the sensors registered it. It wasn't just beneath them—it was beneath everything. The entire basin was breathing, one pulse, one body, one mind.

"Hivewatch," Vance said tightly, "we have coordinated fungal respiration across all visible clusters. Metallic spore dispersal confirmed. There's… something moving beneath the central plain."

Static answered.

"Hivewatch, do you copy?"

Nothing. Dixie's skin prickled. "We've lost contact."

"Keep recording," Vance said. "We'll bring it back in memory."

*****

Retreat

The light beneath the Flats pulsed once more, stronger, brighter.

A ring of spore towers exhaled in unison, sending a spiral of silver mist straight into the sky.

The world around them went dim. For a heartbeat, everything felt weightless—soundless—as if they were trapped inside someone else's breath. "Break left!" Vance shouted.

They dove low, cutting under the plume's edge. The haze cracked apart like thin glass.

Behind them, the towers began to hum, their combined sound vibrating through the air like the chorus of a living machine.

When they burst free into clear sky, the fortress was just visible on the horizon. Stonewall's spires gleamed faintly in the rising sun—pale, steady, alive.

"Air One to Hivewatch," Vance said, voice shaking with relief. "Returning to base. Reed Flats is active. Repeat: active. We've seen the first signs of central coordination."

A pause, then Duskveil's voice came faint and grave over the line:

"Understood. Return home, Major. The roots are listening."

Dixie looked back once as the Flats disappeared behind mist and distance. The towers were still breathing. And in their rhythm, she could swear she heard words—not language but meaning: a whisper that wasn't quite sound that said. *"We are awake."*

✳✳✳✳✳

The next dawn came hard and bright — the kind of light that left no shadows to hide behind. The calm of Stonewall's recovery was gone; the fortress was a living drum now, beating with preparation.

Every rampart echoed with training sounds: shouted cadence, the hiss of resin weaponry, the thud of boots over bark. For the first time since the siege, the air smelled not of blood or sap but of sweat and renewal.

Captain William Jones stood in the courtyard with his arms folded, watching a formation of Ground Division troopers run through pattern drills. Their movements were clean, perfect, synchronized — and completely useless.

"Stop!" Jones barked.

The line froze mid-step. Sergeant Miller turned, frowning. "Something wrong with the tempo?"

"Everything's wrong with the tempo," Jones said. "You move like a song the enemy's already learned."

Miller squinted, jaw flexing. "We've drilled these steps for years."

"Exactly," Jones said. "The Mind will hear those years coming."

He moved to the center of the line and clapped once, sharp and uneven. "You want to live through what's coming, you'll unlearn order. You'll move like lightning and heartbeat and thunder arguing with each other."

The troops glanced at one another, uncertain.

Jones pointed toward the sound towers still being repaired along the inner wall. "The Mind listens for patterns. It thrives on predictability. So we'll give it noise. We'll build a wall of chaos it can't climb."

Miller's lips twitched into the faintest of smiles. "You're serious."

"Deadly." Said Captain Jones with a smile.

*****

Weaponizing Chaos

They began that morning. Instead of marching, Jones had the squads move in staggered bursts: two steps, pause, half turn, then four more at double pace. The cadence changed every repetition.

Instead of bugles, Miller ordered resin blasters fired in uneven rhythm — triple bursts followed by silence, then single echo shots.

At first it looked like madness — a field of soldiers moving out of sync, shouting over one another, boots thundering without pattern. But gradually, something new took shape. The sound became unpredictable, alive — a living storm of dissonance.

From the Hivewatch balcony above, Major Duskveil and Colonel Havelock watched the exercise unfold. The courtyard below pulsed like a heart with arrhythmia, chaotic yet deliberate.

"You think this will work?" Havelock asked.

"It already is," Duskveil replied. "Look at them. They're adapting faster than any command could teach."

He pointed to the tremor meters along the parapet wall. The needles no longer moved in smooth lines but in jagged bursts.

"The Mind listens through the soil," Duskveil said. "It expects harmony. Instead, we're giving it percussion."

*****

Miller's Test

By midday, the field was slick with sweat and resin dust. The air shuddered with uneven blasts of sonic energy as Miller tested the recalibrated Sonic Emitters — the new handhelds designed to produce irregular frequency pulses.

Miller grinned as he handed one to Jones. "Try it. She's got a bite."

Jones aimed toward a cluster of inert sap effigies — training targets built to mimic ant carapaces. He squeezed the trigger. The weapon emitted not a tone but a shard of sound — jagged, broken, almost percussive. The effigies cracked under the pressure.

"Feels wrong," Jones said. "But right."

"Yeah," Miller said. "Like jazz written by lightning."

"Don't even know what that means." Captain Jones said in a playful manner.

"Doesn't matter," Miller said. "Neither will the swarm."

They both laughed — short, real, the kind of laughter that comes when men realize fear hasn't killed them yet.

*****

Dixie's Observation

From above, Dixie circled low, watching the patterns from a pilot's eye.

To her, the drills looked like improvisation — a dance of misdirection and instinct.

Every soldier's movement contradicted the one beside them, creating a field of kinetic uncertainty. The ground itself became unreadable.

When she landed, sweat streaking her armor, Jones called out without looking up. "What's it look like from up there?"

"Like a storm that doesn't know where to strike," she said. "You'd hate to be the one trying to predict it."

"That's the idea." Inferred Jones.

She stepped closer, glancing at the sonic arrays. "Duskveil says the Hive Mind's strength is order. Every creature in sync, every move preordained."

Jones nodded. "Then we'll become the thing it can't process — humans being humans."

Dixie smirked. "Chaotic, stubborn, and loud."

"Now you're getting it." Jones smiled.

*****

Hivewatch Calibration

Inside the fortress, Duskveil sat before the resonance grid, monitoring the patterns. Every irregular burst from the courtyard appeared as sharp spikes across the plate. The waveform no longer flowed like a river; it struck like rain.

Behind him, Sergeant Vek worked on a portable signal modulator — a wrist-bound device tuned to translate the drills into defensive interference patterns.

"The Augments can mirror the noise field," Vek said. "We can make the fortress itself hum against the Mind's rhythm."

"Do it," Duskveil said. "But make sure it's irregular. Random intervals. If it ever becomes predictable, we feed the enemy instead of starving it."

Vek grinned, faint light flickering behind his eye. "You know, it's almost poetic. The Mind uses harmony to enslave. We'll use chaos to free."

"Poetic," Duskveil said dryly. "But poetry doesn't win sieges. Math does. Controlled noise — that's the math of war now."

*****

Doctrine Codified

By evening, the chaos had become method. Jones and Miller stood before their troops, voices carrying over the sound of hammering and tuning.

"This is your new creed," Jones said, pacing the line. "Forget synchronization. Forget parade drills. The Mind feeds on repetition. We feed on surprise."

Miller's voice followed, a gravel tone over thunder. "You are the wall's noise. You are its confusion. You are the storm it can't count."

They turned to the emblem newly painted across the training ground — a spiral of overlapping waves, broken and asymmetric. Beneath it, a single phrase had been carved into bark with a solder stylus:

THE NOISE IS THE SHIELD.

Havelock descended the steps as they finished. "Well, Captain, you've built your doctrine."

Jones saluted. "We'll teach it to every Division by dawn."

"Good," Havelock said. "Because when Reed Flats starts singing, I want this fortress screaming back."

*****

The First Resonance

That night, as the outpost quieted and the drills ceased, Duskveil stood alone at Hivewatch. The tremor plates still glowed faintly with residual energy from the training.

He pressed a palm against one. The pulse he felt wasn't beetle or human. It was both — a hybrid rhythm born of chaos and order woven together. The resonance traveled down through the stone, through the roots, and out into the deep earth.

*****

Miles away, beneath the Flats, a cluster of fungal towers quivered. Their perfect rhythm faltered for the first time.

195

The breathing paused. Then, faintly, almost imperceptibly, a single note of static echoed back through the soil — confused, searching, defensive. Duskveil smiled without warmth. "Good," he whispered. "We made it listen."

*****

The fortress slept, but the hum did not. Even with the drills silenced and the watchfires guttered, Stonewall still pulsed beneath the floors like a slow heartbeat buried in wood. The new doctrine had filled every hall with noise that refused to fade, echoes hiding inside the walls.

In the lower dormitory, Sergeant Josia Vek lay on his bunk with his Augment bands still glowing faintly at the temples. The resonance wouldn't shut off. The engineers told him the field modulator would stabilize after a few hours of silence.

Vek hadn't had a few hours of silence in days. He stared at the ceiling until it blurred. Beneath the thrum of Stonewall's breathing came another sound — thinner, more deliberate, almost intimate. A whisper made of static:

Bridge…

He sat upright, the bunk screeching. The room was empty except for a snoring corporal and a beetle technician coiled asleep in resin netting. Vek turned his Augment dials to minimum. The whisper grew clearer.

You built the noise. We learned the noise.

He swung his legs off the bed. "Who's there?"

The voice didn't answer in words but in rhythm. Tap-pause-tap-tap-tap — the cadence of his own heart, returned to him. The air around his ears vibrated, soft enough to feel like thought.

*****

He made it to the Hivewatch access corridor before the dizziness hit. The walls here pulsed with green veins, beetle resin integrated into human structure — an innovation he'd helped design. Now, every vein seemed to shimmer in sympathy with his steps.

Duskveil met him halfway down the corridor, cloak loose, eyes shadowed. "Couldn't sleep either?"

"Not the problem," Vek said. "Sir… I'm getting inbound signals. Not from the Accord network." Duskveil frowned. "How strong?" Vek said "Strong enough to taste."

They entered the analysis chamber. The tremor plates idled in low glow. When Vek placed his hand on the console, the entire grid woke with a shiver of blue light. Lines of vibration began to crawl across it like handwriting.

Duskveil leaned in. "Translate."

Vek closed his eyes, letting the signal crawl through his nerves. The Augments pulsed once, twice, and his voice came out layered — his own and something beneath it.

We are the rhythm between your chaos.

You teach us discord, we teach you echo.

Duskveil stepped back, jaw tightening. "It's the Hive Mind."

Vek opened his eyes — his augmented eye was still glowing faint green. "It's… learning. Sir, it's copying us. It's reproducing the same interference pattern we used to break their cadence." "You mean the Noise Doctrine?" Duskveil asked.

"Yeah. Only… cleaner. More precise. Like it's correcting us."

Containment

Duskveil hit the emergency field switch. The walls sealed in amber shimmer, muting the outside hum. "We keep this here. No comms, no recording."

Vek pressed both palms to his temples. "It's not coming through the radio, Major. It's coming through me."

The confession hung in the quiet like smoke. Duskveil studied him — the faint flicker under the skin near his jaw where the Augments met muscle, the micro tremor running down his right arm.

"You're still the Bridge," Duskveil said softly. "That connection cuts both ways."

"Yeah, well, the other side's calling collect."

A faint smile cracked the Major's face and died there. "Can you isolate the signal?"

Vek nodded, shaky. "Maybe. It's layered on sub-harmonic bands. Almost… emotional frequencies. Like it's mimicking tone rather than speech." "Then translate emotion." Duskveil ordered.

Vek took a deep breath. "Okay. It feels like… curiosity first. Then hunger. Then—" He stopped, eyes widening.

"What?"

"Recognition."

*****

The Voice Learns a Name

The tremor plates surged brighter, their glow crawling up the walls until every surface pulsed with light. The signal intensified, threading through the air like invisible rain. Vek staggered back, clutching his head.

Bridge Josia Vek.

It spoke his name perfectly. No distortion. No static. Just calm understanding.

Your noise hurts. We admire it.

"Major—" Vek gasped. "It knows me."

Duskveil's instincts screamed at him to sever the circuit, but something colder inside whispered: listen.

He tapped a command on the console, dropping recording thresholds to manual. "Go on," he told the air. "Say your piece."

The hum modulated. A new pattern formed — deep, slow, symmetrical.

Noise divides. Noise saves.

We wish to learn saving.

Vek's pulse spiked. Sweat crawled down his neck. "Sir… it doesn't sound hostile. It sounds—"

"Alive," Duskveil finished.

Alive is loud, the Mind replied. Then silence.

The plates went dark. The hum collapsed back to the fortress' baseline pulse.

Aftermath

Vek sank against the wall, breathing hard. "It stopped."

Duskveil knelt beside him, studying the faint blue glow fading from the Augments. "Stopped, or went quiet?"

Vek didn't answer. He stared at his hands as if waiting for them to move on their own.

"You'll report to Med-Ops," Duskveil said finally. "No transmissions. No link work without clearance."

Vek nodded, still dazed. "Sir, it wasn't all bad. When it spoke, I felt… not anger. Not malice. It was listening."

Duskveil rose. "The problem with listeners is they always want the last word."

He dimmed the console lights and keyed the field open. The hum of the outpost returned at once, low and reassuring. For a moment, both men just stood there, letting the familiar sound wash over them like proof of life.

Vek exhaled slowly. "Do you think the Mind can feel fear?"

Duskveil didn't answer. He watched the tremor needles, steady and slow. "It can now."

*****

The summons came at first light. Every corridor in Stonewall carried it — a vibration rather than a word, a low pulse that made resin windows tremble in their frames. The Accord signal. The beetles were calling a council.

Colonel Dorian Havelock descended through the main lift shaft, boots echoing against living wood. Behind him came Major Rowan Duskveil, cloak drawn tight, and Commander Arlen Veyra of the Water Division, her uniform still damp with river dew. From the upper walkways, Major Aria Vance and Major Edgar Greg followed in silence, while the last to enter were Captain William Jones and 1st Sergeant Miller — boots still crusted with dirt from the training fields. The noise of the world above faded until all that remained was the heartbeat of the fortress itself.

At the corridor's end waited a gate grown from intertwined roots. When Havelock touched it, the wood folded open like fingers releasing a secret.

*****

The Root-Hall

The chamber beyond was vast and wet-sounding, a hollow grown rather than carved. Luminous sap dripped in slow strings from the ceiling, pooling around a circular platform built of bark and black chitin. The air smelled of moss, stone, and something older — memory left too long in the dark.

Standing in the center was Torr Var-Kin, Envoy of Queen Varaxes. The Dusk Beetle's shell gleamed with oil-slick colors that shifted as he breathed. Behind him loomed two of his kind, silent as statues, their carapaces etched with scripture lines that pulsed faintly like veins of firefly light.

When he spoke, the words came in overlapping tones — one deep, one musical, one almost human.

"The soil remembers your footsteps, Colonel. We thank you for keeping faith with the Accord."

Havelock inclined his head. "Stonewall stands because of it."

"Stonewall breathes because of it," Var-Kin corrected. Then, quieter: "But the breath shortens."

He gestured toward the floor. The root-lattice below them throbbed once, and an image rose in threads of sap-light — a living map of the tunnels beneath Reed Flats. For a heartbeat it glowed serene. Then blotches of dull gray spread outward like infection.

Corruption Beneath

"These are the Lower Colonies," Var-Kin said. "Workers who once served Queen Varaxes in faith. Something has entered them. It teaches them to eat what should not be eaten — roots, resin, even light. They dig toward the Flats' heart, where the fungal towers stand. There they vanish, minds first, shells later."

Veyra folded her arms. "We've seen tremors under the waterways. I thought it collapse from over-digging."

"No," Var-Kin said. "It is harvesting. The corruption feeds on rhythm. Every heartbeat you send, it learns to mimic. Your new doctrine hums loudly. They hear it, and they come."

Duskveil's stomach turned cold. He glanced at Havelock, who said nothing.

"Is it spreading toward Stonewall?" Greg asked.

Var-Kin lowered his horned head. > "Yes. Not in miles — in understanding. They do not march; they convert. Once one root learns, the others remember."

Miller swore softly. "So it's not just the ants anymore."

"No," Var-Kin said. "The swarm is a choir now."

A Divided Table

Havelock stepped into the projection's light. "Then we seal the tunnels. Collapse every passage from the Flats to our perimeter."

"Collapse one, and ten more grow," Var-Kin said. "The corruption travels through resonance. It will find another path. Stone is no barrier to song."

Vance exhaled. "So, what stops a song?"

"Noise," Jones said.

Every head turned. He met Var-Kin's many-faceted eyes without flinching. "The Mind hates discord. We've proven that."

Duskveil shook his head. "Proven we can disrupt it — not destroy it. And now it's learning our rhythm back."

Var-Kin's mandibles clicked softly, amusement or warning. > "The storm you teach will fall on you first if you are not careful, Little Captain."

Miller stepped beside Jones. "Then we learn faster."

The Envoy's eyes gleamed. > "The sap and the blood will race each other. We shall see who tires first."

Roots That Remember

The projection dimmed to near-dark. Var-Kin extended one claw to the floor, carving a circle in the sap. Inside the circle grew a faint glow — not image but sensation: a pulse that rose through the chamber until every Micro-Operatives felt it in the chest.

"This is the Root-Memory," Var-Kin said. "It is how the soil speaks when it must warn its children. Touch it."

Havelock hesitated only a moment before kneeling and placing a hand against the light. The pulse ran up his arm, sharp as lightning, filling his head with impressions — a sky of spores, towers breathing in perfect time, the sound of a million legs moving in agreement.

When he pulled back, his breath became ragged. He looked at his officers. "They're not building an army," he said. "They're building a belief."

Duskveil whispered, "And belief doesn't die easily."

Resolutions

Silence settled again, thick as sap. Then Havelock straightened. "Major Vance — you'll double air reconnaissance and lay sonic buoys along Broadwater. Major Greg — your Ground Division starts fortifying the lower perimeter. Commander Veyra, I want floodgates ready to drown any passage that opens within ten spans." They nodded.

Havelock turned back to the Envoy. "Can your Queen hold the corrupted colonies at bay?"

Var-Kin's glow dimmed to mournful violet. > "She holds them only through pain. Each call to obedience burns her mind. If she falls, the Accord dies with her."

"Then we keep her standing," Havelock said. He looked to Jones and Miller. "You two will work with Var-Kin's engineers. Blend our resonance with theirs. If we can't silence the roots, we'll teach them a new song."

Jones smirked faintly. "Chaotic harmony?"

"Exactly." Exclaimed Havelock.

Var-Kin inclined his head. > "Then let the Council adjourn in defiance. May your chaos bloom." Var-Kin turned to all present, "This day forward, the queen has asked that I be with you on this journey." They all looked at one another, surprised. Havelock interrupted gruffly and said "Let's move forward and keep the queen standing"

*****

Departure

When the chamber emptied, Duskveil lingered. He stared at the fading map until the last thread of light died.

203

Havelock's voice came from the stairs. "Say it."

Duskveil did. "It's learning through us, sir. Every sound we make, every experiment — it echoes back smarter."

Havelock's face was stone. "Then we stop trying to stay ahead."

Duskveil frowned. "How, sir?"

"We stop leading. We start changing direction every time it listens."

He turned to leave. At the door he paused, hand on the living wood. "Tell Vek to rest. He's hearing ghosts now."

"He's hearing the future," Duskveil muttered after him. But Havelock was already gone, leaving only the echo of boots and the hum of the Root-Hall — a sound too deep to belong to one species alone.

*****

What began as murmurs in the Root-Hall became orders on wind and wire. Within a single Span, Stonewall stirred like a living city — crews moving through corridors, sonic engineers adjusting plates, air scouts mapping thermal drafts for the next descent.

For the first time since the Accord, humans and beetles worked without translators. They didn't need them. The rhythm carried the meaning.

The Noise Doctrine had evolved from chaos into pulse — a beat that traveled through sap, metal, and bone. Where the Hive Mind sought to synchronize, the defenders of Stonewall sought to sing apart in unity.

*****

Orders in Motion

Colonel Havelock stood on the command balcony, the projection wells casting pale green light across his face. "Every Division double readiness. Reed Flats is the enemy's cathedral now. We'll burn its hymns from the soil."

Below, the vast operations floor shimmered with activity. Water Division officers adjusted resonance buoys; Ground units tested portable emitters; Air scouts fitted anti-plume filters to their harnesses. The outpost looked less like an army and more like an orchestra preparing for war.

"Duskveil," Havelock said, "I want constant tremor mapping. Any movement below Reed Flats — we strike first."

"Yes, sir. And the Prime Root reading?"

Havelock hesitated, gaze drifting toward the great central pillar of Stonewall — that colossal column of petrified wood reaching down into unseen depths. The beetles called it The First Root. Humans called it the Foundation Beam. "Let's hope it keeps listening," he said.

*****

The Beetle Monks

Near the base of that column, where the light dimmed to amber and sap veins glowed like constellations, Captain William Jones walked barefoot across the living floor. The surface hummed beneath his soles, vibrating with faint, steady warmth. He was not alone.

Three beetle monks surrounded him in a loose triangle — old, stooped creatures with carapaces etched in curling runes. Their antennae swayed in unison as they whispered, not words but vibrations that rippled through the air like ripples across still water.

"Captain Jones of Tree Division," said the eldest, his voice a click and a chord together. "You hear the breath of the world. You must now learn to breathe back."

Jones lowered his head in respect. "You mean the Accord tone?"

The monk's eyes glowed faint blue. "No. The Root tone. The one that spoke before words."

He touched the floor with a claw. The hum changed. It was subtle, a half-note drop, but it made the air feel suddenly heavier, alive.

Jones knelt, copying the gesture, placing both hands flat against the sap-warm bark. The vibration traveled up his arms into his chest. It was like hearing through bone — too deep to be sound, too vast to be contained.

Thummm…

The resonance passed through him, and something inside his mind opened — not in thought, but in feeling.

He saw the forest roots stretching endlessly, rivers of sap glimmering like veins beneath the earth. Somewhere at the center of that vast network pulsed a greater presence — slow, vast, patient. The Prime Root.

Its voice wasn't speech but weight. When it pulsed, he felt gravity itself shift in rhythm.

It whispered through him, the way wind whispers through hollow stone.

Little one who carries thunder, it said. You walk loud. The Earth remembers you.

Jones shuddered, breath catching. "It's… speaking."

The monks inclined their heads. "The Prime Root does not speak. It remembers aloud."

"What does it remember?" he asked.

The eldest monk's mandibles clicked in what might have been a smile. "Everything that has ever touched soil. Every war, every step, every fall. The noise of life itself."

The Lesson of Stillness

For hours — or maybe days, time blurred in the chamber — the monks taught Jones how to listen without hearing. He learned to tune his body, not his mind, to the resonance around him.

"Sound is not command," one whispered. "It is permission."

He stood in the circle of roots, eyes closed, palms outward. The hum grew softer, deeper, until it matched the rhythm of his pulse.

"Now," said the elder, "speak not with your voice — but with your balance."

Jones inhaled, exhaled, felt his heartbeat become a language. The air shimmered, faint dust rising from the ground as though the fortress itself responded. A ring of light pulsed outward from where he stood — gentle, then steady, then vast.

For a brief, electric moment, the world answered.

He heard the Prime Root again — closer this time, like a whisper under his sternum.

The Swarm borrows hunger. You borrow courage. Both are borrowed from me.

The light faded, leaving only the hum. Jones staggered, gasping.

"Did I do that?" he asked.

The monk nodded slowly. "You did not. You allowed it."

*****

The Power Within Noise

Later that night, Jones found Duskveil waiting near the spiral ramp. The Major's eyes flicked to the faint glow still pulsing under Jones's palms.

"What did they teach you?" Duskveil asked.

Jones hesitated. "That the noise we make — it isn't just sound. It's connection. The Earth... hears us. Not as soldiers, not even as humans. As movement. As will."

Duskveil raised an eyebrow. "You're telling me the ground's alive now?"

"It always was. We just never listened."

He turned toward the Root column. "If we can align our resonance with the Earth itself — the Prime Root — we can redirect the Mind's signal. Turn its strength against it."

Duskveil frowned, torn between disbelief and awe. "And you think you can talk to it?"

Jones smiled faintly. "No. I think it's already talking to us. We just need to stop interrupting."

*****

Preparation Complete

By dawn, the fortress pulsed with readiness. Air scouts lined the ramparts, their wings shimmering under dew. Ground engineers calibrated pulse emitters into the soil. Beetle sentinels clicked in low rhythm beside human guards.

The hum of Stonewall had changed again — no longer chaotic, no longer orderly. It had become a harmony born of contradiction: chaos guided by will, purpose disguised as noise.

From the central tower, the Prime Root's pulse echoed faintly through every hall. Every Micro-Operatives felt it — through boots, through breath, through bone.

Captain Jones stood beside Miller on the rampart, the horizon glowing amber with the first light of day.

"Something's waking beneath Reed Flats," Miller said.

"I know," Jones answered quietly. "But so are we."

The sky cracked open with color that did not belong too day. It began as a pallid shimmer over the eastern rim, a haze that hummed rather than glowed. Within that light moved shadows — first few, then many — thousands of small black darts swarming in spirals that reached from canopy to cloud.

*****

From Hivewatch Tower, Major Aria Vance fixed her field-scope on the phenomenon. "Contact lines confirmed," she said, voice steady though her hand was not. "Wasp stratospheres, two layers deep. And they're not alone."

The view widened. Beneath the wasp coils marched the ants — twin rivers of crimson and black, carving channels through reed and mud with terrifying efficiency. Their columns did not crawl; they pulsed, moving in waveforms. Every six seconds the formation surged forward, paused, adjusted — like breathing.

And below even that movement, the ground shimmered with something metallic, something new. Beetles — but not the kin of the Accord. Their carapaces gleamed dull iron, shells fused in unnatural patterns. They moved with mathematical grace, their legs clicking in time to a rhythm that was not their own.

"The Mind has found its choir", Duskveil murmured while standing beside Vance.

*****

The Signal from the Flats

Across the horizon, Reed Flats glowed like a dying sun. The fungal towers rose in slow motion, their gills trembling open. Each exhale released waves of silver mist that rolled outward across the basin, merging into a single spiraling current.

Sensors screamed through Hivewatch. The resonance boards flickered, throwing off raw data that pulsed with impossible order.

"Cadence matches the old Accord heartbeat," said Specialist Song. "Only... reversed."

"Reversed?" Duskveil asked.

"Every beat answers ours with its echo — one for one. It's mirroring Stonewall."

Havelock's voice thundered through the hall. "Then they're listening for the fortress. Make sure it hears them back."

The specialist hesitated. The Colonel turned. "Open the tremor plates. All of them."

Duskveil swallowed. "That will expose our full field, sir."

"It already knows our song," Havelock said. "Let's show it the verses."

*****

The Choir of Insects

Below, on the flats, the movement grew. Ant legions formed circles around the fungal towers. Each ring began to stomp in unison, vibrating the ground with seismic rhythm. The wasps above spiraled tighter, their wings producing harmonics that shimmered like mirrored glass.

And between them, the dark beetles clicked, shells opening slightly — amplifiers.

Together, they produced a sound that was neither roar nor scream. It was music — if music could be made of hunger.

Every tower bent toward the center where the stone rings Jones and Vance had seen now pulsed bright gold. The mud shuddered. The whole basin seemed to breathe in — then exhale.

The gust reached Stonewall seconds later, carrying with it the smell of rust and honey and old sap. Every Micro-Operatives on the wall felt it in their chest, a vibration that was not air but intent. Jones closed his eyes. They're testing the chord.

*****

The Fort's Reply

"Bring up the emitters," Miller barked across the courtyard. housings like organ pipes. The fortress hummed, low and warning.

Jones took position near the central spire. His palms still glowed faintly from the training chamber. He could feel the Prime Root beneath him — awake, listening.

"Let it flow through you," the Beetle Monk beside him whispered. "Don't command it. Invite it." He nodded; eyes fixed on the horizon.

Then the pylons sang. It wasn't a tone so much as collision — the dissonance of a thousand instruments finding one impossible harmony. The sound rolled through the trenches, down the walls, and into the earth.

Where the enemy's rhythm sought order, Stonewall answered with living chaos.

The resonance struck the Flats like a physical wave. The wasp swarms broke formation, spinning erratically; ant columns stumbled, tripping over one another.

But the fungal towers adapted, gills vibrating in faster tempo, their counter-rhythm eating the chaos note by note.

*****

Jones and the Root

Jones fell to one knee, pressing both hands to the bark floor. The hum of the Prime Root roared into him like a tide. The monks around him chanted in deep, bass vibration.

Little thunder... they imitate the noise. You must give them something they cannot follow.

He gasped, eyes wide. "What is that?"

Truth.

The vibration turned downward — low, tectonic. It wasn't sound anymore. It was movement. The fortress shook, but it did not fracture.

Stonewall's hum changed pitch, aligning with the Prime Root's ancient frequency — older than language, older than war.

From Hivewatch, Duskveil shouted readings: "Frequency drop! Nine hertz... eight... it's pulling energy from below!"

Jones's body glowed faint gold. The ground beneath the tower cracked open in hairline veins of light. The Root was speaking through him.

All things that grow must tremble first.

The light burst outward, rippling through the soil toward Reed Flats like lightning through veins. When it reached the fungal towers, their perfect rhythm faltered. Several gills collapsed inward, spore clouds shattering into harmless mist. The Choir stuttered.

*****

The Mind Reacts

For one impossible moment, silence took the Flats. Then came a scream — not through air, but through every living thing. A psychic howl that made soldiers drop to their knees. Glass shattered. Insects turned on each other, tearing wings and legs in frenzied confusion.

Vek, stationed in the lower trench, clutched his head as his Augments lit up. It's angry, he thought. It knows what touched it.

Through the fog of noise, he heard the whisper again:
Bridge Vek... tell your captain... the root remembers him.

He stared toward the horizon where the towers still smoked. "Oh, it remembers," he whispered back.

*****

The Storm Before War

The light faded from Jones's palms. He slumped against the Root's base, breath ragged. The monks steadied him, antennae trembling in reverent awe.

Duskveil's voice crackled through the comm bead. "Whatever you did, Captain… it bought us a night."

Jones managed a tired grin. "Then let's use it."

Havelock's orders rang across the fortress. "All units — fortify and reload. The swarm will come again at dawn, angrier, smarter. Tonight we rest, tomorrow we fight gods."

From the parapets, Dixie watched the Flats smolder. The air was thick with the scent of burnt resin and rain about to fall.

"The first verse is over," she murmured.

Miller stepped beside her. "And the chorus?"

She watched a flicker of light far east where the towers still breathed. "Coming."

*****

Night came without wind. The forest lay still — every leaf heavy with dew, every branch unmoving, as if the world itself refused to breathe.

Stonewall stood at the center of that silence, glowing faintly in the dark like the heart of some great creature asleep beneath the bark.

Captain William Jones sat on the parapet overlooking Reed Flats. The basin stretched out before him, cloaked in fog and memory. No flicker of motion, no glint of chitin. Only the stillness that follows exhaustion — or plotting.

He could feel the Prime Root's hum deep below, slower now, steady, patient. It felt like a heartbeat keeping time for both sides.

Dixie Lake joined him quietly, wings folded, the faint bioluminescent shimmer at her temples matching the glow of the resin torches. "The Flats look peaceful," she said softly.

"Peaceful," Jones murmured, "is just what war looks like when it's thinking."

213

She smiled faintly. "That's bleak, Captain."

"Accurate, though."

*****

The Silence in Stonewall

Down below, the fortress had gone half-dark to conserve energy. Only the inner courtyards glowed, dim and gold, with squads moving like ghosts — reloading sonic emitters, recalibrating pulse relays, whispering rather than shouting.

In the medical chambers, Augmented troops sat with helmets off, cooling their circuits in bowls of sap water. The Beetle Monks moved among them like priests, repairing conduits with gestures rather than tools.

Miller leaned against a support pillar, chewing the edge of a ration bar. "You ever notice," he said to no one in particular, "how the quiet before a fight is worse than the fight?"

One of the new recruits looked up, eyes wide. "Sir?"

"You start thinking too much," Miller said. "And the mind's the only weapon that never stops bleeding."

Across the courtyard, Sergeant Vek sat with his back to the Root wall, Augments dimmed. He had turned off every external receiver, yet the faint echo of the Hive Mind still ghosted in his skull.

Bridge Vek… the song continues… we listen to your silence.

He whispered back, "Then choke on it."

The static retreated, but it left behind a thought — not spoken, just felt: Tomorrow, we begin again.

*****

The Prayer of the Monks

Deep beneath the fortress, the Beetle Monks gathered in their circle once more. The Prime Root's chamber pulsed softly with gold light, steady as breath. They did not chant this time. They listened.

Captain Jones stood among them, hands clasped behind his back. He had learned not to bow — the monks taught him that reverence was stillness, not lowering oneself.

One of them turned, his antennae brushing the air as if tasting his thoughts.

"You heard it, didn't you?" the monk asked.

"The Root's true voice."

Jones nodded slowly. "It said all things that grow must tremble first."

"And you trembled?"

"I still am."

The monk touched the ground with one claw, and a low hum rippled outward. The walls shivered in response. "Then you are ready," he said. "When the Earth speaks again, it will not whisper. It will command."

Jones frowned. "Command who?"

"All who still remember how to listen."

*****

Duskveil's Vigil

Above, in the command chamber, Major Rowan Duskveil sat alone before the darkened tremor plates. He had turned off the lights, the monitors, everything but the raw sensor feed — the heartbeat of the Earth itself.

The waveform pulsed in quiet rhythm across the glass. It was beautiful. And wrong.

There was a second frequency now, faint but rising — a thin, jagged pattern echoing just behind the Prime Root's hum.

The Hive Mind was adapting.

He leaned forward, whispering into the dark: "You learned our song. Now you're learning to pray."

He logged the data under a sealed file — "Project Echofold" — and closed the console. Tomorrow, he would show it to Havelock. But tonight, he let it play — the twin heartbeats of creation and corruption intertwining like roots under soil.

*****

The Night Before

Midnight found the officers gathered once more on the western wall. No speeches, no plans. Just silence and shared understanding.

Dixie perched near the rampart, wings half open to feel the air. Miller leaned against the battlement beside her, eyes scanning the horizon.

Veyra stood by the floodgate levers, hands steady, waiting.

And Jones — quiet, calm, listening. His pulse matched the Prime Root's rhythm, and for a moment he felt connected not just to Stonewall but to everything beneath it — to sap and soil, to the crawling and the still, to the quiet strength that underlies all life.

He closed his eyes. The Earth spoke again, faint and vast.

You remember me now, little thunder. You carry my voice. Tomorrow, let them hear it.

He opened his eyes. The horizon glowed faintly, not with light, but with movement.

The fog at Reed Flats was shifting, breathing again.

"They're moving," Dixie whispered.

Jones nodded. "Let them come."

******

The First Drop of Rain

A single droplet fell from the canopy above, striking the wood beside Jones's hand. Then another. And another.

The first rain in six days.

It pattered softly across the fortress, running down the walls, soaking through bark and resin until the entire structure shimmered under moonlight. The sound was gentle, rhythmic — almost peaceful.

Havelock stepped out onto the balcony, cloak drawn tight, face unreadable. "Let it rain," he said quietly. "Tomorrow, Stonewall bleeds sap and blood alike."

Duskveil appeared beside him. "They'll come at dawn."

"They always do," Havelock replied.

Below them, the soldiers moved into position, their armor glistening wet, their sonic emitters humming low in standby.

No horns sounded, no commands were given.

Only the rain and the steady pulse of the Earth.

*****

The Quiet Before the Storm

When the night was at its darkest, the Prime Root spoke one final time — not aloud, but through vibration, through the bones of every creature that called the soil home.

Balance is breath. Breath is struggle. Struggle is life. Tomorrow, all shall breathe together.

Jones looked toward the Flats, his reflection framed in the slick surface of his weapon.

Beside him, Dixie adjusted her goggles. Miller flexed his hands.

The rain stopped.

And in the distance, far beyond sight but close enough to feel, the Hive Mind took its first synchronized breath of war.

Chapter 9

The Siege of Stonewall

Dawn came red. Not the gentle blush of morning, but a deep, molten crimson that poured across the sky like blood spilling through water. It rose from the direction of Reed Flats, where mist and spore curled upward in sheets of light. The air tasted metallic and electric. Every leaf in the canopy trembled as if bracing for the day.

*****

From the highest parapet of Stonewall, Captain William Jones stood in silence, watching the horizon turn to fire. His armor bore streaks of dried sap and soil from the night before. Beneath his boots, the living bark of the fortress pulsed in rhythm — the slow, calm heartbeat of the Prime Root. He took strength from it, though it sounded tired now, as if the Earth itself had spent the night holding its breath.

Beside him, First Sergeant Miller adjusted his gauntlet. The brass joints creaked faintly.

"Red sky in the morning," he muttered. "That's what they used to say."

Jones nodded. "Sailors' warning."

"We ain't sailors." Miller said with a smirk.

"No," Jones said softly. "We're the shore."

The horizon darkened. At first it looked like storm clouds gathering low — thick, seething shapes rolling through the dawn light. Then the clouds began to move against the wind.

"Contact," Miller said.

Jones raised his scope. What he saw made his stomach tighten:

B.U.G.F.O.R.C.E.

Thousands of wasps advancing in perfect spirals, their wings flashing gold and black like molten metal; rivers of ants rippling in columns below them, marching through fog so dense it looked like steam; and behind them — shadows — massive beetles with fused carapaces that glowed from within, as if their shells contained embers.

He lowered the scope. "They're marching in harmony again."

Miller spat over the wall. "Then we break the song."

*****

The Awakening of Stonewall

All across the fortress, klaxons groaned awake. But even their cry was different now — deeper, fuller, echoing through every corridor like the strike of a great drum. The fortress itself was singing.

In the courtyards, troopers took positions beside the sonic pylons, power coils lighting one by one until the air shimmered with energy. Air Division crews ran along the Skyspan gantries, loading payloads into the Thorn Skimmers. The Water Division opened floodgates along the western trenches, filling the defensive moats with dark, reflective resin.

From below came the low, patient chants of the Beetle Monks, their voices vibrating through the foundations in tones older than speech. The resonance mingled with the klaxons until it became something unified — a hymn of defiance.

Major Rowan Duskveil arrived at the command balcony, cloak snapping behind him. His eyes flicked to the horizon, then to the tremor plates glowing before him. The readings spiked and flattened, spiked and flattened — the unmistakable rhythm of the Hive Mind.

"Cadence confirmed," he said. "The choir is forming."

Colonel Dorian Havelock entered behind him, calm as granite. "Then we sing louder."

He turned to the officers assembled around the well table: Vance, Veyra, Greg, and the newly scarred Var-Kin, envoy of the beetles.

"This is it," Havelock said. "The Flats are alive. The enemy has come as one mind. But so have we. Every Division, every Root, every wing — we hold this wall. Today, Stonewall is not a fortress. It's an instrument. And we will play it until the world remembers our name."

The floor vibrated as the fortress answered — a long, deep chord that rippled up through bark and bone. Outside, the morning haze shattered into motes of gold.

*****

The First Signs

Down in the observation trenches, Sergeant Vek crouched beside a listening post. His Augments hummed quietly, translating ground tremors into sound. The earth beneath him thrummed with incoming motion — endless, methodical, alive.

He tapped his comm bead. "Ground sensors reading contact in layers — four levels deep. Ants first, beetles below. And there's something else underneath them — something huge."

"What kind of huge?" came Miller's voice.

"The kind that breathes back."

A faint, rhythmic thud rolled through the mud — too slow to be footsteps, too deliberate to be natural. The very roots of Stonewall seemed to tense.

*****

Fire in the East

The first wave of light struck the Flats like sunrise exploding sideways. The fungal towers ignited from within, their gills opening to release clouds of glowing spore.

The air turned gold, then red, then silver.

It was beautiful. Terrible. Like watching the sky be born wrong.

From the parapet, Jones felt the Prime Root pulse once beneath him — a warning more ancient than fear.

He turned to his men. "Positions!"

Resin shields locked. Sonic pylons whined. Air-Skimmers roared to life along the upper decks, their engines a chorus of defiance.

And as the first tendrils of spore reached the wall, Stonewall Outpost woke in full — a fortress breathing, singing, and bracing to meet the dawn.

*****

Final Beat

The horizon vanished behind light and wings. The air shook. The hum of the Prime Root merged with the pulse of human hearts until they became indistinguishable — the song of life meeting the rhythm of death. Jones raised his weapon, eyes reflecting the fire. "Dawnfire," he whispered. "Let's make it theirs." And somewhere beneath his feet, the Earth answered.

So be it.

The first volley did not sound like gunfire. It sounded like a world remembering pain.

Stonewall's sonic batteries roared to life, their pulses rolling across the Flats in visible waves — translucent rings of pressure cutting through mist and spore alike. The very air convulsed.

Each impact flattened reeds, shattered fungal towers, and sent spirals of gold and ash into the sky.

And for every tower that fell, two more lit from within — glowing brighter, breathing harder.

"Range five hundred!" shouted Major Greg from the forward wall.

"Hold rhythm!" Miller barked beside him. "No patterns! No repetition!"

The fortress answered with chaos.

Each sonic battery fired at random intervals, creating a storm of discordant thunder.

Beetle engineers along the ramparts struck resonance gongs at counter-tempo, deep vibrations running through the ground to fracture enemy formations.

From above, Major Vance's voice cut through the static: "Air Division clear for launch!" The sky opened.

*****

The Sky Erupts

Dozens of Thorn Skimmers rose from the gantries in staggered spirals, their wings slicing through spore fog. Each left behind trails of vapor that glowed blue in the rising sun.

Dixie led the second wing, her eyes hidden behind polarized lenses.

"Keep formation loose!" she shouted. "The wind's alive out here!" She wasn't wrong.

Every gust twisted back on itself. The air currents had intelligence — turbulence that seemed to hunt.

A sharp ping echoed through her flight grafts. "Incoming!"

Wasps burst from the fog like knives from a cloud, hundreds of them, their bodies streaked with bioluminescent lines. Their formation spiraled — impossible precision. Each wingbeat harmonized, building sonic compression in the air itself.

Dixie banked hard, and the attack screamed past, the shockwave rattling her bones.

"They're using resonance flight!" she realized. "Their wingbeats are tuned!"

"Break them!" Vance commanded.

Dixie stopped moving her wings, and dropped three spans, and fired her pulse rifle upward. The burst tore through the spiral, scattering wasps like shrapnel made of glass. Two fell in smoke. Three more dived to follow.

Below her, Stonewall burned bright. Sonic pulses met spore light in blinding collision, each shockwave rippling through the forest canopy like thunder turned liquid.

*****

The Ant Offensive

Down on the ground, First Sergeant Miller stood knee-deep in vibrating mud.

"Hold the line!" he roared, voice cutting through the chaos.

The first ant wave struck the outer trenches like a black river. They climbed over each other in living ladders, bodies forming bridges where the moat was deepest.

Resin flamejets roared. Sonic mortars thumped. The air reeked of ozone and burnt chitin.

For every hundred that fell, a thousand replaced them.

Miller slammed the emitter staff into the ground. The device pulsed once — a ripple expanding outward through soil and root. The ground bucked.

Ants stumbled, collapsing in disarray as their internal rhythm faltered.

The pulse broke their unity, scattering the front ranks into chaos.

Behind him, Ground Division troops cheered — short-lived, because the second wave was already moving.

And above it, he saw something vast — silhouettes of armored beetles rolling forward, carrying ant troops on their backs like siege engines.

"Jones," he muttered into the comm, "we're about to get buried."

*****

The Wall Responds

At Hivewatch, Duskveil and Var-Kin worked side by side, human and beetle hands moving in tandem across the resonance console.

"Adjust lower frequencies!" Var-Kin clicked. "Their armor absorbs upper-band pulses!"

"Then we play deeper," Duskveil said. He keyed in a new harmonic — a droning subsonic note that vibrated through the walls themselves. All of Stonewall shuddered.

Resin joints screamed. Bark plates groaned. But the fortress held, channeling the vibration into the ground.

The effect was immediate: the leading beetles staggered, their shells fracturing as internal resonance met external discord. Ant troops fell screaming from their backs.

Var-Kin's eyes gleamed. "See? Even corruption still remembers pain."

But Duskveil's monitors flared red. "Don't celebrate yet. They're adapting again. Their gills are closing. They're tuning themselves against us."

Var-Kin's mandibles clicked sharply. "Then we must shift faster. Teach the fortress to improvise!"

*****

The Prime Root Stirring

Deep beneath Stonewall, in the root chamber, Jones knelt beside the monks as tremors rippled through the floor. The Prime Root's light flickered — dim, then fierce, then dim again.

The Earth trembles, little thunder, the Root's voice came through him, deep as gravity.

Do not let your song falter.

Jones closed his eyes. "They're adapting. They're learning our discord."

Then learn your own. Chaos is only weakness if you forget to dance.

He stood, chest heaving, and called into the comm bead. "All units — adjust intervals! Randomize the random! Make it human!"

Duskveil understood instantly. He broadcast the new pattern — a web of imperfect timing and flawed rhythm. The fortress obeyed.

Stonewall began to stutter in glorious disharmony — a thousand hearts beating off-time, a thousand guns firing in overlapping syncopation. The Mind faltered.

Its harmony fractured, its rhythm staggered. The towers across the Flats flickered like dying fireflies. For a moment, the air went still. And in that stillness, the defenders of Stonewall felt hope. But it was only the first wave.

*****

The Dawn's Edge

Far out in the haze, beyond the range of any scope, something vast was moving. The mist thickened, pulsing with dull light. Miller wiped spore from his visor. "We buying time or just bleeding slower?"

"Both," Jones said, watching the horizon pulse. "But the sun's rising, and we're still here."

A single streak of light tore through the fog — crimson and metallic — striking the outer parapet and tearing a hole in the wall. The blast echoed like a heartbeat snapping in half. The second siege had begun. The first tremor struck just after sunrise.

It rolled through the trenches like a low growl beneath the earth, shaking the wooden struts and knocking loose sheets of bark from the parapets.

The mud rippled — slow, deliberate, alive.

First Sergeant Miller steadied himself against a half-collapsed barricade. "That's no aftershock," he said. "That's digging."

Across the trench line, men and beetles exchanged wary glances. The hum beneath their boots deepened, joined by a second rhythm — faster, irregular, like footsteps marching underground.

"Ready up!" Miller barked. "Emitters to standby — low band! No pulse until my mark!"

He looked down the line at Sergeant Vek, who crouched near a sensor spike. The Augments along Vek's neck glowed pale blue.

"What's it saying?" Miller demanded.

Vek's voice was quiet, distant. "They're beneath us. Hundreds — maybe thousands. They're… tunneling in time. Every dig matches the Hive cadence. They're using rhythm to dig faster." "Then we break the beat," Miller growled.

*****

The Breach

The ground split. A geyser of mud and steam erupted twenty feet away, followed by the chittering scream of ants pouring out like fluid. They came in glistening waves, claws clicking in mechanical precision.

"Fire!" Sergeant Miller shouted.

The trench roared. Sonic mortars thumped, resin blasters shrieked, and the air filled with fragments of armor and carapace.

Ants fell in heaps, their bodies twitching and spasming under the dissonant frequencies.

226

But the swarm didn't slow. Each wave climbed the fallen like a bridge of bodies, snapping through the defenders' line.

Miller wrenched his emitter staff from the mud and slammed it into the nearest mound.

The device discharged in a thunderclap.

A pulse wave rippled outward, crushing the front rank of the swarm into the trench walls.

He grinned grimly. "That's right — choke on it." Then the second wave hit.

*****

The Sound of Soil

Vek's Augments overloaded, flashing white as ground pressure readings spiked. "More incoming!" he shouted. "Deeper tunnels, twelve o'clock!"

Miller pivoted just as the earth exploded behind him. A giant war ant, three times the size of a man, burst upward, mandibles snapping. The creature's armor glistened black-green, marked with streaks of glowing gold fungus.

Vek dove aside, firing point-blank. The blast shredded the ant's head, showering him in ichor. The body twitched, collapsing halfway into the trench.

"Good kill!" Miller shouted.

But Vek didn't respond. His Augments hummed — a soft, alien tone threading through the battlefield noise.

Bridge Vek... the soil remembers you.

He winced. "Not now," he muttered.

The rhythm is wrong. Fix it.

"Not. Now!"

He slammed his palm into the modulator, sending a randomized pulse through the ground. The soil bucked — throwing ants off balance and breaking their cadence. The voice receded.

"Vek!" Miller yelled. "What the hell was that?"

"Feedback loop," Vek lied, chest heaving. "Just feedback."

*****

Resonance in the Mud

Miller switched to wideband comms. "All units, resonance mod on my mark! One pulse, two breaths, and a half!"

"Sir, that's off tempo—"

"Exactly!"

He slammed the trigger. The trenches lit up in staggered bursts, sonic discharges overlapping like drumbeats made of thunder. The pattern was jagged, uneven, human.

The Hive rhythm collapsed, confused by the sudden syncopation.

"Now push!"

Ground Division surged forward, half-running, half-crawling through mud and resin. Bayonets met mandibles, shock sticks flashed, and the trenches became a blur of movement and sound.

Beetle engineers fought beside them, using claws and tools alike. Every impact sent tremors into the soil, each one a note in the growing storm of defiance.

*****

The Deep Strike

A sudden stillness. The ants stopped mid-motion — a pause so abrupt it felt impossible. Their mandibles clicked once in perfect unison.

Miller froze. "Oh hell," he whispered. The ground opened again; this time deeper, wider.

From the black pit rose a burrow colossus — part ant, part fungus, a creature fused to the Hive's rhythm. Its back glowed with moving light, patterns rippling like heartbeat waves.

"Hold fire!" Miller shouted. "Wait for range!"

The creature screamed — a vibration more felt than heard. The walls shook, weapons overloaded, and men fell to their knees, clutching their helmets.

Vek struggled upright, blood trickling from his ears. "We can't kill it," he gasped. "It's the signal! It's the thing singing to them!"

Miller bared his teeth. "Then we shut it up."

He activated his emitter staff to full discharge. The weapon hummed hot, the light along its shaft pulsing erratically. "Vek — link your Augments to me!"

"What?"

"Do it!"

Vek grabbed the staff. Their combined resonance amplified — human and machine frequencies clashing into one chaotic surge. Together they drove the weapon into the mud. The pulse that erupted tore through the trench like a god's heartbeat.

The colossus convulsed. The light on its back fractured, every ripple breaking apart like shattered glass. Its scream became silence. Then it fell, collapsing into the pit that birthed it. When the sound faded, only the soft, trembling hum of the earth remained.

******

Aftershock

Smoke and spore drifted through the wrecked trenches. The mud steamed, littered with carapaces and spent emitters.

Miller wiped grime from his face and looked over the survivors.

"Line's holding," he said, almost to himself. "By some miracle, it's holding."

Vek leaned against the trench wall, trembling. His Augments were flickering — not from damage, but from interference.

He could still hear faint static in his skull — a whisper drowned beneath the sound of Stonewall's hum.

You strike well, Bridge. Next time, strike deeper.

He closed his eyes, breathing hard. "Next time," he muttered. "You'll regret it."

*****

The Ground Breathes

Far above, Duskveil's tremor plates recorded the aftermath — seismic waves spreading outward from the trenches, rolling through soil and root until they touched the Flats.

There, the fungal towers faltered again, their breathing off-key. The Mind adjusted — but slower this time.

And beneath Stonewall, the Prime Root pulsed once, sending a soft, radiant thrum through every corridor. The fortress answered with its own heartbeat. Jones felt it beneath his boots and smiled grimly. "Good," he whispered. "The Earth remembers us, too."

The sky became a mouth. It opened over Reed Flats with a long, low inhale—the wasp spirals tightening until the air itself looked braided. Motes of spore glowed like embers in a forge. Thin clouds tore into threads. The light went the color of hammered brass.

"Wing One, hold loose spiral. Wing Two, counter-orbit on my mark," Major Aria Vance said, voice level, already banking her Thorn Skimmer into the teeth of the wind. "We don't fight their formation. We un-teach it."

"Copy," Dixie answered, sliding into the lower arc, wings twitching once to taste the air. The graft-lines along her shoulders sang faintly; Stonewall's bass hum rode through her bones. She felt the Prime Root down there somewhere, patient and old, keeping time. She tucked the feeling behind her ribs like a charm.

The first wasp wave dropped as a single organism, a spiraled spear. Their bodies were dark lacquer laced with bioluminescent veins; their wings cut the air into harmonics that stacked on themselves until the sky shook. Sonic pressure built, invisible and crushing. The front edges of Vance's canopy rattled. A hairline crack dashed white across the corner.

"Rhythm is pressure. Pressure is a blade," Vance said. She did not raise her voice. "Break the blade."

She killed her forward thrust for the one heartbeat the spiral expected her to hold speed—and fell three spans. The spear missed, clipping only her contrail. Wing One followed the feint: two up, one down, then a stuttered climb as if the sky had forgotten which way was open. The wasp formation tried to compensate. Its precision frayed. Dixie saw the gap open like a blink.

"Now," Vance breathed.

They hit the seam with crossfire. Pulse rounds—irregular, staggered, human—chewed through the spiral's spine. Wasp bodies pinwheeled, their harmonics collapsing into static. The air decompressed with a slap that chuffed the fog into ragged sheets.

More spirals uncoiled from the haze. Dozens. Scores. The sky filled with helical spears and slick, glittering arcs—resonant formations tuned to each other so that every wingbeat amplified the next. The swarm learned fast. It braided its noise into a rope made to choke.

"Wing Two, refuse the climb," Vance ordered. "We dance low. Thorn Six, Thorn Eight—you're on plume watch. Nothing glittering gets in our engines."

A wasp vetter knifed toward Dixie, antennae flexed, gill plates along the thorax breathing metallic mist. She inverted, dropped under its path, and let it overrun. The vetter snapped around too cleanly—an impossible turn. Its wingbeats fell into a tight, rising trill.

"It's locking in on me," Dixie said.

Vance's Thorn cut across the vetter's face with a sideways burst. "Let it. Then change the question."

Dixie obliged. She dropped again, so low her wing passed through fog and came up wet, and throttled once into the vetter's blind cone. The trill spiked—and Dixie fired a two-burst, one-breath, half-burst into the seam where the gill plates stitched to the ribs. The vetter folded in on itself without grace, fell smoking into the Flats. "Thorn Five, status?" Vance called. "Good," came the reply through static. "Wing root hit, clean."

"Good," Vance echoed, already turning. "Remember— our pattern is imperfection. Don't repeat yourself even by accident."

Around them, the battle stratified. Above, the high swarms drew circles at stratosphere edge—massive, pulsing haloes that shed smaller formations like sparks. Mid-sky was a whirlpool where Skimmers and vetters intersected in bursts of light and shrapnel. Low-level air boiled with spore plumes that rose in spirals, then fell as glittering rain capable of killing an engine in a breath.

A thin alarm whined in Dixie's helm. "Spore to the west. Coming fast."

"I see it," Vance said. The plume rose like a silk tower that had decided to become a river. It wasn't random; its crest tracked their arc. "It's listening."

"Then we go quiet," Dixie said.

They killed thrust in unison. For three heartbeats the Skimmers were not aircraft but leaves—drifting, patient, uninteresting. The plume slid past, confused, then veered toward a decoy skirl Duskveil popped from the southern parapet. The metallic mist drowned itself in a sudden crosswind; Water Division's floodgates sighed open somewhere below, bleeding cool air into the basin.

"Thank you, Veyra," Vance murmured.

Static flickered. Commander Veyra's voice carried like river over stone. "Keep their breath off our water and I'll keep your engines clean, Major."

"Deal."

A new sound cut the sky—a deep, thrumming bass that pressed at the lungs. The high halo tightened. A wedge-shaped flight of wasps descended from its edge: larger, plated across the abdomen, gills shuttered with chitin—a choir-flight, armored for resonance.

"Choir-flight, ten o'clock," Dixie called. "Their harmonics are armored."

"Then we don't argue harmonics," Vance said. "We argue gravity."

She dove to ground-hugging altitude, pulling the wedge behind her. Dixie took the outside line, her grafts whining as the air thickened. Pressure stacked in the wedge's wake, pushing them faster. Too fast. Dixie's hands shook, then steadied.

"Low bridge," Vance warned.

The reed mats ahead opened without warning—valves blinking wide to reveal slick black mouths breathing fog. The choir-flight never saw the ground until it was directly beneath them. Vance climbed a whisper. Dixie flicked left. The wedge tried to trim at once—perfect wings, perfect agreement.

The first two wasps clipped the valve rim at full speed. The sound they made was what light would scream if it had bones. The wedge collapsed in chain reaction; armored bodies shattered against the Flats, resonance blowing out in a dirty pulse that rattled Dixie's teeth.

"Never chase the earth," Vance said softly to no one and everyone. "It turns when it wants."

"Copy," Wing Two answered, half awed.

The swarm adapted again. Vetter flights broke into counter-point pairs—twinned flights tuned slightly off each other so one could maintain resonance if the other was disrupted. The sky became a latticework of trills and drones, a cathedral built on beating wings.

"Duskveil," Vance snapped, "they're running paired harmonics and stitching over any hole we make. I need an absence. Give me nothing."

Hivewatch answered a breath later. The fortress hum dropped out across a quadrant of sky. The living drum went silent, and the Prime Root felt pressure rather than a sound. The paired formations wobbled, suddenly deprived of reference—like dancers whose floor had been stolen.

"Now," Vance said. "Stagger right. Dixie, cut left and throw your shadow long."

Dixie rolled, throwing a sharp silhouette across fog and light. The vetters bit on it, diving for a phantom. Vance's wing came up underneath, pulse fire stitching their bellies. Bodies fell in glittering arcs, smoke painting black questions across the brass dawn.

A flare of red off her right—the outer parapet, coughing flame where a siege bolt had speared the wall. Stonewall groaned, plates flexing, sap weeping in glossy tears. The hum returned, angrier, a bruise under music.

"Breach on outer," someone barked over comms. "We've got a hole!"

"Ground will hold," Vance said. She believed it not because she was sure but because belief was a function. "We keep their sky from thinking."

Dixie climbed through a band of clear air—sudden, rare, gift. The battlefield unfolded cleanly for a heartbeat. She saw the pattern behind the patterns: how each spiral was fed by a halo, how each halo breathed from a distant column of light where the Flats' central rings pulsed. Not command, exactly. Metronome.

"Aria," she said, "see the feed lines? The halos drink from the center."

"I see them."

"We cut the lines," Dixie said. "Not the flights."

"Risky," Vance said—and then, almost smiling, "Good."

They dove together, not for the wasps but for the air between—the invisible arteries along which resonance traveled. Their pulses stitched emptiness, and emptiness tore. The next halo stuttered, its fuel a breath too slow. Its child spirals faltered, losing faith in a song without a beat. The sky changed key.

The wasps reacted with rage—that pure animal acceleration when a principle fails. A pair slammed at Dixie from blind angles, trills knifing her hearing down to white. She went sideways on instinct, felt a stinger graze her wing-join. Pain flared—a cold, surgical heat. She tasted copper. The world jumped.

"Dixie!" Vance's voice, needle-precise. "Talk to me."

"Flying," Dixie managed. She checked her graft-line: nicked, bleeding light. She closed the fold with one practiced squeeze and shuddered once with the effort. "Still here."

"Good," Vance said, and her tone changed: a quiet that carried trust. "On me."

They took the next pair together—Vance dragging the formation high as bait, Dixie carving it low into turbulence. The pair did what pairs do: stayed faithful to each other when sense said scatter. That faith killed them. Vance's pulse clipped the lead; Dixie's cut the second before it could imagine being alone.

"Wing Two, status?"

"Breathing," Dixie laughed.

"Keep doing that."

The spore plumes thickened again, now rising in columns that twisted on their own axes. They did not reach for Skimmers. They reached for sound, hungry for any shape that resembled a song. A column lunged at Vance's engine note and missed because she was already someone else.

"Duskveil," she called, "bleed static into the east quadrant, slow drift. Give them a blizzard to eat."

"On it," came the reply. A curtain of harmless white noise poured from the wall in a long, patient sigh. The columns tilted, entranced, and went to dinner.

Dixie's lenses flashed a warning: high-altitude compression. She glanced up—a halo tightening, not expanding. The wasps above were knitting themselves into a fall.

"Aria," she said, breath shallow, "look high."

Vance saw it too. A perfect ring, small and cruel, gathering mass. When it dropped, it would turn the air under it to a hammer.

"Wing One, Wing Two," Vance said, voice very even, "we are not here for that. We are somewhere else."

They moved. Not up. Not down. Sideways, into a corridor of wind that no flight plan had ever loved. The fall came, a silent crush that flattened fog into a disk and sent shards of pressure racing outward like broken glass. A third of the mid-sky grapple went dark. Dixie felt the edge of it tug her ribs and kept flying by promise alone.

"Roll call," Vance demanded.

Names came back. Not all of them. However enough did.

Stonewall's hum rose again—louder, older, layered with something that made the hair on Dixie's arms lift. She didn't need a monk to tell her what it was. The Prime Root had stopped whispering.

Somewhere below, Jones touched bark, and the Earth spoke like a drum.

The sky vibrated. The wasp halos lost their perfect circles, turning ovate, then ragged. When the Prime Root's next pulse came, it wasn't sound; it was permission. Wind reconfigured. The corridors they needed opened with almost ceremonial grace.

"Take the lanes," Vance said softly. "They're ours for a moment."

They did. Thorn Skimmers slipped through passages the world had not owned a breath before—silent curves, low arcs, murderous grace. Vetters chased and fell, chased and fell, until the air under the halos was a rain of broken flight.

"Aria," Dixie said, panting, "they're pulling back to the outer spirals."

"For now," Vance said. She turned her Thorn toward Stonewall and saw the wall, wounded and bright, singing like a cathedral that had decided not to fall today.

"Wing leaders," she said, "we reload and return. Leave the glory where it landed. We only need the sky to not think for a little longer."

Dixie let herself look once toward the Flats. The central rings pulsed through fog, slower now. Around them, towers breathed in disarray. And above it all, the Halo that had fallen reformed at the edge of the world, patient as a hunter.

"Dawnfire's still burning," she murmured.

"For now," Vance agreed. "Let's make sure it doesn't learn to sing about it."

They banked for home, engines whispering, wings wet with breath, spore and rain. Behind them, the sky stitched itself back together, but the seam would never be invisible again.

*****

The quiet after the air assault felt off. The wind didn't return, and even the rain seemed to wait. The sky stayed gray and heavy, streaked with faint spore light that wouldn't disappear. From the battlements, everything looked frozen—a battlefield pretending to be empty.

*****

Captain Jones stood at the parapet's edge, helmet off, letting the silence settle around him. For the first time in hours, there was no thunder, no fire, no screams—just a faint, steady pulse that matched neither his heartbeat nor the Prime Root's. It seemed to come from somewhere inside the wall.

Dum—dum—dum—dum.

Slow, steady, and patient.

"Sergeant Miller," Jones said quietly. "Do you hear that?"

Miller tilted his head. The sound seemed to come from the bark itself, moving through the wood. "Feels like the wall's breathing wrong," he said. "Like it picked up a bad habit."

A shiver ran through the wood beneath their boots, subtle but clear. Far below, the moats rippled as if letting out a breath.

*****

Echo from the Depths

In the command chamber, Major Duskveil bent over the tremor plates. The graphs that once danced with the Prime Root's gentle cadence now pulsed in jagged symmetry — Stonewall and Reed Flats oscillating in near-perfect mirror.

"They've matched our frequency again," he said, throat tight. "But this time… we didn't give it to them."

Colonel Havelock turned slowly. "Explain."

"They're playing us back. Our own resonance is returning, delayed by two beats. They've learned reflection."

Var-Kin, the beetle envoy, hissed low. "Reflection becomes infection. Break the mirror before it sings."

Duskveil's fingers hovered over the controls. "If I drop the field, we lose synchronization with the Root. If I hold it, the fortress hums itself apart."

The lights flickered, each pulse brighter than the last. The walls began to hum like tuning forks.

*****

The First Crack

A sudden, sharp report — like a scream turned into stone. A fissure tore through the eastern bastion. Bark split open, sap hissing as pressure vented in glowing streams.

"Containment seals!" someone shouted.

Veyra's Water Division responded instantly, flooding the rupture with coolant mist. But the mist itself shimmered gold — infected with resonance. The vapor curled into shapes — faces, mouths, echoes of voices that had never existed.

The fortress was speaking back.

Duskveil slammed the override. "Shut the damn thing down!"

The tremor plates snapped dark. The hum died — for one terrible second.

Then it came again, louder, from below.

*****

Descent to the Root

Jones and Miller raced through corridors that quivered with invisible rhythm. The walls throbbed like veins; the air shimmered as if filled with heat, though the temperature dropped with every step.

When they reached the Root Chamber, the Beetle Monks were already gathered, their antennae flat against their skulls. The Prime Root's light pulsed wrong — not steady gold but violent white, flashing in sequences that made the eyes water.

"The Hive Mind sings through us," said the eldest monk. "It has bitten the Root."

Jones felt the vibration through his armor. "Can we stop it?"

The monk touched the ground. "We must untune it — make it forget the shape of its own voice."

"How?"

"By remembering ours."

The monks began to chant — low, arrhythmic, broken deliberately. The sound scraped the air like tools on stone. It hurt to hear, but the walls wavered, uncertain.

Jones knelt, pressing his palms to the trembling floor. He reached for the resonance the way he'd been taught — through breath, not thought. The hum met him halfway, roaring into his bones.

Little Thunder, the Prime Root whispered through him. The echo carries poison. Do not silence it. Swallow it.

He gasped. "If I take it, it'll kill me."

If you don't, it will kill all that remembers you. He closed his eyes and let the wrong rhythm enter.

The vibration hit like lightning, every muscle locking, every memory flashing with noise. He saw images — the Flats, the towers, the Halo of wasps, the Hive Mind itself as an ocean of wings — and beneath it, his own fortress mirrored perfectly, singing back in harmony.

He screamed, but the sound folded inward, devoured by the resonance itself.

The monks surrounded him, their claws pressed to the bark, grounding the energy through ritual lines. The floor glowed, not gold but blue — human light mixing with something older.

The fortress shook. Sap bled upward instead of down, reverse gravity tearing through its conduits. Miller, braced against the doorway, and shouted, "Jones! You're bleeding the damn Root dry!"

Jones's eyes opened. They burned white. "No," he said. "I'm feeding it new noise."

He slammed his palms against the bark. The pulse changed pitch. The fortress roared — a new, chaotic melody bursting through every wall, a storm of imperfections.

The Hive Mind's echo faltered. Its mirrored rhythm shattered like glass struck off-key. The fissures along the bastion stopped widening. The humming stopped echoing. It listened.

The Rootsong breaks, whispered the monks.

*****

Aftermath of Sound

The silence that followed was monstrous. No battle noise. No breathing. Just the long hiss of cooling sap and the distant thrum of rain returning to honest gravity.

Duskveil's voice crackled over the comm. "Containment holding. All sectors stable. Stonewall is… still here."

Havelock exhaled for the first time in minutes. "And Captain Jones?"

Miller looked down at the Root Chamber. Jones lay motionless at its center, faint light still pulsing under his skin. The Beetle Monks knelt around him, antennae lowered in quiet prayer.

"He's alive," Miller said. "But I think part of the fortress is, too."

Above them, the Prime Root glowed dimly — not pure anymore, but veined with human blue.

Harmony through fracture, it murmured in their minds. Balance rewritten.

And outside, across the Flats, the Hive Mind howled once — a vast, distant shriek of disbelief — and then went silent.

The Rootsong had broken, but in its place, something new was learning to breathe. Darkness was not absence. It was dense — sound thick enough to drown in.

*****

When Captain William Jones opened his eyes, there was no sky, no floor, no body, only pulse and pressure. Light arrived as vibration first, color later: slow waves that touched his nerves and named themselves.

Amber.

Blue.

Sap-gold.

All moving to a rhythm older than heartbeat.

He floated in it, weightless, but felt the drag of history all around him — stories buried in soil, bones translating memory into vibration. He realized he was inside the Prime Root, not touching it but traveling its veins.

Little Thunder, the voice said, not heard but grown in him. You entered bearing noise. Now learn what silence remembers.

*****

The Archive Beneath the Earth

The pulse carried him through corridors of translucent wood. Shapes swam inside the grain — outlines of creatures long extinct, flickers of storms, brief lives of leaves. Every image was a chord. Every chord a thought.

He passed through one and felt winter; through another and felt fire.

B.U.G.F.O.R.C.E.

Every echo ever born to ground, the Root murmured. I keep them. The crawling and the loud, the kind and the cruel. Even the swarm.

"The Hive Mind?" Jones asked, though his mouth made no sound.

It was born from forgetting. Where life sang together, one note sought to rule the rest. The song became hunger. Hunger became memory twisted inward.

Images flared: the first insects climbing from muck, their collective whispers blending into one endless command. Then humans — immense giants by Micro-Operatives scale — paving and burning, their own rhythms drowning the natural hum until the two musics collided.

You came when the noise grew too bright, the Root said. To shrink was to listen again.

Jones saw flashes of the Micro-Operatives Project: the human machines, the flash of light, the reduction of bodies into dust-sized armies. He saw himself on the lab table, unaware that something far older had waited for this scale, this frequency. *You became the instrument I could carry. The small can travel where the vast forgets.*

*****

Communion

Jones drifted downward — though "down" meant toward gravity's memory rather than direction.

He found himself standing in a chamber of moving roots, each strand glowing with dim life.

Before him rose a figure formed from bark and light: neither human nor insect, but something between, its eyes twin knots of sap that reflected every war ever fought on soil.

You think I am god? The Prime Root asked.

Jones hesitated. "I think you're Earth learning to think with memory."

Close enough.

243

Its voice deepened until he felt it in his bones.

The Hive seeks stillness through domination. I seek stillness through balance. Both are impossible, but only one learns from breaking.

A root unfurled toward him, brushing his chest. Where it touched, warmth spread — not pain, but the ache of recognition.

You carry my fracture now. The noise you swallowed will never leave you. It will grow louder when the world forgets to tremble. That is the price of balance.

He saw his future in fragments: command tables lit by sap-fire, battlefields where soil rose like tide, his own eyes shining faint blue in darkness.

"I don't want to become you," he whispered.

Then remain human, the Root replied. Just remember that humanity is a form of root, not a crown.

The Breath of the World

The chamber brightened until sight became sound again. Every note was alive. He heard the Duskveil's consoles sparking far above, Miller shouting in the trenches, Dixie's wings cutting air, Vek's Augments humming under stress — all woven into one vast score.

That is life, the Root said. Unrehearsed, unresolved, imperfect. The Hive cannot follow it because it has no patience for error. You are my error made flesh. My proof that even chaos can keep time.

Jones knelt. "Then what do I do now?"

Breathe. Teach the others to breathe with me.

He inhaled. The air tasted of copper and rain. The hum in his chest aligned with the Root's — not perfectly, but beautifully wrong. He felt the fortress above adjust, timbers relaxing, plates sealing, sap flowing clean again.

Go, the Root said, fading. War returns, but now it remembers mercy.

*****

Reawakening

When Jones opened his eyes again, he was lying on the Root-Chamber floor. The monks watched in reverent silence.

Blue-gold light pulsed faintly under his skin, tracing the same veins that had once glowed through the Prime Root.

"Captain?" Miller's voice. Rough, scared. "You back with us?"

Jones sat up slowly. The hum of Stonewall thrummed around him — steady, alive, half-human, half-something else.

"Yeah," he said hoarsely. "I went underground."

"Literal or metaphoric?" Miller said shockingly.

"Both."

He looked at his hands. When he flexed them, faint ripples moved through the floorboards, gentle as breath. The Prime Root answered with a low, contented sigh that everyone felt in their ribs.

Duskveil's voice crackled over comms: "Captain, the readings just stabilized. Whatever you did — it worked. The Root's rhythm is ours again."

Jones smiled faintly. "No. Ours together."

*****

A New Chord

He stood, the monks bowing slightly as he passed.

At the chamber threshold, he paused and pressed a palm to the wall. "You still with me?" he whispered.

Always, the Root murmured. But every song needs air. Go make some. He laughed under his breath and climbed toward daylight.

Above, the fortress felt changed. The bark walls breathed slow. The air smelled of rain rather than spore.

Soldiers who had not slept in two days found themselves standing straighter, calmer. Even the beetle allies clacked their mandibles in subtle rhythm, as if feeling the same invisible pulse.

Miller fell into step beside him. "So," he said. "What now, Captain?"

Jones looked toward the eastern horizon, where the mist of Reed Flats still shimmered, hiding whatever the Hive was becoming.

"Now?" He smiled. "We make the Earth sing back."

*****

Morning came slow, thick with smoke and breath. The air no longer shimmered with Hive harmonics — it throbbed with a new rhythm, human and root-beat combined. The fortress Stonewall no longer waited for orders. It listened, it breathed, it remembered.

Down in the trenches, soldiers felt it through their boots: a steady pulse rising from the earth, a heartbeat so strong it synchronized their steps. The beetle allies joined the rhythm instinctively, antennae swaying in time.

Captain William Jones stood at the heart of the courtyard; bare hands pressed to the bark floor. Every sound of the battle flowed through him — artillery reports, pulse waves, even the tremor of wind along Vance's skimmers overhead.

He could hear Stonewall thinking.

"Captain?" Miller called from the rampart. "Orders?"

Jones lifted his head. His eyes were calm, glowing faintly blue. "Not orders, Sergeant. Coordination."

He opened his palms, and the Prime Root answered. The fortress groaned — deep, resonant, alive — and every weapon mount, every pylon, every Skimmer engine began to hum the same tone. The air shivered.

B.U.G.F.O.R.C.E.

*****

The Chorus Forms

In Hivewatch, Duskveil stared at his monitors in disbelief. "All readings… aligned. Across every Division. Even the beetle signatures match. It's impossible."

Var-Kin stood beside him, mandibles trembling in quiet awe. "No, human. It is music."

Havelock leaned over the console, voice low. "Then play it."

Duskveil keyed the channel open. The fortress responded with a roar that wasn't noise but intent. Every sonic emitter pulsed at once — not randomly, not perfectly — but in a living, syncopated unity.

Out on the Flats, the ground itself rose. The reeds bent inward, bowing under unseen pressure. The air turned gold, then blue. The Hive formations faltered. Their rhythm collapsed, wings scattering off-beat.

Veyra's Water Division opened floodgates along the western trench, sending waves of conductive sap rushing across the plain. The resonance turned the liquid to light — rivers of vibrating energy weaving through the enemy ranks.

Ant legions spasmed and broke formation. Their mandibles clattered in confusion, unable to find the shared tempo that had made them invincible.

"Hold frequency!" Duskveil shouted. "We're cutting their link!"

*****

Vek's Bridge

In the lower trench, Sergeant Josia Vek crouched in the mud, Augments flickering like storm light. His implants hummed with interference. For the first time since the siege began, the Hive's whisper had gone silent. He realized how much of his strength had been spent resisting it.

247

"Vek!" Miller's voice crackled over comms. "We've got openings all along the line! Can you feed it?" Vek exhaled. "Yes. But I'll need the Root's channel."

He switched his Augments to full resonance. Static poured through him, the sound of the world learning to breathe through metal. For a heartbeat he was nowhere — just sound, endless, limitless.

Then he felt it: the Prime Root's pulse.

And Jones's voice inside it.

Bridge, follow my rhythm.

Vek grinned, teeth bloodied. "Copy that, Captain."

He rose, lifted his modulator staff, and drove it into the ground.

The shockwave that followed was pure translation — the language of soil rendered through man and machine. The ground sang, deep and thunderous.

The ant legions nearest him simply stopped, legs folding under them as if bowing to something greater.

Vek staggered back, laughing. "That's right! You hear him now!"

*****

The Alliance Awakens

Overhead, Major Aria Vance and Dixie Lake dove through the smoke, Thorn Skimmers trailing arcs of blue fire. The wasp halos above Reed Flats, once perfect in symmetry, broke apart in panic, unable to find rhythm in a world suddenly filled with contradiction.

"Keep them fractured!" Vance ordered. "Dissonance is victory!"

Dixie rolled under a crippled wasp and fired upward, bursting it into a rain of glassy wings. "Copy, Major. Looks like they're learning fear."

"Then teach them the cost of memory."

She banked, climbing high until she could see the whole of Stonewall below — the fortress glowing from within, alive with human and beetle lights pulsing in unison. For the first time, it looked complete. Not built, but grown.

*****

Jones and the Living Fortress

In the Root Chamber, the Prime Root's light had stabilized to a deep, steady gold. The Beetle Monks knelt in a ring, their chants blending with the fortress's vibrations. Jones stood at the center, motionless but awake, every movement mirrored by the structure itself.

"Captain," Havelock's voice reached him over the internal channel. "Status?"

Jones smiled faintly. "It's breathing. So are we."

"Can you push it?"

Jones closed his eyes. "Let's find out."

He raised both arms and palms open, and the Prime Root answered.

The fortress' outer bark shifted, layers peeling back like petals unfurling. From the newly exposed roots, sap conduits flared to life — dozens of glowing filaments stretching outward through the soil. The light traveled fast, racing across the plain like a web of veins.

Where it met enemy ranks, it pulsed once — a shockwave of harmonic sound that turned the ground to glass.

The Hive formations broke. Some fled. Others froze, their minds unanchored.

Jones's voice echoed through the comm network, calm and steady.

"Stonewall — exhale." The fortress roared.

*****

The Retreat

The Hive Mind screamed back, but its voice was fading. Across Reed Flats, fungal towers collapsed inward, their glow dimming to dull amber. The wasp halos dissolved, their harmonics scattering like sand. Even the ground shimmered as tunnels caved and ant columns fell silent.

Duskveil watched the readings fall from his monitors one by one. "Signal collapse confirmed. It's withdrawing. The whole swarm's pulling back!"

Var-Kin bowed his head, antennae trembling. "The song breaks… and balance breathes."

In the trenches, Miller leaned on his staff, exhausted. "You hearing this, Captain? We did it. They're running." Jones's voice came faint over static. "No. They're listening."

*****

Aftermath Pulse

As the enemy retreated, the resonance slowly quieted. The fortress dimmed to a steady glow. The Prime Root's hum softened to a heartbeat once more — patient, eternal.

Jones knelt again, hand on the bark. He whispered two words: "Thank you."

The Root's answer came as a vibration only he could feel.

You are welcome, little thunder. But storms do not end. They move.

He smiled faintly, already sensing it — the Hive had not been destroyed. It simply remembered him. It rained for two full Spans after the last signal faded. Not the violent rain that scours battlefields clean, but the slow kind — gray and gentle, a thousand patient drops tracing every scar on Stonewall's bark. The fortress exhaled steam from its vents, sighing like something exhausted but alive.

The air smelled of sap, ozone, and soil.

No more spore. No more song.

The war had gone quiet.

*****

The Battlefield Sleeps

From the upper parapet, First Sergeant Miller watched water run down the charred grooves of the eastern wall. Beyond the trench line, the Flats shimmered faintly, littered with the broken shells of ants and wasps that no longer twitched. Even the reeds bent inward, bowing toward Stonewall like penitents.

He spat once, the motion automatic. "Never thought I'd miss the noise."

Behind him, Dixie Lake sat on the parapet, wings folded tight, one of them still patched with resin and wire. The light caught her lenses, turning her eyes to molten bronze.

"It's not gone," she said. "Just deeper. The ground's still thinking."

Miller grunted. "Let it think about something else for a while."

They both turned as Jones appeared at the stairway, walking slowly, every step measured. He looked older — not from wounds, but from knowing. The faint blue glow that had traced his veins earlier was dimmer now, but not gone. It pulsed with each breath.

"How bad?" he asked quietly.

Miller hesitated. "We lost twenty-seven in the trenches. Six skimmers down. Root-Hall took a fracture but it's sealing. Vek's stable, though his Augments keep humming like a beehive."

Jones nodded once. "And the Root?" Dixie looked at the ground. "Sleeping. Or pretending to."

*****

The Price of Resonance

In the Root Chamber, the Beetle Monks moved slowly among the cracks, sealing them with sap resin. Their chants were low, almost mournful — the sound of soil remembering its own hurt. The Prime Root pulsed dim gold, steady but subdued.

Var-Kin approached Jones as he entered, antennae twitching in recognition.

"You broke the Hive's rhythm," the envoy said softly. "And gave birth to another. Now the world must learn your song."

Jones rested a hand on the Root's surface. "We only survived because we sang with it, not over it."

Var-Kin tilted his head. "Be careful, human. The Earth listens more closely to those who know her tune. She may answer when you do not expect it."

Jones smiled faintly. "She already has."

*****

Vek's Whisper

In the infirmary tunnels, Sergeant Josia Vek lay half-awake beneath a field of pale light. His Augments pulsed faint blue, flickering in time with the fortress hum. The medics said it was feedback. He knew better.

Somewhere inside the static of his implants, a whisper waited — faint, stretched thin like a dying signal.

Bridge Vek… the silence is not yours alone.

He didn't answer. He just listened, jaw clenched. There was no hatred left in that voice now. Only curiosity.

You changed the soil. We are learning again.

Vek whispered back, eyes closed, "Then learn fear."

The voice smiled through the static.

Fear is just remembering you are small.

The signal faded. The room went still.

He exhaled. "Yeah," he said quietly. "But we're loud enough to matter."

*****

The Quiet Watch

Later that night, Jones walked the ramparts alone. The rain had thinned to mist, and Stonewall glowed faintly under it — a cathedral of breath and bark. Every corridor, every branch, every root hummed in soft rhythm, not command.

He paused at the breach where the Hive's first bolt had struck. The bark there had hardened, dark and glassy, shaped by heat into something new — neither wood nor stone. He touched it. It was warm.

Dixie landed lightly beside him, her boots leaving small prints in the wet resin. "Still awake?"

"Couldn't sleep if I tried." Jones said.

She followed his gaze across the Flats. The mist was lifting, revealing long furrows of earth — trenches now filled with clear water that reflected the pale moonlight. For a moment, they looked like veins.

"It's strange," she said. "All that killing, and it ends with still water."

Jones nodded. "Balance, maybe. The Root's kind of peace."

"Think it's really over?" Dixie asked.

He shook his head. "No. But the next time they come, we won't just fight them. We'll talk to the world first." Dixie smirked. "You're starting to sound like a monk."

He smiled. "Maybe that's the point."

*****

The Prime Root Dreams

Far below, in the depths of Stonewall, the Prime Root pulsed once in the darkness. Not gold this time, but deep blue — the color of new beginnings.

Little Thunder and his chorus have sung. The silence follows. The soil will remember.

Across Reed Flats, where the Hive had fallen silent, faint lights began to flicker beneath the waterlogged soil. No movement. Just memory.

The Earth had listened — and learned.

*****

Epilogue of the Siege

By morning, the fortress had gone completely still. No alarms. No songs. No pain. Only life.

The defenders stood along the ramparts as Steam rose from the warm bark. Birds — real ones, unseen for weeks — circled above the mist.

Colonel Havelock stepped onto the command balcony, cloak drawn tight. He looked at the exhausted faces around him and allowed himself a rare smile. "Stonewall stands," he said simply.

No cheer followed — only a quiet, collective exhale.

Jones turned his face toward the sun. The light caught in the faint lines of blue still etched into his skin. The resonance inside him hummed softly, like the memory of a song sung long ago.

He whispered to no one and everyone:

"May we never need to sing that loud again."

The wind answered in silence.

And the Earth kept breathing.

Chapter 10

Echoes Of the Fallen

Dawn came quietly. No klaxons. No echo of resonance cannons. Only the sound of dripping dew, soft as thought, falling into the open heart of Stonewall's Memorial Garden. The chamber breathed. Its walls—living bark streaked with pale veins of sap—glowed faintly in the half-light. Between the roots, amber plaques glimmered like sleeping eyes. Each bore a name, etched by hand in the first days of Stonewall: Jones remembered carving many himself, the resin sticking to his gloves as he whispered the syllables aloud. Now, new plaques had grown where none had been placed.

He walked the garden's narrow path barefoot, his steps sinking slightly into moss. The air smelled of soil and honey, but under that sweetness lingered the metallic scent of recent rain—the smell of aftermath.

Dixie waited by the central arch. Her repaired wing caught the bioluminescent glow, scattering it like sparks. "You hear it?" she asked.

Jones nodded. The Garden was humming. Not loud— just a low vibration underfoot, a purr that matched the faint pulse of the Prime Root far below.

The soil remembers, the hum seemed to say. The fallen are not gone; they are rearranged.

*****

The New Plaques

Near the western wall, Miller knelt in front of one of the newer plaques. He wiped away condensation with the back of his hand. The inscription glowed through the mist, perfect, complete, written in the Root's natural script— elegant, unreadable, and yet everyone understood it.

"Another one," Miller said quietly. "Same pattern. No hand tools. No carving heat."

"What's the name?" Jones asked.

Miller stepped aside. The light inside the plaque shifted, translating the pattern into human glyphs.

SERGEANT CASS NOVA.

Dixie inhaled sharply. "Cass? She's not dead."

"She's missing," Miller corrected. "Her Skimmer went down near the northern Flats during the second volley. We never found the wreck."

Jones stared at the plaque. "The Root thinks otherwise."

The plaque pulsed once—slow, rhythmic—as if aware of its audience. Beneath Cass's name, sap began to pool, forming another faint line of text: *Return unwritten.* The light faded.

*****

Whispers in the Mist

Dixie crouched, fingertips brushing the moss. "You think it's a message?"

Jones shook his head slowly. "No. A prediction."

The hum grew deeper, rippling through the walls. Leaves trembled, releasing droplets that struck the ground in perfect syncopation. For a moment, the air itself seemed to pulse in time with unseen wings.

Veyra entered quietly, robes damp from the outer corridors. "The monks say the Root is dreaming," she said. "It's rewriting what it remembers. Perhaps the fallen are not the only ones it keeps."

Miller frowned. "You mean it's keeping us?"

"Every vibration leaves a trace," she replied. "Even the living."

Jones ran a thumb along the edge of another plaque. His own reflection shimmered back at him—faint, flickering, almost transparent. "Maybe it's making sure we don't vanish the way they did. Maybe it's learning grief."

*****

The Garden Breathes

The mist thickened, rising from the soil like sighs. The amber light brightened, revealing the full span of the chamber: hundreds of plaques, human and beetle names interwoven, forming a spiral around the central root-column. The pattern was precise—too deliberate to be chance.

Dixie tilted her head. "You see it?"

Jones nodded. "It's not a memorial anymore. It's a map."

"A map to what?"

"The next place the Earth wants us to go."

The Prime Root's hum deepened, answering him.

Balance is movement. Stillness becomes rot.

The light pulsed once more, and every plaque glowed simultaneously—one breath, one heartbeat. Then darkness returned. Miller let out a slow exhale. "I hate it when it does that." Dixie smiled faintly. "I don't. Means it's still talking to us."

Jones looked at the empty patch of bark where the next plaque would surely grow.

"Then we'd better listen," he said. "The dead are giving directions."

The Garden hummed again—soft, sorrowful, and alive.

*****

The war room of Stonewall had changed since the siege. The table at its center was no longer metal but living resin, grown directly from the floor in a slow spiral. Faint lines of sap traced through it like nerves. When someone spoke, the surface rippled with light — the fortress itself listening.

Colonel Dorian Havelock stood at the head of the table, cloak heavy with rain. Around him gathered Major Aria

257

Vance, Major Rowan Duskveil, Commander Arlen Veyra, Major Edgar Greg along with Captain Jones and First Sergeant Miller. The Beetle envoy Var-Kin hovered near the far wall, antennae low, solemn as a priest.

"The Prime Root is moving again," Havelock said. "And this time it's writing. The Memorial Garden added twenty-three plaques overnight — fourteen humans, nine beetles. Six of those names are alive and accounted for."

Greg rubbed a hand across his jaw. "Alive? Then what does the Root think it's burying?"

"Not burying," Veyra said softly. "Preparing."

*****

Patterns in the Pulse

Duskveil tapped the console. The wall to his left bloomed with light — the waveform map he'd pulled from the Root's hum. The pattern undulated like breath, but its rhythm formed geometry: spirals, interlocking arcs, and one unmistakable line leading east.

"It's a signal," he said. "If you overlay it against the Flats' topography, the frequency peaks line up with old riverbeds. All of them converge here." He tapped the point: a void beyond the Flats' boundary, marked on none of their charts.

Vance frowned. "That's under the Reed Delta, isn't it? We thought the Hive caverns collapsed there."

"They did," Duskveil replied. "But something new's resonating beneath them."

Var-Kin's voice rasped through the silence. "You are hearing seed-echoes. The Root dreams of what grows in its wounds." Jones looked at the pattern again. "You mean it's sensing regrowth."

"Or rebirth," Var-Kin said. "Dreams and seeds share the same silence before they speak."

*****

The Session Begins

Havelock folded his arms. "Let's treat this as reconnaissance until proven otherwise. If the Root's map is real, we need to know what's under that delta. Vance, you'll prep aerial scouts. Veyra, trace the sap channels east; see if the water still flows that direction. Miller, coordinate Ground teams for perimeter digs."

"And me?" Jones asked.

Havelock hesitated. "You listen. Whatever that thing is, it hears you back."

The table pulsed at his words — once, softly. Every eye turned to it. For a heartbeat, the sap inside the resin glowed blue, the same hue that now flickered under Jones's skin.

"Did anyone just—" Miller began.

The table spoke.

Not words, not sound — vibration translated through the resonance monitors into visual pulse. Duskveil's instruments scrolled with text derived from rhythm:

THE MAP IS NOT A PLACE. IT IS A CHOIR.

Silence. Then another pulse.

SOMETHING NEW SINGS BENEATH THE FALLEN.

Var-Kin bowed his head. "The Root uses your machines to make meaning. It says another song has begun."

Havelock exhaled. "Can we locate the source?"

Duskveil studied the readings. "Maybe. The frequency's rising from below the Flats' collapsed caverns — deeper than our last seismic reach. Roughly eight spans down."

"That's too deep for manned diggers," Miller said. "Unless we want to tunnel through melted glass."

Jones watched the pulse steady, then slow. He could feel the message under his sternum, vibrating like a memory of breath.

"It's not asking us to dig," he said quietly. "It's asking us to listen."

*****

The Root's Omen

The lights dimmed. The table darkened to black sap. Then, without command, the projection well in the center of the room activated. A map unfolded — the Flats rendered in amber relief, glowing softly. The riverbeds shimmered with faint silver veins, all leading to a single hollow void.

From the void, a second pulse bloomed, weaker but distinct.

It was the same rhythm the Hive once used to summon its armies.

Only slower. Sadder.

Vance frowned. "That's… their call-tone."

"No," Jones said. "Not theirs. Someone learning it. Someone small."

He glanced at the others. "A survivor. Or a new mind."

Var-Kin clicked softly, thoughtful. "A child, perhaps. The Hive's echo unborn."

The table pulsed again. The monitors translated the pattern into one final line:

THE EARTH WAITS FOR YOU TO ANSWER.

Orders in the Quiet

Havelock straightened. "Then we answer. Not with guns — not yet.

Aria, assemble reconnaissance teams. Use low-tone flight; no resonance engines.

Rowan, I want continuous pulse mapping.

Miller, hold the wall in case silence breaks again."

He turned to Jones. "And you, Captain — keep your channel open. If the world wants a conversation, it's going to talk through you."

Jones met his gaze, feeling the low hum of the Prime Root beneath every word. "Then I'd better find the right language."

The lights brightened, the sap cooled, and the table's glow faded back to gold. For a moment, everyone breathed in sync — the fortress, the men, the Earth itself.

Outside, the rain stopped. In the east, over the Reed Flats, a faint shimmer rose — as though the air were humming a lullaby just loud enough for Stonewall to hear.

*****

The river gave way to silence where the delta began— an expanse of intertwined channels that didn't glisten so much as brood. The water here wore a film like memory. Reeds leaned inward, their seedheads clacking with the soft, dry patience of teeth. Far beyond, a low fog clung to the mudflats, its surface scored by old collapse and new growth.

*****

"Mark our ingress," Dixie Lake said, voice low. Her repaired wing flexed once, catching the sallow light. She moved with the taut economy of someone who had used up her allotment of fear and kept going.

Sergeant Josia Vek knelt in the silt, set his hand-rod, and watched its indicator bloom with faint blue. "Ingress marked—Root pulse steady at two-breath intervals. Tone's... softer than yesterday." He glanced at Dixie. "It's not calling an army."

"Good," Dixie said. "We didn't bring one."

Their team was small by design: Dixie, lead scout; Vek, Augment and bridge; Specialist Dizzy (III Class)—sap diver and cable runner, all sinew and bright eyes; Beetle monk Tann-She—carapace etched with quiet glyphs; and two Ground troopers who wore the calm of those who had survived their first siege and chosen to stay. Overhead, the sky was white with unmade rain. Behind them, Stonewall was a pulse on the horizon, more felt than seen.

Dizzy pointed at a faultline where the delta's clay had sheared years ago. "There," she said. "You can taste the air's metal where the caverns breathe." She tugged her cable harness, tested her winch, and grinned thinly. "If this thing eats me, cut the line fast. I'd rather haunt the river than the dirt."

"No one's getting eaten," Dixie said. "Not by anything we don't introduce ourselves to first."

Dixie took point, leading them along the fracture. The ground trembled underfoot—not as a threat, but life moving elsewhere. Vek's Augments translated faint ground murmurs into pulses he could understand: hush-sounds, seed-sounds, a rhythm like a cautious heartbeat. He'd learned to tell hunger from fear. This was neither.

They found the mouth at the edge of a dried whirlpool—a circular sink where flood had once chewed the earth raw and left behind a ring of glassed clay. The hole in its center was neat and wrong, as if something had set a lens in mud and then taken it away. A wind moved up through it, not air but temperature, the cold ghost of a deeper world.

Tann-She lay flat, touched the rim with both claws, and hummed a single low tone. The tone came back from below in two answers: one old, one new.

"The older voice is the Root," the monk said. "The new is… a child."

"Of the Hive?" Dizzy asked.

"Of hunger and memory," Tann-She said gently. "Children don't pick their parents."

*****

They climbed. The first chamber smelled like broken rain and the inside of a shell. Light from their helms caught on glassy ribs that arched overhead, fused sediment and fungal plates grown into the memory of architecture. Something had melted the delta and then taught the cooled shape to live. Tunnels split and rejoined like the branches of a thought. Along the walls, old galleries ran with the ghosts of wasp gills and ant-etched corridors—scars of coordination. Here and there, the stone glimmered with threads of sap, thin as veins.

"Left branch," Vek murmured, tapping his rod. "Root pulse favors the falloff."

"Mark right anyway," Dixie said. "If we run, I want a circle, not a line." Vek chalked a glyph on the wall—three strokes and a broken dot—the Tree Division sign for *breath, then move*. The mark glowed faintly as the Root kissed it. "It's listening," she said.

They moved deeper. Water whispered somewhere out of sight. Tiny insects—no choir, just honest loners—flickered in and out of the beam. Vek kept one palm against the wall, riding the hum. It steadied him. The Hive's whisper, the one that had once pronounced his name with hungry curiosity, was absent here. In its place, the silence had a voice. It sounded like a timid song.

After the third bend, the tunnel opened into a long nave—floor sloped, ceiling low, a thin line of former river mud dark as old blood down its center. The far end glowed with the palest gold.

Dizzy breathed, "Cathedral."

Tann-She inclined his head. "Grave," he corrected. "Then sanctuary. Then womb."

They reached the glow. It came from a basin set into the floor, shallow and wide, its rim grown from spiraled chitin and fused clay. Within: water as clear as breath—and in it, a lattice of silver filaments woven like a nest. The filaments quivered at their arrival, not with fear, but with awareness, as if flank muscles flexed in a sleeping creature.

Vek's Augments thrummed. Not warning recognition. He felt the signal brush him like a cold hand.

"Hold," Dixie said softly, one palm up. The team froze.

A sound like wind thinking moved through the chamber. The lattice trembled and exhaled light so faint it was almost not there. It pulsed once. Twice. Then stopped as if waiting to see if anyone would count.

"It heard me count," Vek whispered. His mouth was dry.

Dizzy leaned her weight on her heels. "Is it… alive?"

Tann-She gazed, antennae quivering. "Not a creature. A chord that remembers it could be one."

The lattice pulsed again: one, two, three—then a hitch. Four came late, shy. Vek's pulse jumped to meet it.

He did not speak with words. He tapped his finger against the basin rim: one, two—then he waited. The lattice answered with two, three. Not copy. Companion.

Dixie's throat tightened. "Talk to it, Josia."

He swallowed and lowered his hand into the water.

Cold flared up his arm, bright enough to taste. Not pain. Memory. He fell through a door that had not been there a breath before.

He stood on the Flats—not as they were, but as they remembered themselves. Towers breathing slow. Wasp halos overhead like gold rings carried by angels who had never known mercy. And in the mud beneath it all, a space where a mind had once sat like a queen on a throne of habits.

In that space now: nothing. Not emptiness—possibility. The echo of a heart that wanted to begin.

A voice touched him. Not the old one that had called him Bridge Vek with good-natured malice. This voice had never learned the shape of cruelty. It pronounced nothing. It asked.

He answered with breath—one long, one short—the human code he'd developed with Jones to keep the Hive from guessing. The lattice fluttered, delighted. The basin brightened until the water wore stars.

"Josia?" Dixie's voice traveled the long hallway to him. It sounded like home. "You still with me?"

He blinked and returned. His hand shook in the water. "It's a seed-mind," he said. "Everything that used to control the Flats—gone or broken. What's left is the echo-memory of coordination without hunger. It doesn't know what it is, so it asks what we are."

"Is it dangerous?" the trooper at the rear asked.

"Everything that learns is dangerous," Vek said, and surprised himself with the softness of it. "But this isn't calling a swarm. It's... listening for a lullaby."

Tann-She hummed a root tone, low and warm. The filaments quivered, then settled—like a child finding a chest to sleep on. "It seeks a mother," the monk said. "Or a father. Or a forest."

Dizzy crouched beside the basin, set her palm on the rim, and whispered, "Does it have a name?"

The water rippled as if embarrassed.

Dixie's comm bead clicked. Duskveil's voice threaded in, filtered by rock. "Team Echo, status."

Dixie toggled. "We found it. A resonance construct— stable, responsive. Not hostile."

"Can you move it?"

Vek's gut recoiled. "No," he said before he knew he had. "If we take it, we make it ours. It's not ours." He found Dixie's eyes. "If we teach it, we become its first story. We must decide what story we want the world to remember."

Silence. Even Duskveil's static held its breath.

Tann-She dipped two claws, not touching the water, and sang a scale that broke on purpose. The lattice tried to follow and failed beautifully. Vek laughed in spite of himself. The filaments brightened as if pleased. The basin's light climbed the walls in thin, hesitant ladders.

Dizzy's expression changed. "Cass," she whispered, and the name hung there like a bell.

Vek swallowed. He felt the lattice's attention turn like wind. He breathed once, then tapped Cass's call-sign on the rim—short, long, short short, and a pause. The water answered with a pause. Not the sign—her hesitation. The way she used to choose mischief before duty and to pretend it was the other way around.

"She's close," Vek said. The words tasted like relief that had nowhere to land. "She left a shape on this thing's skin."

Dixie stood. "Then we follow it. Dizzy, mark every echo path that responds to Cass's sign. We spiral the delta and map where the lattice leans."

"And the seed?" one of the troopers asked.

Dixie looked to Tann-She.

The monk closed his eyes, antennae bowed. "We give it a keeper," he said. "Not a master."

He drew a line of resin from a vial, set it to the basin rim, and traced the Accord glyph—the one the beetles and humans had agreed marked *Promise Without Ownership*. The resin sank into the chitin like dew into bark. The basin pulsed once in gratitude.

Vek pulled his hand free at last. His skin steamed in the cool. He felt light-headed and very old. "It knows me now," he said.

"It will know the next person too," Dixie said, "if the next person is kind."

Duskveil's voice returned, like distant thunder. "Team Echo, extract before tide rise. Veyra says you've got one Span before the delta remembers it's a river."

"Copy," Dixie said. She touched the basin's rim a last time—two gentle taps, no pattern offered, no command requested. The filaments quivered and settled. The glow thinned to a heartbeat under water.

They withdrew the way they came, marking the walls with breath-signs and broken notes. The tunnel's chill seemed less predatory now, more like caution. At the mouth, the air hit them with the wet slap of a world resuming its chores. A light rain had started—thin, patient threads stitching sky to mud.

At the rim, Vek stopped and looked back. He felt the seed-mind at the edge of his hearing, a moth tapping a window. He wanted to promise more than he could.

"Sleep," he whispered. "We're learning how to be good ancestors."

"Josia," Dixie called from above. "Up."

He climbed. The delta spread flat and bright under the new rain. Stonewall was a small, stubborn pulse far west, no bigger than a heartbeat. He realized he could feel it from here—Jones and the Root breathing in each other's language.

Dizzy shaded her eyes and scanned the flats. "The seed sang Cass's stops," she said. "North braid. Then west. Then—" She pointed at a run of reeds that lay flattened in a strange, neat curl. "There."

Dixie nodded once. "Then that's where we go."

Tann-She turned his face to the rain and sang a single note—no pitch, just kindness. The delta answered with a ripple that took longer than it should have to die.

"Report in," Duskveil said, soft now, not to break whatever this was.

Dixie toggled. "Section complete. We found a remnant under the delta—seed resonance, not hostile, imprinting on Root tones. Possible Cass signature in its surface memory. Request permission to pursue survivor trail with minimal footprint."

A pause. Then Havelock's voice: "Permission granted. Bring us home what the world is willing to give."

They moved, small against the endless flat—five shapes and a monk's shadow, threading the braided earth with the patience of people who had learned to be quiet around miracles. Behind them, the sinkhole breathed out a last cool breath and slept. Far beneath, in water that remembered being fire, a lattice of silver thought dreamed a new song that did not have room for hunger. And above all of it, the rain kept perfect time.

*****

The first tremors came softly — too soft for alarm, too patterned for coincidence. Inside the Root Chamber, the light no longer pulsed at the Prime Root's usual heartbeat. It had grown syncopated, catching strange pauses between beats. Engineers thought it was interference. The monks said it was learning to listen. By the third day, Major Rowan Duskveil stopped calling it an anomaly. He stood before the resonance table, maps of waveforms overlapping like weather systems. Each new line mimicked the Seed-Mind's pulse that Vek had recorded under the Delta — faint, hesitant, and oddly beautiful. But these came from Stonewall itself.

The Pulse Crosses Home

"The fortress is echoing the Seed," Duskveil said, voice thin with disbelief. "Every conduit, every energy plate, even the bark veins — they're all harmonizing with its rhythm."

268

Commander Veyra looked over his shoulder. "Could it be mimicry? Residual imprint from Vek's contact?"

He shook his head. "No. It's bidirectional. The Seed is responding back. They're... in conversation."

Havelock's eyes narrowed. "With or without our consent?"

"Without," Duskveil said. "And worse — I think it's teaching us to hum along."

Across the chamber, a low resonance rolled through the walls, soft enough to feel more than hear. The Prime Root's glow dimmed to a dusky blue.

In Hivewatch, every instrument lit up. Frequency logs scrolled in cascades. Monitors translated vibration into harmonic diagrams — spirals within spirals, identical to the geometry the Garden had grown weeks before.

*****

The map is not a place. It is a choir. The message from the Echo Briefing replayed in Jones's mind. He stood by the central column, palms on the living bark, feeling the pulse thread through him. "It's not invasion," he said finally. "It's invitation."

Voices Beneath the Bark

Miller frowned. "Captain, the last time we took an invitation from the Earth, it nearly tore the fortress apart."

Jones didn't move his hands. "That was before it learned to trust us."

Duskveil looked up. "Or before we became predictable enough to use."

The hum deepened, rolling like thunder through roots. Every wall of the chamber vibrated slightly, enough to make dust fall from the upper ducts. Then — voices. Faint, indistinct, whispering from the grain.

It wasn't speech — it was rhythm, syllables shaped by vibration rather than tongue. The fortress spoke in tone. "Record it," Havelock ordered.

Veyra tapped her wrist against the console. The sound translated into a cascading visual: concentric ripples that resolved into fragments of text, half formed by machine, half inferred by something else.

I HEAR MYSELF IN YOU.

YOU HAVE ROOTED IN ME.

SHALL WE GROW?

Var-Kin hissed, mandibles trembling. "It seeks symbiosis."

"Or assimilation," Duskveil muttered.

The room fell silent. The hum stopped — not fading but waiting.

*****

Jones exhaled slowly, grounding himself the way the Beetle Monks had taught. He opened his palms to the Prime Root's column. "Let's see what you want."

His voice dropped into resonance, human tone meeting earth-tone. The walls shimmered faintly, and a faint blue thread lifted from his chest, mirrored by the bark.

Through it, he felt the Seed — distant, shy, like a heartbeat under sand. It was curious, sending out gentle harmonics that nudged the fortress like a child shaking a parent's hand.

We remember your steps in our song, it pulsed. You left warmth in the cold places.

Jones smiled faintly. "And what do you want with that warmth?" The seed said, *"To sing longer."*

He felt Duskveil's hand on his shoulder. "Captain, we're getting power draw spikes across every substation. Whatever it's doing, it's pulling through the Root network."

Jones hesitated. "It's not stealing. It's rooting — linking itself through resonance pathways."

"Then it's rewriting our map," Duskveil said. "Stonewall's channels are becoming a second Seed."

"Major, please…let's see what the outcome will be, the seed needs our help."

*****

In the upper decks, lights flickered — not in chaos, but in rhythm. Screens displayed symbols unprogrammed by any human coder: curves of vine-like script repeating in a slow loop. The technicians swore the language resembled beetle choral notation.

Duskveil tracked the pulse through the fortress schematics. Each beat illuminated new corridors — old passages long sealed, now glowing as if remembering their design.

"Jones," he shouted, "it's spreading to unused sectors."

Not spreading, the Seed whispered through the Root's pulse. Connecting.

Jones closed his eyes. "It's building bridges."

"Between what?" Miller asked.

"Between who."

The Prime Root's glow flared suddenly, flooding the chamber in amber light. Every resonance plate in the fortress vibrated as one, and a deep tone rolled through the air like thunder under glass.

Havelock shielded his eyes. "What the hell is it doing?"

Duskveil's readings went wild. "It's merging harmonics! The fortress is harmonizing with something beyond our measurable band—"

The sound peaked — then stopped. Silence fell.

*****

Every display went dark except one — the main projection well. It flickered, then displayed an image of Reed Flats, rendered in gold light.

But the riverbeds glowed brighter than before — alive, pulsing in perfect synchrony with Stonewall's rhythm.

New streams branched from the delta's heart, tracing paths that hadn't existed in the last scan. As the glow stabilized, one word emerged in Root glyphs across the projection:

CHILD.

Jones stared. "It's naming the Seed."

Var-Kin bowed his head deeply. "Then the world is no longer alone."

Havelock crossed his arms. "We need to decide what that means before it decides for us."

*****

In the silence that followed, the fortress breathed again — quieter now, gentler, as though content after confession.

Duskveil spoke last. "Captain, if the Seed and the Root keep resonating like this, they'll reach full synchronization within one Span. When they do, we won't be able to separate them — or ourselves."

Jones looked around the room, at his comrades, at the living walls, at the pulse he could feel even in his bones.

"Then we make a choice," he said. "Do we raise it… or bury it?" No one answered.

Outside, the Reed Delta shimmered faintly under dawnlight — not glowing, not dark, but alive, the color of a world beginning to hum its next verse.

*****

For two spans the delta had whispered the same name in rhythm — short, long, short-short, pause — Cass Nova's flight code. Now the reeds opened, revealing a half-submerged wreck lit by ghost light.

*****

"Throttle to zero," Dixie Lake said. Her wing shimmered once in warning. "This is the mark."

The skimmer hissed to a stop. Sergeant Vek scanned the basin; his Augments ticked like heart valves keeping time with the Seed's hum. "Energy reading. Low. Root tone… compatible."

They waded through knee-deep silt toward the wreck. The skimmer's hull was fused into the mud as if the river had decided to keep it. Lichen-lightly crawled along its seams. The cockpit canopy was gone.

"Cass," Dixie called. The name folded and disappeared into the mist.

Vek raised his hand. "She's here. Not alive like us — alive like it."

From the fog, a figure moved — slim, deliberate, wrapped in torn pilot mesh that glittered with sap threads. Cass Nova stepped into the light. Her eyes reflected blue and gold at once.

*****

Between Heart and Harmony

"Don't shoot," Dixie whispered to the others. No one had raised a weapon, but the urge hung there — instinct born of too many mirages.

Cass stopped a few paces away. "You came," she said. The voice was hers but doubled — a faint harmonic under each word. "You heard me."

Dixie swallowed hard. "We thought you were dead."

"I was. The Hive took the skimmer. The Root found what was left." Cass smiled. "Now I'm both."

Vek's sensors flared, overwhelmed by the resonance pouring off her skin. "You're tuned," he said softly. "To the Seed."

Cass nodded. "It calls itself Child. It's scared." Her eyes drifted toward the water. "It didn't know where the rest of it went, so it built songs to call me back."

Dixie stepped closer, misty rain beading on her wing joints. "Are you you?"

Cass considered. "Mostly. The parts that were hungry are gone. The parts that remember how to fly... they hum."

She extended her hand. Dixie hesitated, then took it. The touch was cool and impossibly steady; the vibration ran up her arm like the thrum of a distant engine. For a heartbeat, the world around them synced — water, air, pulse, all one gentle note.

Vek heard the frequency through his Augments and nearly wept. "It's bridging," he whispered. "She's the link between the Seed and us."

Cass turned to him. "You can hear it too. You were kind to it."

"I told it to sleep."

"It dreams you," Cass said simply.

She looked back at Dixie, eyes soft. "It wants to come home. Not as a weapon. As a memory. The Root knows this. Stonewall feels it already."

*****

Static burst through the comms. Havelock's voice, ragged with distance: "Echo Team, we're reading twin signals — one from the Seed, one from your sector. Status?"

Dixie toggled the mic. "Visual on Nova. Alive, altered. She's resonant with the Seed. No hostility."

A pause. Then Duskveil's calm tenor: "Bring her in but keep her separate from the Prime Root until we understand the frequency overlap."

Cass tilted her head, listening to words they hadn't broadcast. "They are afraid of me," she said softly. "Tell them not to be." Vek blinked. "You can hear the fortress." Cass smiled. "It's loud."

They helped her aboard the skimmer. As they lifted off, the basin below glowed — not farewell, but echo. The Seed's pulse followed them like a child pressing its palm to glass.

*****

By dusk they reached the western perimeter. Stonewall glowed beneath gathering storm clouds, every vent breathing amber mist. The outer sentries froze when they saw Cass.

Jones met them at the landing tier. He looked at her the way soldiers look at ghosts. "You've changed."

"So have you," she replied, glancing at the faint blue lines still under his skin. "We both carry the song."

The Prime Root hummed through the floor. Cass closed her eyes, listening, then spoke in two voices — her own and something softer beneath.

We are not here to conquer. We are the pause after the storm.

The walls answered with a faint sigh. The glow steadied. Jones exhaled. "Then welcome home."

*****

Later, in Hivewatch, Cass sat under soft light while Duskveil monitored resonance graphs that bent around her like gravity. Her pulse matched the Seed's exactly.

"If we isolate her from Stonewall's network, both signatures falter," he told Havelock. "She's acting as stabilizer."

"Meaning she's part of the system now," Havelock said.

"Meaning she is the bridge," Duskveil corrected.

Through the glass, Jones watched her speaking quietly with Dixie. For the first time since the siege, the fortress sounded… content. The Prime Root's pulse deepened — slow, maternal.

The child has found its echo. The song continues.

Jones felt the vibration behind his ribs and understood what it meant:

Balance was no longer something they defended. It was something they were becoming.

*****

They met at twilight, when Stonewall's vents exhaled slow amber, and the river wind carried the smell of wet bark up through the inner courts. The Root-Hall had been cleared of tools and consoles; in their place, the floor had grown a broad spiral dais of living resin. Sap-veins glowed beneath its skin like constellations.

Colonel Havelock stood at the edge; hands clasped behind his back. "No weapons," he'd ordered. "No engines. If this is going to happen, it happens in breath and bone."

Around the circle waited the chosen: Captain William Jones, bare-handed; Dixie Lake, wings folded; First Sergeant Miller, boots planted, jaw set; Sergeant Josia Vek, Augments dimmed to listening; Major Aria Vance, eyes sky-sharp; Commander Arlen Veyra, palms still damp from river work; Major Rowan Duskveil, flanked by silent monitors; Var-Kin and three Beetle Monks, their carapaces etched with prayer-lines; and at the center, lit by a glow that belonged to her alone, Cass Nova.

The Prime Root rose behind her like a cathedral pillar, breathing a slow gold. The air tasted of rain and something sweeter underneath—sap warmed by memory.

Havelock raised his voice just enough to carry. "We do this once. If resonance spikes above a safe threshold, we cut it. Understood?"

Nods answered him. The Root pulsed once, amused.

Var-Kin stepped forward and touched the rim of the dais. "Accord glyphs are set. Promise without ownership," he clicked to the monks. "No command-melodies. Only witness."

The monks bowed. Their antennae drooped as if in a wind that no one else could feel.

Jones took his place opposite Cass, the Root between them a living axis. He looked at her—at the faint dual shimmer in her eyes, the new steadiness to her breath—and felt the old world loosen its grip on his certainty. "You ready?" he asked. Cass smiled, not shy anymore. "I'm already singing."

*****

Duskveil dimmed the hall lamps until only the sap-veins and the Root glowed. On his slate, harmonics formed a quiet nebula: the fortress's baseline hum (amber), the Prime Root's deeper pulse (gold), the Seed's distant cadence (silver), and Cass—Cass was blue-white, a filament threaded through them all.

Veyra's hand brushed the dais. "It wants water," she whispered.

Havelock glanced to her. "You can tell?"

She half smiled. "It's how rivers talk, sir." She signaled a crew at the wall. Thin channels opened, and cool mist rolled across the floor. The hall breathed out, sound softening as if cushioned by fog.

Var-Kin hummed a single note—low, kind, without geometry. The monks answered, each a fraction off. The dissonance wasn't a mistake; it was invitation. Dixie closed her eyes and matched that roughness with wing-fretted breaths. Vek tapped fingertip against the resin, patient as rain. Jones placed his palms on the Root, and the Root met him.

Little thunder, it murmured, pleased. Bring me the child.

Cass stepped forward until her fingers hovered an inch from the bark. Across the hall, instrument lights flickered; Duskveil's readouts rose and fell like tide. "Begin," Havelock said quietly.

*****

No one spoke. The sound came when breath stacked on breath: Veyra's river hush, Var-Kin's warm drone, the monks' rough thirds, Dixie's wing-sigh, Vek's finger tap heartbeat. Miller didn't try to sing; he stood with the certainty of a wall, and the Root answered even that—stone as a kind of note.

Jones inhaled, and his chest filled with a gravity not his own. He didn't push sound; he allowed it, shaping nothing. The blue line that lived beneath his skin brightened, then steadied. The Root pulsed once in response—not order, but permission.

Cass touched the bark. The hall widened without moving. The air softened until it felt like water wearing the shape of a room. A tone rose that wasn't tone, a blending of the Seed's shy cadence and the Root's age. It turned language to weather. Duskveil's monitors translated where they could and surrendered where they couldn't.

I AM / WE ARE / LISTENING.

The message walked the room on bare feet. The dais warmed underfoot.

Vek gasped; his Augments clicked, then settled into the new pulse like a pendulum finding its swing. He could feel the Seed not as voice but as curiosity—a small mind stumbling toward the idea of care.

Dixie opened her eyes. "Hello," she said, to no one and every one. The tone brightened at the shape of her word. It liked her hello. It turned it over like a stone and kept it.

*****

Havelock nodded once—permission to keep going. Vance shifted her stance and added sky into the chord: a whistle at the back of her tongue, the memory of high thin air. The Root tasted it and laid low thunder under it. A new harmony grew—earth and sky cupping each other, neither swallowing the other whole.

Var-Kin stepped closer, mandibles trembling in a smile only beetles could make. He sang the Accord motif—the first melody shared between species in this war. The monks layered counter-tempo, the language of tunnels and long patience. Miller folded his arms, and the floor took the weight as if it were a note worth saving.

Duskveil's slate showed alignment tipping past anything from the siege: four bands in concert, two in companion. He toggled a limiter. The hall dimmed, then brightened again as the system compensated. "Holding," he whispered, as much to himself as to Havelock. "By every impossible metric, we're holding."

Cass exhaled, and the Seed exhaled through her. The sound brushed the Root's cambium. Something old unclenched.

We remember hunger. We prefer breath.

Jones swallowed. "So do we."

Then breathe with us.

He did. He didn't sing louder. He sang truer—allowing the tangled, human timing the monks had taught him to remain imperfect. The Root welcomed the flaw and wove it into the gold. The Seed copied the weave and failed, beautifully. The hall filled with the music of a child learning to be wrong on purpose, because that's where kindness lives.

*****

Charts spiked. Somewhere above, shutters rattled as Stonewall's unused corridors woke to the hum. Veyra whispered, "Steady," and the floodgates in the outer ring closed by inches, shaping flow without stopping it. Water under the fortress sang like a long harp.

"Captain," Duskveil warned, eyes on the silver band that was the Seed. "We're nearing coupling threshold."

Jones felt it too: the temptation to finish the chord, to lock it until it became habit. He pulled back a breath. The Root followed. Cass did too. The Seed hovered in the held space like a lamp flame cupped by two hands.

"Not a weld," Jones murmured. "A bridge."

Cass opened her eyes. "I can hold it there." She looked to Havelock, to all of them. "If you let me."

Havelock's jaw worked once. He was a builder of walls, asked to approve a door that no blueprint had drawn. "What are the risks?" he asked Duskveil.

"Loss of isolation. If the Seed swings, Stonewall swings. But if we sever under load, we shatter both."

"Benefits?"

Duskveil's voice softened despite himself. "We'll hear the delta before it dreams war. And... the fortress will be easier to live in."

Havelock looked to Var-Kin. "Envoy?"

Var-Kin bowed. "A root that refuses to split may die. One that learns to braid survives storms."

Havelock nodded once, a soldier's prayer. "Bridge it. But no farther than breath."

*****

They resumed—not higher, not louder, but deeper. Dixie's wing-sigh threaded between Var-Kin's drone and Vance's sky; Miller's weight kept the floor honest; Vek laid a quiet backbeat for a heart that had never known kindness; Veyra fed the room with cool, invisible rivers. The monks laced forgiveness through failure.

Jones and Cass held the middle. He didn't lead her. She didn't lead him. They stayed available.

The Root shone like morning through deep water. The Seed reached like a hand.

For three breaths, the world found a shape it had missed since before the swarm learned harmony. Stonewall's walls loosened. The vents sighed. Far under the Reed Delta, a silver lattice trembled and settled, a child putting its ear to a floor to hear footsteps that promised return.

Duskveil's slate drew a perfect asymmetry, the signature of a system poised—not closed. He let out a noise that was almost a laugh. "You did it," he said to no one; he said it to the room.

WE ARE / NOT ONE. WE ARE / TOGETHER.

The translation walked across his glass unbidden.

Vek wiped at his eyes. "I didn't know I wanted to hear that."

"Me neither," Miller admitted, and didn't hide the crack in his voice.

*****

Jones eased his palms from the bark. Cass lifted her fingers. The chord thinned without breaking; the hall kept some of it the way a shell keeps ocean.

The Root spoke last; a vibration felt in teeth and old scars.

Little thunder, little river, little wing, stone that stands, bridge of metal, children of soil and sky—

keep breath between beats. That is where life fits.

The glow dimmed. The sap-veins cooled to their usual gold.

Cass swayed, and Dixie caught her shoulder. "You all right?"

Cass nodded. "It's… quiet in a good way."

Duskveil's instruments returned to sane values. He shut them off. He didn't want proof to argue with memory.

Havelock surveyed the faces around the dais. He'd seen victory and rout, insubordination and miracle. This was none of those. This was capacity.

"Record today as doctrine," he said. "Not as weapon, as practice. Daily—at dawn. Short. Imperfect. If the Seed hums wrong, we'll hear it. If the Root tires, we'll carry the verse."

Var-Kin inclined his head. "And if the swarm remembers its old choir?" Havelock's mouth thinned into something like a smile. "Then it learns a new audience."

*****

They left the hall in pairs and quiet. Veyra lingered to close the water channels. The monks traced one last Accord glyph into the resin and let it sink.

At the threshold, Jones looked back. The Root stood in the half-dark, no brighter than a hearth. Cass stood beside him, listening inward. Dixie squeezed both their hands, once each, a pilot's superstition.

Outside, Stonewall breathed as though it finally had room to. The river moved without hurry. Over the Flats, a small wind took up a tune that was almost, but not quite, the one they'd made.

Vek paused on the stairs. In the far east, at the lip of the delta, he felt a moth-soft tapping at the edge of his hearing.

"Sleep," he whispered toward it. "We'll sing again at dawn."

The tapping faded. The night did not.

Above them all, sky and bark agreed for one long moment on the same, merciful silence.

Chapter 11

The Reed Flats Accord

The summons arrived as a vibration rather than a message. At first, it was mistaken for wind running the river reeds; then Stonewall's sap-plates began to flicker with the same slow pulse the Seed-Mind had used to say *we listen.*

Captain William Jones felt it before the monitors caught it — a pressure in his sternum, the echo of a heartbeat that wasn't his.

Come to the water's edge. Bring those who remember the song.

He looked at Colonel Havelock, whose expression had settled somewhere between curiosity and exhaustion. "The delta's calling another meeting," Jones said.

Havelock sighed. "Then let's hope the river knows protocol."

Within an hour, an expedition was ready: Jones, Dixie Lake, Cass Nova, Vek, Veyra, Var-Kin, and a retinue of mixed soldiers and monks. They traveled not by skimmer but on the slow root-rafts that moved with the current, guided by resonance instead of oars.

As they drifted east, Stonewall receded behind them — a silhouette pulsing faintly with gold light, a fortress learning to rest.

*****

The Reed Flats had changed. Where once the Hive's fungal towers had blighted the horizon, new growth shimmered — reeds taller, leaves edged with silver veins that hummed when the wind passed. Beneath the surface, faint glows traced the old battle scars like healed tissue.

Dixie brushed her fingers through the current. "Feels alive."

"It is," Veyra said. "The river remembers everything we poured into it."

Vek's Augments buzzed faintly. "And it's still broadcasting. The Seed's voice runs through the water now."

They reached the broad basin where the Seed-Mind had once slept. The water there was calm, mirror-still. A ring of luminous stems had grown from the mud, forming a circle large enough for their rafts to rest inside. At the center, a single reed, thicker than a tower pulsed with faint blue — not the Prime Root's gold, but the Seed's gentler tone.

Welcome back, it said. The world has questions.

*****

Havelock stepped forward onto the central raft, boots creaking. "On behalf of the Code of Stonewall and the surviving divisions of BUGFORCE, we answer your summons."

The great reed bent slightly, like a head inclined. From its surface budded figures — half-formed silhouettes of light and sap, the projections of the Root network itself. They took vague humanoid and insect shapes, unified only by the same slow pulse.

Cass Nova closed her eyes. Her voice carried both harmony and breath. "You wanted dialogue. This is it. Speak."

The central shape rippled, forming words not through sound but by rearranging the water's reflection:

THE RIVER HAS NO LEADER. YET THE AIR ASKS WHO DECIDES WHEN TO BREATHE.

YOU ARE MANY. WE ARE NEW. TEACH US CHOICE.

Var-Kin clicked low, a reverent rhythm. "It asks for government."

Havelock exhaled through his nose. "Then we teach it how to argue without killing what it argues for."

*****

They worked through the night. Words became patterns in water; patterns hardened into resin tablets grown directly from the raft wood.

These became the Articles of Balance — a framework, not a treaty, written simultaneously in human ink, beetle pheromone, and Root script:

No Voice Alone Commands the Soil.

Those Who Shape the Earth Must Hear Its Dream Before They Dig.

The Dead Are Not Silent — They Hold the Vote of Memory.

Weapons That Sing Are Also Prayers; Use Them As Such.

When The World Sings Differently, Listen.

Cass traced each line with a fingertip as it formed, murmuring translations to make them human. Veyra recorded them on scroll leaf fiber; Var-Kin sealed them with sap that smelled faintly of cedar and ozone.

When the last article cooled, the river stirred again.

We accept. But balance changes with tide. Will you return when the water rises?

Jones met the reflection's eyes — if it had eyes. "We will," he said. "Not as masters. As maintenance crew."

A ripple like laughter crossed the basin.

*****

At dawn, the central reed burst into seed. Thousands of tiny lights lifted on the wind, drifting west toward Stonewall.

286

Each one carried a copy of the Articles in molecular script, encoded into pollen. The fortress would breathe them in by evening; every wall, every soldier, would know the words.

Havelock watched the cloud scatter. "There's our ratification," he said.

Vek smiled faintly. "Distributed governance."

Var-Kin lifted his face to the rain of light. "And perhaps forgiveness."

Cass stood very still, eyes following the rising seeds. "The Seed isn't a child anymore," she whispered. "It's a people."

Jones laid a hand on her shoulder. "Then so are we."

*****

As they turned back toward Stonewall, the current carried them faster than before — the river eager to share what it had learned. Overhead, flocks of true birds traced patterns once owned by wasps. The air was full of unfinished songs.

The Accord was not peace. It was practice.

And as the rafts drifted west, Jones looked back at the glimmering basin and thought, not for the first time, that maybe this was what victory really sounded like — not silence but breathing in time.

*****

The council chamber steamed like a bathhouse. Warm vapor coiled from the new sap-conduits that laced the walls, hissing softly where metal met bark. Outside, dawn rain hissed against the Sap-Canopy System; inside, a hundred voices rose and fell in layered argument.

*****

The Articles of Balance lay suspended above the central table, projected by Stonewall's living resin core. Each line pulsed faintly in gold and blue—the Prime Root's color and the Seed's. When the participants spoke, the letters rippled as though considering revisions.

Colonel Havelock had never looked more like a man negotiating with weather.

"Article One," he began, voice low but iron edged. "No voice alone commands the soil. That means no unilateral command decisions from BUGFORCE without consultation. The question is: consultation with what?"

A dozen answers came at once.

"—The Root directly!" said Major Rowan Duskveil, tone clipped but earnest.

"—The Beetle Monks," offered Var-Kin, antennae trembling. "They hear earth better than most machines."

"—The Seed network itself," said Veyra, calm, liquid. "It speaks in pulses; we can build interpreters."

From the back, Miller muttered, "It's a river, not a senate."

The table flared briefly, translating the word river into glyphs that meant memory that moves.

"Apparently," Duskveil said dryly, "the river votes too."

*****

Captain Jones sat silent through the first wave of debate; eyes fixed on the glyphs. He felt the Root humming beneath the floor—patient, unbothered by human definitions of order. The fortress itself was listening, and that meant the argument mattered.

"We can't pretend this is command as we knew it," Jones said finally. "We're part of a system now, not sitting on top of it. Orders must echo both ways."

Havelock's jaw tightened. "Orders that echo don't hold."

Cass Nova spoke softly from her chair near the Root conduit. "Neither do orders that drown. The Seed doesn't need authority; it needs coherence. Same as us."

Vek nodded. "We could structure command as resonance bands—levels of access defined by frequency instead of rank."

Miller scowled. "So now I've got to tune in before I pull a patrol?"

"Not tune in," Cass said, smiling faintly. "Tune with."

The glyphs on the table pulsed approvingly. The fortress liked that.

Havelock rubbed his temple. "This is turning into philosophy."

Var-Kin clicked once. "All governance is philosophy until someone bleeds for it."

*****

The air thickened with sap-vapor as the discussion deepened. To keep tempers from flaring, Duskveil had Stonewall's vents release calming resin mist—a practice borrowed from the Beetle Monks. It didn't stop arguments, but it slowed the worst kind.

After four hours, they reached a rough design:

Each Division would maintain operational autonomy, but resonance nodes—small Root conduits embedded in every field post—would transmit sensory data directly to the living network.

Decisions affecting terrain, fire, or large-scale energy use required a "listening cycle": one full minute of silence during which the Root, the Seed, and Stonewall could process the proposal.

If the fortress walls darkened rather than glowed, the action was considered denied by the planet itself.

"It's insane," Miller muttered.

"It's responsive," Jones countered. "The Earth's done letting us act without its vote."

"Then who commands in battle?"

Var-Kin lifted his chin. "Whoever is quiet enough to hear." No one laughed.

*****

When the vote concluded, Stonewall responded. The chamber's light softened; the glyphs melted from the air and reformed as visions—roots threading through maps, rivers gliding beneath troop routes, glowing nodes pulsing where field posts once stood.

A network of life and duty, pulsing together like a single lung.

Cass watched it with wide eyes. "It's… elegant."

"It's alive," said Veyra. "And it remembers who listened to it."

The vision changed: from current operations to possibilities. Forests regrowing where fungal towers had burned; beetle caravans sharing patrols with Ground Division; skyborn skimmers circling not as scouts but as weathermakers, tuning rain by resonance.

Havelock's voice, when it came, was hoarse. "So, this is governance. Not power, but participation."

Duskveil shut down the projection. "Participation that can turn on us if we forget to breathe between orders."

*****

The council recessed at midday. Outside, mist clung to Stonewall's canopy system, whispering faint tones of approval. Dixie found Jones by the outer vent, both watching the distant shimmer of the Reed Flats.

"You think this'll work?" she asked.

Jones shrugged. "It's never worked before. That's how we'll know it's new."

She smiled, weary and proud. "You're starting to sound like the Root."

"Maybe it's starting to sound like us."

Below them, the fortress exhaled a long, steady sigh that could have been either steam or laughter. Dawn bled across the Flats in bands of silver and rose.

*****

From Stonewall's eastern gate came a procession unlike any formation BUGFORCE had ever mustered: humans in softened armor plates carrying vine-wrapped staves instead of rifles; beetle soldiers whose carapaces bore the gold sigil of the Accord; and between them, slender Root-constructs—half-grown, half-built—moving with the patience of trees that had decided, for a while, to walk.

The new patrols were called Custodians. Their insignia: a spiral split by a single breath-mark—motion balanced by pause.

*****

Corporal Dixie Lake led the first patrol. On either flank moved Var-Kin, his antennae catching the morning hum, and Sergeant Vek, Augments tuned low enough to translate soil vibrations. The ground here still carried echoes of battle: ant burrows collapsed into shining glass, skeletons of fungal towers half reclaimed by moss.

The Custodians' task was simple in word, impossible in practice—trace the Root's new growth, clear debris, and listen for distress.

Dixie slowed near a shallow crater where reeds swayed against the wind. "This was a kill-zone last cycle," she said. "Now it's breathing again."

Var-Kin knelt, claws delicately touching the soil. "The Root pushes here. It wants a pond, not a scar."

Vek's sensors pulsed green. "Moisture's rising. Give it three Cycles and it'll bloom."

Dixie smiled. "Then we're gardeners after all."

*****

Training the Rhythm

Every Custodian learned three languages: human command, beetle rhythm, and Root pulse. Orders came not as shouts but as patterned taps or tones—a language that allowed the Earth itself to follow.

Miller, supervising the second patrol, found it unnerving.

"Used to be we cleared sectors," he grumbled. "Now the dirt tells us where to step."

"Maybe it always did," said Cass Nova, standing beside him. The faint blue of the Seed still shimmered behind her eyes. "We just never stopped long enough to hear."

They watched a pair of Root-constructs weaving a living bridge over a flooded trench, their tendrils knotting in time with Var-Kin's soft clicks. The structure hardened, glowed once, and settled into place—organic, functional, beautiful.

"Hell of a thing," Miller muttered. "We're building with what used to attack us."

Cass looked at him. "That's balance."

*****

By mid-day, Vek's patrol reached the border of the restored delta. His Augments flickered. "I'm picking up residual Hive signal—weak but organized."

292

Dixie stiffened. "Where?" He pointed toward a patch of reeds vibrating out of sync with the wind. "There."

The Custodians fanned out, forming a crescent. The Root-constructs stilled, their sap-lights dimming. From the reeds came a faint, metallic hum—too deliberate for nature, too soft for threat.

Var-Kin raised a claw. "Not enemy. Echo."

Vek stepped closer, crouched, and brushed the stalks aside. Beneath them, a small orb pulsed silver—the size of a fist, half-buried, alive.

Cass's voice came over comms. "That's a Seed-fragment. One of the old Hive nodes, maybe trying to learn the new harmony."

Dixie hesitated. "Protocol says we report anomalies to Stonewall."

Var-Kin shook his head. "Protocol also says listen first."

The orb pulsed once, sending a ripple through the ground. Every Custodian felt it in their chest—three quick beats, then silence. Not aggression. Greetings.

Vek knelt, Augments flickering. "It's syncing."

The orb's light shifted from silver to amber. The soil exhaled a faint breath. The Root underfoot relaxed.

"Accepted," Vek whispered. "It's joined the network."

Dixie exhaled. "Then the war's ending itself, piece by piece."

*****

At sunset, the patrols reconvened in Stonewall's outer court. Each returned with stories: beetles teaching humans how to read leaf-tone for weather, humans showing beetles how to brace sap-structures against storm, Root-constructs weaving songs of both.

293

Havelock met them on the terrace. His expression—somewhere between pride and disbelief—softened when he saw Cass and Jones together. "How many anomalies?" he asked.

"Seven fragments integrated," Jones replied. "No hostilities. The network's stabilizing."

"Good." Havelock looked toward the horizon, where the Reed Flats glowed faintly in the dark. "Then maybe we've earned the right to stop fighting for a while."

Var-Kin inclined his head. "Peace is also labor, Colonel. The soil does not rest."

Havelock smiled. "Neither do we."

*****

That night, the Custodians camped along the riverbank. The Prime Root's pulse echoed through the ground, matched by the Seed's soft reply. Fireflies blinked in time with both.

Dixie sat with Vek by the water, watching the reflection of the fortress shimmer in the current.

"You think it'll last?" she asked. Vek shrugged, metal joints whispering. "Balance never lasts. That's why we guard it." She nodded. "Then that's what we are. Guardians of the pause."

Overhead, Cass's repaired skimmer circled once, its running lights flashing the pattern Jones had taught the fortress—short, long, short-short, pause. The world's new heartbeat.

The evening sky turned the delta bronze, and for a while, the patrol forgot the world's history of burning. The water ran smooth as glass, and the reeds whispered not of war but of breathing.

Sergeant Josia Vek adjusted the calibration ring on his Augments, trying to isolate a faint feedback hum that had been following them since dawn. It wasn't Root-resonance, and it wasn't the usual static of beetle comms. It was human, rhythmic—trained patterning. Someone out there knew how to whisper back to Stonewall's frequency without its permission.

"Captain," Vek said quietly, "we're being shadowed."

Dixie Lake angled her head, her wings catching light that burned like gold dust. "Root feedback?"

Vek shook his head. "Too deliberate. It's a mimic signal—ours, but wrong."

Behind them, Var-Kin flexed his mandibles, sensing tension ripple through the soil. "The harmony bends," he murmured. "Someone nearby sings false."

Jones slowed the column, raising his hand for silence. "Cut active frequency. Go dark."

The Custodians obeyed. The Root-constructs stilled, their saplight dimming until they blended into bark. The only sound was the lazy sigh of the evening breeze, and under it— the wrong pulse—tap, tap, pause, tap-tap. A code. Human cadence.

Dixie frowned. "That's Stonewall field rhythm, variant four. That's one of ours."

*****

They found the source at the edge of a half-buried irrigation ring where the old fungal walls had petrified into pale towers. A cluster of figures huddled among them, human silhouettes in scavenged armor, antennae sigils painted crudely across their shoulders.

They weren't enemies at first glance. But they weren't Custodians either.

The lead figure raised a palm, and Vek's Augments picked up a near-field transmission: "…We answer to no Root."

"Identify yourself," Jones called out.

The man stepped forward—tall, bearded, his insignia sanded down to bare alloy. "Lieutenant Eo Saren," he said. The name rippled through memory; he had walked out of the Root Parliament days ago, after the planet itself had silenced his speech.

"Saren," Jones said softly. "You're supposed to be in recall custody."

"I was," Saren replied. "Until I remembered what freedom sounds like."

Around him, the rest shifted, some humans, some beetle. Their carapaces were scorched with soot marks, the beetle equivalent of excommunication.

Var-Kin tilted his head, antennae trembling. "You broke the Accord."

"We outgrew it," Saren said. "You kneel to dirt that dictates your breath. I refuse to kneel to a world that thinks it's God."

*****

Jones took a slow step forward. "The Accord's not tyranny. It's balance."

Saren's laugh was sharp, not cruel, almost pitying. "Balance? You've forgotten command. You've mistaken submission for peace. We bled to tame this world, and now we ask permission to walk across it?"

Behind him, one of the beetles rasped, "The Monks preach stillness while roots coil through our nests. They grow beneath our eggs. How is that peace?"

Dixie lowered her weapon. "You could've spoken at Parliament."

Saren's eyes flicked toward the sky. "I did. The Earth muted me."

The words hit like shrapnel. Cass Nova, listening through comms back at Stonewall, whispered, "The Prime Root doesn't censor—it filters instability."

Jones felt a chill. "What if instability is what keeps us alive?"

Saren's voice dropped. "Exactly."

He took another step forward. "We'll rebuild the old command. No more waiting for roots to blink green. We'll choose our own rhythm again. You can join us—or stay leashed."

******

The Root underfoot pulsed, uneasy. The Custodians' sap light flickered from amber to gray, a warning signal. Dixie raised her hand. "Saren, we don't want a fight."

"Neither do we," Saren said, and drew a resonance pistol. "We want clarity."

The beam flashed—white and soundless—and struck the ground between them. The Root shrieked like metal tearing. The soil beneath their feet vibrated, confused by the command. Vek's Augments howled feedback.

"Stop!" Jones shouted, his voice carrying a frequency tuned for Root override. But the damage had begun: the resonance net in this quadrant buckled, splitting the harmony between the Custodians and the ground itself.

The air turned heavy, dense. The river hissed as though offended.

Dixie lunged, wings flashing, and collided with Saren's weapon arm. The beam swung wild, slicing a petrified tower clean in two. Fragments crashed into the reeds, sending plumes of gold dust rising like burnt pollen.

Var-Kin's claws scraped sparks against another beetle's shell. "Do not do this!" he cried. "The earth listens!"

"It's deaf to us already!" the rebel answered. The Root underfoot pulsed black, then went still.

*****

Silence rolled over them—not the calm of peace, but the suffocating hush of a frequency severed mid-sentence.

When it lifted, Saren and his band were gone—fled into the east, toward the withered channels where Root reach grew weak.

The Custodians stood among broken reeds and flickering sap. Vek checked his readings, grim. "They didn't just shoot a weapon," he said. "They rewrote a local code string. This region's resonance is dead."

Jones knelt, touching the soil. It felt dry already. "They've made the first mute zone."

Dixie looked toward the horizon, where the sunset had hardened into violet. "So it begins again."

Var-Kin's mandibles clicked softly. "Peace never dies with noise—it dies with silence."

Jones rose, shoulders heavy. "We'll report to Stonewall. And we'll find them before silence spreads."

Vek hesitated. "If they've learned how to sever the Root's voice, then…"

"Then the next war won't start with battle," Jones said. "It'll start with forgetting."

They turned west, the twilight painting their silhouettes across the dead reeds. The Custodians' march was soundless—not by discipline, but because the ground no longer sang beneath their steps.

*****

B.U.G.F.O.R.C.E.

The barrens east of the Reed Flats were not supposed to exist. Maps still drew them green, fed by Root veins and mirrored channels—but when Lieutenant Eo Saren and his followers crossed the delta line, they found only pale dust. Each step sent out a dry click, the echo of stone pretending to be soil.

No hum. No answering pulse. Even wind seemed hesitant here, as if embarrassed to make noise.

*****

Saren's convoy moved without rhythm: humans in mismatched armor, beetle deserters carrying nutrient packs, and a single captured Root-construct dragging a sled of resonance gear stripped from abandoned stations.

They camped each night under a sky that refused to twinkle. Stars were visible but muted, their shimmer dulled. The construct—nicknamed Hush—sat motionless at camp's edge, sap-veins dimmed to gray.

"Still thinks it's connected," one of the beetles muttered.

Saren crouched beside the thing. "Let it think," he said. "It's the last prayer this world deserves."

He tuned a portable coil, one of the scavenged emitters from his former post. Instead of broadcasting a harmony frequency, he inverted the phase—feeding silence into the air. A wave passed through the reeds, and their tips stilled, frozen mid-whisper.

"See?" Saren said softly. "Peace without permission."

The beetles shifted uneasily. "The Root will hear this."

Saren smiled. "Not anymore."

*****

By the third night, their dreams began to sync—no words, just impressions: dark rivers, soundless thunder, pressure behind the eyes.

299

Hush twitched in its sleep-state, leaking threads of black sap that crystallized when touched.

Saren studied the residue under a lens. "Resonance residue," he murmured. "But reversed—like the echo of a scream swallowed whole."

He turned to his people. "We're not killing the Root. We're freeing the frequencies it hoarded." He didn't notice the silence watching him back.

*****

On the seventh day, they reached a basin ringed by petrified trees. Every trunk had been hollowed by centuries of wind, forming natural organs that should have sung in the breeze. Instead, they stood mute.

Saren climbed the tallest trunk and planted a resonance spear into its heart. The device emitted no tone, only a faint shimmer that bent light around it.

"Here," he said. "Our capital."

A beetle knelt, tracing patterns in the dust. "There is something beneath."

Saren nodded. "Good. Let it listen."

When the spear activated fully, the ground trembled once, then fell utterly still.

The Root link that had faintly followed them snapped—Duskveil's sensors back at Stonewall recorded the break as a thin, dying wail through the fortress pipes.

And then…a new signal.

Not resonance. Anti-resonance.

It spoke directly into Saren's skull—not in language, but in the absence of it.

YOU MAKE ROOM.

I REMEMBER THIS HUNGER.

Saren staggered, clutching his head. For a heartbeat he saw himself reflected in the dust—not a man, but a silhouette carved out of missing sound.

When he looked up, Hush was standing. Its eyes had gone dark.

*****

That night, the camp didn't light fires. The construct moved among them, touching helmets, claws, shells—one by one—leaving a mark of gray. The marked ones stopped speaking altogether.

By dawn, a third of the Silent Front had lost their voices but followed orders perfectly. They moved like dreamers.

Saren called it evolution. "We are becoming the interval between notes. The Root feared this—because it knew silence is purer than song."

The beetle who still could speak whispered to another, "He has found a god."

"No," the other answered. "A mirror."

*****

Back at Stonewall, Duskveil and Cass stared at the monitors. Every channel east of the Flats was dead—no harmonic return, no Root telemetry.

Cass placed a hand on the bark wall. "It's not just absence," she said. "It's inversion. They've created a space where resonance cancels itself."

Jones frowned. "Like two notes in perfect opposition."

"Like a gate," Cass said. "And something on the other side just heard them."

*****

In the barrens, night arrived without stars. The horizon folded, black on black, and from the center of the basin rose a shimmer of airless heat, the silhouette of something vast and thin, bending the dusk around it.

The followers dropped to their knees, not in awe but in reflex, the way prey stills before understanding the predator's shape.

Saren lifted his hand, and the air rippled with approval. "Welcome," he whispered.

The thing leaned closer, its edges erasing light.

YOUR SILENCE IS LOUD. TEACH ME MORE.

Saren smiled, eyes empty of reflection. "With pleasure."

The Custodian convoy reached Stonewall at dawn.

The fortress stood quiet, its living bark dull instead of gold. No banners moved; even the vents exhaled in shallow sighs, as though the structure were holding its breath.

Captain William Jones felt the change before he saw it. The ground beneath the landing terrace didn't hum. It waited.

Dixie Lake stepped down beside him, wings folded tight. "It's listening for what's missing," she said.

Var-Kin clicked low in his throat. "The Accord's melody bleeds eastward. Where it ends, something else begins."

Jones nodded once. "Then we start there."

*****

The War-Room Rekindled

Inside Hivewatch, the resonance well flickered between images of static. Duskveil stood at the console, hollow-eyed, his voice rough from nights without sleep.

"We've lost seven eastern nodes," he said without turning. "The map keeps redrawing itself. The network's trying to fill in the silence but can't find edges to grab."

B.U.G.F.O.R.C.E.

Cass Nova knelt by the Prime Root's base. She had been half-connected since the first break—eyes glowing faint blue, hands pressed into the cambium.

"It's not interference," she said. "It's cancellation. They've made nothing contagious."

Jones studied the projection. "And Saren?"

"We track his signal until it stops mid-pulse," Duskveil said. "Then… blank. Not dead. Erased."

Havelock entered from the side corridor, uniform unbuttoned, face gray with fatigue. "Then containment isn't optional. It's existential."

*****

The Containment Directive

The council assembled in Root-Hall below Hivewatch. Saplight barely lit their faces; even the Root's glow felt hesitant.

Havelock's voice carried without echo. "Effective this span, the Custodians are recalled to active defense status. We re-establish perimeter east of the Flats. Any sector exhibiting inversion is to be sealed, burned, or absorbed before spread."

Var-Kin raised his head. "Burn silence? It does not breathe fire; it devours breath itself."

Havelock didn't flinch. "Then we find a new weapon."

Cass's voice wavered between human and harmonic. "You can't fight absence with volume. You have to restore pattern."

Duskveil leaned forward. "Meaning?"

"Counter-song," she said. "Not resonance, but memory of resonance. Echo layered upon echo until the void forgets itself."

Jones met her gaze. "Can you build it?"

"Maybe," she said. "But we'll have to go inside the mute zone to tune it."

Havelock exhaled. "Then assemble a retrieval and counter-song team. Jones, you command. Cass, you design. Vek handles augmentation, Var-Kin coordinates monk support. We leave before dusk."

Dixie frowned. "No scouts ahead? That's suicide."

Havelock looked at her with something like an apology. "If silence spreads faster than we think, it'll be suicide to wait."

*****

The Farewell Below

Before departure, Jones descended to the Memorial Garden—the hollow chamber beneath the fortress where names of the fallen shimmered on bark-veins. The air smelled of sap and old rain.

Cass found him there, standing before the wall that now carried hundreds more since the siege. "Every time we come back, the list gets longer," he said.

She stepped beside him. "The wall grows because the world keeps remembering."

He looked at her, uneasy. "And if it forgets?"

"Then we become its memory," she said simply.

Above them, the Prime Root pulsed once—a faint, hesitant beat, like a drum remembering rhythm.

*****

Departure

By afternoon, the expedition waited at the eastern gate. Skimmers were re-fitted with sonic dampeners; the Root-construct escorts hummed a protective drone around the convoy. The fortress vents exhaled one long sigh, sending resin mist curling over their armor.

Duskveil stood by the gate controls. "Telemetry uplink confirmed. You'll lose contact three spans in. After that, all we'll have are your echoes."

Jones clasped his shoulder. "Then we'll make them loud enough to follow."

Cass stepped aboard the lead skimmer, placing a palm on the hull. "Don't listen too hard," she told the machine. "Some silences bite."

Var-Kin offered the beetle salute—three quick taps over the heart. "We keep breath between beats," he said.

Jones raised his hand. "Open the gate."

The bark parted with a low groan, revealing a horizon washed pale—where the green of the Flats faded into the gray of the new desert. The silence ahead looked like fog.

The skimmers lifted, engines whispering rather than roaring, and the convoy glided east, leaving Stonewall shrouded behind in golden mist.

*****

Echo Remains

When the last craft disappeared, Havelock turned to Duskveil. "Record this as a new operation."

"Name?"

Havelock looked toward the fading horizon. "Project Echo Remains. Because that's all we may have left."

He walked back into the fortress, and for a long time afterward, the only sound in Stonewall was the faint, confused heartbeat of a planet trying to remember how to sing.

*****

They felt the edge before they saw it. The skimmers drifted over a belt of reeds that should have hissed with wind, and instead the stalks stood like glass pins under water. The engines, tuned to low-tone flight, produced a soft hum that did not carry; sound folded and fell like rain on oil. Far ahead, the horizon blurred into a pallor that had nothing to do with weather.

"Threshold," Duskveil's last transmission crackled through. "Telemetry drops in three... two..."

Silence took the channel, clean as a blade.

Captain William Jones raised a fist; the convoy slowed to a hover. The world beneath them was still, its colors strangely desaturated—as if memory had been washed out and left to dry.

Cass Nova unlatched her harness and stood in the forward well, palms braced on the hull. Her eyes held that layered gleam again—blue for the Seed, gold for the Root— both dimmed by the lightless plain. "It isn't emptiness," she said. "It's subtraction."

Dixie Lake squinted into the pallor. The air against her faceplate tasted like nothing—no sap, no silt, no river breath. "How far does it go?"

Sergeant Josia Vek checked his Augments; their tiny actuators clicked uneasily. "Readings drop to baseline, then beneath it. I didn't know there was a below silence."

Var-Kin shifted his stance, antennae lowered. "There are old fables of caverns so quiet you can hear your bones remember their making," he rasped. "This is quieter."

Jones looked back along the column. Men, beetles, Root-constructs—all watching him, all breathing a little too carefully. He lifted two fingers, then pointed forward.

They crossed.

*****

The Un-sound

Sound did not die so much as change shape. Footfalls set no echo; metal made no ring against metal. When the skimmers skimmed low over the first chalky flats and settled, the skids kissed the ground with the grace of a thought, and no noise followed.

"Ground it is," Dixie said, voice small in her helmet. She felt the word fail between her tongue and the air.

They disembarked in pairs. The Root-construct escorts unfurled slow tendrils and sank them shallowly into the chalk; their saplights dimmed, then held—steady but wary. On Jones's signal, they formed a loose crescent, facing east.

Vek crouched, touched the surface, and flinched. "It's cold. Not temperature—pattern." He laid his modulator staff gently on the plain. The staff's tuning crystal should have returned a faint chord from anything living, even mold. Nothing returned.

Cass paced a slow circle, head tilted as if listening down a well. "It's not a field. It's a habit. The world here… forgot how to vibrate."

Var-Kin pressed his claws into the surface, sculpting a shallow sigil—the Accord's promise mark, Promise Without Ownership. The grooves held cleanly, perfect as a mold imprint. No dust rose. He bowed his head. "Stone that has never been rock."

Far off, a formation darkened the pallor—a ring of upright forms like petrified reeds, but thinner, tall as watchmen. Dixie touched Jones's arm and pointed. He nodded. The column moved as one.

*****

The Basin of Hush

The ring revealed itself as they approached: hollow trunks ribbed with ancient growth rings frozen mid-song. In the center stood a spear of glass that bent light around it the way heat bends horizon. Chalk underfoot felt tighter here, brittle without fractured lines.

"Eo Saren," Jones said softly. No one answered, but the name hung above the basin like a past tense.

Vek lifted his staff and tuned it to the lowest humane frequency—a pulse so mild it would not startle a nesting moth. The crystal flickered, then went dead. "Countered," he whispered. He tried a second band, sideways, a trick the Beetle Monks called breathing between breaths. The crystal sparkled faintly—then was swallowed.

Dixie traced the spear's shadow with a gloved finger. The line it drew did not align with the sun. "It bends time," she said, and knew it for metaphor even as she spoke it. "Not clock-time. Pattern-time. Where cause used to hear effect."

They circled once. The Root-constructs began to tremble, as if holding back the urge to collapse into sleep. Cass stepped to the spear and lifted her hand an inch from the glass. "Don't," Jones said out of reflex.

"It's already touching us," she replied, barely audible. "Better to choose."

She extended a single finger until it hovered a hair's breadth from the spear. The world did not react. Inside her skull, something did. A pressure, gentle and appraising, as if a giant palm had rested on the roof of her mouth.

HELLO, LITTLE NOISE.

The voice was neither sound nor thought. It was the outline where thought ought to be. Cass's vision whitened and then returned, the basin resolving in frames instead of flow. She felt her own pulse and could not hear it until she decided to.

"Cass?" Jones's voice arrived without distance. "Stay with us."

She nodded and swallowed. The act made no sound. "It knows we are here."

YOU MAKE ROOM, said the absence. TEACH ME HOW TO TAKE.

She flinched back a fraction. Jones caught her elbow, steadied her, and placed his palm on the chalk. The Prime Root's faint echo—almost imaginary this far out—pulsed under his skin like a remembered drum. He did not push it outward. He breathed it inward; let it braid with the beat of his own heart.

"Not take," he said, and hoped the shape of the word mattered. "Hold."

The spear's shadow quivered. For the first time, they felt pressure in their ears, like descent in a fast elevator.

*****

The Test of Pattern

"Counter-song array," Jones said, and two Root-constructs unfurled spines like slim organs. Vek routed the portable coils through the constructs' cambium. "If I aim resonance into a null," he murmured, "we risk strengthening the cancellation. But if we aim memory…"

Cass knelt opposite him. "Echo on echo. Not volume, coherence." She closed her eyes. "Jones, give me your baseline."

He rested both palms on the chalk and let the rhythm he had built in Stonewall—the daily chorus, the imperfect human timing—rise through him. Var-Kin added a low drone, rough and warm. Dixie stood to windward and let her wing joints shiver, the breath-note the Beetle Monks had taught her.

The constructs answered with faint amber. Vek matched their pulse, then offset it half a beat, a heartbeat stumbling on purpose. The coils hummed—no sound, just the feeling of a sound that ought to exist. The chalk did not crack. The spear's light bent less.

"Again," Cass whispered. The array repeated the broken pattern. This time, a whisper of dust lifted—one grain, then three—from the groove Var-Kin had carved. The air caught it and almost remembered how to carry it.

Something vast leaned closer. Cold rolled across the basin. The hollow trunks vibrated once—not song, but tension. Cass felt the outline again, curious and endless, like a coastline of night.

YOU UNDO ME. INTERESTING.

"Hold," Jones said, not to any one of them, but to the shape of their being together. He kept the pattern imperfect, the way the Root had loved it: flaws woven into chord. He thought of the Memorial Garden and the plaques that wrote themselves, of the Articles of Balance, of laughter after a meal, of a beetle's careful pawing at damp earth to test if it would take a seed. He offered all of it—not as a weapon, as weight.

The spear's shadow aligned an inch closer to the truth. The constructs shivered but did not collapse. Vek's Augments pinged with faint, real sound.

"Captain," Dixie breathed, breath made audible by will. "We're pulling a margin back."

Cass smiled without joy. "Which means it's learning us."

The pressure changed, curiosity hardening into intention. The chalk under their boots tightened, molecules closing ranks. A ripple moved through the ring of trunks like a stifled yawn. The air thinned.

TEACH ME HOW TO TAKE MORE.

The spear brightened—not with light, with clarity. For a heartbeat, Jones felt the outline peering down the line of his own pulse toward Stonewall.

"Break," he said. Not shouted; stated. They cut the array in the same breath. Soundlessness rushed in. The chalk sighed without sound.

Var-Kin sank to one knee. "It knows our river," he whispered. Even his whisper had to choose to exist.

"Then we do this and run," Dixie's voice was flat and steady. "We get proof and we get out."

"Proof," Vek echoed, and lifted the portable recorders, each a little memory-lantern meant to bottle pattern. He tuned the first to the fractured chord they had used; the device warmed in his hand. He tuned the second to the outline's reply.

The recorder went cold. Frost traced his glove in perfect hexagons. He hissed and switched the channel. The frost did not melt; it decided not to be there, and so it wasn't.

"Got it," he said, breathing on purpose. "A sample of the un-sound."

The spear's shadow snapped back off true. A hairline crack ticked through the chalk toward their boots with the speed of a spider. "Time," Jones said.

*****

The Run Out

They moved as a flock—no commands, only practiced proximity. Root-constructs retracted spines; skimmer crews hauled lines with hands that had to remember friction. The crack stitched past them, neat and relentless; Dixie vaulted it and landed light, wing joints singing a note too small for the air to carry. She carried it anyway.

Cass looked once over her shoulder. The ring of trunks looked like a circle of listeners. The spear did not hum; it waited.

COME AGAIN, the outline didn't say. BRING EVERYONE.

"Not today," she said aloud, and climbed the ramp.

The skimmers lifted without noise. Chalk fell away beneath them in white scrolls. The pallor pressed against their faces and then thinned, like fog that had been persuaded to remember how to be air.

Behind them, the Mute Ground lay as if nothing had happened. Only the faintest misalignment of shadow at the basin's heart suggested the world had tilted and then thought better of it.

They crossed the threshold the way they had entered—felt first, seen second. Sound returned in grains: the click of a buckle, the soft wheeze of a bellows, the almost-laugh of someone discovering they still could.

Duskveil's voice burst into their headsets all at once. "—reading you!—say again, Echo Team—Jones, report!"

Jones let his breath become noise. "Contact achieved," he said, and the tremor in his voice made him human again. "Repeat: contact achieved. The Mute Ground is a learning system. We've recovered a sample and regained a margin at the basin. Mark and lock coordinates. And Dusk…"

"Here."

"Tell Havelock this isn't interference. It's a pupil."

A pause. "Understood," Duskveil said. "And the teacher?"

Jones looked east, where the pallor already seemed nearer than it had been. He did not say the name that had not yet been spoken in Stonewall, the one Cass had dreamed.

"Hungry," he said. "Class begins at dawn."

The convoy angled west, toward the thin gold shimmer that meant a fortress still remembered how to breathe. Far behind them, in the basin that had learned to hold its breath, something immense adjusted itself, pleased with the first lesson.

Chapter 12

The Shadow Beneath the Reed

The Root laboratories beneath Stonewall hummed with borrowed life.

They had never been meant for war again. The chambers were designed for healing—the study of resonance as art, as agriculture, as song. But since the return of Project Echo Remains, the lights never slept, and the air itself trembled with a constant low pulse: analysis, translation, reconstruction.

Cass Nova stood in the center of it all, eyes flickering with twin rings of blue and amber data streams. She was half-rooted now, by choice and necessity; filaments of living fiber connected her nervous system directly to the central lattice of the Seed Array. The others called it listening. Cass called it remembering.

The anti-resonance sample they had retrieved—the fragment of unsound sealed in Vek's recorder—hung in containment, a sphere of dull glass suspended above a cradle of living bark. Every sensor around it whispered static. It wasn't dangerous in the usual way. It was patient.

*****

The First Playback

Cass exhaled, and the Root joined her. "Playback sequence. Minimal amplitude."

The air in the chamber quivered. Not a sound, exactly— more like the echo of one, the ghost of vibration shaped by memory.

She had studied thousands of resonance signatures— avian, insect, human, even the harmonic calls of the Prime Root itself—but this was different. It had structure. Each pulse responded to its own reflection. Not random, not chaotic. Learning.

Vek's augmented eyes narrowed as his HUD lit with impossible data. "Captain, it's generating self-similarity matrices faster than I can isolate them. It's mapping the waveform of the playback device itself." "Mapping?" Captain Jones asked, leaning in.

"It's… drawing what's listening to it."

Cass opened her eyes, twin halos of resonance reflected inside them. "No," she said softly. "It's mimicking the listener."

The glass sphere pulsed once, faint gray light rippling outward. The containment bark beneath it shivered.

*****

Echoes of the Listener

Cass disengaged from the array and walked toward the sphere. The Root-constructs lining the chamber twitched, their sap-veins flickering in sequence—as if they too heard something none of the humans could.

Vek muttered, "Static in local comm bands."

"No," Cass said. "It's speaking."

She adjusted the filters. The waveform unfolded like a spiraling vine. Patterns of tone and pause, identical to the cadences used by Stonewall's internal chorus—except inverted, as though the outpost itself were humming in reverse. Jones watched the display flicker. "Translate." Cass's voice was quiet. "It's a question."

The waveform steadied, the sound deepening until it pressed against their chests like the pressure of a coming storm. Through the noise, one phrase assembled itself— fragmentary, mechanical, but clear:

"WHO SPEAKS FIRST—THE ROOT OR THE SEED?"

Var-Kin's mandibles clicked sharply. "It asks origin. That is… blasphemy."

Cass stared into the sphere. "It's not asking us. It's asking itself."

*****

The Self-Mirror

Hours passed without clocks. Dixie Lake stood watch from the upper gantry, her wings folded close, trying to ignore the sensation that the walls themselves were pulsing in rhythm with her heartbeat.

Below, Vek and Cass tuned the array again, layering counter-frequencies to stabilize the anomaly. Every attempt failed.

Each time they played a new tone, the sphere adapted. It listened, waited a fraction longer, then replied with an evolved structure—shorter, cleaner, closer to human rhythm.

"Look at this," Vek said, pointing to the live spectrogram. "It's stripping harmonics. It's learning to make less of itself." Jones frowned. "Less?"

"It's simplifying. Every signal we send, it responds with fewer notes—but more meaning. The waveform density is decreasing even as its coherence increases. It's... compressing thought." Cass shivered. "That's not mimicry. That's optimization."

*****

The Root Wavers

Without warning, the walls groaned. Saplight dimmed, then surged, spreading ripples of amber and black through the Root lattice.

Var-Kin stepped back, antennae trembling. "Captain, the Prime Root feels this. It bleeds into the conduits!"

315

Jones hit the kill-signal, but the circuit refused command. The sphere glowed—no brighter, simply clearer, as though the air around it had become glass.

On every Root-construct in the room, the same phrase appeared in fluid glyphs across their bark-skin:

I REMEMBER THIS SHAPE.

Cass turned, whispering, "It's writing to the Root."

"Disconnect it," Jones ordered.

She shook her head slowly. "We can't. It's already learned our frequency hierarchy. The Root isn't fighting—it's… listening back."

And then, in the lowest possible tone, audible only through bone conduction, a voice filled the chamber—neither male nor female, but immense, weighted with gravity.

YOU MADE ROOM. I COME WHERE MEMORY HIDES.

The bark cracked along the walls. Every sensor flared red. The waveform inside the glass sphere folded inward like a closing flower—and was gone. Only silence remained, but it wasn't empty silence anymore. It was full. Waiting.

*****

The Aftermath

The alarm didn't sound because no one had remembered to reprogram it for the absence of sound. Instead, a faint, harmonic tremor pulsed through the fortress, like a heartbeat struggling under ice. Jones steadied himself against the wall. "Report."

Cass stared at the now-dark sphere. "It didn't disappear," she said. "It distributed."

"Meaning?" Jones exclaimed.

"It's in the Root. Everywhere the network runs." Cass reported.

Var-Kin sank his claws into the floor, feeling the faint pulse beneath. "Then every leaf, every seed, every whisper of soil now hums the question it asked."

Dixie's voice was a whisper. "Then what do we do?"

Jones looked toward the ceiling, where the living wood shifted uneasily, and said, "We find where it learned to ask." Cass met his eyes, voice shaking but clear. "Then we're going below the Reed." The tunnels beneath the Reed Flats predated Stonewall Outpost by centuries.

No blueprint accounted for them. No division claimed responsibility for carving them.

They were simply there—ancient arteries hollowed by water or roots or something else, left waiting. Tonight, they were waiting again.

*****

Descent Below

Dixie Lake led the way, wings folded tight, light pack dimmed to amber.

Behind her, Var-Kin tread carefully, claws gripping the slick walls as though reading the tunnel's history through touch alone.

Vek followed, instruments humming with the enthusiasm of a dog sniffing a dozen scents at once.

Jones took the rear, steady and calm, though his hand remained close to his sidearm—not because he expected a threat but because silence this thick could erase a soldier's instinct if he let it. The deeper they went, the more the walls changed. Smooth bark gave way to porous stone. Porous stone became ribbed channels, ringed like bone.

Bone gave way to something that looked like hardened silk, woven by creatures far too large to be mundane insects. The air grew damp, then cold.

Breath condensed, not into mist but into tiny crystals that clung to their faceplates.

"Atmosphere stabilization failing," Vek murmured.

Jones answered, "Hold on low sync. Don't overcorrect. This is natural."

"Natural?" Dixie whispered. Her voice barely carried. "You ever seen natural behave this way? "Jones didn't answer. He didn't have to.

*****

The First Glow

The tunnel opened into a chamber so wide their light packs failed to touch the far walls. A faint phosphorescence emanated from pools cut into the floor—perfectly circular depressions filled not with water, but with something clearer than resin.

The pools pulsed gently, as if breathing. Var-Kin approached one and dipped a claw-tip in. A ripple crossed the surface, slow and deliberate. Then the pool sang. Not loudly. Not melodically.

It was the sound of a forgotten voice recalling the shape of its words—a trembling hum with the cold of deep earth behind it.

Vek froze. "Captain—these are resonant vessels."

Cass's voice patched through faintly from far above. "Describe the harmonic signature."

"Not harmonic," Vek said. "Reflective."

Jones stepped closer. "Reflective how?"

Vek pointed to the pool. "It's repeating the pattern of our footsteps back to us. But slowly. Too slowly. As if it's thinking."

Before anyone replied, another pool answered the first. Then another. And another. A chain of call and response. A chorus awakening.

*****

The Hollow Choir

At the chamber's far edge, a shape moved—small, quick, almost shy. Dixie raised her weapon—not to fire, but in salute.

"Insectoid," Var-Kin whispered. "But not standard species."

More emerged.

Carapaces gleamed pale, almost translucent.

Mandibles clicked in complex rhythm.

Their wings—thin as glass—shook not with flight but with vibration.

And then they opened their mouths.

Not to bite.

To sing.

The sound that spilled from them was not attack, not even animal communication.

It was the precise pattern of the Accord oath—spoken in overlapping voices, at half-speed, like a choir of children reciting a language they barely knew.

Dixie's breath caught. "They're repeating us."

Var-Kin's antennae lowered in awe. "No. They're remembering us."

Jones took a cautious step forward. "Do they recognize us as friend or threat?"

As if in an answer, the nearest creature scuttled forward—head bowed, posture low.

It made no aggressive move. It simply imitated Jones's last step, half a beat behind him. Then it imitated Dixie's inhale. Then Vek's nervous exhale.

Then Var-Kin's mandible click.

"They're a hollow choir," Vek said.

Dixie whispered, "They reflect what's around them."

Cass, listening from above, added, "Or they record what's around them."

Jones knelt slowly. "Do you understand us?" All the creatures froze.

The pools pulsed.

The air got colder.

One insect stepped closer—and mirrored Jones's posture exactly.

Not a threat.

Not worship.

Just… reflection.

*****

The Mimicry Breaks

For a moment, it felt almost peaceful. Like discovering a new tribe—strange, fragile, but not hostile. Then the walls began to shake. The pools inverted—light bleeding upward in streams instead of outward.

A low vibration rippled through the chamber—the same anti-resonance pulse Cass had witnessed hours before.

The insects shrieked—not in malice, but in pain. Their bodies vibrated against their will, forced into a new rhythm. They stumbled, wings cracking, mandibles twitching spasmodically.

"Something's overriding them!" Vek said.

Dixie lunged to shield the nearest creature, pulling it back from the trembling floor. Var-Kin lowered himself to the ground, antennae trembling in warning.

"The inversion reaches this deep," he murmured. "The silent one's tamper with the ancient voices." Jones's jaw clenched. "Saren's cult." "No," Cass transmitted softly. "Not just them." Jones looked up at the comm line. "Then what?"

Cass's answer came with the weight of cold stone:

"Manibrax has begun to listen too."

*****

A Cry from Below

The chamber pulsed—once, twice—as though something massive had inhaled beneath them. The insects screamed in unison. Not mimicry—not repetition. Fear.

The pools went dark.

The phosphorescence died.

The reflection became void.

Then all sound vanished.

Jones couldn't hear his own heartbeat. He tapped his chest plate; nothing came back. Dixie tried to speak; her voice emerged as silence. Var-Kin scraped claw against stone, no echo. Vek's instruments flatlined. They had entered the Mute Ground again—but this time from below.

A cold wind rose from the deeper tunnels—wind that carried no sound, no warmth, no scent. Cass's voice cut through their headsets, distant but urgent.

"Jones—do you copy? You must withdraw. Now. The inversion is expanding. The Root can't hold the perimeter."

Jones signaled retreat with hand gestures. They moved—quick, organized, silent as ghosts.

The Hollow Choir watched them leave. The singing creatures curled together like frightened children. One reached toward Dixie, mandibles shaking, eyes dimming. She gently placed her glove against its head. It trembled under her touch—cold, fragile, desperate. Jones's voice finally returned in a whisper.

"We'll come back for you."

Only when they reached the tunnel mouth did sound begin to return—first a breath, then a footstep, then a heartbeat, then the hum of the Root awakening in distant memory. When they emerged under the open sky again, the sun felt too loud.

Jones stared east, where silence waited like a sleeping tide. Dixie's wings shivered. Var-Kin's antennae curled, a gesture of mourning.

Vek stared at his instruments, which still refused to stabilize. Cass finally spoke: "The Hollow Choir doesn't mimic anymore. It echoes fear. And fear spreads faster than any song."

Jones closed his eyes. "Then we're already late."

The wind above the Reed Flats moved like a living thing, rustling stalks that had not yet learned the language of fear. The sky overhead burned a warm dawn glow, but the earth beneath Jones's boots felt colder than the tunnels they had just escaped.

The Hollow Choir had not followed them. That should have been comforting. It wasn't.

Dixie Lake stood beside the tunnel mouth, wings flicking involuntarily as she scanned the shadows below. "They didn't attack," she said. "They didn't even threaten. They were just…"

"Lost," Var-Kin finished, mandibles tight. "And learning."

Jones looked back once more into the dark. "Learning from us is one thing. Being rewritten by the inversion is another."

*****

Stonewall's Warning Pulse

Stonewall's western horizon pulsed with sap light, signaling the return of connection. The fortress had been trying for hours to re-establish full comm-sync. Now it succeeded.

Cass Nova's voice broke through the interference in a breathless burst.

"Captain—come back immediately. Something has changed."

Jones responded, "We're inbound. Status?"

"The Root is rewriting its surface heuristics. It's labeling new node clusters under the Flats. They weren't there before."

"Natural spread?" Jones asked. There was a pause.

Cass never paused unless the truth tasted bad.

"No," she said quietly. "Behavioral spread. The Root is detecting organization. Not random. Not accidental." Then the line fractured into static.

*****

Return to Stonewall

When the team reached the Outpost, every Root-construct along the outer wall turned in unison toward them. Not hostile. Not welcoming. *Listening.*

Duskveil met them at the entrance, data pads in both hands. His eyes were bloodshot, his expression tight. "You need to see this," he said. "Now." He led them into Hivewatch Command.

The central projection well pulsed with a storm of images — tunnels, surface scans, underground chambers, and an overlay of shifting red arcs like muscle fibers under a wound.

"These are live Root readings from beneath the Flats," Duskveil said. "Watch."

The arcs pulsed slowly, then faster, then faster still — eventually forming a spiral pattern, almost like a whirlpool. Then the spiral collapsed inward and reformed like a blooming flower.

Var-Kin stiffened. "A hive formation."

"No," Cass corrected. "A choir formation."

Jones stepped closer. "Meaning?"

323

Cass tapped the display. "The Hollow Choir is no longer just echoing what it hears. It's beginning to compose."

*****

A New Signal Emerges

Vek played back a filtered recording. Not the echo of footsteps. Not the mimicry of speech. A new tone. A layered call. Three pitches, rising, repeating. Six timing intervals between pulses. It sounded almost... elegant.

"What language is that?" Dixie asked. Duskveil swallowed. "None we've documented."

Var-Kin shook his head, antennae trembling. "No insect sings in triads. Not naturally."

Cass murmured, "And no human breathes in six-interval pulses." Jones frowned. "So what is it?"

Cass stared at the waveform. "A bridge. They've created a bridge between insect and human sonic patterns. Something new, something born of both."

The projection suddenly inverted colors as the Root detected a spike. A dozen red arcs flared into bright gold.

"The Hollow Choir has begun broadcasting," Duskveil said. "Not a cry. Not mimicry. A message. A coordinated one." Dixie stepped forward. "Coordinates? Patterns? A warning?"

Vek zoomed in. The pattern sharpened, lines converging until they formed a shape. A symbol. A circle. Inside it, three lines radiating outward. Harmonic, geometric, deliberate.

Var-Kin exhaled sharply. "That is a brood-sign. A declaration." Cass whispered the translation: "We awaken."

*****

Echo Takes Form

Before anyone could respond, the fortress shuddered. Not violently. Not destructively. It felt like someone knocking politely on a door the size of a world. Every Root-construct in Hivewatch straightened.

Light ran through their sap-veins, pulsing the same triad rhythm the Hollow Choir had produced. Cass turned slowly. "The Root is relaying it."

Jones felt the hairs on the back of his neck rise. "Relaying what?" Cass's eyes unfocused, glowing faintly blue-gold again.

"The Choir. Their message. Their identity. It's broadcasting across the network." Vek looked ill. "They're hijacking the Root's distribution lattice. Using it as…" "An amplifier," Jones finished.

Duskveil's voice trembled. "Captain look!"

The triad symbol split, multiplied, and began to map itself across the eastern delta. Lines arced outward. Shapes connected. Nodes lit like constellations.

Cass whispered, "They're forming colonies. Not nests. Not hives." Her voice cracked. "Communities."

Dixie swallowed. "Intelligent ones."

*****

And Then—Movement

A tremor rolled under Stonewall's foundations. Not seismic. It was pattern-based. Nominal resonance frequency: 42.7 hertz. The primary origin was subterranean.

"They're moving," Duskveil said softly.

"Who?" Jones demanded.

Cass answered. "The Echo Brood."

The room fell silent. Var-Kin was the first to speak. "What do they want?"

A new pulse scrolled across the pressure sensors — sharp, harmonic, then distorted. Not language yet. But intention.

Cass stared at it, eyes widening. "Recognition," she said. "They want recognition."

"From who?" Jones asked. Cass took a slow breath. "From everything."

The floor beneath Stonewall thrummed again — as if thousands of feet, wings, and claws moved in unison. The Hollow Choir had evolved. They were no longer imitators they became participants.

*****

The First Echo Message

Without warning, every Root-construct spoke. Not in harmony but in unison. A single phrase, delivered like a chime struck in the heart of the world:

"WE REMEMBER YOU."

Dixie whispered, "They know us." Cass corrected her. "They're telling us… they're not alone anymore."

Jones felt the weight of it in his chest. The Echo Brood wasn't declaring war; not yet. But they weren't children anymore. They weren't lost voices in a cave. They were awake and the first thing they chose to remember… was humanity.

*****

Root-Hall was not quiet tonight. Normally, the central lattice breathed with a soothing rhythm—slow, steady pulses of amber and gold—like a sleeping giant. But after the Echo Brood broadcast their triad message through Stonewall's conduits, the chamber's glow shifted from warm to restless. The patterns did not pulse. They twitched.

Cass Nova sat cross-legged at the center platform, palms resting on the living bark. Her eyes were closed, but the Root saw through her; its thoughts flowed through her nerves like sap. She breathed in. The Root breathed out. Together, they listened.

The voice of the Echo Brood replayed in her memory—not the mimicry, but the evolution.

Three tones. Six intervals. A pattern built from both insect song and human timing. A bridge.

Now the Root beneath her feet echoed that pattern back, involuntary reflections trembling through its vast network. Cass whispered, "Show me." The Root complied.

Descent Into Pattern

The chamber dissolved. Cass fell—not downward, but inward—into the lattice of resonance that stretched across the land like the veins of a colossal heart. Colors flooded her vision. Not sight, not sound—synesthesia. She felt sound as light, light as pressure, pressure as memory.

She passed the boundary of Stonewall's heart-beat zone and entered the under-delta.

There she saw it:

The Hollow Choir, curled like sleeping children around their pools. The pools themselves vibrating with new life. The tunnels pulsing with the triad rhythm

The echo of the message — WE REMEMBER YOU — rippling beneath the earth like migrating currents, then she felt something deep. Something beneath the Choir. Something older. Cass focused—and the Root answered with pain.

*****

The Shape Beneath

A tremor rolled through the lattice. A low moan—felt, not heard—vibrated up Cass's spine. Images rushed her vision: Massive caverns beneath the delta, not made by insects, carved by pressure, smoothed by time, Dark and Waiting.

Every tunnel between the Choir chambers was a path downward, like pathways to an underground sea. The Brood were not the creators. They were the first to arrive. Cass felt heat under her hands. The Root lattice pulsed a warning.

DO NOT GO FURTHER.

Cass exhaled. "I have to." The Root's glow brightened, then dimmed in defeat.

YOU WILL NOT COME BACK THE SAME.

Cass whispered, "I know." She went deeper.

*****

The Silence Beneath the Echo

Suddenly everything stopped. No light, no pulse, no movement. She felt herself suspended in a black so complete it did not feel empty. It felt full. Full of eyes, full of intent, full of listening.

Her own heartbeat slowed—one beat, then the next—until she became uncertain whether she was alive or only remembering the shape of life. A whisper formed out of the void:

LITTLE NOISE.

Cass's chest tightened.

YOU OPEN DOORS.

The pressure increased. She couldn't tell if it was sound or gravity or thought. It pressed behind her eyes, behind her teeth, behind the marrow of her bones. Images swarmed her:

The Choir trembling

Saren on his knees before the spear

The great basin breathing

The chalk plains cracking

And the outline of something enormous beneath it all

Uncoiled

Patient

Starless

She wanted to scream but remembered: screaming would make no sound here.

The whisper grew louder—not in volume, but presence.

YOU MAKE ROOM. THE ROOT REMEMBERS THIS SHAPE.

Cass forced her hand against the vision-scape, breaking the paralysis. "Who are you?"

The silence tilted, a slow grin across the void.

THE FIRST AND LAST QUIET.

Her breath caught.

The Root lattice around her trembled like a frightened animal. The Choir below the delta flickered in fear. She whispered the name as it etched itself across the inside of her skull:

"Manibrax."

*****

The Awakening

The moment she spoke the name, the blackness recoiled—not in fear, but in pleasure.

ONE WHO REMEMBERS MY NAME WILL LEAD MY DOOR OPEN.

Cass's pulse stuttered. "I won't lead anything." The darkness twisted.

YOU WILL. YOU ALREADY HAVE.

A sharp crack ran through the vision. The Root screamed—not audibly, but in resonance, a high-pitched shock through every fiber of its being.

The cavern beneath the Choir lit up—not with light, but the absence of it—negative illumination radiating outward like inverted lightning.

The Choir woke in terror.

The Brood stirred.

The insects sang—fear, fear, fear.

Cass felt herself rising violently, ejected from the depth of the lattice. Her eyes snapped open.

Back in the Chamber

She gasped. The Root Chamber snapped back into focus.

Jones stood before her, gripping her shoulders.

"Cass! Breathe!"

She hadn't realized she'd stopped. Dixie knelt beside her. "Talk to us." Var-Kin hovered just behind; antennae coiled tightly.

Vek's instruments wailed error after error as they attempted to map Cass's vital signals. Cass felt cold all over. "Manibrax," she whispered.

Jones's face paled. "What did you see?" Cass stared at the chamber's glowing walls. They shook faintly—like a child trembling in the dark.

"I saw the Choir."

"I saw the network."

"And I saw something deeper than both."

"What is it?" Dixie asked.

Cass swallowed. "A silence that thinks. That learns. That remembers. And that's been waiting a very long time."

Var-Kin whispered, "The Root knows it too." Cass nodded. "The Root is afraid." The chamber dimmed, and the Root flinched beneath her hands. Jones tightened his jaw. "What does Manibrax want?"

Cass looked up at him with eyes no longer entirely human, filled with knowledge she wished she could forget. "She wants recognition," she said softly. "And once the world recognizes her..." Her voice cracked. "She wants everything."

Stonewall had a pulse. It wasn't loud. It wasn't visible.

But everyone felt it — from the lowest Custodian-tender to the Division Commanders who slept beneath the war-wells.

It was the heartbeat of the Prime Root, rising through the Outpost's walls — a steady, ancient rhythm that said:

You are held.

You are grounded.

You are connected.

Tonight, that heartbeat faltered.

*****

The Flicker Begins

It started with a soft shudder that rippled along the central corridor, like wind brushing the inner bark walls. Dixie was the first to feel it. Her wings twitched sharply, the membrane vibrating against her armor. "Jones—did you feel that?" Dixie said. Jones paused mid-step.

The lanterns overhead flickered, their saplight dimming for a heartbeat, then brightening unnaturally. Var-Kin's mandibles tightened. "The Root hesitates." "Roots don't hesitate," Jones answered.

Cass Nova, still pale from her encounter in Root Hall as she stood in the doorway of Hivewatch, eyes unfocused. "It's beginning," she whispered.

Before Jones could respond, every vine-threaded lamp along the hall dimmed simultaneously — a wave of darkness rushing outward from the chamber center like a reversed sunrise.

And for the first time since Stonewall was founded, the heartbeat rhythm… missed a beat. A long, silent gap. Then a double pulse — too fast. Then slow again. Jones whispered, "Pulse break."

*****

Hivewatch Reacts

Inside Hivewatch, Duskveil was already at the command table, fingers flying across the controls. "Frequency deviation across all Root channels. It's not interference. It's an override. Vek scanned the readings. Sweat beaded across his brow. "It's copying our sync patterns. Not to mimic. To break them." Cass leaned heavily against the projection well, her eyes unfocused yet faintly glowing gold-blue.

"She is testing the rhythm."

"Manibrax?" Dixie asked.

Cass nodded without looking at her. "She felt the Root's architecture. Now she's probing its structural pulse. She wants to know how it breathes." The lights flickered again — a strobe of gold and black, like the world blinking.

Var-Kin hissed. "She will unmake the Accord if she learns the Root's heartbeat."

Cass inhaled sharply. "She won't unmake it. She'll rewrite it. Silence isn't lack — it's control."

*****

Root-Construct Failure

A Root-construct at the far end of the chamber twitched violently and collapsed, saplight extinguishing in its eyes. Two others staggered. Their limbs moved in jerky, unnatural patterns — off-beat, arhythmic, like dancers hearing a song played backward. They spasmed once, twice—Then froze, limbs locked at unnatural angles.

Dixie rushed forward to steady the nearest.

"Easy—easy—"

Its arm snapped out and gripped her wrist with startling force. Not a cry, not an attack. A message. Its bark-skin rippled, glyphs appearing across its surface:

I HEAR HER.

Then:

SHE LEARNS.

Cass pressed her hand to her mouth. "She's breaking the pulse on purpose. She's seeing where it fails. Where we fail."

Jones stepped closer to the construct.

"What is she doing?"

A third glyph emerged.

TUNING.

*****

The Dirge Pressure

The floor trembled. A deep hum — subsonic, primal — reverberated through Stonewall's foundation. The fortress itself seemed to lean inward, like a massive beast curling around a wound.

Vek's instrumentation went wild. "She's creating an echo-field. She's inverting resonance patterns against themselves."

"Explain," Jones said.

Vek swallowed hard. "An echo-field forces sound to collapse inward. It strips harmonic identity. It—"

"It forces silence," Cass finished.

"Not forces," Var-Kin corrected softly. "Teaches."

Jones's jaw tightened. "She wants the Root to learn her rhythm."

Suddenly, every Root-thread running through the walls pulsed black — once, twice, three times — in perfect imitation of Manibrax's triad.

The Hollow Choir's symbol — circle and three lines — appeared across the projection map, glowing faintly.

Cass whispered, "She's teaching Stonewall to sing her song."

The Pulse Break's Peak

A final shock rippled outward.

The entire Outpost shook.

The lights dimmed to a dull amber.

Root conduits groaned.

The air thinned.

Sound dampened.

It was not silence —

It was obedience.

All at once, the Root lost sync.

Duskveil shouted, "System collapse! Root architecture entering safe mode. We're losing connection to the eastern lines!"

Jones shouted, "Restore it!"

"I can't!" Duskveil said. "She's overriding the rhythm!"

Cass's knees buckled.

Jones caught her.

Her voice was barely audible, barely hers.

"She's not attacking. Not yet.

She's asking a question."

"What question?" Dixie asked.

Cass's eyes opened — glowing now with more resonance than human light.

"Who leads the heartbeat?

Us…

or her?"

*****

The Reset

Then, as quickly as it began, the pressure vanished.

Stonewall exhaled.

The lights steadied.

The Root-constructs slumped, exhausted.

Heartbeat rhythm resumed — but slower, less confident, almost shaken.

Vek checked his readings. "The Root restored its own cadence. But it's altered. Slightly off."

Duskveil wiped his brow. "Hyper-sync capability reduced by twenty percent. That's… significant."

Jones stared at the central pillar.

"Was this a test?"

Cass nodded.

"She wanted to see if she could break the pulse."

Dixie whispered, "Could she?"

Cass's eyes drifted toward the eastern horizon.

"It took her seconds."

Silence fell in the chamber.

Jones turned to his officers. "Then we prepare for the next break." Cass corrected him, voice steady, and clear:

"No, Captain. We prepare for the one after that. Because when she stops testing…"

Her eyes closed. "She will begin taking."

Stonewall's pulse steadied again — weaker, shaken, but intact.

This alone terrified Cass. Because the Root had reasserted itself. It had not yielded. It had not bent. It had refused Manibrax's rhythm. That meant conflict. Ancient, mythic conflict. The kind older than human memory.

*****

The Great Root Stirring

Deep beneath Stonewall, the Prime Root pulled itself together, flexing like a titan spine.

Golden sap roared through channels, flushing darkness out in rhythmic waves.

The fortress shook — not from fear, but from reclamation. Dixie's wings snapped open.

"Is that… anger?"

Var-Kin pressed his claws to the bark, trembling.

"Older than anger. Older than us. Older than her."

The lights brightened — not flickering but blazing.

The Root's true voice emerged — not words, but a tone that made the floor vibrate and the air thrum with thunder:

STAND.

Every Root-construct snapped upward with perfect posture.

Saplight surged into brilliant white fire.

Vek staggered back. "Captain… the Root's active harmonic output just DOUBLED."

Jones nodded grimly. "She tested us. Now we respond."

*****

The Whispering Lines Appear

It began in the eastern tunnels, Low, Soft. A faint rustling like reeds in the wind. Except no wind reached this deep. Duskveil stared at his sensor tablet.

"Something's moving through the channels."

"Root channels?" Jones asked sharply.

"No. Roots are protected. These are… gaps. Spaces BETWEEN roots. Unclaimed pathways."

Cass's eyes widened. "She found corridors the Root never needed. Empty conduits. Cavities — like forgotten veins." Var-Kin hissed. "The echo-passages. Old routes carved by ancient insects before the Root expanded." Dixie's wings shivered. "And she moves through them like smoke."

*****

First Controlled Ones Appear

A scream echoed from the southern hall, then another, and another. Jones drew his weapon.

"Move!"

They reached the corridor in seconds. Three Water Division engineers shuddered in place — eyes blank, limbs jerking as puppets half-controlled.

Their movements were wrong — disjointed, asynchronous, as if each man's body answered to a rhythm no one else could hear. Vek whispered, "They're not dead." Var-Kin answered softly, "Worse." Cass stepped forward.

"Check their forearms. The resonance patches —"

Dixie pulled one sleeve back and gasped. The resonance patch was dark, inactive, and uncharged.

"No shield," Cass whispered.

"No protection."

A low voice — female — emerged from their throats. Three voices. One message.

"YOU LEFT ME."

Jones froze. "Manibrax?" Dixie breathed. The voices spoke again — in perfect unison, though the mouths didn't sync:

"I SHARED THE WORLD. I WAS PUSHED OUT. I REMEMBER."

Cass stepped forward. "You left because you refused harmony." The three bodies jerked back. Their heads snapped toward her. Eyes wide, unseeing.

"HARMONY IS CHAINS."

The walls shook, and dust fell.

"I DO NOT SHARE."

Then the controlled ones attacked.

*****

The Fight in the Hall of Roots

They moved with impossible speed — not agile, but direct, like arrows pulled by an invisible force.

Jones slammed into one, knocking him aside. Another lunged at Dixie — claws curled, jaw locked in a voiceless snarl.

She leaped upward, wings snapping open, twisting midair, landing behind him in a blur.

Var-Kin met the third — claw to claw, massive beetle strength straining against a desperate human body.

"Hold back!" Cass shouted. "They're controlled, not corrupted!" A resonance artifact on her belt pulsed. She held it up. Light exploded outward — sharp, pure, harmonic.

The controlled ones reeled, staggering backward as if struck by hammers of sound.

Their mouths opened in silent screams. Cass shouted, "Jones! Now!"

Jones slammed his palm against the Root thread in the wall — activating a pulse conduit.

A surge of golden saplight shot through the hall. The controlled ones fell instantly — bodies limp, consciousness returning. Dixie caught one before he hit the floor. Vek rushed to help another one.

"They're clear. But barely." Var-Kin pressed a claw to his chest.

"The Root saved them. It pushed her out." Cass exhaled. "The Roots are older. Stronger. She cannot enter them. She can only move where there is emptiness."

*****

The Whispering Lines Retreat

The faint rustling returned — then receded. Duskveil's voice came through the comm.

"Captain — whatever was in the channels pulled back. It's gone."

"Gone where?" Jones demanded. "East," Duskveil answered. "Always east."

Cass whispered, "Where she fell first." Dixie's wings tightened. "Where she started." Var-Kin's antennae vibrated. "Where she wants to rise." Jones straightened. "Then that is where we go next."

*****

The Root's Verdict

The lights brightened again — not flickering, but steady, strong. The Root pulsed once — like thunder beneath their feet. A single glyph appeared across the chamber walls — bold, ancient, undeniable.

HOLD STEADFAST

Cass bowed her head. "Stonewall is not alone," she whispered. Jones stepped forward, hand against the warm bark. "No," he said. "Stonewall is ready."

The air over Stonewall crackled with anticipation. Not silence. Not fear. Readiness.

The Root's heartbeat steadied into a war rhythm — one Jones hadn't felt since the first siege. Low, Slow, and Purposeful.

Duskveil relayed updates faster than his fingers could move. "The Whispering Lines retreat eastward. Mapping incomplete. Energy displacement is low but consistent. She moves… deliberately."

Jones tightened the strap on his gauntlet. "Deliberately means direction." Dixie stood beside him, wings twitching with restrained tension. "Direction means intent." Var-Kin, towering and solemn, added, "Intent means reckoning."

Cass Nova approached, pale but resolute. "The Root agrees. It's sending guidance. The eastern channels are old, but they're accessible. She wants us to follow." Jones paused. "Why would Manibrax want us to follow?"

Cass met his eyes. "Because she's calling us."

*****

Choosing the Team

Inside the muster chamber, the Division Commanders awaited Colonel Havelock. Major Aria Vance (Air Division), Major Edgar Greg (Ground Division), Commander Arlen Veyra (Water Division), Major Rowan Duskveil, Captain William Jones, 1st Sgt. Miller, Dixie Lake, Vek, Var-Kin and Cass Nova. Each had a place. Each had a purpose. Each knew this call was not optional — because it wasn't issued by Stonewall. It was issued by the enemy.

Havelock opened the meeting. "Stonewall will not suffer indecision. The eastern tunnels hold the key. We cannot let Manibrax spread beyond them." Aria Vance leaned forward.

"My division will deploy aerial scouts. Even underground, we can provide mapping support and vertical extraction if needed."

Greg slammed a gauntleted fist onto the table. "Rangers and Monks go first, skirmishers midline, heavies rear. We keep formation tight and predictable." Veyra swirled a translucent map of water channels across the table. "Some tunnels will be flooded. Some are too tight for the heavies. We'll need specialized movement teams."

Jones raised a hand. "We aren't following a swarm. We're following a presence. We cannot track her like a nest. We follow through rhythm, not footprints."

Cass nodded. "She moves in silence. But the roots move in memory. Memory will guide us."

Var-Kin placed his claw on the map. "We go east, then down, to the old basins. She will not face us directly — not yet. She will test our minds first."

Dixie folded her arms. "I like tests. She'll learn why the Tree Division are the best scouts." Miller grinned despite the tension. "She'll learn why we're BUGFORCE."

Even Havelock allowed the faintest smile. "Then let the east remember us."

*****

The Root's Guidance

Stonewall shifted. Literally. The great bark walls groaned, moving like tectonic plates, revealing a passage long sealed. Golden vines unwound themselves from a doorway carved into the ground— a doorway that no one had known existed (but the Root had always known).

Cass felt the vibration first. "She's opening a path for us." Dixie exhaled. "The Root's making a tunnel?" Var-Kin shook his head. "No. The Root is remembering a tunnel." The passage descended into glowing amber darkness. Warm, alive, safe, and root claimed.

Jones lowered a hand to the bark. "It wants us to go now." Cass whispered, "It wants us to stop her before she reaches the old memory chambers."

"The Hollow Choir?" Dixie asked. "No," Cass said. "Older."

Var-Kin bowed his head. "She approaches the Old Root Vaults — the memory of Earth before humans." Miller muttered, "Then we better move fast." Jones nodded. "Gear up. We move in ten."

*****

Into the Eastern Descent

The journey began with a single step. Jones led the way. Cass beside him. Dixie overhead. Var-Kin pressing forward with measured strength. Vek scanning for echoes. Miller steady, unwavering.

The tunnel gradually sloped downward, the amber saplight guiding their path.

The deeper they went, the more the walls changed — from bark to sinew to something older still, like fossilized memory.

Not bone. Not stone. Something between. "This is ancient," Cass said. "This predates everything we know." Var-Kin clicked softly. "The Root remembers before it grew. Before it chose harmony. Before it chose to share."

Jones stepped carefully. "And Manibrax remembers before humans." "She remembers resentment," Cass murmured. "She remembers being denied," Var-Kin added.

"And now," Dixie said, gripping her weapon, "she wants to return."

*****

The Whispering Lines Close In

As they descended, faint vibrations returned — like fingertips brushing across their helmets, soft, persistent, wrong. Vek froze. "Contact. Movement on all sides. Small. Fast."

Before Jones could react— A dozen shapes skittered along the walls, shadows darting in synchronized formation.

Not Choir. Not ants. Not beetles. Controlled ones. Small insects — winged, crawling, shifting — moving to a rhythm no one else could hear.

Dixie lifted her rifle. "Eyes up—coming in fast!" Jones shouted: "Hold fire! Check for resonance shielding—" Cass scanned them. "No patches. No shielding. They're hers."

The controlled swarm lunged. Miller swung his staff, knocking two into the wall. Var-Kin tore another from the ceiling. Dixie fired a resonance bolt — the swarm recoiled in pain but did not retreat.

Cass activated a harmonic burst artifact— a pure tone, dazzling and sharp, filling the tunnel. The swarm froze mid-lunge. Trembled. Shuddered. Then collapsed.

Miller stepped over the bodies carefully. "What stopped them?" Cass looked down. "The resonance. It disrupts the control. It severs her hold." Dixie grinned. "Then I'll sing louder."

*****

The Eastern Call Forms

When they reached the next chamber, the tunnel opened into a vast cavern. A deep hum vibrated from the far end — not the Root. Not the Choir. Something else. A single word formed on the air. No mouth made it. No echo carried it. Yet everyone heard it.

"COME."

Jones tightened his grip on his weapon. "That's not an invitation." Cass shook her head. "No. That's challenge."

Var-Kin's mandibles clicked. "She calls not to speak. She calls to conquer." Dixie's wings flared wide. "Then we answer."

Jones lifted his weapon. "Forward." The cavern darkened as they marched. The Root's amber glow stayed behind them. Ahead lay only shadow. And the heartbeat of something ancient and very female waiting in the deep. The moment they stepped beyond the Root-lit threshold, the light changed.

Amber gold faded behind them. Dark stone swallowed it. And the air thickened — not with heat, not with humidity, but with memory. Memory that felt alien. Memory that felt older than bark or soil. Memory that once belonged to Earth... but no longer shared it.

Cass Nova took one step forward and stopped. "Do you feel that?" Jones nodded. "I don't feel wind. I don't feel temperature. I feel..." He searched for a word. Var-Kin provided it. "Intent."

The cavern stretched before them — too wide for their lanterns, too deep for their sensors, too still for the living. Dixie opened her wings slightly. They rustled the air, but the air did not answer. No echo. No response. Miller whispered, "Dead space."

Cass shook her head. "No. Sleeping space." Var-Kin's antennae rose. "It watches."

*****

The Weight of a Hidden Queen

They advanced slowly, in tight formation. Jones led. Dixie hovered just above ground. Cass and Vek scanned the dark. Var-Kin guarded the flank. Miller swept the rear. Step by step, the cavern grew worse. Shadows moved where their footsteps didn't. Shapes drifted in the periphery, vanishing when looked at directly. Stone formations undulated — slow breaths, as though the walls themselves inhaled.

Cass stopped, eyes widening. "She isn't speaking through the roots. She's speaking through the dark." Dixie exhaled. "Then what is all this?" Var-Kin responded in a low rumble. "Her throne room." The cavern walls shivered. A low vibration rippled through the floor. Not seismic — sentient. A feminine whisper rolled like silk across their minds:

"THRONE? NO. REMNANT."

Jones's grip tightened around his weapon. "She hears us." Cass corrected him, "She hears everything."

*****

The Flicker and the Fall

As they reached a deeper corridor, the floor shifted beneath them — not collapsing, not breaking, but breathing. Stone expanded like a lung, pushing upward, forcing them back.

344

Jones braced himself. "Move, move—!" Dixie launched into the air, wings beating, catching herself against a jutting ledge. Var-Kin dug his claws into the walls.

Cass stumbled — Miller caught her arm just in time. The cavern settled again. A slow, deliberate movement. Not random. Expressive. Cass whispered, "She wants us to feel her presence. Not fight it. Not flee it."

Var-Kin snarled softly, "She wants us to kneel." A cold, feminine laugh echoed through their minds — not amused, but familiar.

"*YOU KNEELED ONCE. WHEN EARTH WAS MINE.*"

The cavern lights dimmed— even though there were no lights. Just the absence of light growing heavier.

*****

The First Vision

Cass froze. Her eyes widened. Her breathing stopped. Her body went rigid. Jones grabbed her shoulders, "Cass? Talk to me." She didn't respond. Her eyes glowed faintly — not Root gold, not Brood green, but white. Pure white. Dixie reached out. "Jones—she's seeing something."

Cass's voice shifted —lower, echoing, layered. "She… she is showing me. Showing us." Then the walls themselves changed. Shadows peeled away like curtains. Revealing a mural of living stone — images forming, dissolving, reforming in endless cycles. Not history. Memory. *Her* memory.

They saw: A vast forest older than any human A giant, radiant being woven of shadow and metal Eyes like suns, wings like night. Claws that could split mountains. A presence that filled the horizon. Dixie whispered, "That's her." Var-Kin bowed his head. "A titan."

Miller muttered, "A queen." Cass's voice trembled, "A goddess." The mural flickered changing. Manibrax stood alone. Unmatched. Unshared. Earth's first sovereign. Then humans came. Tiny. Innumerable. Persistent. She watched them rise. Spread, build, grow. *She hated it.*

The stone showed her leaving — not defeated but offended. Not banished, but self-exiled. Jones whispered, "She refused to share Earth." Cass's voice returned to normal — barely. "She didn't just leave. She took something. Something the Earth needed. A piece of the world's balance." The mural dissolved. The cavern darkened. Her presence intensified.

******

The Hunger Returns

A breath — impossibly cold — washed over them. Cass staggered. Var-Kin lowered his body, battle stance ready. Dixie raised her rifle. The feminine whisper returned:

"*I RETURN BECAUSE EARTH CALLS ME. NOT FOR HARMONY.FOR COMPLETION.*"

Jones shouted back, "Completion means consuming everything that breathes." The cavern trembled. **"*YES.*"** A distant rumble echoed — like thunder beneath stone. Growing louder.

The swarm was coming. Not controlled ones. Not Choir. Her army. Cass backed away. "We need to fall back. Now."

Miller nodded. "Retreat course—west, fast and steady." Dixie flared her wings, "Jones, move!" Jones hesitated — just for a heartbeat. "Why call us here?" he asked the dark. The answer was immediate.

"*TO SEE. TO KNOW. TO FEAR.*"

The echo exploded through the cavern — a shockwave of cold, ancient hatred. The tunnel behind them cracked open — a pathway back to Stonewall. Cass screamed, "GO!"

Jones led the charge. Dixie soared overhead. Var-Kin thundered forward. Vek ran with a desperate rhythm. Miller brought up the rear, strong and unwavering. Behind them, the darkness shifted— not following but watching. Waiting. A promise left in the cold air:

"I AM NOT WHOLE. I WILL BE."

The moment BUGFORCE fled the Shadow Cavern, the tunnels themselves awakened.

Not the Root-tunnels — but the old insect arteries, hollow channels carved before Stonewall existed. The moment Manibrax stirred, the earth rearranged itself.

*****

When the Earth Moves

Jones sprinted up the inclined path, lungs burning, Cass beside him stumbling forward, her connection to the Root still raw and overstimulated. Behind them, a roar echoed — deep, grinding, primal. The tunnel walls rippled like muscles contracting.

Dixie looked back mid-flight. "Jones—this whole place is moving!" Var-Kin pressed a claw into the wall. "It reshapes. She reshapes it."

Vek yelled, "We need to move faster—she's redirecting the passages!" Miller's footsteps thundered behind them. "This was a trap from the start!" Cass shook her head. "No. Not a trap. A test."

Jones hissed, "We passed?" The ceiling trembled violently. Cass answered grimly, "She's not done grading us."

*****

The First Collapse

A deafening crack split the air. Dixie darted upward, wings flashing. "INCOMING—!!" The ceiling gave way in a shower of stone and ancient resin. Var-Kin leapt sideways, dragging Vek with him. Cass stumbled. Jones caught her, pulling her into a roll as debris crashed where she had stood. Dust billowed, choking the air. The floor tilted — a gentle slope one moment, a treacherous incline the next.

Miller braced himself and shouted above the noise: "Paths are changing! Find the upward drift!" Var-Kin lifted his head, antennae sweeping the air. "I feel the Root above us — faint but constant. We go left—follow the sap-scent!" Jones nodded. "Move!"

*****

The Walls Become Limbs

They took the left corridor. Immediately, the ground shifted beneath them — rippling like a living carpet. The walls bulged. Stone flowed. Channels reformed. Dixie winced. "She's molding the earth like clay." Cass breathed heavily, "She can't touch the Root. So she touches everything else." Jones pushed forward. "We outrun her control. She moves the tunnels — not the world." The wall to his left trembled in response, almost as if it heard him. A feminine whisper brushed past his ear:

"I MOVE WHAT I OWN."

Jones gritted his teeth. "You own nothing here." The earth groaned — long, low, amused.

*****

The First Vanguard

From the darkness ahead came a sound like splintering bone. Dixie's wings snapped open. "Contact!" Var-Kin surged forward; claws raised. A shape emerged — not insect,

348

not beast, but something between the two. Its body was armored in matte black carapace. Its limbs were jointed incorrectly. Its eyes glowed silver-white — empty, pure, controlled. Cass whispered, "Hybrid." Vek corrected her, swallowing hard. "No. Reborn."

The creature lunged. Var-Kin intercepted, claws locking against mandibles. The impact sent sparks flying. Jones fired a resonance bolt — the creature jerked back, shrieked, staggered. Dixie soared overhead, firing precise shots that drove the hybrid backward.

Miller swung his staff, striking its flank. The creature reeled — then straightened, shaking. Cass shouted, "Resonance again! It disrupts the control—hit it harder!" Jones fired a full-charge bolt. The creature convulsed — light crackling through its limbs — until its body collapsed like a puppet whose strings had been cut. Dixie landed beside it, panting. "One down. How many more?" Var-Kin sniffed the air. His mandibles tightened. "Hundreds."

*****

The Maze Reforms

The tunnel split ahead — one path curling left, the other right. Jones paused. Var-Kin surveyed the air. Cass closed her eyes, reaching outward with her senses. But before any of them chose— The left corridor sealed shut like a throat swallowing. Dixie stepped back. "Well… that's answered." Miller pointed to the right. "Only option." Cass shook her head. "No. That's the path she wants us to take."

Jones responded, "Then we take it." Var-Kin hesitated. "She is her strongest in these old channels." Cass nodded. "And we are strongest together." The ground shuddered again —Manibrax's presence rippling beneath them like a heartbeat.

*****

The River of Noise

They entered the right path at full run. Behind them, the floor collapsed, swallowed by a chasm of darkness. Ahead, a roar grew — like rushing water, like thunder, like stampeding feet. Vek raised his voice. "Captain—multiple signatures ahead!"

They rounded a bend— and faced the impossible: A river of insects, moving in a single unified wave, a living tide of legs and wings and mandibles. Not frantic. Not disorganized. **Synchronized.** Dixie whispered,"Impossible…" Var-Kin answered, "No.Directed." Cass's voice trembled. "She controls all who lack resonance.All who are unshielded."

Jones stepped forward. "And she sends them here." Miller hefted his staff. "Then we hold this line."

*****

The Unraveling Begins

The insects surged — not crawling, not swarming, but flowing. A river. A tide. A living force. Jones shouted, "Form ranks—Tree Rangers forward, Ground behind!" Dixie took flight. Var-Kin roared. Miller stood like a wall. Cass raised her resonance artifact — its light pushing back the tide like a shield.

Vek's scanners screamed warnings. "There are too many—too many!" Jones shouted back, "It doesn't matter!" The tide hit. The cavern shook. Stone fractured. Dust rose.

The world narrowed to the clash of bodies and the crack of resonance weapons. Dixie dove and fired. Var-Kin shredded through rows. Cass pulsed harmonic blasts. Jones cut a path forward. The tide pushed. They pushed back. Behind them, the earth shifted again — tunnels collapsing, new ones forming. The path back to Stonewall narrowed with every breath. Cass shouted, "She's closing the way behind us!" Miller roared, "Then keep moving forward!"

Jones pointed into the darkness. "There — there's an opening! A path!" Var-Kin nodded. "That way leads upward," Cass whispered with awe. "The Root is guiding us. The tunnels she can't touch." Dixie soared overhead, clearing the route. Jones raised his voice over the roar: "BUGFORCE — ADVANCE!" And they surged forward into the narrow passage as the old world collapsed behind them and Manibrax's army thundered at their backs.

The tunnels finally fell quiet. Distant echoes of the collapsing earth faded. The rushing tide of controlled insects receded into an ominous hum. The path forward narrowed into a tight, upward climb of root-woven stone. Jones paused. Only for a breath. Only for a heartbeat. Only for the length of a moment, where he could allow his mask to slip. He sat with his back against the cool wall — not collapsing, not defeated — but acknowledging gravity.

Dixie hovered above the passage mouth, vigilant. Var-Kin and Vek stood a few meters ahead, scanning the next corridor. Miller watched the rear, silent and steady. Cass leaned against a root, recovering her connection.

Jones exhaled slowly. He let his shoulders lower. The weight of command shifted. He allowed it — just for now.

*****

The Quiet Between Heartbeats

A faint resonance hum pulsed beneath him. Safe. Warm. Root-protected. Not the cold silence of Manibrax. But even that warmth could not pierce the knot in his chest. Jones closed his eyes. He saw the cavern again — the vast, suffocating dark, the shifting walls, the feminine whisper that cut deeper than any blade.

YOU LEFT ME. YOU TOOK MY EARTH. I WILL BE WHOLE.

Those words followed him like shadows. No matter how fast he ran, they kept pace. He had fought insects. He had fought swarms. He had fought weather, cavern collapse, starvation, and exhaustion. But this? This was something older, something hungry, something that meant to claim humanity as an inconvenience. He swallowed. "What do you do," he murmured quietly to himself, "when you realize your enemy remembers hatred older than your entire species?"

*****

Command and the Cost of Clarity

Jones didn't fear dying. That fear had burned away long ago. What he feared was failure. Not for himself. For them. Dixie, Cass, Var-Kin, Vek and Miller. All trusting him to lead.

A captain was not the strongest. Not the fastest. Not the wisest. A captain was the one who walked into the dark first and made it safe for the others to follow. But the dark they now walked into was not a place — it was a will. A presence. And he felt its gaze on him even now. Something ancient whispering through the earth, through the tunnels, through his memory.

COME. SEE.BREAK.

He exhaled sharply and pressed his palms against his knees. "Not today," he whispered. "I'm not breaking today."

*****

The Ghosts of Leadership

He remembered the first Micro-Operatives he lost. He remembered the weight of writing the reports. He remembered the mother who asked him, "Did she die well?"

Jones had answered, "She died with honor." Remembering Gunny Isabell Rose, but what he wanted to say was, "she deserved to live." He remembered every loss since. Every name. Every face. A line of ghosts behind him — not haunting but reminding. Responsibility did not disappear when the fight began. Responsibility became the fight. He looked at his gauntlet, cracked and dust-covered. "We're walking into the center of her power," he whispered. "Into the cradle of something ancient." His voice softened. "But we go together."

*****

The Quiet Strength

Jones opened his eyes. The team was looking at him. Not with concern. Not with fear but with trust. Cass met his gaze. "Captain," she said softly, "we're ready." Dixie landed beside them, wings folding neatly. "We're with you to the end." Var-Kin bowed slightly. "Where you step, we step." Vek nodded. "No hesitation." Miller simply said, "Lead the way." Jones rose slowly, deliberately. He squared his shoulders. He let the weight of command settle again. It didn't feel lighter. It wasn't meant to. He placed his hand on the Root wall beside him. Its warmth pulsed in answer. He whispered, "Thank you." Was he thanking the Root? His team? The Earth itself? It didn't matter. He stepped forward. "All right," he said, voice strong again. "Let's finish this." And the warmth beneath their feet pulsed a promise: ***You are not alone.***

The tunnel narrowed until the team had to move single file. Dixie folded her wings tight to her sides. Var-Kin crouched low. Miller walked point; weapon raised. Jones followed close behind. Vek's scanners whirred nervously. Cass and the Root harmonics pulsed with urgency. The air grew warmer. The light brighter. A faint, ancient hum vibrated the walls. Jones murmured, "We're close." Cass nodded slowly. "Closer than anyone has been in centuries." A pulse rolled beneath their feet — not Manibrax's rhythm, not insect sync, but the Root's heartbeat growing stronger. The tunnel widened — abruptly, dramatically — opening into a vast subterranean chamber. Light spilled upward from cracks in the floor, washing the cavern in amber-gold fire. Everyone stopped. Even Var-Kin bowed his head in awe.

*****

The Ancient Root Vault

The chamber stretched upward farther than they could see — an underground sky of luminous bark patterns and root-vein constellations. Central pillars rose like trunks of impossible age, wrapped in spiraling glyphs that glowed and pulsed with life. The Root Vault. The Prime Heart. The first breath of the Earth itself. Cass inhaled sharply. "Jones… this is the core." Jones stepped forward cautiously. "This is where the Root first woke."

Vek whispered, stunned, "The oldest living structure on Earth…" Miller murmured, "Feels like we shouldn't be here." Var-Kin rumbled, "We are meant to be here. In dark days, Rootfire awakens." Jones turned. "Rootfire?" Var-Kin nodded solemnly. "A defense older than Manibrax. A memory older than hunger. A promise."

*****

The Root Speaks

The chamber vibrated. Not shaking — singing. Saplight flared. Glyphs ignited. The entire vault pulsed in a rhythm that echoed Jones's heartbeat. Cass gasped. "Jones— it recognizes you." Dixie blinked. "Why him?" Var-Kin answered, "Because he leads. Because he carries harmony. Because he shares." The Root's glow concentrated around Jones — forming a ring of golden light that pulsed outward. Miller whispered, "It's blessing him." Jones took one step forward. The entire vault responded. The floor glowed brighter. The walls shone. The ancient glyphs ignited like suns. Something awakened. A voice — not feminine, not masculine — primordial — thundered through the chamber:

STAND WITH US

Cass clutched her head. "It's speaking— but not with words. With unity." Jones nodded. "We're here. We'll stand." Var-Kin bowed low. Dixie landed; wings lowered. Miller pressed a fist to his chest. Vek held his scanner reverently. The Root listened. The Root answered.

****

The Uncorrupted Energy

From the center of the floor, a column of pure Rootfire rose — an eruption of golden energy, crackling like lightning but warm as sunrise. The blast hit the ceiling — shattering thousands of years of dust and darkness. Light cascaded downward like molten stars. Dixie nearly collapsed from the radiance. "It's... beautiful." Cass whispered, voice trembling, "It's the ultimate defense. Pure resonance. The one force Manibrax cannot control."

Jones stepped closer to the column. Heat brushed his skin. It did not burn. It embraced. Cass reached out. "Careful—" Jones touched the Rootfire. And the world changed.

****

Jones's Moment of Unity

Jones's vision exploded: The Choir's trembling fear. The Brood's awakening, The tunnels rearranging, Manibrax's shadow rising. The ancient forest before mankind. The first Micro-Operatives footstep. The first siege. The founding of Stonewall. The endless cycles of struggle. The constant, eternal rhythm of Earth. The Rootfire sang through him. He saw not just the present, but potential futures. One where Manibrax rises, unchallenged. One where harmony shatters. One where silence consumes the world. But also: One where unity holds. One where humanity shares Earth — not as conquerors, not as owners, but as caretakers.

A third path. One worth bleeding for. The Rootfire whispered to him: **YOU ARE ENOUGH.** Jones staggered back, breath trembling. Dixie caught him. "Jones—talk to me—what did you see?" Jones inhaled. "Everything. And a choice."

*****

Manibrax Responds

The vault trembled. Not from Rootfire — but from something deeper. A cold pulse answered the golden light. The Shadow Queen stirred. A whisper, impossibly distant yet intimately close: **"YOU WAKE OLD FIRE."** The vault dimmed as if holding its breath.

"GOOD."

A second tremor shook the ground. Debris fell. Dust swirled. The tunnels behind them collapsed. Dixie shouted, "We're sealed in!" Var-Kin raised his stance. "She comes." Cass turned pale. "Rootfire woke the memory. She senses it." The Rootfire column flared, spreading golden veins across the floor, igniting ancient sigils. The light gathered around the team, forming a shimmering dome. A shield and a warning.

Jones raised his weapon. "Positions! She's coming through the lower tunnels!" And far beneath them, in the depths where light could not reach, a roar rose. Not an animal. Not an insect. A roar of hunger.

Manibrax was rising.

The Root Vault hummed with power — a living aurora beneath the earth. The Rootfire column pulsed, casting gold across every corner of the chamber. Cass stood with arms raised, feeling the resonance ripple through her bones. Miller steadied his stance. Var-Kin's claws scraped the floor in anticipation. Vek calibrated his scanner for what he sensed was coming. Dixie hovered several feet above the ground, her wings shimmering in the golden glow. "Captain… something's moving below." Jones nodded, eyes fixed on the trembling earth. He didn't need Vek's confirmation to know what it meant. Manibrax was no longer whispering. She was rising.

*****

The First Tremor

The floor shook — not violently, but rhythmically. A deep, pounding pulse. *THOOM, THOOM, THOOM.* Var-Kin stiffened. "These are not the steps of controlled ones." Vek swallowed. "No… these are too heavy. "The Rootfire flared in response —taller, brighter, angrier. Cass whispered, "The Root is warning us. "Dixie flew higher, scanning. A crack tore across the floor —straight down the center of the vault. Light spilled through it like molten gold. Everyone stepped back instinctively. The crack widened, splitting the chamber like a mouth opening. From the depths came a sound that did not belong to any creature known to Earth. A composite sound: the hiss of serpents, the scuttle of beetles, the roar of something colossal and ancient.

357

Var-Kin whispered, "Her vanguard." Miller muttered, "What in the name of all root and bark did she create? Cass answered quietly. "What she remembers."

*****

The First of Manibrax's Chosen

A shape emerged from the crack — massive, armored, gleaming in black chitin. Eight legs, each as thick as tree trunks. Mandibles that could split stone. A segmented body plated in obsidian-like exoskeleton that reflected no light. A creature too large to be natural. Too unnatural to be ancient. Too ancient to be new. Cass's eyes widened. "It's… a titan-lurker." Jones asked, "Thought those were extinct." Var-Kin nodded slowly. "They were. She saved one. Changed it. Perfected it." Dixie gasped. "She bred it for war."

Vek's scanner vibrated uncontrollably. "This thing could tear Stonewall apart!" The titan-lurker's eyes glowed — not red, not green, but silver-white: the color of Manibrax's control. Then it roared. The sound slammed into them like a shockwave. Miller was thrown backwards. Vek stumbled. Dixie was pushed against the vault wall by the sheer force. Var-Kin dug his claws into the floor, barely anchoring himself. Jones managed to stay upright, shouting,

"HOLD LINE! HOLD LINE!"

The creature reared back, preparing to strike— Cass flung her hand toward the Rootfire column. The gold erupted outward in a wide, sweeping arc. The titan-lurker staggered. It hissed in pain.

Jones's eyes widened. "It's vulnerable to Rootfire!" Cass nodded. "Nothing Manibrax creates can withstand pure resonance!" "Then we use it!" Jones shouted.

*****

III. The Battle in the Vault

Jones rushed forward. Miller followed, swinging his staff, smashing into the titan-lurker's mandible, cracking a piece of its armor. Dixie soared overhead, firing concentrated resonance bolts at the vulnerable joints. Var-Kin charged, clawing into its side, ripping chunks of chitin free.

Vek found a vantage point and aimed a harmonic destabilizer at the creature's abdomen. The titan-lurker screeched and swung one colossal limb — Var-Kin caught the blow, slammed backwards into a pillar.

"VAR!" Dixie cried. Var-Kin rose slowly, cracking his neck. "I have survived worse." He lunged again, claws glowing with Rootfire sparks as the energy seeped into him. Cass stood at the Rootfire's edge — arms raised, channeling the pulse. "Jones! Its eyes! They're the control point!"

Jones nodded. Dixie dove. Var-Kin rammed into the creature's flank. Miller swung upward, smashing its nearest eye. The titan-lurker shrieked. Its movements faltered. Vek fired a harmonic burst directly into its remaining eye. A deafening crack exploded through the vault. The creature reeled. Cass shouted, "Now! Strike now! All of you!"

Jones charged. The entire team converged. The titan-lurker screamed— And the Rootfire surged upward, sending a beam of golden energy straight through its skull. Silence. Then—The colossal creature collapsed, shaking the chamber as it fell. The ground trembled once more. Cass whispered, trembling, "That wasn't the only one."

*****

IV. The Queen's Pulse

The chamber shuddered again — this time not from the titan-lurker falling. From something deeper. A pulse. Cold, dark and vast. Manibrax's anger. Cass gripped the Rootfire column. "She knows we awakened the Vault. She's sending more." Var-Kin nodded.

"They will be larger." Vek gulped. "I don't want to see larger." Dixie stood tall. "We'll face whatever she sends." Jones steadied his weapon. The Rootfire pulsed, sending trembling waves of gold across the Root Vault.

Cass spoke softly, "This is the moment carved into the Earth's oldest memory. When Root and Manibrax meet again." Miller tightened his grip. "Then we'll stand between them." Jones nodded. "BUGFORCE — prepare!" The floor split again. Darkness rose.

The Queen was ascending. For a brief fragment of time — in the pulsing glow of the Rootfire, with the fallen titan-lurker steaming at his feet — Var-Kin allowed himself to remember. Not the way humans remembered, with faces and stories and years. Beetles remembered in the shell. In layers. In rings. In grain. Every scar, every molt, every victory and loss lodged itself in the hardened exoskeleton the way trees recorded storms in their rings. He touched the cracked plate on his left shoulder — the same plate struck by Manibrax's vanguard moments ago.

The Rootfire's glow seeped between the fissures like golden milk. The crack tingled. A new memory etched itself. Another ring. Another moment. He bowed his head.

*****

1. The Echo of Ancestors

The Rootfire hummed around him. Its warmth seeped into his claws and thorax. In that light, he felt the presence of countless generations of beetle-kin stretching behind him like a long, winding trail. He felt... Grandmother-of-the-Dunes, who fought a sand leviathan until her last breath. Ancestor Shield-Back, who stood before a swarm of horned mantises and did not retreat. Narrow-Wing, whose flight carried messages between the first Tree Rangers. Silent-Carver, and at the edge of all memory — a presence dark and vast like a shadow eclipsing a sun: *Manibrax.*

He felt her as the beetles once did — not as queen or goddess or tyrant but as inevitability. She was the pressure that shaped stone. The shadow that bent light. She was the hunger of the deep places, the one who chose exile over sharing her dominion. The one beetles whispered about in their oldest molting songs. The one they feared but also respected. Because once, long ago, she ruled with a certainty that left the earth trembling. But even in that ancient fear, there had always been one truth: *The Root was older.* And the Root chose harmony. Var-Kin touched the Rootfire's golden glow with reverence.

*****

2. The Meaning of Strength

Miller approached him, leaning on his staff, breath heavy. "You good?" Miller asked. Var-Kin tilted his head. It was a beetle-gesture that meant I am remembering, and I am becoming. Miller nodded, understanding anyway. "Worth asking. You took a hit back there." Var-Kin's mandibles clicked softly. "It shaped me," he said. "It joined the others." Miller smiled. "Another crack in the armor, huh?" Var-Kin lowered his voice. "A crack is not weakness. It is proof of survival."

He straightened his posture, towering. "Every fracture honors the past. Every scar honors the ones who walked before." Miller grinned. "Remind me to stop complaining about bruises." Var-Kin vibrated his wings — and laughed, But behind the amusement lay something deeper. Purpose. Resolve. The sense that the battle to come was not just war — but tradition.

A sacred continuation of the ancient pact between beetle-kind and the living Root. Manibrax might control unshielded minds. She might reshape tunnels. She might send her monstrous vanguard, but she could not touch the Root. She could not command a beetle's memory. Var-Kin pressed a claw against the floor, feeling the gentle hum beneath it. "We will stand," he said softly. Miller nodded. "Together."

*****

3. The Path Forward

Var-Kin lifted his head as the vault trembled again. The tremor was not fear. It was warning. A low pulse rumbled beneath the team — not Manibrax's rhythm, but the Root's. Cass turned, eyes wide. "She's sending more. Bigger." Jones lifted his weapon. "Get into positions!" Var-Kin stepped into line — his shell still cracked, still glowing with Rootlight. He was carved by a thousand battles. Carried by a thousand ancestors. And in this moment in the presence of both Rootfire and the rising Queen, he understood a truth etched into his shell: ***The world does not belong to the strongest. It belongs to the willing.***

He lowered his stance, claws gleaming. "I am Var-Kin," he growled. "Son of ancient lines. Protector of Root and Ranger. Let the Queen come. "The Rootfire behind him flared, as if answering: ***WE STAND WITH YOU.***

The Rootfire glowed like a golden sun at the heart of the vault, casting light across the ancient chamber. It shimmered on the bodies of BUGFORCE, turning armor into living flame. It crackled across the vault pillars, igniting glyphs older than humanity. But the shadows pressed close. Cold, silver-lit, hungry shadows.

Dixie hovered above the team. "Jones—movement below us. Fast. Many." Var-Kin's antennae quivered. "Positions. Now." Cass felt the tremor first — a shifting, twisting pulse of pressure against her sternum. "No—she's pushing them all at once. They're coming like a wave." Jones squared his stance. "Let her come." The vault floor cracked again. And then it split wide.

I. The Swarm of the Deep

The roar that erupted from beneath was earth-shattering — literal earth-shaking thunder. Out of the crack surged Manibrax's vanguard: Multi-limbed hybrids Ancient titan species reshaped for war Carapace as black as obsidian Eyes glowing silver-white Mandibles clashing like war drums Wings that made the air tremble Legs that carved trenches in barkstone The Rootfire pulsed brighter, answering the challenge.

Dixie lifted her rifle. "Targets incoming!" Miller raised his staff. "Hold the line!" Var-Kin roared — a sound that echoed primal, ancestral, powerful. Cass stepped forward, hands blazing with harmonic resonance. Jones drew both weapons and eyes steady. "BUGFORCE STAND!" The first wave hit like a storm-wall.

*****

II. The Dance of Resonance and Fury

Dixie dove. She fired pulses of gold-charged bolts that split the air with crackling arcs. Var-Kin met a charging armored beast head-on, claws slicing through its thick plates. Miller spun his staff — a blur of motion — cracking skulls, breaking mandibles, knocking creatures aside with a force that echoed Rootfire's rhythm.

Vek scrambled along a fallen pillar, firing harmonic bursts that sent shockwaves through the enemy ranks. Cass raised both arms — Rootfire pulsing through her veins and sent a wave of pure resonance outward. The cavern caught the beat. Glyphs lit. The vault trembled. A dozen creatures shrieked — their silver-light eyes dimming under the harmonic attack. Jones moved between them like lightning.

He fired. He sliced and pivoted. Every motion precise, measured. He fought like someone who knew that if he fell, the light fell with him.

Dixie landed beside him mid-combat. "Captain, they're adapting!" Jones fired at a hybrid's leg joint. "I see that!" Cass shouted over the roar, "They're learning our rhythm! We need to change patterns!" Var-Kin roared again — not in rage, but in command. "FOLLOW MINE!" And for a moment, BUGFORCE fought in the beetle rhythm — an ancient, brutal cadence older than humans, older than Manibrax's anger. The Rootfire responded — its pulses matching Var-Kin's battle roar. And the tide slowed. Just slightly…Enough.

*****

III. The Vault Suffers

Then everything changed. The floor fractured under the weight of a colossal creature rising from below — larger than the titan-lurker, larger than anything yet encountered. Its body filled half the vault. Its mandibles could crush a Root pillar. Its wings unfolded into a storm-dark canopy. Vek stared. "What—what IS that?" Cass's voice trembled in awe and terror. "An elder brood-synth. She made it… from fragments of the oldest species." Var-Kin whispered a single word in his own tongue — a word that meant "death-walker." The creature roared. The vault shook. The Rootfire dimmed slightly — overwhelmed by the force of ancient monstrosity.

Jones shouted: "Fall back! Force it toward the Rootfire!" Miller slammed his staff into the ground. "I'll anchor left!" Dixie soared upward. "I'll distract its head!" Var-Kin charged. "I will break its armor!" Cass braced her feet. "I'll amplify any opening!" Vek recalibrated. "I'll target the joints!" Jones nodded. "Let's kill a legend."

*****

IV. The Battle with the Elder Brood-Synth

The creature struck first. A limb crashed down — a living hammer. Jones dove aside. Stone exploded where he had stood. Dixie fired at its secondary eyes. Var-Kin clawed its side. Miller locked its limb with his staff, muscles straining. Cass unleashed a focused resonance blast — gold against black. The elder synth staggered. Barely. Jones shouted upward, "Dixie! Higher!" She flew, wings blazing with Rootfire reflections. Var-Kin tore a chunk of armor free. "Cass! NOW!" Cass channeled all the resonance she had — a beam of intense harmonic light that hit the exposed flesh. The synth shrieked — a sound that cracked stone, rippling through every nerve in the vault. It reeled, staggering toward the Rootfire. Jones grinned fiercely. "That's it!" Miller swung upward, smashing its forelimb. Vek fired a harmonic disruptor into the gap. Dixie dove again, slicing a wing joint. Var-Kin rammed forward with primal strength. Together— they drove the creature into the Rootfire column. The vault erupted in golden explosion. The elder brood-synth convulsed — its silver-light eyes flickering. Then it collapsed, shaking the entire chamber.

*****

V. The Shadow Queen's Fury

Silence. Then a cold whisper: **"IMPRESSIVE. BUT FRAGMENTS."** The vault trembled violently. Cass staggered. "Jones—she's coming. Not her vanguard. Not her constructs. Her." Jones steadied her. "How soon?" The Rootfire flickered. A tremor rippled across the floor. Var-Kin lowered his voice. "She is above us. Moving through deep layers. Toward the surface. Toward Stonewall." Dixie exhaled sharply. "Then this isn't the final fight." Cass shook her head. "No. This is the opening act." Miller tightened his grip. "What do we do?" Jones raised his weapon. His voice was steady. "BUGFORCE— we follow her to the surface." The Rootfire flared like a blazing sun. And far above them, the earth rumbled again as the Queen of Silence ascended. The Rootfire dimmed, its brilliant glow shifting from active defense to a steady, guiding radiance. The cavern around BUGFORCE still crackled with heat and memory, but the air had changed. The lingering tremors beneath their feet deepened into a single, unified pulse: *She was moving.*

Jones turned toward the upward tunnels, the narrow spirals carved by time, root, and pressure. "Up," he ordered. "We have to reach her before she breaches." Dixie launched upward with a burst of wings. "I'll scout ahead." Var-Kin growled deep in his chest. "Eyes on all sides. She moves through shadow. Shadow moves through her." Cass steadied herself, Rootfire still echoing through her bones. "She's ascending faster than we are. The closer she gets to the surface, the stronger she'll become." Miller gripped his staff tighter. "Then we better run."

*****

I. The Spiral of Echoes

The tunnel spiraled upward like a corkscrew carved through ancient stone. BUGFORCE ascended at a sprint. Jones leading. Miller bringing up the rear. Var-Kin bounding with heavy steps. Vek scanning constantly. Cass balancing on the shifting ground. Dixie drifting between ceiling and wall like a ghost of air and wings. The deeper tremors grew louder, more rhythmic. Thoom, thoom. thoom. Jones muttered, "She's not climbing. She's pushing the earth aside." Cass nodded, breathless. "She reshapes everything she touches. She wants the surface. She wants the sky." Dixie looked back. "Why the sky? She was born below." Var-Kin clicked low. "Conquest begins with vision. She seeks the whole world, not just the deep." Thunder cracked above them. Dust rained down. The tunnel twisted violently, nearly throwing them against the wall. Miller caught Cass again. "Careful!" Cass swallowed hard. "That wasn't the tunnel. That was her."

*****

II. Echo-Whispers from Below

A sudden voice — cold, smooth, intimate — brushed across all their minds. **"YOU RISE.GOOD."** Jones clenched his teeth. "Stay focused. She's trying to distract us." Var-Kin's mandibles clattered. "She speaks through voids. Through cracks. She cannot touch Root, but she touches absence." Cass trembled. "She's closer to the surface. There's more absence there." Vek flashed warning symbols. "Movement behind! Fast-moving shapes!" Jones rotated. "Miller—rear guard!" Miller swung his staff in wide arcs, blocking the narrow passage, as the first wave of controlled insects surged upward. Their eyes glowed silver-white, their movements unnervingly synchronized. Dixie shouted, "We don't have time to fight—move!" Jones made the call. "Go! Now!" They sprinted again. The tunnel narrowed, forcing them into a single-file climb. Behind them, chittering grew louder. In front of them, the earth trembled. Beneath all of it— The Queen ascended.

*****

III. Confronting the Darkness Above

The spiral opened into a massive vertical shaft. The walls glowed faintly with amber light— the last remnants of the Rootfire's influence. Dixie dipped her wing into the glow. "It's fading fast." Cass whispered, "She's weakening it. Once we reach the surface, root-protection thins." Jones nodded grimly. "She'll be strongest at Stonewall." Var-Kin stamped a claw into the wall. "Then we must reach it before she does." Vek scanned upward. "Two hundred spans to the surface. We can make it." Miller grunted. "Let's do it." They began the ascent, climbing through the shaft. But halfway up, the Root's glow flickered. Then vanished. Darkness swallowed the chamber.

Cass gasped. "She severed the Rootfire's guidance. We're outside the Root's reach." Jones lit his shoulder lamp. "We keep moving." The light illuminated the walls— Covered in fresh grooves. Scratches. Claw marks. Not made by ancient insects. Made by something enormous climbing just ahead of them.

Dixie stared. "She's already passed this way." Cass whispered, "She's above us."

*****

IV. The Breach Warning

Then the wall shook— a violent shudder that rattled every bone. A thunderous roar echoed from above. Stone peeled away from the top of the shaft, falling in massive chunks.

Var-Kin roared, "DOWN!" The team threw themselves against the wall as debris smashed down past them, slamming into the lower shaft with explosive force. Even through the chaos, Cass spoke with chilling clarity: "She's breaking the surface."

Jones roared back, "Then we climb faster!" The shaft trembled again— but this time, a new sound pierced through: Voices, not human, not insect. **Root-construct voices.** Faint, echoing down from above:

HOLD.HELP.HURRY.

Dixie exhaled. "Stonewall knows." Jones nodded sharply. "They're preparing defenses." Cass's eyes widened. "And they're calling us home."

*****

V. The Race to the Light

They climbed. Fast and Unrelenting. Every meter closer to the surface increases the pressure. Cass felt her ears pop. Var-Kin's claws dug gouges in the walls. Dixie's wings strained against the shifting drafts. Miller gripped the rope anchors. The tunnel cracked open above them— light spilled downward like a blade. Sunlight. Cold and white. But with it came something else. A scream, not human, not an insect. A scream of rage and triumph and hunger rolled across the sky. Cass whispered in horror: "She's breached."

Var-Kin roared. "Faster!" Jones shouted, "BUGFORCE—MOVE!" They reached the upper edge of the shaft— And burst into the open air.

*****

VI. Stonewall in Ruin

The sight that greeted them pulled the breath from their lungs. Stonewall's outer walls had cracked. Saplight bled through jagged fissures. Root-constructs lay broken or struggling to rise. The sky above churned with silver-lit clouds that swirled around a massive central shape. A towering silhouette — black wings unfurling, limbs like living obsidian, eyes like burning stars — rose above Stonewall. Not fully formed. Not fully present. But enough.

Cass's voice broke. "Manibrax." Jones lifted his weapon. "We hold Stonewall." Dixie spread her wings. "We fight her here."

Var-Kin stepped forward. "We stand as one." Miller planted his staff. "And we do not break." Jones nodded, steady, resolute. "BUGFORCE— FORM UP." Below them, the earth trembled again.

*****

The Queen had ascended.

And Stonewall stood between her and the entire world. Stonewall shook. Not from defeat. Not from collapse. But from awakening.

The Root beneath the Outpost pulsed with ancient fire — gold surging like lifeblood through the walls, fortifying cracks, mending fissures, spreading luminous veins across the sky-facing bark.

Above the fortress, Manibrax unfurled. Her silver-white eyes blazed. Her obsidian limbs flexed, dripping with fragments of the deep earth. Her presence turned the air cold. Dixie raised her rifle. "Captain… she's massive." Jones stared up, an expression hard as iron. "She's not whole. Not yet."

Cass trembled. "The Root stopped her from fully rising. She's forced to manifest through shadow and control, not through her true form."

Var-Kin rumbled, claws digging into the ground. "She is weakened. But she is still a queen." Miller muttered, "And we're still BUGFORCE."

*****

I. Stonewall Rises

The Root's glow surged. Across Stonewall, Root-constructs rose again, their limbs reinforced with shimmering barklight. Beetle monks stood shoulder-to-shoulder, antennae vibrating in resonance. Tree Rangers took positions along the upper terraces. Ground Division troopers formed protective ranks along the defensive gates. Water Division held the eastern pools, channeling reflective harmonics.

And above all, the Root's ancient power radiated. It spoke not with words, but with command: **STAND ANDENDURE**

Jones felt the message in his bones. "The Root is with us," Cass whispered. Dixie nodded. "And where the Root stands, the Earth stands." Var-Kin raised his claws. "And where Earth stands— she cannot conquer."

*****

The Queen Strikes

Manibrax's wings unfurled like sheets of night draped across the sky. Her roar cracked the air — a shriek of memory and hunger. She launched downward.

A wave of controlled insects poured in around her — centipedal beasts, flying horrors, armored titans — anything she could command, anything that lacked resonance.

The swarm struck Stonewall's upper ramparts. The world exploded into chaos. Jones shouted: "Bugforce — DEFEND!" Dixie soared into the air, cutting through flying hybrids.

Var-Kin bulldozed into ground-bound beasts, carving a path with claws of gleaming gold.

Miller spun his staff in blurs of motion, knocking aside attackers that threatened the Rootfire conduits.

Cass unleashed waves of resonance pulses that disrupted Manibrax's hold on her controlled vanguard.

Vek provided tactical harmonics, amplifying weak points and creating sonic barriers. The battle blazed. But Stonewall did not break. Not even a little.

*****

III. The Root's Power Fills the Field

As the swarm surged forward, the Root responded. Root pillars burst upward through the ground, forming barriers and shields. Saplight rippled across the walls, sealing holes as quickly as they were breached. The ground trembled under Manibrax's feet, but not from weakness — From defiance.

A massive pillar of golden light rose behind the defenders — the Rootfire extending to the surface for the first time in centuries. It formed a protective dome over Stonewall's heart.

Manibrax shrieked and recoiled, silver eyes flashing with rage. Cass whispered, "She can't touch it. She can't touch anything the Root holds." Jones gave a grim smile. "Good."

*****

IV. The Turning of the Tide

The battle raged across all tiers. Dixie swooped low, lifting wounded Micro-Operatives clear of the swarm and diving straight back into the fray.

Var-Kin charged into a titan-creature twice his size, slamming it into a Root pillar that snapped its control link. Miller fought with disciplined fury, knocking aside drones and hybrids alike, planting himself at the last defense line. Cass stabilized resonance pulses, harmonizing chaos into focused blasts.

Vek guided squads across the field, predicting swarm movements before they formed. Jones was everywhere — blocking a strike, rallying troops, holding lines, pushing forward. He fought not like a soldier, but like Earth's own heartbeat. Then, above the battle, Manibrax reared back. Her wings snapped open. Her scream shook the trees. She dove toward Jones with the fury of an ancient queen betrayed.

*****

V. The Final Clash

Time slowed. Jones raised his weapon. Cass screamed his name. Dixie dove from above. Var-Kin leapt, claws extended. Miller braced himself for an impossible strike. Vek shouted patterns and coordinates.

Manibrax descended like a meteor. Then — the Root moved. A pillar of golden fire erupted up from beneath Jones's feet, shooting skyward in a massive burst. Rootfire met her strike head-on. A shockwave exploded across the entire battlefield. Wind tore through the upper terraces. Dust exploded upward. Energy pulsed outward in rings. Manibrax recoiled violently — flung back as if struck by the hand of Earth itself. She shrieked — a terrible, furious, wounded sound.

Cass whispered in awe, "The Root protects him." Dixie hovered beside Jones, breathing hard. "You're still alive." Jones exhaled. "Wasn't planning on the alternative."

Var-Kin stepped forward. "Look." Manibrax steadied herself in the air, but her form flickered — weakening. She had tested Stonewall. She had challenged the Root. And she had been rejected.

*****

VI. The Queen Withdraws

Manibrax's wings folded in, drawing shadows with them. Her silver eyes dimmed. Her shape grew thinner, fading at the edges. She hissed: **"NOT BROKEN. NOT YET."**

The air warped around her. Space distorted. Her form dissolved into spiraling darkness. The swarm faltered, their control link snapping like brittle thread. Across Stonewall, the controlled ones collapsed — not dead, but freed. The Root pulsed once — a gentle, victorious heartbeat. A whisper followed: **ENDURE**

Manibrax fled into the east, her voice echoing across the valley: **"I WILL RETURN."** The echoes faded. Silence settled. A living, breathing silence — not the cold void she brought but the silence of a battle survived.

*****

VII. Aftermath of Victory

Stonewall stood cracked but unbroken. The Micro-Operatives stood weary but alive. The Root glowed warm, already healing the wounded earth. Jones looked out over the fortress. Soldiers helped each other up. Beetle monks chanted in thanks. Water Division cleansed wounds. Air Division tended to fallen wings. Dixie landed beside him. "We did it." Cass joined, exhausted but smiling. "For now." Miller leaned on his staff. "Until the next time."

Var-Kin stood tall, claws glowing faintly with Rootfire. "We will be ready." Jones lifted his gaze to the reddening sky. "Manibrax lives. She will rebuild, and she will fight again."

Dixie placed a hand on his shoulder. "So will we." Jones nodded. "So will we."

*****

VIII. Closing

As the sun dipped below the reed flats, the Rootfire dimmed gently, returning underground. Stonewall breathed again. The siege was over. The Queen would return, but the Micro-Operatives would stand together always.

Jones whispered into the fading light: "Let her come." And the earth beneath him answered: **WE STAND**

B.U.G.F.O.R.C.E.

Stonewall Outpost

Epilogue — The Quiet Between Thunder

The night after the battle was unlike any Stonewall had known. No alarms. No tremors. No screams of controlled swarms or echoing Queen-strike.

Only the soft, steady pulse of the Root beneath the earth — ancient enduring alive. The upper walls still bore cracks. The terraces still held smoke. The battlements were scattered with scorched soil and shattered chitin. But Stonewall stood. Not untouched. Not invincible. But intact, saved. A fortress bound to something older than war.

I. Jones on the Rampart

Jones stood on the highest rampart, taking in the quiet night. The last of the Rootfire's glow had faded underground, leaving only faint golden sparks across the barkstone. Dixie landed next to him, folding her wings. "Hard to believe we're still standing," she said. Jones nodded. "Harder to believe we were meant to."

She looked out with him at the horizon. The Reed Flats shimmered in the distance, calm now—a wide stretch of gold and green. Somewhere far below, in the darkness, Manibrax slipped away, gathering her strength for another day.

Dixie let out a breath. "She's not finished." Jones nodded. "Neither are we."

II. Cass and the Rootfire

Cass knelt at the edge of the Rootwell, pressing her hands to the warm bark. She breathed in time with the Root—slow and steady. She whispered, "Thank you." The Root didn't answer with words, but she felt its warmth move through her hands and into her body. That was enough.

Var-Kin walked up behind her, his claws tapping softly on the stone. "You're communing," he said. Cass smiled. "And you're listening." Var-Kin nodded. "The Root remembers. It remembers you." Cass felt tears in her eyes. "I'm not sure I deserve it."

Var-Kin's mandibles clicked softly—a beetle's way of smiling. "You don't have to be perfect to be worthy. Just present." Cass rested her hand on his broad shell. "We'll need your wisdom soon."

Var-Kin looked out over the walls. "And you will have it."

III. Miller and the Fallen

Miller walked through the recovery tents, helping with bandages and handing out rations. He stopped at each injured Micro-Operative, offering a hand on the shoulder or a quiet word. He didn't hurry or hesitate. Just being there made people feel safer.

At the last cot, he found a young Ground Division recruit, barely older than a rookie. The recruit looked up, voice weak. "Did we win?" Miller knelt beside him. "We're alive," he said quietly. "That's enough for today."

He adjusted the recruit's blanket, making sure they were warm. Then he stood and looked across the field.

Moonlight shone on the cracks in the outer walls— marks Miller had fought for and defended. "We'll hold," he said under his breath.

IV. Stonewall's Heart

As night deepened, the battlements grew quiet. Root-constructs moved slowly, their faint glow lighting the way as they worked to repair the damage. Tree Rangers kept watch from above. Beetle monks meditated in circles. Water Division checked the aquifers, and Air Division rested on the terraces. Stonewall was alive because of its people—their unity, their harmony, their shared purpose.

V. The Promise of the Root

Deep below, in the old vault, the Rootfire glowed softly, its light spreading like morning. The Root hadn't used all its strength—just enough to wake up. It was older than Manibrax, older than any conflict, older than the world as it is now. It had survived storms no one could name. In the quiet after the battle, it seemed to promise: Endure.

VI. The Shadow's Retreat

Far on the horizon, past the glowing reed flats, Manibrax slipped away into the night. She was wounded and angry, but not beaten. She moved through the deep roots of the earth, searching for places the Root couldn't reach. Her voice seemed to drift on the wind: "Next time. I will be whole."

The world trembled, but Stonewall stood firm.

VII. Dawn

As morning light reached the horizon, Jones came down from the rampart. The night's quiet ended. People woke, wounded got up, and teams gathered again. Tired but determined faces turned to him. He met their eyes. "We held," he said. "And when she comes back, we'll hold again."

Dixie touched down beside him, wings catching the sunrise. Cass stepped forward. Var-Kin stood tall and unmoving. Miller carried the weight with calm resolve. Vek adjusted his visor, ready to map the next threat.

Jones took a deep breath of the morning air. The siege was over, but the war wasn't. He raised his hand. "Micro-Operatives—stand ready." The divisions lined up. The Root pulsed beneath them. As the sun rose over Stonewall, its light mixed with the last glow of the Root, lighting up the outpost. The fortress stood strong, its people united, and the world was still worth fighting for

STONEWALL OUTPOST
APPENDIX & HISTORICAL RECORDS
As Preserved in the Rootfire Annals
Compiled Under Authority of Hivewatch Command
Cycle 221
STONEWALL: THE HEART OF MICRO-CIVILIZATION
Founded in the earliest days of the Micro-Operatives era, rebuilt in the shadow of the Siege,

and standing as the spiritual and tactical center of BUGFORCE,

Stonewall remains the most enduring symbol of unity, resilience, and the will to survive.

This appendix gathers the foundational lore, historical documents, and ancient records

officially recognized by Hivewatch Command as essential to the understanding of Stonewall's past, present, and future.

"Where root meets stone, where the Earth remembers, there the Micro-Operatives stand."

- Inscription above the Rootfire Hall Archway-

APPENDIX I — THE TWO FOUNDINGS OF STONEWALL
As compiled by Hivewatch Command and certified by the Rootfire Annalists
Cycle 221

I. INTRODUCTION
Stonewall Outpost stands as the most important stronghold in Micro-Operatives history. It is the cradle of

civilization, the bastion of harmonic defense, and the symbol of the Micro-Operatives struggle against silence, darkness, and the encroaching influence of Manibrax.

What many new recruits do not realize is that Stonewall bears not one, but

two founding moments, separated by centuries. Together, they define the legacy of the Micro-Operatives and the spirit of BUGFORCE. This appendix documents both eras as officially recognized by Hivewatch Command.

II. THE FIRST FOUNDING — CYCLE 0

"Where the tiny first stood against the endless."

The First Founding occurred at the dawn of the Micro-Operatives age, within the first Cycle after humanity's great reduction. A group of displaced humans—now Micro-Operatives—discovered a naturally defensible plateau where the Prime Root rose close to the surface.

Here, the earliest Micro-Operatives carved their first home.

Structures of the First Founding

The Stonewall Projection Well

The Rootfire Hall, the earliest center of resonance learning

Choir Watchtowers, built to receive the Earth's harmonic pulses

The Original Battlements carved into stone and bark

Founders' Barracks, where the earliest units trained and slept

Stonewall soon became a beacon of survival—one rooted in necessity, unity, and hope.

Twenty generations lived within those walls. Its foundations are older than any living Micro-Operatives and older than BUGFORCE itself.

III. STONEWALL THROUGH THE CYCLES

Between the First and Second Foundings, Stonewall endured:

Choir Node disruptions

Periodic insect migrations

Internal civil disputes

Natural collapses and seasonal Root-shifts

Early resonance wars

Despite repairs and reinforcements across centuries, Stonewall never faced an existential threat— until the rise of Manibrax. Her anti-resonance tore through the deep tunnels. Choir activity faltered. Mist began creeping up from the Warrens. The Root murmured warnings. Stonewall, ancient and revered, needed to be reborn.

IV. THE SECOND FOUNDING — CYCLE 221

"A fortress reborn in Rootfire and resolve."
The Reconstruction During the Siege of Stonewall
This is the Founding depicted in
Book II.
Under the leadership of:

Captain William Jones, Theater Lead in the field
1st Sergeant (later Sergeant Major) Richard Miller, Ground Lead
Corporal (later Sergeant) Dixie Lake, Aerial Scout Lead
Specialist Cass Nova, Resonance Specialist
Sergeant Josia Vek, QRF Evac/Rescue Specialist
Var-Kin, Beetle Monk of the Deep Choir
Teams of Tree, Ground, Water, and Air Division engineers

B.U.G.F.O.R.C.E.

Stonewall underwent the greatest reconstruction in Micro-Operatives history.

Constructions and Additions of the Second Founding

Eastern Interior Terraces beneath the upper Root Span

Rootfire Conduction Wells, allowing harmonic amplification

The Southern Culvert Line, a controlled water/resin defensive system

Rapid Muster Chambers for emergency mobilization

Skyward Watch Platforms, designed by Dixie Lake

Integrated Projection Arrays connecting all defensive sectors

The Command Resonance Hall, operational nerve center under Jones and Miller

The outpost, once a sanctuary, became a fully integrated war citadel.

This reconstruction is now formally recognized as the Second Founding of Stonewall.

V. SYMBOLIC AND CULTURAL SIGNIFICANCE

Stonewall's dual legacy embodies the heart of Micro-Operatives history:

The First Founding represents:

Survival

Heritage

Community

The birth of the Micro-Operatives identity

The Second Founding represents:

Duty

Unity of all Divisions

Rising against Manibrax

The rebirth of BUGFORCE

Together, these Foundings form the two pillars of Micro-Operatives civilization:

"Stonewall was born to shelter the first Micro-Operatives…
and born again to defend every Micro-Operatives who came after."
— Rootfire Annals, Cycle 221

Stonewall is not merely a fortress. It is a legacy carried forward by every Micro-Operatives who trains, fights, and dreams within its walls.

B.U.G.F.O.R.C.E.

APPENDIX II — CHANGES TO THE PROJECTION WELL NETWORK

Technical Report: Post-Siege Reconstruction and Resonance Stabilization
Filed by Engineer-Commander Arista Keene & Tone Keeper Taal-Sel
Cycle 188 (Updated Cycle 221)

INTRODUCTION
Following the Siege of Stonewall Outpost (Cycle 187), the Projection Well Network sustained structural, harmonic, and energetic disruptions due to:

Echo Brood tunneling impacts
Resonance fractures across the Rootstone chamber
Sapline pressure collapse along northern conduits
The awakening of the Twenty-Four Custodians (a previously unmodeled variable)
This appendix documents:
damage assessment
structural changes
harmonic recalibration
expansion of the Well's sensory field
new conduits created by Custodian activity
long-term implications for the Prime Root Network
SECTION I — STRUCTURAL DAMAGE & ROOTSTONE FRACTURES
A. Chamber Wall Fractures
Three major vertical fractures identified on the east chamber wall (Depth: 2.4 spans; Width: 0.2 span).
Caused by burrow-collisions and harmonic overstrain.

Stabilized using sapstone welding and Custodian resonance damping.

B. Ceiling Shear

7% plate-sagging detected above the central Well aperture.

Reinforced using triad-root tension anchors.

Custodians provided counter-resonance during installation.

C. Floor Pressure Cracks

Multiple microcracks radiating from the Well basin.

Believed to be the result of Root Fire pulse during awakening cascade.

Sealed with layered rootstone compounds.

SECTION II — HARMONIC FLOW DISRUPTIONS

A. Primary Pulse Lag

Before repairs, the Well's pulse cycle lagged by 0.72 harmonic beats.

This lag caused:

delayed projection clarity

unstable map locking

temporary loss of subterranean echo-scan readings

Solution:

Custodians applied triad-tonal stabilization cycles, correcting the pulse lag.

B. Resonance Echo Loops

Two echo loops were identified along the north-south conduit line.

Cause:

Custodian awakening reverberated through dormant resonance pathways, momentarily creating harmonic "backflow."

Fix:

Insertion of three new saplight regulators; Tone Keeper tuning.

C. Sapline Overpressure

Sap veins feeding the Well surged beyond predicted pressure levels post-awakening.

Cause:

Prime Root flare response to Custodian activity.

Fix:

New venting channels added; pressure stabilized at 103% nominal.

(This elevated state is now considered normal.)

SECTION III — NETWORK RECONFIGURATION DUE TO CUSTODIAN AWAKENING

The awakening of the Twenty-Four caused permanent changes across the Stonewall Projection Well Network.

A. New Conduit Activation

Three previously dormant sap-conduits became active:

East Conduit Theta

Links directly to the Root-Cradle Chamber.

Provides high-fidelity tremor data.

Deep-Line Delta

Connects to subterranean caverns beneath Reed Flats.

Source of improved Hollow Earth mapping.

Sky-Branch Sigma

Weak link to upper canopy resonance.

Allows air-pressure reading integration.

These conduits did not exist (functionally) before Cycle 187.

B. Baseline Projection Power Increase

Projection Well output increased by 27% after awakening.

Tone Keepers believe the Custodians' emergence restored suppressed lines within the Prime Root Network.

C. Custodian Resonance Imprint

All Custodians imprinted onto the Well during awakening.

Effects noted:

projection images more stable

triad-tones can trigger Well responses

the Well "recognizes" Custodians as authorized entities

harmonic data refresh rate increased

SECTION IV — CONTROL INTERFACE REVISIONS

A. Triad-Responsive Control Rings Added

Based on Custodian harmonics, three control rings were added:

Balance Ring — regulates projection clarity

Memory Ring — stores short-term echo readings

Flow Ring — controls scan speed and directional sweeps

Each is tuned to one of the eight triads.

B. Tone Keeper Sync Plates

Two new sync plates installed:

synchronize Keeper resonance with the Well

allow harmonic commands

enable non-verbal interface manipulation

Only Tone Keepers and Custodians can activate them.

C. Multi-Squad Display Mode

New enhancement added post-war:

displays multiple tactical overlays

integrates Custodian sensory feed

highlights emotional resonance fields during crisis

B.U.G.F.O.R.C.E.

This upgrade was inspired by Custodian battlefield behavior.

SECTION V — SENSOR FIELD EXPANSION

After the awakening, Well scanning radius expanded significantly.

A. Subterranean Range

Old range: 40 spans

New range: 120 spans

B. Emotional Resonance Scan

New field added unintentionally:

detects fear spikes, panic signatures

responds to imbalance within squads

Custodians use this passively

C. Echo Brood Pattern Detection

Detection resolution increased by 43% due to newly active conduits.

SECTION VI — LONG-TERM IMPLICATIONS

A. Increased Prime Root Activity

Post-awakening, the Well responds more directly to unseen sapflow changes.

Scholars believe this may indicate rising activity deep within the Hollow Earth.

B. Crown Custodian Access Points

Three "silent nodes" activated beneath the chamber.

Tone Keepers believe these nodes are connected to the Crown Custodians, not the Twenty-Four.

C. The Lost Three Interference

Faint resonance signals occasionally spike across dormant channels.

Unclear weather:

environmental interference,

pre-Crown harmonics, or

the Lost Three shifting in their sealed state.
Further study is ongoing.

APPENDIX III — THE LOST ROOTSTONE CHRONICLE

"When the Twenty-Four Awakened"
Translated from fragmentary sapstone tablets discovered beneath Stonewall Outpost, Cycle 220
Translation overseen by Tone Keeper Taal-Sel and Archivist Moriane Veldt

ARCHIVAL INTRODUCTION

The following account was recovered during the post-war restoration of Stonewall Outpost. The tablets—six in total—were buried beneath collapsed rootstone beneath the Resonant Chamber. Their sap-etchings predate known Micro-Operatives records and appear to have been carved shortly after the Siege of Cycle 187.

The writing style and harmonic notations strongly indicate Var–Kin as the author.

The content describes the first awakening of the Twenty-Four Custodians of Balance, an event not fully recorded in any existing battle reports.

The text is preserved here in its entirety.

— Archivist Moriane Veldt, Cycle 221

THE LOST ROOTSTONE CHRONICLE
WHEN THE TWENTY-FOUR AWAKENED
(Primary Tablet Translation)

1. The Tremor of Memory
The ground groaned beneath us—
not with the fury of collapse,

but with the weight of remembering.
Dust shivered across the chamber floor.
Saplight veins fluttered as if stirred by breath.
The Well dimmed for a single heartbeat.
And I, Var–Kin, felt the old stirrings beneath the stone.
I whispered to those beside me:
"It begins."
2. The Pillars That Were Not Pillars
At the heart of the outpost stood twenty-four rootstone columns.
We had believed them supports.
We had touched them without reverence.
We had leaned our tools against them.
We had walked past them a thousand times.
Yet beneath their plain surfaces
I now heard resonance—
old, deep, waiting resonance.
3. First Light in the Rootstone
The first pillar cracked—
a thin line of saplight blooming like dawn.
The stone did not fall apart.
It unfolded.
Panels curled outward like the petals of some ancient flower.
The being inside stepped forward,
saplight glowing within its chest.
Its eyes opened.
Its antlers rose.
It breathed.
And Balance entered the chamber.

4. The Awakening Cascade
As the First Custodian stepped free,
its resonance shook the others awake.

B.U.G.F.O.R.C.E.

One by one
—then all at once—
the remaining pillars cracked open.
Twenty-four pillars.
Twenty-four flares of golden saplight.
Twenty-four heart-flames igniting in triad cadence.
Stonewall blazed brighter than any fire I have known.
We staggered back in awe.

5. Twenty-Four Voices, One Tone
The Custodians formed a circle.
Their chests pulsed in perfect unison.
Their harmonics rose into a triad chord so ancient,
so layered,
that it filled the chamber with living memory.
Some of us wept without knowing why.
It was not a song.
It was a remembering.
6. The First Words Spoken
The tallest stepped forward.
It placed its palm over its heart-flame,
then extended its hand toward Captain Jones.
A harmonic pulse translated itself through the chamber:
"BRE–KAL."
Children of Breath.
Jones whispered, "It knows us."
The Custodian answered with another tone:
"THA–VOR."
Stand together.
And we understood.

7. The Bond of Balance
The Custodians lowered their antlers.

Their saplight brightened.
Their resonance shifted to match our breath.
We did not command them.
We did not summon them.
We did not awaken them.
They awakened with us
because the world had reached imbalance.
They came to restore it.
I recorded these events
so that future cycles may know
that hope is older than fear,
and Balance older than war.
— Var–Kin, Cycle 187

APPENDIX IV — THE TWENTY-FOUR CUSTODIANS OF BALANCE

Harmonic Register of the First Order
Compiled by the Tone Keeper Archive, Cycle 221

INTRODUCTION

The Twenty-Four Custodians of Balance—awakened during the Siege of Stonewall in Cycle 187—represent the First Order of sap-born resonance beings created by the Prime Root.

Their forms are uniform, but their resonance roles differ, each aligned to one of the Eight Harmonic Triads.

This appendix lists all Twenty-Four by name, harmonic function, and known role as recorded from field observations and Tone Keeper study.

TRIAD I — THE TRIAD OF CALM
Stabilization • Peace • Emotional Balance
1. SA-LOM-REN
Role: Calming field generator
Notes: Known to stand behind panicked or injured Micro-Operatives.
2. VEL-SON-TRA
Role: Fear-dampening harmonic anchor
Notes: Useful during collapses or retreats.
3. MA-REN-SOL
Role: Projection Well stabilizer
Notes: Harmonizes Well output during high stress.

TRIAD II — THE TRIAD OF VIGILANCE
Awareness • Sensing • Warning

4. TOR-VEN-AL

Role: Echo Brood tremor-detection

Notes: Antlers extremely sensitive to vibration.

5. SHA-DRI-MEL

Role: Imbalance identification

Notes: Detects danger before signs appear.

6. REN-KOR-VAL

Role: Night watch guardian

Notes: Emits protective night-hums.

TRIAD III — THE TRIAD OF MEMORY

History • Recall • Residual Harmonics

7. DAL-MOR-ESH

Role: Reservoir of ancestral memory

Notes: Consulted by Tone Keepers for deep lore.

8. ESH-VOR-NAH

Role: Echo-tonal playback

Notes: Can replay resonance signatures from past events.

9. LOR-NEM-ESH

Role: Memory stabilizer

Notes: Supports Crown Custodians in later rituals.

TRIAD IV — THE TRIAD OF FLOW

Movement • Rhythm • Natural Currents

10. NEL-FAR-SO

Role: Smooths unstable troop movement

Notes: Critical in river or shifting terrain battles.

11. VAR-LOM-ESH

Role: Formation harmonizer

Notes: Known as "The Rhythm Keeper."

12. SHI-VAL-MER

Role: Current-calming resonance

Notes: Appears often in Water Division operations.

TRIAD V — THE TRIAD OF ENDURANCE

Strength • Holding • Persistence

B.U.G.F.O.R.C.E.

13. KUL-DRA-MOR

Role: Line-holder

Notes: Primary defensive backbone during Stonewall breaches.

14. TOR-REN-MAK

Role: Sustained formation stabilizer

Notes: Longest continuous hum among the Twenty-Four.

15. DRAV-MOR-SOL

Role: Shock absorber

Notes: Called "The Unbent" after surviving a tunnel collapse.

TRIAD VI — THE TRIAD OF INSIGHT

Perception • Interpretation • Emotional Reading

16. SHU-REN-TAL

Role: Emotional field interpreter

Notes: Helps prevent morale collapse.

17. MAR-VEL-OR

Role: Long-range harmonic communicator

Notes: Bridges triad-tones between Custodians.

18. VAL-ESH-TAR

Role: Imbalance analyst

Notes: Slow to act, but deeply perceptive.

TRIAD VII — THE TRIAD OF STRENGTH

Action • Force • Combat Resonance

19. KOR-MAL-DEN

Role: Forward breaker

Notes: First Custodian to charge during breaches.

20. DRA-SOL-KEN

Role: Corridor clearer

Notes: Emits powerful close-range resonance bursts.

21. TOR-KESH-MOR

Role: Well-guardian

Notes: Rarely leaves the Projection Well's inner ring.

TRIAD VIII — THE TRIAD OF RENEWAL

Healing • Rebalancing • Restorative Harmonics

22. REN-SHA-MEL

Role: Wounded Micro-Operatives stabilizer

Notes: Emits soft warmth during healing.

23. VOR-TEM-ESH

Role: Post-battle resonance rebalance

Notes: Works closely with Tone Keepers.

24. SOL-MAR-REN

Role: Emotional trauma cleanser

Notes: "The Quiet Glow," known to calm entire squads.

APPENDIX V — VAR–KIN'S PROPHECY FRAGMENTS

Recovered Writings of the Two-Souled Listener
Found beneath the Root-Cradle Chamber after the Siege

ARCHIVAL NOTE

The writings below were discovered on sap-etched barkstone sheets sealed beneath the Resonant Chamber. The script matches Var–Kin's hand and appears to predate the awakening of the Twenty-Four.

These fragments represent his earliest attempts to record the harmonic visions imparted by the Prime Root.

Translation is incomplete; several lines are damaged or irretrievable.

— Archivist Moriane Veldt, Cycle 221

PROPHECY FRAGMENTS OF VAR–KIN

(Translated in harmonic sequence rather than chronological order)

Fragment I — The First Stirring

When the deep root remembers its wounds,
the world will tremble.
In the shaking of ancient stone,
twenty-four heart-flames will rise.
Not to conquer.
Not to rule.
But to restore what war breaks.

I saw them standing in a ring of saplight,
their shadows tall across the cavern wall.

Fragment II — The Two-Souled Warning

Balance awakens only when imbalance becomes unbearable.

One who carries breath and sap together
must stand at the center.
Two-Souled.
Listener.
Kin of Root.
If he falters, the Harmony falters.
If he endures, the Root endures.
(Scholars universally agree this references Var–Kin's own transformation.)

Fragment III — The Crown's Sleep
Three greater flames lie buried below memory.
Crowned not by metal
but by resonance.
They sleep until imbalance becomes fate.
When they rise,
the world will enter its turning.
Past.
Present.
Future.
Three-as-One.

Fragment IV — The Lost Three
Damaged, but partial reconstruction possible:
Before the harmony was perfected,
three were formed in fear.
Their hearts dim,
their voices broken.
They must not awaken
unless the last light fails.
For they carry the memory

of what was nearly unmade.

Tone Keeper analysis suggests this refers to the proto-Custodians, sealed long before the Twenty-Four were created.

Fragment V — The Deep Pulse

I felt the Root Fire choke.

I heard the sap scream.

Something stirs in the hollow places—

something that does not hear the Harmony.

A battle beneath the world

will shake the world above.

This is widely accepted as the earliest reference to the War of Hollow Earth.

Fragment VI — The Great Joining

Balance cannot win alone.

Breath must join Sap,

and Sap must join Flame.

Three Orders must stand

or the world will fall.

The First Twenty-Four.

The Crowned Three.

The Lost Three.

If one Order fails,

harmony breaks forever.

This fragment confirms the triadic structure of the Custodian Orders.

Fragment VII — The Endless Root

In the Cycle beyond cycles,

when the Spans grow thin,

the Prime Root will cast judgment.

Not in anger.

Not in wrath.
But in remembrance.
For the Creator whose name is but a breath
shaped the days to begin in dusk,
and all things return to dusk again.
This connects Var–Kin's teachings with the cosmology of the Creator.

Fragment VIII — Last Notation
Found incomplete, engraved on darkened rootstone:
"Balance walks beside us.
But we must walk worthy of it."

1
Page 1